A Map of the County of

BARSETSHIRE

Shewing the Situations of the

various great Estates and Seats

HOGGLE END

HOGGLESTOCK

Rising Castle

WINTER OVERCOTES

Pomfret Madrigal

River Rising

High Rising

SHEARING JUNCT.

Little Misfit

Low Rising

Hatch End

Bolcar's Knob

Scannington

Pomfret Towers

Greshamsbury Hall

Obelisk

Winter Underclose

Boxall Hill

EAST BARSETSHIRE

Ruddingdale

Lambton

THE RIVER

Stogpingum

Beliers Priory

Eiderdown

Fleece

Worsted

Crabtree Canonicorum

Staple Park

Skeynes

Laverings Fm

Great Hump

Pooker's Piece

PRIVATE ENTERPRISE

A Novel by

Angela Thirkell

MOYER BELL
Wakefield, Rhode Island & London

Published by Moyer Bell
This Edition 1997

Copyright © 1947 by Angela Thirkell
Published by arrangement with Hamish Hamilton, Ltd.

LIBRARY OF CONGRESS
CATALOGING-IN-PUBLICATION DATA

Thirkell, Angela Mackail, 1890–1961.
    Private enterprise : a novel by Angela
Thirkell. — 1st ed.
       p.   cm.
    1. Barsetshire (England : Imaginary
place)—Fiction.   2. World War, 1939–
1945—England—Influence—Fiction.
I. Title.
PR6039.H43P75   1997
823'.912—dc20   96-36739
                                      CIP
    ISBN 1-55921-189-X

Cover and chapter illustrations:
Details from *Apple Blossoms* by
John Everett Millais

Printed in the United States of America
Distributed in North America by Publishers Group West, P.O. Box 8843,
Emeryville CA 94662, 800-788-3123 (in California 510-658-3453).

PRIVATE ENTERPRISE

CHAPTER I

Mrs. Noel Merton looked out of the dining-room window with considerable displeasure. It was mid-May and for at least the one hundred and thirty-fifth time that year the day was beginning with cold grey sulks accompanied by a highly unsympathetic wind. Every tree looked as if it had been blown inside out, the grass was as leaden as the sky, the river at the bottom of the garden looked like a cross between mud flats and dirty pewter. A few melancholy birds, their tails blown almost over their heads, their breast feathers untidily ruffled, were lounging aimlessly on the terrace. Not as it used to be, thought Mrs. Merton; a thought which was in the minds of all her elders and most of her contemporaries by day and by night. Since the glorious summer which marked the days of Dunkirk warmth and light had been withdrawn from England, and the peace, which certainly passed everyone's understanding, had not had the faintest influence on the weather which had got the bit well between its teeth and was rapidly heading for the ice age.

Mr. Noel Merton, who had been out of the army for more than a year and was back at the bar doing extremely well, came into the room and put an arm round his wife's shoulders.

"It's like Horace," said Lydia, rubbing her face against her husband's coat.

"I'm sure it is," said Noel. "But why?"

"You remember that summer you came home when I was at

the Barchester High School," said Lydia, "and that beast Pettinger set us some odes of Horace to do in the holidays and Everard helped me. I suddenly remembered it."

"If you could explain yourself a little better, my precious love," said Noel, "I might begin to have some idea what you are talking about. What is like Horace?"

"Well, I can't remember any of the words," said Lydia, "but it was something about everything being pretty awful and everything being much awfuller than it used to be but it will be much awfuller presently. You know what I mean."

Noel said he did. Though why, he added, Lydia should think she was much worse than her parents and expect her progeny to be yet more corrupt than herself, he could not see.

"It isn't so much the children," said Lydia, at once up in arms to defend her young. "Lavinia does scream sometimes, but she is an angel, and I don't know how anyone could say that Harry is corrupt. He has got two teeth. At least it was a tooth and a half last night and I am sure it is through this morning."

"I am glad I am not likely to have to cross-examine you," said Noel. "Come and have breakfast."

So Lydia sat where her mother used to sit, behind what used to be called the breakfast equipage, and poured out her husband's coffee. But Noel did not sit opposite her at the other end of the handsome mahogany table where old Mr. Keith used to sit, for he did not approve of a table coming between him and his wife, preferring to be near her and have his back to the wood fire which an English spring made so necessary.

"Another of the horrid things is the post not coming till after breakfast," said Lydia, "and even when it does come it usually brings horrid letters. It was almost nicer when you and Colin and everyone were fighting, because we did get letters."

"Well, if you really want another war," said Noel, "doubtless someone will oblige soon. Only in the next war I shall be a red-tabbed Colonel at the War Office instead of a dashing Major in a hush-hush job. And where is Colin, by the way?"

Lydia looked at her brother's empty chair and not seeing him very sensibly said she supposed he wasn't down yet.

"It is very nice to have Colin here for Whitsun," she said earnestly. "But I can't help thinking what fun it was that Whitsun you and Everard were here and Colin was a master at Southbridge and it was sunny. It's all different now."

"We will try to go back if you like," said Noel, always willing to oblige his Lydia, "but it might be a bit hard on Colin. He likes being a barrister much better than schoolmastering. And Everard mightn't like it much now that he is to be headmaster next year, and he wouldn't be married to Kate. And come to that, you wouldn't be married to me or have Lavinia and Harry."

"And there would be Dunkirk," said Lydia, her eyes darkening as she remembered the long vigil till news of Noel's safety reached her. "Sorry, Noel. I simply adore everything as it is. Only I do wish we could sometimes be warm."

And this modest wish was but the echo of millions of men and women who could have forgiven an all-wise and all-merciful Creator, also all-bounteous and all-seeing if all that was said were true, for all their hells and purgatories, if only he had allowed the sun to shine as of old.

"Yes, it's the ice hell of Pitz-Palu all right," said Noel, referring to a pre-war film in which a man became frozen to death with great nobility because the hero had tried to climb an Alp with no guide and no previous experience and the heroine had gone to his rescue without her pullover. "Never mind, my precious love. We'll saw some wood this morning. And thank God the hens are laying."

He then applied himself to a boiled egg and began to discuss with Lydia the thousand interesting jobs to be done about Northbridge Manor.

"Buying this place back from your brother Robert was the best thing we ever did," said Noel. "I still can't think why he parted with it."

"I don't think he wanted to very much," said Lydia, "but

Edith never liked it. She thought the children might be drowned and this isn't the right side of Barchester. She likes the Omnium Castle side. Hullo, Colin."

And in came Colin Keith with a bundle of letters and newspapers.

"I went down to Twicker's cottage before breakfast to talk about these new apple-trees," said Colin, who spent a good deal of his spare time at his parents' old home and knew nearly as much about its working as his sister Lydia, "and I met the post and the papers so I brought them in. I thought you'd like to have them for breakfast."

The three breakfasters then disembowelled their letters, or prised them open with the handle of a spoon, or very neatly slit them with a small knife, according to the temperament of each. Noel, who never had a large post in the country as his letters waited for him in his chambers and were sorted by his clerk, had finished his first and idly ate bread and their own honey, speculating without much interest upon his wife's and his brother-in-law's expressions.

"If I didn't know you better, Lydia," he said, "I should suspect you of having run up a monstrous bill at your mantua-maker's or lost prodigiously at cards, and having pawned your diamonds or your honour to meet your creditors. What is it?"

"It's from Kate," said Lydia, laying down her elder sister's letter. "They have got mumps in the House and she hopes the children won't get it. Do you think I ought to go over and see, Noel?"

"Certainly not," said her husband. "Kate is a very good mother and she has a very good nurse and if you go into the mump-house you'll give them to Lavinia and Harry. Besides they probably won't get them. Anything else?"

"Only Lavinia Brandon," said Lydia. "Francis is out of the army and is back at work in Barchester and she is having a party for him on Monday. It will be rather fun to go to a party, only one's hands are so horrid."

"So are everyone's," said Noel. "It is a shocking sign of these degenerate times, but whenever I see a woman with very clean, elegant hands I find myself saying automatically, 'What did you do in the Great War, Mummy?'"

"Some of those evacuated teachers in the war had such awfully clean hands that one felt quite ashamed," said Lydia thoughtfully.

"Of them or of yourself?" said Noel.

"First of them," said truthful Lydia, "because it did seem horrid to have clean hands when everyone else was dirty—I don't mean dirty really, but not being able to get the dirt off however hard one washed—and then of oneself for thinking such beastly thoughts. And I expect they had special orders that they weren't to do anything that would dirty them. I often think I'll stop washing altogether," said Lydia, gazing ruefully upon her capable, well-shaped hands, indelibly marked by every kind of war and peace work, by hospitals, by farms, by machinery, by the continual round of house and garden.

"I like them," said Noel, who to his own amusement and deep pleasure became more fond of his Lydia with every day of his life. "Anything in your post, Colin?"

"Nothing particular," said Colin in a voice so off-hand as to rouse even Lydia's suspicions. "Just the ordinary kind of things. Oh, there is one that might interest you," he added, making a pretence of looking among his correspondence in a way that deceived nobody. "It's from Mrs. Arbuthnot—I don't think you know her. She is looking for a house. Oh yes, here is the letter. She says do I know any nice small house in a village or a small town within reach of Barchester."

Lydia asked who Mrs. Arbuthnot was.

"You'd like her very much," said Colin. "Her husband was with an Indian regiment."

This hardly seemed to Lydia sufficient ground for liking the unknown Mrs. Arbuthnot, but her fondness for Colin made her ready to accept any friend of his, so she asked what kind of house the Arbuthnots wanted.

"Arbuthnot was killed," said Colin rather impatiently, "in the East. She was extraordinarily brave about it. She wants a small house, because she isn't very well off. I think Arbuthnot had some money and ran through it, though of course she never told me about it. She isn't that sort. So I said I'd look round when I came down here and let her know."

So much were Noel and Lydia one in mind that they did not even look at each other, but each knew that the other was having the same thought. Colin Keith, the ex-schoolmaster, the lawyer, the soldier, and now again the lawyer, immersed in his profession, his chief recreation to visit his sister Lydia at their old home, by no means a hermit, dining out a good deal in London where he had a comfortable flat; this Colin, who as far as either of them knew had never felt Love's wound apart from a few trifling irregularities such as wishing to marry his mother's hideous under-housemaid when he was seven and being in love with a little girl with a gold band round her front teeth at the dancing-class when he was nine; this Colin, marked by heaven as a bachelor uncle, had evidently been smitten by the charms of this Mrs. Arbuthnot. Lydia did not mind. Much as she loved her favourite brother, or perhaps because she loved him so much and was herself so happily married, she had always hoped that he would present her with a very nice sister-in-law. And now perhaps this Mrs. Arbuthnot was to be she. If so, by all means let Mrs. Arbuthnot come to Barsetshire and have a small house to be not very well off in. And if she were nice enough for Colin, then Lydia would forward their affairs by all means in her power. Noel, knowing his Lydia well and having already had much the same thoughts, caught her eye and exchanged an amusing conspirator's glance.

"We must find some nice houses," said Mrs. Noel Merton, putting her elbows on the table and twining a leg round each of the front legs of her chair, much as Miss Lydia Keith used to do.

"Isn't the Hollies to let?" said Noel, thinking of the pleasant stone Georgian house in Northbridge High Street where Mrs. Turner and her nieces used to live.

"It was when Mrs. Turner went to live in Norfolk with her niece Betty Topham," said Lydia. "But it got taken a few weeks ago by some people from the new aerodrome. Mrs. Villars told me when I went to tea at the Rectory. Besides it's not small. What about that cottage down at the Ferry next to old Bunce's?"

"My dear girl," said Noel, "it's out of the question. If only it were on Pomfret's property one might get it put into order, but you know as well as I do that the Duke, or the Duke's agent, will not do a thing about repairs. One might try Pomfret Madrigal."

But Lydia had heard from Mrs. Brandon that there wasn't so much as a hen-house unoccupied in the village, partly owing to the increasing age and size of the evacuees who had never been claimed by their parents, and partly because the Government Department housed at Brandon Abbey had overflowed into neighbouring villages, including Pomfret Madrigal. Several equally unfelicitous suggestions having been made and squashed on both sides, the Mertons agreed to make further inquiries and let Colin know the result.

"I'm sure we'll find something," said Lydia to her brother. "I'll tell Kate to ask at Southbridge and I'll ask Nurse. She might know of something at Worsted or Winter Overcotes. Come and see the children, Colin."

So Lydia and her brother went upstairs and as they went Colin thanked Lydia for taking so much trouble about a cottage for Mrs. Arbuthnot, adding that he was sure Lydia would like her; a statement with which Lydia was quite prepared to agree, though reserving for Noel her own private opinion of Mrs. Arbuthnot whenever she should meet that lady. She also had at the same time a faint feeling that if Colin said even once more that she would like Mrs. Arbuthnot she might, for the first time in her life, find her beloved Colin a little exasperating. But the nursery door opened onto a delightful warmth smelling of milk and biscuits, and these darker thoughts vanished.

Nursery breakfast had of course been finished some time ago. Miss Lavinia Merton was seated on a small chair near the window, a small table in front of her, playing industriously with some small wooden cubes painted a different colour on each face. Master Harry Merton was lying on his back on a rug, waving his hands about with a general air of wondering where on earth these starfish creatures had come from. From time to time he gave a few convulsive kicks with his firm fat legs and smiled a broad almost toothless smile.

"Well," said Nurse, a middle-aged woman of uncompromising appearance, coming in with a tray of breakfast things which she had been washing up, "isn't it nice to see Uncle Colin, Lavinia? And baby is ever so pleased to see Uncle Colin, aren't you, baby?"

Master Merton, who had managed to catch one of his fat feet in his fat hands and was a good deal surprised by what he had done, made a bubbling and quite unintelligible remark.

"He's saying how do you do to Uncle Colin," said Nurse.

This was so palpable a lie that Lavinia pushed all her bricks onto the floor and said, "Silly Harry," in a very clear voice.

"Now you know that's not the way to talk, Lavinia," said Nanny, "in front of Uncle Colin too. Pick your bricks up nicely, there's a good girl."

"Uncle Colin," said Lavinia, turning upon her uncle a bewitching and appealing smile.

Colin began to pick up her bricks.

"Now don't you trouble yourself, sir," said Nurse. "She's just seeing how far she can go. When I was with Mrs. Dean, Jessica was just the same. Always a smile for the gentlemen. No wonder she took to acting. I expect you've seen her, sir. She gave me seats for her last play and I went with Mrs. Laurence Dean's Nanny and we had ever such a nice tea between the acts, and the young lady took us round to Miss Jessica's dressing-room afterwards.

'Well, Jessica,' I said, 'what's the use of my telling you times without number that there's a place for everything and everything should be in its place and you keep your room in a mess like this.' But she only laughed and then she gave Mrs. Laurence's Nanny and I cocktails and cigarettes and we had ever such an interesting time and she wrote her name on her photo for me."

"Do you mean Jessica Dean?" said Colin, his opinion of Nurse suddenly rising to fever height.

"I had all Mrs. Dean's younger children, sir," said Nurse. "Jessica was the baby. I'll never forget the day we met the bull in the lane and Jessica fell off the donkey, Neddy we called him. Young Mr. Tebben saved her life. We did think there was something between him and Miss Susan, that's Miss Jessica's next elder sister, but it seems there wasn't. Miss Susan is working for the Barsetshire Red Cross Hospital Library. You would like Miss Susan, sir."

And that, thought Lydia, as she watched her brother reeling slightly under so much information about a family whom he hardly knew intimately, will learn you not to say you know people will like people. But Colin for the moment appeared to be entirely absorbed in Nurse's connection with Jessica Dean, looking upon her with a reverence which amused Lydia, who had not realized that her brother was such an admirer of the young actress. For Lydia, having spent nearly all her life in the country, first working and then being married and very much occupied in running Northbridge Manor, knew little of London. Now that Noel was working so hard at the bar they had a flat in town, but she did not often leave Northbridge and was not in touch with London events, and the name Jessica Dean meant little to her. Still, if Colin liked her she must be a good actress and if Nurse approved of her she must be nice.

"Oh, Nurse," she said. "A friend of my brother's is looking for a small house or a nice cottage. You don't think Mrs. Dean would know of anything at Winter Overcotes or Worsted, do you?"

"I'm sure I couldn't say, madam," said Nurse. "But I can ring up Miss Susan and ask. She stays in Barchester for the week, at the Deanery, but she's always at home at the weekends. Would it be a real cottage the gentleman wants, sir, or a nice one?"

Colin said he thought a nice one. It was for a lady, a widow, he added nervously and then felt that his character was ruined in Nurse's eyes. A war widow, he added even more nervously, and knew he had damned himself for ever.

"Well, poor things, they can't help it," said Nurse charitably. "But I must say it was all much better when we didn't have these wars and things and ladies could live quietly without their husbands being killed. It doesn't seem natural. And so many of them were babies too, sir, and no more fit to look after them than Mrs. Merton is."

"Oh, I say, Nurse," said Lydia. "You know I look after them frightfully well on your day off."

"Now Mrs. Carter," said Nurse, "there's a lady that does understand children. Really, the way Mrs. Carter looks after the young ladies and gentleman, you'd think she'd been in the nursery all her life."

Much as Lydia loved her sister Mrs. Everard Carter this unfairness was more than she could bear, so she made a diversion by telling Nurse that mumps had broken out in the Carters' House.

"I did want to go over and see Kate," she said, "but Mr. Merton didn't want me to."

"Quite right, madam," said Nurse. "You might bring them back with you. Now Mrs. Carter, that's a lady that wouldn't have mumps. Don't you worry, madam, just leave it all to Mrs. Carter and I'll be sure to ring Miss Susan up about a cottage. But I don't think there's much chance, sir. Is it a young lady, sir? Some of these war widows are very young, poor things, and it doesn't seem right. Before the war a lady that was a widow *was* a widow, sir. These poor young ladies they really don't hardly know what they are."

"I think you would like Mrs. Arbuthnot very much, Nurse," said Colin. "She is very lonely. Her husband was killed in Burma and she hasn't any children."

But if Colin thought he could win sympathy by this appeal he was wrong.

"Tschk, tschk," said Nurse (which but feebly represents the sounds we wish to convey). And this appeared to damn so irretrievably the unlucky Mrs. Arbuthnot that Colin hardly dared to speak for fear of making matters worse. But speak he did and immediately regretted it.

"They had only been married a year," said Colin.

On hearing this Nurse kept silence with a vigour that was quite terrifying and was so obviously making Gampish calculations that Colin felt the nursery was no place for a man and said he ought to answer some letters.

"Say good-bye to Uncle Colin, Lavinia," said Nurse.

Lavinia looked at the floor and then looked up under her long lashes at her uncle.

"I think," said Colin to Lydia, "that Mrs. Brandon gave your daughter more than her name. Mrs. Brandon herself couldn't have given me a more alluring look. Good-bye, Lavinia."

He picked his small niece up and hugged her, a most pleasurable sensation. He then set her down and she ran to Nurse and hid behind her, looking round Nurse's skirt at her uncle.

"That's enough, Lavinia," said Nurse. "Come and get your things on to go in the garden, there's a good girl."

She withdrew her young charge to the night-nursery. Master Merton, who had lost his foot and given it up as a bad job, smiled broadly at his uncle and chuckled to himself.

"Come on," said Lydia. "We'll go and see Nanny Twicker."

She put her arm through her dear Colin's and led him away from the nursery.

Mrs. Twicker, as all Lydia's friends must know, was the wife of Twicker the gardener, a North-countrywoman who had been nanny to the Keith family and still treated them as if they were her adored young charges, thinking but poorly of her own grown-up children because they were not gentry. Already did Miss Lavinia Merton know that in Nanny Twicker's cottage she could break all nursery rules with impunity. As for Master Harry Merton, we should not like to take it upon ourselves to say what went on in his fond and foolish mind, but though a placid and silent child at home he burst, whenever taken to the cottage, into such a spate of melodious and unintelligible conversation as made his mother fall into helpless laughter, though Nanny Twicker indignantly said that she understood every word Master Harry was saying.

Though Robert Keith, Lydia's married brother, was Nanny's favourite as her first nursling she felt very affectionately towards the rest of the family. Her welcome to Colin took the form of a large cup of cocoa with cream on the top and to Colin's mind quite nauseously oversweetened, accompanied by two large slices of bread and dripping.

"Oh, I say, Nanny, you shouldn't," said Colin, appalled by the sight of this rere-breakfast so soon after coffee, boiled egg, toast, butter and honey.

"Now you sit down, and eat what Nanny's given you," said Mrs. Twicker. "It won't do you no harm. It's not that nasty dripping you get at the shops," said Nanny, who as a North-countrywoman had the deepest contempt for everything that was not made, grown or reared on the estate. "That's the old gander, Mr. Colin. We fattened him up for Christmas and he ate like a young pullet," said Nanny, alluding to the quality of the gander's flesh rather than his appetite, "and the fat I got off him would have surprised you. I did it all down and put it in a nice jar and greaseproof paper on the top and made it air-tight with some candle grease the way the Women's Institute showed us and I put it on a nice cool shelf in the larder. Many's the time Twicker made sheeps' eyes at it, but 'No, Twicker,' I said. 'No.

That's meat for your betters,' and I gave him a nice bit of pork dripping Twicker got off that little runt in the old sow's last litter. You remember, Miss Lydia, the one that had such a funny shaped back and died. There was a gentleman come from the Government or somewhere said Twicker must kill the runt and burn the body, some rubbish or other about making you ill, and then the poor thing died, so I said to Twicker, 'You humour the gentleman, Twicker, and say you killed the runt and leave the rest to me,' and he cooked beautiful. I don't like gentlemen interfering round my place, Mr. Colin, and by this one's boots he'd never so much as set foot on a midden."

So enthralled was Colin by this story of village Hampdenism that he had eaten all the goose-fat slices and drunk the rich cocoa without noticing.

"That's right, Mr. Colin. You do as Nanny says and you won't go wrong," said Nanny approvingly.

Then they made a tour of Nanny's little dairy, her hens, her bees, her vegetable plot exquisitely kept by her husband, her jam, her dried apple rings, her little laundry. Here Nanny paused.

"Whenever I do a bit of washing, Miss Lydia," she said, "I think of the summer Mr. Tony and Mr. Eric and Mr. Percy were here. They all helped me turn the mangle and I had a lovely time washing their shirts and underpants and mending their socks. I often wish they were here, Miss Lydia. Have you any news of them?"

Lydia said she thought Tony Morland had been in the East and was now demobilized.

"I don't know where Swan and Hacker are now. Do you, Colin?" she asked.

Colin said he thought Hacker had been in some Ministry or other during the war and was now a Fellow of his own college, Lazarus. Of Swan no one had any news.

"Oh, Nanny," said Lydia. "Colin has a friend that wants a

little house or a cottage somewhere about here. If you hear of anything I wish you'd let me know."

Nanny, eyeing her ex-charge piercingly, said was it a lady or a gentleman, as of course it all depended.

Colin feeling himself getting hot, much to his own annoyance, said it was a lady. The widow of an army friend, he said, and he was sure Nanny would like her.

"They say liking goes by favour," said Nanny oracularly. "Still, if she's a real lady, sir, I'm sure we'll find something."

"I should have thought that was exactly the way not to find anything one wanted," said Lydia with what was for her unusual bitterness. "The more one's a lady or a gentleman, the less chance one has."

"Now, that's quite enough, Miss Lydia," said Nanny. "You know it says in the Bible that you don't see the righteous forsaken nor his seed begging their bread."

"Nous avons changé tout cela," said Colin, addressing a distant imaginary audience.

"Look at Geraldine Fairweather," said Lydia. "She's got two babies and can't get any help. And three of the Dean's grandsons are demobbed and can't get jobs. And Noel knows *millions* of young lawyers that are back from the war and have to live on their parents. And I know heaps of girls that were Wrens and things and can't find work. And all their people were pretty righteous."

"I suppose," said Colin, "that there is a difference between being righteous and being a lady or a gentleman. As a matter of fact there are uncommon few people in the Bible that one would want as paying guests, or to marry into one's family. Come to that, of course, there are very few people anyhow now that one wants to see much of. All the nice people seem to have got into holes or been submerged. I don't know."

"That's quite enough, Mr. Colin," said Nanny. "Now don't you worry about the lady, sir. I'm sure we'll find her a nice little house and a nice steady woman to look after her. Is she bedridden?"

"Lord, no!" said Colin, startled. "She's quite young. If she can get a bit of rough help she'll manage splendidly. She loves the country and dogs."

Nanny's icy silence made her disapproval of young widows who liked the country and dogs and were befriended by Colin all too plain. But in a few moments her kind heart reasserted itself and she began to plan a spider's web of inquiries all across the country via the Women's Institute. Then Colin and Lydia said good-bye to her. Colin said he would walk about the place till he found Noel. Lydia recommended him to go to the bailiff's cottage and then returned to the house and her duties.

Northbridge Manor included a small farm with a good dairy herd, some pasture, some arable land, and a small wood. Old Mr. Keith, a wealthy Barchester solicitor, had never attempted to manage the property himself, nor had his son Robert who inherited the place. For the last few years the management had been in the hands of a middle-aged naval man who had left the service after the 1914 war to take up farming, rejoined for the 1939 war and been invalided out of the service after Dunkirk. When Noel and Lydia bought the place back from her elder brother they were very glad for him to stay on, and Mr. Wickham was glad to stay, and had been accepted by the countryside and the Close and elected to the Country Club. He came to supper at the Manor on most Sundays, for Noel was usually at home for the week-end and Lydia hardly ever went away. And once a year he was with great difficulty forced to take a holiday which he spent in Norfolk, watching birds with great affection and interest all day, sometimes through a telescope, sometimes in a flat-bottomed boat with a kind of camouflage of rushes, and sitting up all night in the middle of a fen in gum-boots and lovingly shooting hundreds of birds as they flew over at dusk and dawn. But such are bird-lovers, a peculiar race, apart from the ordinary run of mankind, self-sufficing, slightly inhuman, absorbed, their eyes almost as distant and expressionless as those of the birds they adore and kill.

Colin went by the side door into the agent's office where he found Noel and Mr. Wickham talking about their possible entries for the Barsetshire Agricultural Show in the autumn.

"Cheerio, Keith," said Mr. Wickham. "A spot of navy rum? A pal sent me some from Bombay. Queer place to get rum from, but you never know."

"On any other morning there's nothing I'd have liked better," said Colin, "but I've just been to see Nanny Twicker and she made me drink a cup of very strong sweet cocoa and eat two huge pieces of bread and goose dripping."

Mr. Wickham said navy rum would settle anything. He had a pal, he added, who used to top off a binge with a spoonful of Epsom salts in hot rum and water and always came up bright and smiling. Rum, he said, navy rum, was the thing, but if Colin didn't feel like it, what about a finger of whisky? Whisky, he said, wasn't rum, but its settling properties were notorious wherever the Flag flew. Colin thanked him very much but said he had made a promise to himself not to drink anything before lunch.

"Well, if you won't, you won't," said Mr. Wickham. "Merton?"

Noel also declined.

"Then," said Mr. Wickham, who had already opened a well-stocked corner cupboard, "it will have to be a Johnny Woodser."

He poured some rum into a tea-cup and drank it.

"What is a Johnny Woodser?" Noel asked.

"I don't know who he was," said Mr. Wickham, "but when I was at Sydney in the last war I heard his name a lot. He was a fellow called Johnny Woods who wasn't sociable and always kept his drink for himself, so if any fellow stood himself one and didn't shout his pals he was called Johnny Woods and the drink was a Johnny Woodser. I daresay there never was such a person.

Mythical, you know. Like the old gods and goddesses, what?
Well, one more for luck."

He poured himself a second drink, drained the tea-cup, and
put the bottle in the cupboard.

"And now, what about that heifer?" he said.

Had Colin not been used to the agent's peculiarities he might
have thought eleven o'clock on a Saturday morning a bad
moment to drink two very large navy rums, especially when the
choice of the local representative at the Barsetshire Agricultural
was under discussion. But experience had taught him, and
taught Noel and Lydia, that Mr. Wickham had a power of
absorbing rum, gin and whisky without being even faintly
affected by them, only equalled by the amount of whisky, gin
and rum that came to him not only from pals in every corner of
the globe, but from mysterious sources all over England and
most of Scotland, for it was Mr. Wickham's proud boast that he
had never visited a pub without making a pal of the proprietor.
Every year when he went to Norfolk the little post office at
Duchess Loose (said by philologists to be a corruption of Dutchie's
Sluice, so named in the years of Dutch draining) had to engage
the services of the village idiot (for the old civilization had not
yet been throttled by Progress at Duchess Loose and each little
village jealously conserved its idiot, thinking but poorly of the
idiots in rival hamlets) to help to carry down to the station the
birds that Mr. Wickham had shot overnight and was despatch-
ing to his friends, which gifts came back to him in the shape of
drink from Christmas to Christmas every year. Noel had at first
been a little shy of asking the agent to supper, for his own stock
of drink was scanty and he felt he could not entertain Mr.
Wickham as he would wish. But, as Mr. Wickham cheerfully
explained to him, he only drank for courtesy and good comrade-
ship when he dined out, preferring to do his serious drinking at
home, so Noel found it simpler to fall in with the agent's views,
give him the glass of sherry or claret that he could provide and

accept without false pride the drinks he offered in his own cottage.

"You'd better come and look at her," said Mr. Wickham. "She's as nice a heifer as we've had here."

He shepherded his guests to the door and led the way down the garden.

"I'll come with pleasure," said Noel, "though you know as well as I do that you'll send whatever you like."

"Of course I shall," said Mr. Wickham. "It's no use keeping an agent and barking yourself. But I'd like you and Keith to look at her. Mrs. Merton was down at the farm on Friday and I asked her to pick the likeliest heifer and, by Jove, if she didn't pick Verena at once. She's got the Nelson touch about heifers."

"What an unusual name for a cow," said Colin.

"After the Rector's wife," said Mr. Wickham. "Not that she knows anything about cows, but she knows Duchess Loose, and that's enough. She was as bucked as anything when I asked if I might call the heifer after her. I wondered afterwards if I ought to ask the Rector to christen her, the heifer I mean. I don't mean really christen, but just give his blessing on the whole thing, so that he'd feel he wasn't being left out of it."

"And did he?" asked Noel, amused.

"Well, I thought it over," said Mr. Wickham, "with a good tot of navy rum to help the brain to function, and I came to the conclusion I'd better leave it alone. Queer birds, clergymen. You never know with them. Daresay it's the clothes they wear or something. But I asked old Tubby."

"You asked who, or do I mean whom?" said Noel.

"Father Fewling. Tubby Fewling," said Mr. Wickham. "You know him. The high church padre at St. Sycorax. He was in the Navy in the last war. A Commander he was and I only got as far as Second Lieutenant, but he's one of the best. When the rum begins to get out of hand I have old Tubby down to the cottage and he helps me to straighten things out. At Easter," said Mr. Wickham thoughtfully, "the cupboard was quite full and there was one bottle I couldn't fit in, though I had them head to tail and double-banked. Now it's a principle of mine never to leave spirits lying about and never to have them in the bedroom. So on Easter Monday I got old Tubby down here and we showed that bottle what the Navy is made of."

"Was Father Fewling all right?" said Noel, who though he had never attended St. Sycorax, being put off by the ferocious smell of incense that came rushing out of it, had liked the hard-working, selfless priest-in-charge.

"The British Navy is always right," said Mr. Wickham. "As a matter of fact it did him a lot of good. Easter must be plain hell if you go at it baldheaded like old Tubby. That bottle just saved him from a good old breakdown. Well, what do you think of her?"

They had by now reached the Home Farm where a number of cows were standing about in the yard, whisking their tails in a perfunctory way and chewing sideways.

"I told Bunce to have them here for you to look at," said Mr. Wickham. "Come over here, Bunce."

The cowman slouched across the yard. It was at such moments that Noel Merton, the very successful barrister, a man of the world equal to almost any occasion, able to tip exactly the right amount, felt how insignificant he really was. To Wickham and Bunce his legal fame, the large retaining fees marked on his briefs, his acquaintance with the best of what is left of London's good society, his delightful and competent wife, his two excellent children, his position (through his wife) as practically Lord of the Manor, including the right of presentation to the living of St. Mary's, Northbridge, alternately with the Bishop of Barchester, meant absolutely nothing. It is true that most of these things were quite unknown to them, but had they heard of them they would have been equally unmoved. A man who did not know cows, or was incapable of talking as if he knew about them, was not worth considering. Deeply did he envy Colin who had lived at Northbridge most of his life and knew who everyone was. Colin could ask Bunce how his wicked old father Bunce the ferryman was, and how Mrs. Bunce's rheumatism was doing, and whether his disgraceful sister Effie Bunce had had her baby christened yet.

"Well, no, sir, not rightly christened," said Bunce to Colin. "She's expecting again, sir, and she don't rightly know who the father is. I seed her coming out of the bushes at Christmas with young Hibberd, that's old Hibberd's son that's gardener at the Rectory leastways it's his father that's gardener if you take my meaning, and I reckoned it was him, but Mum she caught our Effie in that old air-raid shelter outside St. Sycorax with that young Syd Fitchett and she gave Effie a rare old beating. I did laugh. So did Dad. He laughed till his teeth got crossed-like in his mouth and Mum she had to hit him on the back to stop him. So Effie says she'll have them both christened together and Mrs. Villars is going to be godmother and Effie says she's going to be confirmed now she's got two to work for, if it costs her the last penny she's got."

"Splendid," said Colin. "Tell your father I'll be coming down to see him before I go back to London. And now let's see the heifer you're showing."

"That's her, sir," said Bunce, pointing to a group of four cows all exactly alike.

"Well, you've never bred a nicer one," said Colin approvingly and fell into technicalities with Bunce and the agent.

Noel thought seriously of emigrating, and had he not been extremely fond of Lydia might have done so at once, except that he had not the faintest idea how to set about such a thing, assisted passages for emigrants not being one of the subjects in the law curriculum. He also thought of suicide and of catching the next train to town. By this time the inspection was over. Bunce opened the yard gate and the herd moved slowly out, elbowing each other with their large hip-bones with a kind of lazy spitefulness.

"Here's good luck to Northbridge Verena," said Colin, handing half a crown to Bunce.

"All the best to you too, sir," said Bunce and went back to whatever he was doing.

"Come back and have a drink before lunch," said Mr. Wickham.

Noel thanked him but said they ought to be getting back.

"By the way, Wickham," said Colin, as they took the path back by the water-meadows. "You don't know of any small house or cottage anywhere in the neighbourhood, do you? Or really anywhere round about Barchester. It's for the widow of an army officer, a friend of mine. She's not very well off."

Mr. Wickham said he would look out, but the outlook wasn't too bright. What with Government offices still occupying the big houses and the wrong kind of people sticking like leeches to the small ones, he didn't see where the right kind were going to have a look in.

"Does she need much looking after?" Mr. Wickham asked. "I know Miss Talbot and Miss Dolly Talbot have taken a lodger from time to time since their old father died. An aunt of Mrs. Villars's who had arthritis stayed with them last winter and said they were most kind and made her very comfortable."

Damn people, thought Colin, why on earth do they think widows must be old. Aloud he only said, with a forced cheerful patience that amused Noel and put him back into his usual good temper again, that Mrs. Arbuthnot was quite young and would manage splendidly if she could get a woman to help in the mornings. She was very nice, he rashly added.

"Veuve Clicquot, eh?" said Mr. Wickham. "Well, let's hope she'll click with someone. I can't think of anything at the moment, but I'll keep my eyes and ears open in Northbridge. I'll ask at all the pubs. They know what's going on."

Colin's desire to call Mr. Wickham out for his coarse witticism was cancelled by his gratitude for Mr. Wickham's evident wish to be of use. So instead of offering him a choice of rapier or pistol he thanked him very much. They then separated; the agent to look at a sluice that needed repair, Noel and Colin to go in by the little gate from the water-meadows and on through the garden.

"Funny how one remembers things," said Noel. "Do you remember the summer Everard and I were here, before the war, while you were still a schoolmaster at Southbridge? I fell very slightly in love with Kate, really nothing to mention, but then I saw her give Everard a piece of honeysuckle from this bush and I realized that I wasn't in love with her at all."

"When did you begin to fall in love with Lydia?" said Colin.

"Not for quite a long time," said Noel. "I was very much attracted to her all along and thought she was an extremely good sort. It wasn't till your father died and I suddenly found her looking lonely that I knew."

"Does one always know?" Colin asked.

"I couldn't say," said Noel, pausing at the garden door. "I knew at once when I saw her looking sad. I expect everyone knows in a different way. Lord! how glad I am I didn't marry Kate. She is quite perfect, bless her heart, but it would be like being married to a warm fire and a feather bed and sixpenny-worth of toasted crumpets swimming in butter."

"I suppose," said Colin, in a rather legal voice, as if asking counsel's opinion, "that it sometimes comes on one by degrees."

"I expect it does," said Noel, adding rather unkindly, "but in any case it sticks out a mile when one is in love with anyone. I do hope we shall be able to find a house for your charming friend. I feel sure we shall like her."

He then escaped into the house, rather ashamed of himself, and hoping that Colin would not detect the parody.

Lunch was not marked by any special incident unless it were that Lydia nearly choked over a fishbone and had to be beaten on the back by Colin. After lunch the sun came out, though in a very amateurish way, and Lydia said they ought to clean out the boatshed in case it ever got warm enough to go on the river, so they went down the water-meadows carrying the cushions for the punt and the rowing-boat. The boat and the punt were well dusted, the cushions put in their place, the punt pole and the sculls brought from the shed where they hibernated, and everything was ready. But no one felt much inclined to do anything.

"It's quite dreadful," said Lydia, "but I suppose we are all too grown-up. Or else it's the war."

"More probably the peace," said Noel. "When we were at the Warings—was it three winters ago?—we were at least ten years younger than we are now. Apart from my work in London, which I do really like, I feel I am an old, old man, doddering about the haunts of my childhood."

"I don't a bit want to punt up to Parsley Island," said Lydia. "And I'd hate to fall into the river. What's wrong?"

"I'll tell you, my precious love," said Noel sententiously. "We have seen the end of a civilization. It began to crash in 1789 and this is its last gasp. It's a sickening thought, but there it is. All our scrabblings and scutterings, our trying to save a bit here and a bit there are useless. We are out of date. All we can do is to bring up our children to have nice manners and not tell them how much they have missed. They'll never believe us; no more than I believed my father when he told me that life was much happier before motors were invented. Perhaps Horace was right."

"Some people," said Lydia, "think exercise is a good thing if one feels depressed. Let's take the punt up as far as the Rectory and call on Mrs. Villars. We do owe her a call."

At this moment the sun emerged from behind a cloud and a perceptible feeling of warmth stole over the river. Everyone's spirits rose, Lydia's plan was adopted and the punt set out on its journey. For the first time since 1939 the authorities responsible for the river had been at work. A large elm that had been blown down near the ferry and had accumulated such a mass of weed and rubbish in its branches as almost to constitute a dam had been in great part removed and the sight of a tractor on the bank, neatly tarpaulined against the weather, with a heap of chains and other tackle beside it, gave hopes that the course of the river would be cleared before long. Beside the tractor old Bunce was sitting on a log while a grandchild of shame, the child of the disgraceful Effie Bunce, was making mud pies at his grandfather's feet, just as if he knew his father's name. Lydia and Colin shouted greetings to old Bunce. The child, with the engaging friendliness of the State-protected young of to-day, threw a handful of mud at them and yelled a few words of fine old Anglo-Saxon obscenity. Its grandfather gave it a hearty cuff. The child returned to its mud pies.

"How's Mrs. Bunce's rheumatism?" Lydia shouted.

"Main bad, Miss Lydia," said old Bunce. "When I do hear her groaning about the house of a morning I do laugh till my cough fair chokes me. Main bad my cough is, but I'll carry it to my grave with me, Miss Lydia, and that's more than our Effie will do with her load of trouble. Mother and our Effie had a rare old turn-up last night. Couple of gert sillies. If I'd a made a song and dance about all my bits of trouble when I was young, I wouldn't be here now."

And upon this old Bunce, who was well known to have assisted materially in increasing the population in his younger days, fell into a fit of wicked reminiscent chuckling which rapidly developed into a terrifying cough. The grandchild of shame, using most unsuitable language for one so young, threw a handful of mud at its grandfather who gave it another hearty cuff. The child yelled. Effie Bunce came down from the cottage, slapped the child, said a few highly unfilial words to her father, and sketched a kind of rough salute or obeisance to the punt.

"Hullo, Effie, how are you?" Lydia shouted, as Colin began to push the punt up-stream again.

Effie, apparently pleased by their informal afternoon call, shouted across the water that she was fine and not to take no notice of father because he wasn't nothing but a gormed old fool. As the punt swung round the bend in the river the child of shame could be seen hitting with malicious vehemence at its mother's legs, while Effie's voice, hurling abuse in a mixture of American filmese and the authentic language of King Alfred, came to them across the water.

"At least," said Lydia rather proudly, "that's something this Government can't spoil."

This was one of the moments when Noel Merton suddenly felt the immense guilt that still exists between the city-bred and the true countryman. A boyhood in Barchester, by now so large as to be almost entirely urban in its outlook, and a life of hard concentrated work in London, made a gulf between himself and the world of Bunce which neither his goodwill nor his intellect could span. For the friendly, practical, unillusioned attitude of Lydia and Colin he felt admiration and some envy. Never would he be entirely at his ease with the Bunces of this world. Among townspeople, among the well born, well placed, or highly intelligent people of his own world he could move in complete freedom and security. But never, he knew, in spite of his position as a landowner and his serious attention to his county duties during the Law Vacations and at week-ends, never would Bunce look upon him as anything but Miss Lydia's husband.

"It's a pity there aren't more like old Bunce in the Government," said Colin. "We need a more eighteenth-century set to see us through this mess. If they were gentlemen in the proper sense of the word, if they drank and gambled and whored— excuse me, Noel, and I do hope I pronounced it properly, but one always feels a bit nervous about it—and put people in the pillory or cut their ears off and encouraged child-labour, I'd feel some faint hope for England. But as their one idea appears to be that everyone should do no work and be highly paid for not doing it, I don't see where we are going."

"What I really mind is their trying to burst up the EMPIRE," said Lydia, whose deep if undigested patriotism made her use words which her more sophisticated friends were too self-conscious to tolerate. "I mean like leaving Egypt and trying to give India to the natives. If they try to do anything to Gibraltar I shall put on a striped petticoat and a muslin fichu and murder them all in their baths, because TRAITORS ought to be murdered," said Lydia, the single-minded.

Chaotic though Lydia's speech was, her loving husband and her very fond brother had to admit that she had evoked the figure of Charlotte Corday in a very striking way.

"I believe you would, Lydia," said her husband, gazing upon her with deep admiration and the affection that her mere existence perpetually kept warm in his heart. "And I'll get you off. I am not quite sure though," he added, "whether a husband is allowed to defend his wife on a capital charge. You might look that up for me, Colin."

"Our sort are the worst TRAITORS," said Lydia, pursuing her own peculiar train of thought. "I mean the ones that aren't our sort don't know any better and of course they want to show off by making a lot of laws and making children stay at school till they are too stupid to learn anything sensible. But the ones that were properly brought up like us are the real betraying ones. I expect their wives are frightfully ashamed of them."

"What worries me," said Noel, "is the deliberate extinction of the upper middle class. We aren't running to seed yet, as some of our betters are. There are some very honourable families of old title who really need suppressing altogether, because all the brains and vigour have gone to the women, and the men are spineless or fanatics. But I think we have still a few generations of good work to do. The people in power know it, and they are frightened of words like patriotism, or integrity, or incorrupt- ibility. So they hope to tax us till we die out. I daresay they will."

"Meanwhile," said Colin, who as punter had the advantage of seeing where they were going, "here are the Rectory steps, and owing to being out of practice I am probably going to make a very bad landing and fall into the water, and then you'll have to get me out."

His deeds belied his words, and in another minute the punt lay-to neatly at the bottom of the Rectory garden.

"I suppose," said Lydia, as they landed, "we'd better put the cushions and the paddle in Mr. Villars's boatshed. One never knows."

It was, her hearers felt, too sadly true. Nothing was safe now. Being a half-holiday it was quite on the cards that a boatload of the conceited, half-educated oafs and louts from Barchester might pass and help themselves to portable property. Or the village school, red forcing-ground for revolution, might steal what it could carry and throw the rest into the water. In neither case would the police dare to prosecute, for very few magistrates dared or wished to support their own police.

"Blast," said Colin. "But I expect you are right."

So all stealable parts of the punt were carried into the Rectory boatshed and Colin took the precaution of putting the key in his pocket.

The Rectory garden sloped pleasantly down to the river with the handsome church in the background. Outside the drawing-room window they found Mrs. Villars pulling up weeds and grass from the flagged terrace. She was pleased to see her visitors. Northbridge Manor and the Rectory had always been on friendly terms and during the war, with her own house full of billeted officers, her sons away and the Manor taken over by a business firm, she had missed the friendly intercourse with the Keiths. Now the Rectory was her own again and the Mertons were established as neighbours, and though her sons could not often visit her, she was content.

"I will not," said Mrs. Villars, who had got up from her knees, taken off her gardening-gloves and apron and given herself a general shake, "offer you tea on the terrace, because if I did the sun would go in at once. There is a fire in the drawing-room."

She stood aside for her guests to go in by the french window. The drawing-room was full of the afternoon sunshine, a large wood fire was burning and everything looked worn yet comfortable.

"If you would shut the window," said Mrs. Villars to Colin, "I think we shall be safe. Ever since this peace one cannot trust the sun for a single moment. Gregory is in the study, supposed to be writing a sermon for tomorrow, but I think he is really asleep. At least I went in a quarter of an hour ago and he was pretending to read *The Times*. The Bishop was speaking in the House of Lords yesterday and Gregory thought he might find something useful in his speech."

"Does the Bishop ever say anything useful?" said Colin.

"What Mrs. Villars meant," said Lydia, "was that the Bishop might have said something silly like loving the Germans."

Her explanation appeared perfectly clear to her hearers, who were all anti-Palace to the death.

Mrs. Villars then rang for tea, a proceeding which impressed her guests deeply, and the faithful though rather tyrannous parlourmaid Foster brought it in, followed by the Rector. Conversation flowed mildly on such original subjects as the defects of the Government, how nice it was that Mr. Churchill had not taken a title, the probable shortage or complete disappearance of coal, electricity, gas, coke, candles, oil and matches during the ensuing winter, and, as always, food rationing.

"I know," said Mrs. Villars, staring straight into infinity in a sibylline way, "that the next thing they will ration is bread."

"And how do you know, my dear," said her husband.

"Because they said they wouldn't," said Mrs. Villars.

A discussion then arose as to whom one meant when one said "they." Lydia, the single-minded, said she meant the present Government. Mr. Villars said that if he took the trouble to examine his own thoughts, which he rarely did because he had other things to think about, he would probably find that "they" was the equivalent of person or persons unknown. Mrs. Villars said there were all sorts of different theys and the ones she was talking about were, she supposed, the people who were responsible for all this rationing. But not, she added, Lord Woolton, because he had done the rationing so well and so fairly that one couldn't possibly call him They.

"'There is example for't: the lady of the Strachey married the yeoman of the wardrobe': *Twelfth Night*," said Colin and then apologized, adding that he didn't know why he said it and hadn't the faintest idea what it meant.

"Everyone knows why you said it," said Lydia. "It's because Mrs. Villars was talking about Lord Woolton. That's cause and effect or conjunctivitis or something of the sort. But if it's in Shakespeare it must mean something, because what he says always means something, even if you can't understand it. I expect he didn't always understand what he was saying either. I mean a thing like what Colin said must mean *something*, because if it didn't there would be no sense in saying it."

"After Mrs. Merton's masterful exposition of the subject," said Mr. Villars, "I feel that there is hardly anything to add. I would merely suggest that Mr. Keith, though his remark has thrown no light at all upon a quotation which is one of the permanent puzzles to Shakespeare scholars, has at least given what journalists call a new slant on the question."

Colin hastened to disclaim any kind of theory as to the literary or historical meaning of the quotation, adding thoughtfully that the worst of the name was that there were no rhymes to it, so one could not write scurrilous lampoons in rhymed couplets.

There was a brief silence while each of the party tried to think of a rhyme, in silent but fruitless emulation.

"Oh!" said Lydia suddenly. "Arbuthnot."

"Darling, Lydia, 'tis a pity, You have lost your wits, my pretty," said Noel. "Spell it as you may, it does *not* rhyme with Arbuthnot."

"Well, Mr. Villars said scurrilous lampoons, so of course I thought of Pope. Not that I've read him, except a bit we had to do for that foul School Certificate and that beast Pettinger made us learn it by heart," said Lydia vengefully, "but Arbuthnot was

a doctor or something. Anyway Pope or someone wrote about
him. So it reminded me about the cottage, Colin, and I thought
you might ask Mrs. Villars."

No single member of the party had been able to grapple with
Lydia's speech as a whole, though several of them had thought
they understood parts of it. Colin, realizing that his sister was
thinking about the little house that Mrs. Arbuthnot wanted,
threw her a grateful look and said to Mrs. Villars that he was
looking for a little house for the widow of an army friend of his,
a Captain Arbuthnot, and would be very grateful if she knew of
anything suitable.

"I do wish I did," said Mrs. Villars, quite truthfully, for she
had a high standard for the duty of a Rector's wife and felt
herself mildly responsible towards anyone who needed help. "I
am afraid little houses are very difficult to find."

"Or a cottage," said Colin. "She's not very well off."

Mrs. Villars nearly said Don't be silly, for very few people
were well off and the difference between a cottage, at any rate
the kind of cottage Colin meant, and a little house existed
entirely in the imagination.

"I know that Mrs. Dunsford, the General's widow, you know,
sometimes lets the first floor of Hovis House, with service. But
perhaps Mrs. Arbuthnot would find the stairs too much."

"Mrs. Arbuthnot," said Colin, goaded beyond patience, "is
quite young and I'm sure you'd like her. And she is awfully
good-looking," he added, coming out into the open.

Noel and Lydia almost winked at each other. Mrs. Villars
apologized for her mistake. Ever since that idiotic poster of a
widow wearing a hat and weeds that no self-respecting woman
would be seen dead in had been stuck up everywhere to stop
people walking straight into buses and cars as they always will,
one had been apt to think of widows as being at least fifty, she
said. Of course if Mrs. Arbuthnot could do her own housework
and cooking it would be easier to find a home for her, and she
would certainly make every possible inquiry and let Colin know.

"As a matter of fact," said the Rector, "that very over-dressed woman in the poster never cared about her husband in the least. She is looking like that because she voted Labour and suddenly saw what she had done."

The guests looked at Mr. Villars with a respect they had not hitherto felt. Immersed in his own work and in learned articles on patristic literature, the Rector seemed to most of his acquaintances rather aloof and unconcerned with daily life. But he had been taking notice all the time and had just offered a valuable contribution to—well, no one could say exactly to what, but they all felt it had helped to clarify things in general.

Colin then thanked Mrs. Villars for her offer of help and the party broke up. Mr. Villars aid he would walk down to the river with them, which made Colin have to confess that he had pocketed the boathouse key.

"Quite right," said the Rector. "Some friends who came from Southbridge left their boat tied up with some soft cushions in it. They were all stolen by the school children who sold them in the village. I met several of the cushions in various cottages where I was visiting, but the police couldn't or wouldn't take action although the children were boasting openly about the money they had got for them. It was quite useless to preach a sermon about it, for none of them go to church, nor do their fathers and mothers. One often thinks of Herod with sympathetic understanding."

"And of Elisha," said Noel. "Even one she-bear would be a help; she would account for twenty-one of them."

The Rector, pleased to find the brilliant lawyer so well brought up, fell into conversation with him about their favourite characters in Holy Writ. Noel said that after a long day in court he often wished he was the Tachmonite that sat in the seat, and was delighted that his pastor could not immediately place the reference.

When they got back Lydia went upstairs to assist at the baths and suppers of her offspring, while Noel and Colin split some wood for kindling and discussed in all its bearings an incredibly dull case of company law. Dinner was chicken and vegetables and fruit, all grown on the place. Then they read newspapers and were comfortably silent till the telephone bell rang.

"It's for you, Colin," said Lydia, who was nearest to the instrument. "I'll switch you through to the pantry."

Colin was absent for a considerable time and came back with the air of one who had just stepped out to look at the sky and see what the weather was like. Noel and Lydia, half-asleep in their chairs, very naturally made no comment and no inquiries.

"Sorry I was so long," said Colin, with an expression that an ill-wisher might have called fatuous.

"That's all right," said Noel lazily. "The other end pays."

"Oh," said Colin, "I told them to charge it to this end. I hope you don't mind."

"Of course not," said Lydia. "I'm going to bed."

Colin, apparently hurt by his sister's want of interest, said he didn't suppose she wanted to know who it was.

"It wasn't to say Kate's children had got the mumps, was it?" said Lydia, suddenly alert.

"Good Lord, no," said her brother. "It was only Peggy ringing up to ask if I'd got anything. It was awfully nice of her to ring up so late."

"Than God it wasn't any later," said Noel, "or Lydia would have jumped to the conclusion that all the young Carters had swelled and died. Well, good-night."

He turned out his reading-lamp and got up. Lydia did the same.

"It doesn't matter of course, but I thought you might just care who it was," said Colin.

"You said it was Peggy, darling," said Lydia. "Good-night."

"How did you know her name was Peggy?" said Colin suspiciously.

"What on earth are you talking about?" said Noel. "Come along, Lydia. See that the lights are out when you come up, Colin, like a good chap."

"I only thought," said Colin with the patient articulation of a gentleman suffering from drink or the tender passion, "that you'd be pleased that Peggy Arbuthnot rang up. She was awfully grateful that you are going to find a house for her. I wanted her to wait and talk to you, but she rang off. You'd have liked her voice awfully."

"I am sure we would," said Lydia and quickly shut the drawing-room door upon her brother. She and Noel looked at each other and laughed, though carefully, for they didn't wish to seem unsympathetic.

"Poor lamb," said Lydia, suddenly feeling a great deal older and more worldly than her elder brother. "It's the first time as far as I know. I do hope she is nice. But even if she isn't I shall like her very much so long as she is nice to Colin. I must say though that I think Peggy is a dull sort of name."

Noel said that Lydia appeared to him to be distinctly the name of a cat and upon this they went upstairs to bed.

CHAPTER 2

On the following day beyond church, Sunday lunch at which Lavinia was allowed to assist and behaved very well, Sunday coma, a Sunday walk after tea and Sunday supper to which Mr. Wickham came, nothing of note occurred. The question of a house or a cottage for Mrs. Arbuthnot was discussed at intervals. Kate Carter rang up from Southbridge to say that the mumps had been a false alarm and it was an impacted wisdom tooth which had caused the swelling and the boy was in the Barchester General and doing nicely and would be back at school in a few days, so when would Lydia and Colin come over. As everyone was going to Mrs. Brandon's party on Monday, Kate suggested that the Manor should come back to supper at Southbridge and meanwhile she would inquire about a small house, adding that she didn't know Mrs. Arbuthnot but if she was a friend of Colin's she was sure she was very nice.

As there was no fine or warm weather that summer and there will obviously never be again, we will try not to allude to it. Monday was slightly colder, wetter and windier than Saturday or Sunday, and the same holds good for every other day. Luckily for Mrs. Brandon's party the house faced south and so had what daylight there was, and in any case the presence of a number of human beings all out-talking each other has a warming effect on the atmosphere. During the war Mrs. Brandon had housed at Stories a small private nursery school and enjoyed it very much.

The school had now gone back to its own home, but two or three of the more delicate babies had remained with the nice teacher Miss Feilding in charge of them. The reason for this was twofold. The ostensible reason was that if They knew that Mrs. Brandon was being so capittleist and undemocratic as to have a drawing-room and a spare bedroom They would probably, nay certainly and deliberately, have billeted Mixo-Lydians or hands from the Hogglestock iron-works on her. The second reason and the really important one was that Mrs. Brandon's ex-Nurse, who had brought up Francis and Delia and remained as a kind of general utility, having tasted the joys of power over a series of babies was not lightly going to give up this power.

"Very well, Nurse," said Mrs. Brandon. "Miss Feilding and the three little ones can stay and keep the Green Room and Dressing-room and they can go on using the drawing-room for I really do not see how we could ever get the furniture and carpets put back. But the Pink Room I must have, because if anyone came to stay with me I would need a room for them."

"I quite see what you mean, madam," said Nurse condescendingly, "and I am sure Miss Feilding will be quite agreeable. Really, madam, when we remember how poor Baby Collis wasn't quite the thing when first he came here and what a fine little fellow he was when he left us, it does seem as if it was meant."

"It was your idea of putting him onto Toddlefood that made all the difference, Nurse," said Mrs. Brandon, basely pandering to the tyrant.

"Well, madam," said Nurse pityingly, "one couldn't expect Miss Feilding to know a thing like that. Those trained ladies, madam, they don't study the babies. It's all out of books with them. Still, she's a nice lady, for a nursery-teacher, and I'm sure we have always got on very well. Of course the ideas she has, they are all right for the babies that come here, but I wouldn't dream of letting her do anything for Miss Delia's children. Our babies need someone who really does understand them. It's to be hoped that Miss Delia and Mr. Grant and the children will be visiting us again soon. I found an old dress of yours, madam, that chiffon you had the first year of the war, sweet-pea colour and sweetly pretty, and I was thinking that I could make a lovely little frock for Miss Felicia out of the skirt. And that green tweed skirt that Rose scorched, though I told her at the time she ought to do it with a damp cloth, would just be enough to make some nice knickers for Master Freddy."

As usual Mrs. Brandon submitted, and indeed to what better use can one's pre-war clothes be put than to be cut up for one's grandchildren. For one will not wear them again. One is too bony, one's skin is coarsened, one's hands are not fit to show, one's neck and shoulders are better covered than uncovered; the very dresses look strange and out of place in the Foul New World. Better to cut one's losses, to make frocks and knickers, to cover cushions or reline coats, to relegate sentiment to the attic or the dust-bin. It is of no use to look back. Lear's fivefold "Never" is our lament for the lost douceur de vivre.

The first arrival at Stories on Monday afternoon was Sir Edmund Pridham, Mrs. Brandon's old friend and trustee, an indefatigable worker for every good public cause in the county, a champion against all bureaucratic oppression. He had once, sorely against his will, almost offered honourable matrimony to Mrs. Brandon under the misapprehension that she was about to contract a second and most unsuitable marriage, and seldom had he been more relieved than when he found his offer was not necessary.

"Well, Lavinia, so you're having a party," said Sir Edmund. "I can't stay long. Some damfool official is trying to get that land round Starveacres Hatches for a sewage farm. I'm meeting Pomfret about it. That bit was flooded in '23 and half the vixens in the county were drowned. If these fellers get their way all the vixens will be drowned. If I had my way the whole of this Government would be drowned. Not one of them knows about the country and none of 'em want to know. You're looking your age, Lavinia. Why don't you wear one of those pretty dresses you used to have? Mustn't look an old woman before your time."

Mrs. Brandon did not resent his criticism. For a delightful and stupid woman she had flashes of great insight, and she knew quite well that her once entrancing good looks were gone for ever. It was all very well to take more care of one's hair, to cream one's face, to add quietly a little more make-up; youth was gone long ago, and the young, graceful middle age which had adorned her had become a little withered. Short sight helped one to forget, but she had to put her spectacles on now when she made up her face, and sometimes she wished her spectacles did not show her the ravages of the long war and the hateful peace so clearly. And then, having never taken herself seriously, she couldn't help laughing at her own face and thinking how very little it really mattered and how very nice it was that she still had Stories, and Delia could come to stay with her babies, and friends had more petrol and could visit her again. What she did not see was the elegance of the bones in her face, the distinction that had taken the place of her young-middle-aged beauty. Some saw and admired it who had never admired her looks before. Sir Edmund saw a pretty woman who had lost her bloom, but he found her as charming and irritating as ever.

"Nurse won't let me," she said. "She has just told me that she is going to make an evening dress and a tweed skirt into a frock for Felicia and knickers for Freddy."

"Damned interfering woman that nurse of yours, said Sir Edmund. "Tell you what, Lavinia, you ought to wear black. My old mother always wore black. You looked very nice with a black lace affair on your head that night we dined under the Spanish chestnut years ago."

"I don't remember that," said, Mrs. Brandon.

"Don't be stoopid, Lavinia," said Sir Edmund. "You were wearing the ring old Miss Brandon gave you and I told you you ought to get it insured. By the way, you ought to insure it a bit more now. Price of diamonds is up."

"I wish you would see about it for me," said Mrs. Brandon, feeling that if she was to be called an old woman she might at least have the advantage of being treated like one. And she lifted her tired but beautiful eyes to Sir Edmund.

"All right, Lavinia. No need to make eyes at an old feller like me though," said Sir Edmund. "You've a fine pair of eyes, my dear, even if you've lost some weight. You ought to fatten up, you know. Well, I must be off."

But even as he spoke a crowd of visitors came into the room all at once and Sir Edmund, who preferred to do business by word of mouth, was detained by one and another county friend till at last he got away and went off to Pomfret Towers.

As always happens at a party, the empty room suddenly filled and the hostess's ears were gladdened by the parrot-house screeches of successful entertainment.

"And where is Francis?" said the Dean's wife. "Josiah wants him to come and dine with us. We have that nice girl of Mrs. Dean's living with us during the week. I haven't seen him since he came back."

Mrs. Brandon said she couldn't see him at the moment, but if Mrs. Crawley made for the noisiest bit of the party he would probably be there. Mrs. Crawley did as she was told and came face to face with her hostess's son who was looking after the drinks.

"Francis! This is nice. You've grown," said Mrs. Crawley.

"I never quite know if I have grown or my clothes have shrunk," said Francis. "With nearly all my suits I feel as I did in the growing-years, when one went back to school every term looking rather like Smike, with one's coat sleeves and one's trouser legs too short. The tailor in Barchester has been very nice about trying to let things out, but there are limits, and two perfectly good suits are doomed to the rag and bone man."

"You wouldn't think of selling them privately, would you?" said Mrs. Crawley. "Some of my grandsons are perishing for want of decent clothes and they will grow so fast that no one has

any coupons. Look here. The Dean wants you to dine with us.
Bring over any suits you can't wear and I'll get the girls," by
which Mrs. Crawley meant various daughters with large school-
boy sons, "to make you an offer for them. Have you any shirts or
underwear?"

"I wish I had," said Francis. "Most of them are in such a state
that Nurse has taken them to use for dusters."

"Well, if you can grow out of any before next week, do bring
them," said Mrs. Crawley. "What about Tuesday week?"

Francis said Tuesday week would be very nice indeed, and he
didn't know what the world was coming to when the Dean's
wife had to tout for old clothes at the back door.

"One just can't help it," said Mrs. Crawley. "Josiah is really
very lucky, because the kind of clothes and hats he wears are so
unsuitable for ordinary life that his grandsons can't take them,
though my eldest grandson did borrow his grandfather's second
best gaiters last Christmas to keep goal in a hockey match."

Francis said he didn't think gaiters would be much good as
hockey pads.

"Oh, not to keep the balls off," said Mrs. Crawley. "Only to
keep his legs warm. The dreadful thing was that they were too
tight and he burst three buttons off. Not the buttons just coming
off in the ordinary way, but a bit of the gaiter coming off with
them. I managed to get them repaired, but it was very awkward
because Josiah was looking for them everywhere and you cannot
say that gaiters are at the wash. Really, this Government does
make life very difficult."

"Though I regard His Majesty's present Government with a
fascinated mixture of fear and loathing," said Francis, "one must
be fair. Much as I should like to accuse them, collectively and
individually, of having abstracted—I will not say stolen—the
Dean's gaiters to play hockey in, I cannot believe that they have
the wits to do it."

"Well, Tuesday week then," said Mrs. Crawley, her eye
already on the next person she wanted to talk to. "I have the

Deans' youngest girl—no, the youngest but one—staying with
me during the week."

Francis could not think why Mrs. Crawley should allude to
one of her daughters as her husband's youngest but one girl, and
must have looked as perplexed as he felt, for Mrs. Crawley
added hastily, "A daughter of Mr. and Mrs. Dean at Winter
Overcotes. A sister of Jessica Dean the actress. She is working
for the Barsetshire Red Cross Hospital Library and goes home
for the weekends, or I would have brought her today. Kate, I
want to talk to you about my third girl's second boy. He is going
to Southbridge Junior School next term and I hope you will let
him come to tea one day." For Kate Carter and the Dean's
daughters had all been at the Barchester High School and the
families of Crawley and Keith were old friends.

Francis had returned with renewed vigour to the mixing and
shaking of such drinks as his mother had been able to hoard or
to acquire by unblushing and open bribery. As he surveyed the
company he felt it was very nice to see them again but he
somehow didn't much mind if he did or not. He was glad to be
out of the army, for though he had much enjoyed the fighting,
he had found the post-war interlude of peace-time soldiering
quite intolerable. But though he was truly pleased to see his
mother and his home again, though he looked forward very
much to seeing his sister Delia Grant and her husband and
children, though it was very pleasant to meet old friends and
revisit familiar places, the fact remained that it was all a little
dingy; more than a little depressing. That no one would wish to
hear about his soldiering experiences in the Near and Middle
East he quite realized and had taken considerable pains not to
mention them. That his mother's friends and indeed most of his
own would prefer to tell him about the bomb that fell six miles
away, and the night they weren't in London when Aunt Edith's
house was totally destroyed only luckily she wasn't there; for all
this he had allowed and took it very well. But what he did resent
was the ceaseless preoccupation with food. Everyone, so far as

he could judge, had enough to eat, but they could not stop talking about it. The rations, the meat, the fish, the milk and eggs, the awfully dull recipes that people would give each other at meal-times, the even duller though more pretentious recipes that people cut out of newspapers and waved at each other; all these in his own simple words got him down. Had he stopped to think, he might have reflected that with a mother who still had a cook, with vegetables and eggs on the premises and a friendly farmer who despised the milk regulations as far as he dared and always saw to it that Stories didn't go short, he had not any real grounds for complaint. But he saw his mother, of whom he was really very fond and proud, looking worn and being very ready to go to bed soon after their evening meal, which one could hardly call dinner, though Mrs. Brandon usually had a very sketchy lunch so that Francis should have two large helpings at night; he found that many of the neighbours were too tired or too busy to go out much; drink went by luck or outright bribery; furniture, walls, cushions, curtains looked worn and exhausted. It was not amusing for a hero returned from the nastiest war yet known, and Francis, for all his natural good-temper, was sometimes more depressed than he would have wished to admit. So he mixed and shook harder than ever and poured rather weak cocktails with a very good appearance of cheerfulness.

"My dear boy," said a voice at his elbow. "My *dear* boy. Indeed, indeed this is a pleasure. Welcome, welcome."

Francis turned and shook hands warmly with Mr. Miller, the Vicar of Pomfret Madrigal.

"I did see you in church yesterday," said Francis, "but I didn't like—I mean it didn't seem quite the moment——"

He paused, slightly embarrassed, a feeling to which he was as a rule a stranger. Dash it all, why couldn't one explain that though one was awfully pleased to see Mr. Miller again one couldn't exactly get up in one's seat and wave, and if one's mother had hurried off after the service to get on the roof and see what it was that had blocked the pipe that carried the rain water off the leads to the water-butt, one could not say how do you do to the Vicar.

"I know, I know, my dear boy," said Mr. Miller. "I too saw you and I rejoiced, for I felt your return was in a way an answer to my earnest prayers—you don't mind I hope," he added, fearing an excess of zeal.

"Rather not, padre. It was jolly decent of you," said Francis, "and it was awfully nice to see everyone in church and the organ still with that note missing. I say, hope you didn't mind my calling you padre, Mr. Miller. One just got into the habit in the army."

Mr. Miller, who had been called padre during the whole of the 1914–18 war (or First World War, or First War for Universal Freedom, or War to End War), said he liked it very much and it made him feel quite young again.

"Have a drink, Mr. Miller," said Francis. "I've made this one a bit stiffer for you. It's a bit of a blow to come back and find one can't offer people proper drinks. How is Mrs. Miller?"

The Vicar, much gratified, said that his dear wife was very well and would be coming to the party a little later. She had, he said, been a tower of strength to the whole village during the war. He then enumerated some of the many war jobs that Mrs. Miller had done with her usual quiet efficiency.

"But this small beer will not interest you," said Mr. Miller, "I am most anxious to hear about your war experiences. You were in the Holy Land, so your mother told me. What a privilege. And what impression did you receive from it, my dear boy?"

Francis said he didn't exactly know. Quite often, he said, he didn't really know where he was and all the natives seemed much alike. He remembered Jerusalem because of the hotel there.

"Jerusalem," said Mr. Miller. "And what was it like?"

"Pretty mouldy, sir," said Francis. "And the hotel where they billeted us was quite ghastly. The Barsetshires got so fed up that they nearly wrecked the dining-room."

The Vicar looked dashed. Francis's heart smote him for his tactless remarks and he cast about for something to say that would cheer Mr. Miller up.

"Of course we saw all the sights, sir," he said, "only it was a bit difficult to know what was what with a lot of guides all gabbling, and we had a pretty awful padre. Gosh, he was awful. Oh, I'm sorry, Mr. Miller, but I forgot you were a padre. I mean he was quite different. He would be human all the time, at least I don't exactly mean that—but you understand, sir."

Never had anyone appealed to Mr. Miller in vain. He partially understood his young friend's difficulty and embarrassment, and in any case did not suspect any intent to be discourteous.

"I quite understand, my dear boy," he said. "Have you a little more of that delightful mixture? Thank you, thank you. It is but rarely that I see the wine when it is red now," said Mr. Miller, eyeing the pale watery fluid which had to take the place of a proper cocktail. "Was he the religious kind or the cheerful kind?"

"Both, sir," said Francis. "That was the awful part. And we all wondered where he had been brought up, because he knew absolutely nothing. He said one day in mess, sir, that he was all against foul-mouthedness, but when the men used meaningless oaths was less offensive. He said he could not but shudder when he heard a man say 'Cripes'—he really did say that, sir—but he didn't mind a bit if they said a work that meant nothing, like——"

Here Francis paused, horror-struck to find just in time that a word was bursting out of his mouth which would certainly shock his mother's guests, though most of them were pretty tolerant and many of them, under the stress of war and peace, had become foul-mouthed in a way quite unsuitable to their years and sex.

Mr. Miller not only smiled, but laughed.

"It is curious," he said, "how that very unpleasant nation's name has become a synonym in more than one language for vice. It is, of course, largely a matter of religion."

"I don't understand, sir," said Francis, much relieved that the Vicar had not excommunicated him.

"They, in common with other Eastern European nations if one can call them European, belonged, in so far as they could be said to have any religion," said Mr. Miller, "to the Orthodox Church. The Church of Rome therefore very naturally attributed to them every vice they could think of and so the name stuck. And, as you say, Francis, it is deplorable that such uneducated men should be sent to minister to our fighting forces. They should all spend at least six months in a place where the inhabitants are habitually profane. I had the great good fortune as a very young man to live in the slums of a large seaport for a year, which taught me a great deal. In fact, during the last war—I am not boring you?—I was able if necessary to swear longer and more foully than anyone in the regiment. It took the heart out of the most profane when the padre beat them at the job," said Mr. Miller with justifiable pride.

"Thanks awfully sir," said Francis, feeling quite forgiven. "I didn't mean to be rude about Jerusalem, but it was really pretty grim. And I brought a lot of picture postcards for you, sir, if you'd care to have them."

Mr. Miller said he was deeply touched by the kind thought and would find them most useful for his confirmation classes which, he was glad to say, were the largest this year he had yet had, and so passed on to talk to other friends, while Francis attended to old Lady Norton who had to be asked and modelled her dress, hair and hats upon the Queen Mother with overpowering effect.

"How is everything going, darling?" Said Mrs. Brandon, finding herself by the sway and movement of the party, now one huge indistinguishable hubbub, suddenly brought face to face with her son.

"Splendidly," said Francis. "The drink in particular is going

like anything. In fact if it weren't for the way your tall hero son
is watering it down, it wouldn't be here at all by now. Hullo,
Lydia."

"It's Francis!" Lydia exclaimed, grasping his hand with her
old vigour. "I haven't seen you since the Pomfret Madrigal
Flower Show. Do you remember the roundabout?"

"Lord! yes," said Francis. "You rode on the cock and Delia had
the ostrich, and I was helping Mrs. Miller in the refreshment
tent, only she was Miss Morris then. What a long time ago."

"Eight years," said Lydia.

"It all shows there is something in relativity," said Francis. "At
least I don't know if that's what I mean, but I mean the same
amount of time can be longer or shorter. I say, how is your
husband? My dear mamma used to flirt with him quite shockingly. It impressed me, because I looked upon him as a man of
the world. I daresay he wasn't much older than I am."

Lydia said Noel was very well and very hard worked and was
somewhere about in the room and Francis must meet him again
and then a great wave of Birketts and Carters from Southbridge
School descended upon the drinks and Francis returned to his
duties. As most of the guests had to cook their own dinner or be
home early in case the person who was cooking it for them took
offence, the party did not linger as parties had lingered before
the war. With a great final roar most of them went away. The
Mertons were among the last to go, for Lydia had not forgotten
about the house for Colin's friend.

"Do come and sit down for a minute, Mrs. Brandon," she
said, refraining from the words 'how tired you look.' "I wonder if
you could help us. My brother Colin has a friend, a Mrs.
Arbuthnot, whose husband was killed in the war, and she wants
a little house somewhere near Barchester. If you ever hear of
anything, will you let me know?"

Colin, hearing his own name mentioned, came and sat down
by them.

"Poor young thing," said Mrs. Brandon. "I was left a widow very young, you know, though it was only pneumonia."

"Never mind, mamma dear," said Francis, who had brought the lees and dregs of the drink for consumption on the premises. "We can't always have a war and I am sure my father would have been killed if he could have managed it. And you didn't tell Lydia that the pneumonia was at Cannes. That makes it more distinguished."

His mother said he shouldn't say things like that.

"She isn't very well off," said Lydia, "so it will have to be a small house or cottage, only not a draughty one."

As the Millers the last remaining guests were trying to say good-bye, Mrs. Brandon told them about Colin's young widowed friend who wanted a house, and at once enlisted their help. That is in a general way, for Mrs. Miller, who knew the country within bicycling radius inside out, said it was practically impossible to find any house or cottage. Even the cottage next to the Thatchers' down at Grumper's End, condemned by the sanitary inspector before the war, had been bought for an immense sum by a rich businessman on the Town Council who had installed a septic tank and a swimming pool and was getting the drains brought down the lane. All she could do was to promise to keep her eyes and ears open and report any possibilities to Colin. Then she and her husband went away.

"Has Mrs. Arbuthnot any children?" said Mrs. Brandon. "No? That is very sad, and now I don't suppose she will."

"Really, mamma," said her outraged son, "you must not say things like that."

"Posthumous children," said Mrs. Brandon, with an air of sibylline wisdom, "are perfectly practicable."

"For children read progeny," said Noel Merton, "and you will beat Peter Piper hollow. But Captain Arbuthnot was killed more than a year ago, so if his widow hasn't had a child by now it is highly improbable that she will have one later. And I beg you," he added, seeing a calculating gleam in his hostess's eyes, "not to think of elephants, for that is quite, quite different."

He was standing while he spoke and looking, his Lydia thought, very handsome, with the growing likeness to an admiral that so many lawyers have; something perhaps in the habit of command. Mrs. Brandon, a little flushed by her party and the unwonted cocktails, the light behind her, looked up at Noel with an appealing glance, smiled, and examined thoughtfully the exquisite hands which she had managed to keep fairly soft and white in spite of a very busy war life. Noel, looking down from his considerable height, saw with a pang of remembrance for a dead world, how she pensively admired her own hands as of old and, as of old, could make eyes in an adorable way. For a moment he was back in the summer before Munich. He had come through the sun-drenched garden into Mrs. Brandon's cool, flower-scented drawing-room and had indulged in a delicate flirtation, conducted with great skill, no emotion, and considerable amusement on both sides. She had admired her lovely hands, she had raised her lovely eyes to his. Lydia was still a hoyden then, though a very dear one. The glass clouded, the vision changed. The goddess was now a charming middle-aged woman, and would be a very good-looking elderly woman, but the years of war and peace had destroyed too much. His eyes moved to his Lydia and there he saw all he could ever need. Lydia, who had chiefly been thinking that Mrs. Brandon looked as if she ought to rest before dinner, got up and said they must go as they had to go to Southbridge. Good-byes were said, Mrs. Brandon promised to inquire about houses, and the party was over.

"And now, mamma darling," said Francis, "you are going to lie down, and your handsome demobilized son is going to clear the remains of the orgy away if Rose has no objection."

Mrs. Brandon sighed as a hostess and obeyed as a mother, secretly feeling glad to be ordered about and told to rest. Rose had already put a hot-bottle on the sofa in her bedroom and

Mrs. Brandon gladly lay down, grateful to Providence that had sent Francis back to her in safety. She hoped he would marry someone very nice, but not just yet. Only it must be fairly soon, for Delia had only two babies so far and if Nurse was to stay she would require more nanny-fodder. Then, thought Mrs. Brandon sleepily, the rest of the nursery school could go and Stories could have relays of grandchildren all the year round. And there was Colin's friend who was a widow. Perhaps Colin would marry her and they would have babies too. And in a dream of Francis in his nursery chair with yellow hair and a green linen suit and Delia in her tall chair in a yellow muslin frock with a yellow ribbon in her brown hair having their nursery tea, she comfortably went to sleep.

Meanwhile the Manor party were driving to Southbridge to sup with the Carters. Colin was loud in praise of Mrs. Brandon, the first person who had had the wits to realize that Mrs. Arbuthnot was not an old woman, mentally and physically defective. So loud indeed was he that Noel and Lydia exchanged glances of resigned amusement and almost wondered if Mrs. Arbuthnot was going to find a rival already in possession of Colin's affection. Noel said he was sure Mrs. Arbuthnot would like Mrs. Brandon very much and felt ashamed of himself when Colin cordially agreed.

When they got to Everard Carter's house they found Kate Carter full of the exciting news that a small house in Southbridge was just coming onto the market.

"It is still quite a secret," she said, "and the Vicar only told me because it is so important to get the right people. It is one of the cottages in Wiple Terrace where the Vicar's aunt lives. She is giving it up and going to live at the Vicarage with her nephew for the present. The School is most anxious to get a nice tenant, so I thought we might go down before supper and look at it. The Vicar's aunt said we could come whenever we liked and if she is out the key will be under a flower-pot by the back door."

On hearing this exciting news Colin begged to go at once, so Kate got into the car and they drove down to the village.

Wiple Terrace, as everyone should know, is a little block of four red-brick two-story cottages, lying back from the road with a strip of grass in front of them. The Terrace belongs to Paul's College, Oxford, who also own the Vicarage and the living and are very good landlords. The four cottages are called after the daughters of Mr. Wiple, a small master builder whose name and the date 1820 may be seen on a stucco pediment which surrounds them: Maria, Adelina, Louisa and Editha. Adelina Cottage was inhabited by two spinster ladies, Miss Hampton and Miss Bent. Maria and Louisa were now occupied by masters from the School, and Editha Cottage by the Vicar's aunt.

The journey only took five minutes. The key was under the flower-pot. Kate opened the back door and they entered a neat kitchen with a small scullery off it. Beyond them were the dining-room and the drawing-room, which had one window upon the road and another upon the little side-garden. A steep narrow stair led to a bedroom overlooking the street, a smaller bedroom behind it, and a tiled bathroom. The whole house was spotlessly clean.

"I didn't know," said Lydia, awestruck, "that one could have so many hideous things in one small house. I simply must see the drawing-room again, Kate."

Kind Kate led the way downstairs again so that Lydia could sup full of horrors. The monstrous armchairs covered with richly embossed velvet and quite incredibly with thick lace antimacassars; the ball fringes on the mantelpiece; the painted vases with coloured pampas grass in them; the rickety bamboo tables; the tinted family photographs in plush frames; the round table with photograph albums on it; the one hanging bookcase made of bamboo; the china dog in a top hat with a pipe in its mouth; the small easel holding a large photograph of a man with a huge beard, a piece of Indian embroidery draped across one corner; the heavy Nottingham lace curtains: it was hardly to be believed.

"I know the rooms are a bit full," said Kate anxiously. "But the Vicar's aunt is taking all her things to the Vicarage and I am sure we can get the walls distempered and some light paint. Paul's are very obliging landlords and if there is any difficulty we can usually get things done through the School. Our odd-man is very handy. What do you think, Colin? Mrs. Arbuthnot could have the front bedroom and the other little room would do for a maid or a guest."

"I don't think she will have a maid," said Colin. "She isn't very well off and her sister-in-law is going to live with her because she isn't very well off either."

This sudden introduction of a sister-in-law surprised Noel and Lydia, but they said nothing.

"I hardly know Miss Arbuthnot," said Colin apologetically, "but I believe she is awfully nice. She was very good to Peggy when her husband was killed and she is very sensible. I didn't know they were going to live together till Peggy rang up last night. It was after you had gone to bed, Lydia, and I didn't want to disturb you and Noel, so I switched the telephone through to the pantry. I am awfully glad she will have someone with her, because she seems so alone and defenceless."

Miss Lydia Keith, if she had heard these fatuous words from her beloved brother, would have stigmatized the whole thing as sentimental rot, but Mrs. Noel Merton said it all sounded very suitable and she was sure Editha Cottage would be very nice when it was distempered and painted and not quite so full. Kate said they ought to be getting back or they would be caught by the Vicar's aunt and have to drink damson gin made with a special war recipe that had hardly any sugar. So the back door was locked, the key replaced under the flower-pot, and they all went towards the car.

"Good God!" said Noel, who had lingered to look at the front of the house, "the door is real imitation oak with grained twiddles and six coats of varnish. Colin, your friend simply must have it."

Kate said they would talk about it after supper and she would give them all details about rent, rates and so forth, and so hustled them into the car and back to the Carter's House. Here they found Everard Carter talking to a pleasant young man whom he introduced as Robin Dale, an assistant master, and then Mr. and Mrs. Birkett, the Headmaster and his wife, joined them. For the Birketts and the Carters supped together at one or the other house every Sunday of the school year, but owing to Whitsun and the fact that the Mertons and Colin were coming, the engagement had been altered to Monday.

The talk at supper was mostly about School affairs, for as the Birketts and the Carters saw each other every day and supped together every week, they naturally had a great deal to discuss. Colin, who had taught classics at Southbridge for a term before he began to read law, was interested by the talk and the various changes in the School, so Noel and Lydia found themselves a little out of it. But they were quite happy to listen, and when kind Kate looked at either of them to see if they had enough food on their plates, they smiled back and were quite content. The principal subject of conversation was the approaching retirement of the Birketts and the appointment of Everard Carter as future Headmaster.

"It is such a blessing," said Mrs. Birkett, kindly bringing Noel into the conversation, "that Kate knows the very worst of the Head's House. If an outsider had been chosen, I should have been obliged to be rather truthful and tell his wife that no one has ever been able to repair the lead roof over the bathroom that was added in Dr. Damper's time satisfactorily, so that there is always a damp patch on that ceiling, and to explain that the door into the scullery and the door to the cellar stairs can't be opened at the same time or they bang into each other, and the way servants always trip up over that stupid little step outside the old nurseries. And though we have got quite used to the House and are very fond of it, I feel that the wife of any new Head might be put off by its inconvenience."

Kate, who had never yet been daunted by any domestic difficulty or inconvenience, said she was sure everything would be perfectly comfortable and the only drawback would be that the Birketts would not be there.

Noel asked Mrs. Birkett what their future plans were. She said they had taken the Dower House at Worsted which was just unrequisitioned by the military, and high time too.

"I know the Dower House far too well," said Noel. "I was there for a winter during the war on hush-hush work. Apart from being full of the most unpleasant officers the British Army can produce, it seemed to me a delightful place and was obviously longing to have a proper family in it."

Mrs. Birkett said she had felt exactly the same, and that was partly why they had taken it.

"You see," she added, "Rose and Geraldine may have to go abroad at any time on account of their husbands' jobs, so we want to be able to have all the grandchildren. It is really extraordinarily lucky that the Fairweather granny died last year. She was a delightful person, but she spoilt the children quite shockingly, and she left quite a nice sum of money to my sons-in-law. Both the girls' Nannies disapproved of her, so it would have been very difficult. It is really a very good thing," said Mrs. Birkett with the complacent air of a housewife who has for once been able to get her allocation of imported eggs. "And do tell me, Mr. Merton, did you ever notice anything about the drains when you were there? The surveyor's report is quite satisfactory, but if you had noticed a smell or anything I should feel much safer."

Noel, who quite saw her point, had to tell her that he had never lived in the Dower House, as he and Lydia had stayed as paying guests with the Warings at Beliers Priory. "And that," he added, "is partly why our second child is called Harry."

Mrs. Birkett asked why partly.

"Because we can then kill three birds with one stone," said

Noel. "First we can pretend he is called after Lydia's father, whose name was Henry and not Harry at all, secondly he is called after Sir Harry who was never Henry, and thirdly Lady Waring is Harriet."

"Amurath an Amurath succeeds," said Robin Dale.

No one took his allusion (partly we must confess because they were not listening) and he thought with pleasure that Anne Fielding, whom he hoped to marry within the year, would have taken it at once.

"There is," said Mr. Birkett, "one point upon which I shall be adamant. For one year after my retirement I shall not visit the School."

This pronouncement struck the whole table into respectful silence.

"But you must," said Kate. "You and Amy are to be our first guests. That is quite settled. And if you aren't, I shall invite the Bishop and his wife and Everard will ask him to preach in chapel on Sunday morning."

"I absolutely forbid it," said Mr. Birkett.

"You can't," said Mrs. Birkett placidly. "Kate will be the Headmaster's wife and the Bishop is one of the Governors, so it will all be quite reasonable."

Mr. Birkett, almost angry, said that at least that Woman, if woman she could be called, was not a Governor, though doubtless the Bishop found she was a monstrous Governess, and he absolutely inhibited Kate from letting her cross the sill of the Headmaster's House. Noel said he believed that Bishops were technically the only persons who could inhibit people. Mr. Birkett fumed, laughed, and finally said that he and his wife would come as the Carters' first visitors but only under threats and coercion, and everything was smooth again.

The men did not linger over the port, for there was no port to linger over and not very much beer, so the whole party settled comfortably in the drawing-room to talk about the drink shortage which had never been more acute. Even Miss Hampton and

Miss Bent at Adelina Cottage, said Everard, had found it difficult to keep themselves in gin, whisky, rum and beer; and what Miss Hampton did not know about getting drink was just about the size of the Food Minister's brain.

"Perhaps he can't help it," said Kate, always ready to make allowances. "Some people just haven't much intelligence. You can't blame them. And often they are quite clever in other ways. Do you remember Jessie, Colin, the House under-house maid? She is almost mentally defective, but she can mend linen quite beautifully and darn the boys' socks like an angel, if only she would remember to wear her spectacles. But she will not, and Matron is always scolding her about it.

"If spectacles would help, I'd subscribe at once to give a pair to the Food Minister," said Mrs. Birkett. "Poor fellow; it must be dreadful to have a job you can't do. But I daresay he needs the money."

Kate, ever on the side of the oppressed, said perhaps he had a wife and children and of course a man would do anything to support his family. But Mr. Birkett, in whom the matter of beer still rankled, said that in this particular case he did not see the necessity.

"I remember," said Everard, looking at his wife with the besotted look of a devoted husband, "that before Kate and I were engaged she mended a sock of mine, a black sock that Jessie had darned with blue wool. She undid the blue and darned it quite beautifully with black."

"Darling, it was *dreadful*," said Kate, her kind eyes growing misty at the remembrance.

Luckily all the company present were well accustomed to the Carters' mutual adoration. Colin, with great presence of mind, reminded his sister Kate that she had promised to tell him more about Editha Cottage.

All that Kate had to tell about it was in its favour. The rent was very moderate. The walls, roof and drains were in good condition, for Paul's College insisted on a yearly examination by

their own surveyor and were generous about all structural repairs. The Vicar's aunt, a keen and vigorous amateur gardener,
had the little strip of grass in front and the lawn and vegetable
garden at the back in excellent order. There was a jobbing
gardener in Southbridge who worked for her every Saturday
afternoon and proposed to work for any subsequent tenant of
Editha Cottage whether the said tenant required him or not.
There was a fair stock of coal and coke in a locked shed at the
back of the house and the Vicar's aunt was willing to sell it at cost
price. Mr. Brown at the Red Lion would always do his best to
oblige with beer, or an occasional half-bottle of spirits, but could
only do his best under the present restrictions. When even Miss
Hampton and Miss Bent were finding difficulty in stocking
their cellar, said Kate, it was very lucky that Mr. Brown was so
nice.

"When you say cellar," said Noel, "I suppose that is a figure of
speech."

"Dear me, no," said Everard, taking up the challenge for his
wife. "Didn't you show them the cellar, Kate?"

Kate apologized. She was thinking about supper, she said,
and didn't want to keep the Birketts waiting, but she was sure
the Vicar's aunt would give them permission to look at it
another day if Mrs. Anstruther——

"Arbuthnot," said Colin, faintly offended that so beautiful a
name should be confused with another.

Kate said she was so sorry, of course it was Arbuthnot and
how stupid of her. If, she continued, Mrs. Arbuthnot wished to
look at the cellar it could be arranged at any time. Colin, torn
between a determination that Mrs. Arbuthnot should have
every inch of her rights and a wish to explain that she was not a
heavy drinker, began to speak, but Everard got in first.

"Mr. Wiple, the man who built the cottages," said Everard,
"must have been a very good builder. You know the river is apt to
overflow near Southbridge in the winter and that part of the
village can be rather damp. He must have known this, and he

made the foundations very deep. You will have noticed that there are three steps up to the front door, so the whole house is well raised above ground level. And the cellars are so well built and aired that, so Miss Hampton tells me, she has never seen a sign of damp or mould on any barrel or bottle in her cellar. The Vicar's aunt found it so dry that she stored some of her trunks there."

Mr. Birkett, whose face had been darkening while Everard spoke, said there was a diabolical plan on foot to tap some of the head waters of the river for a new reservoir. In that case, he said angrily, they wouldn't get any more winter floods at Southbridge.

"But wouldn't that be rather a good thing?" said Lydia.

"It means the end of skating," said Mr. Birkett gloomily. "In the first winter of the war we had the best skating I remember. The whole of the playing-fields were flooded. Well, now we've got this wretched peace we shan't have any more frosts, I suppose. Look at the weather this Government has brought on us. No summer and no proper winter. Just one long run of nasty chilly wet weather. Why we were ever born I don't know."

"It would have been so disappointing for our parents if we hadn't been," said Kate, "and one must think of one's parents."

Never had Kate's universal benevolence of soul been more apparent; seldom had her hearers, though all devoted to her, been more inclined to shake her, with the exception of course of her husband, who gazed at her with more than his usual devotion and looked almost pale as he reflected upon the disappointment it would have been to himself and his wife if Miss Angela Carter and the Masters Philip and Bobbie Carter had refused to be born.

The telephone rang.

Everard, putting aside in Roman fashion all thoughts of family life, got up and took the receiver off.

"It's for you, Colin," he said. "Long distance."

"Who on earth would ring me up here?" said Colin, at the

same time going bright red in the face, a symptom which did not escape the lynx though loving eye of his sister Lydia.

Colin, for the first time in his life looked almost coldly at his younger sister and went to the telephone. In the ordinary course of things no one would have paid much attention, but there was something in his manner, a mixture of pleasure, annoyance, uncertainty and a kind of boorishness very foreign to him, that made it almost impossible for the rest of the party not to listen. They made, it must be said to their credit, praiseworthy attempts to talk among themselves in voices low enough not to disturb the telephone, yet loud enough to make one another hear; but most of them found their attention sorely distracted. Robin Dale, the only guest who had no particular personal interest in Colin, naturally remained unmoved, but it was plain to him that the Carters, Birketts and Mertons were secretly devoured by curiosity and the ladies in particular talking quite feverish nonsense.

Colin hung the receiver up and returned to his seat with the face of unconscious and sheepish triumph that a long-distance talk with a lady one is not in the least in love with—oh no, not at all, far from it, but one must be civil to the widow of a dead brother officer—is apt to induce in gentlemen of all ages.

He carefully pulled his trousers up enough to prevent that bag at the knees and sat down with meticulous care.

"Was it Mrs. Abernathy?" said Kate.

Her husband looked at her with amused despair.

"I was just going to tell you," said Colin, in a voice which but ill concealed a sudden dislike and contempt for his elder sister, "that it was a long-distance call from MRS. ARBUTHNOT."

"How stupid of me," said Kate.

Robin Dale said not stupid at all. Arbuthnot and Abernathy were both doctors, and the only difference was that Dr. Abernathy invented a biscuit and Dr. Arbuthnot didn't.

"I don't see why not," said Kate, her thoughts as usual flying to the nursery. "I think an Arbuthnot biscuit might be very nice.

Rather a fat one, a bit like a cracknel. Isn't it dreadful to think that none of the children know what a cracknel is. I haven't seen one since the first year of the war."

Mrs. Birkett said she had seen practically no biscuits of any kind since this Government came in.

"Probably we are selling them all to the Argentines," said Mr. Birkett. "If we ever are allowed to make anything nice we are never allowed to buy it. It all goes abroad."

Lydia, Kate and Mrs. Birkett, all talking at once, said what made them more cross than anything were fashion magazines full of pictures of delightful suits and frocks for export, to people who had practically been Germans all the time. The conversation became loud and confused, everyone lamenting his or her favourite luxuries, for necessities they did not ask nor expect, which were flowing in a steady stream to foreigners: clothes, hand-bags, shoes, whisky, gin, tweeds, silks, a thousand other things.

"Well, God help us all," said Mr. Birkett. "We need it."

Kate, always ready to see the best of everything, said she didn't think it was really as bad as that. Robin Dale said one couldn't expect things to get better while the present Government was in Downing Street and the present Bishop of Barchester in the Palace, a remark which went down very well.

Colin meanwhile had been getting sulkier and sulkier and only his really good heart prevented his throwing his glass of thin beer on the floor and walking out into the night. Kate saw his expression, blamed herself for having fiddled while Rome was burning, and asked Colin in her quiet comfortable voice if Mrs. Arbuthnot was well.

"Yes, thank you," said Colin, who was very fond of his sister and beginning to be ashamed of himself. "It was awfully good of her to ring up. When she rang up last night I told her that I was dining here this evening and I was sure she would like you. She took a lot of trouble to find your number," said Colin, his face lit by a holy rapture. "But she managed it at last."

60 Angela Thirkell

Kate said how perfectly splendid and she did hope Mrs. Arbuthnot was pleased about Editha Cottage.

Colin said she was very much pleased and wanted to come and see it as soon as possible. She was, he added, rather badly off but frightfully brave about it, and Kate would like her very much. Kate, who had long ago scented romance and was always enchanted by the idea of any two people, however unsuitable, falling in love, said she knew she would like her and it would be so nice to have the right kind of tenant at Editha Cottage.

"Her sister-in-law who is going to live with her is very nice too," said Colin. "She isn't sensitive like Peggy of course." After which exquisite tribute to Mrs. Arbuthnot he fell into a kind of trance, well known to those who study the tender passion.

"I do hope your friend will be able to have Editha," said Robin to Colin. "I rather had my eye on it myself, as I'm getting married within the year. But I believe I am getting the Junior house, so we shall at least have a home. And there is central heating. I've never felt warm since I was in Africa."

Colin asked if he had been anywhere near Sadd-el-Bak. Robin had. They fell joyfully into soldiers' talk, discovering that by an extraordinary chance they had both known a man called Benson. Colin said he had got demobbed last year and was back at the bar, in his brother-in-law's chambers.

"I've been out for ages," said Robin. "One of my feet fell off at Anzio, so I became a beggarly usher."

Colin was sorry, and then they talked again about Benson who collected butterflies and had hair growing out of his ears, and Colin, we are relieved to say, quite forgot about Mrs. Arbuthnot and enjoyed himself very much.

Then Lydia said they must go. The party drifted out into the hall and good-byes were said.

"Oh, Everard," said Colin, who had lingered in the drawing-room, "I told Mrs. Arbuthnot to charge the trunk call to your account. I hope you don't mind. I have just rung up the exchange and it is three and fourpence. Here you are."

He handed a half-crown and a shilling to his brother-in-law.

"If you will be so pernickety," said Everard, "you'll have to take the consequences. Here you are. Twopence change."

Colin refused to take it, saying that it would pay for his ringing up the exchange.

"Rubbish," said Everard. "It's only a penny farthing or something of the sort to subscribers."

Kate, with unsuspected malice, said how like men to squabble over twopence, and as it is well known that this peculiar and irritating form of honesty is the prerogative of females, her attack quite flabbergasted her husband and her brother.

"Let me know as soon as Mrs.—as Peggy can come and see the house," said Kate, which Colin took to be a very beautiful expression of affection towards Mrs. Arbuthnot, though Everard knew that it was merely to avoid calling that lady by some other name beginning with A. "Perhaps she would like to spend a night here. The spare room mattress is away being remade, but there is always the little room and I can have it ready whenever she likes."

Overlooking the appalling slight of offering the little room to a Mrs. Arbuthnot, Colin thanked his sister and got into the car. Being by himself in the back seat he was able to concentrate on the extreme beauty, nay heroism, of Mrs. Arbuthnot's action in ringing him up in somebody else's house at half-past nine o'clock at night; also upon the sweetness of disposition which had made her submit to his plan of charging her telephone call to people she didn't know; which lover's thoughts made time pass so quickly that they were back at Northbridge manor before he had time to reflect more than once upon the wonderful trust she was showing in him by letting him advise her about a house.

"Burglar in the drawing-room," said Noel as they drove up and saw light through the curtains.

Lydia said she expected it was Mr. Wickham, who had a way of dropping in if he had any news to give. And so it was.

"Have you see this?" he said, flourishing a copy of the *Barchester Chronicle*.

"I haven't," said Noel. "What is it?"

Mr. Wickham laid the paper on a table and put his finger on a paragraph headed 'Death of Well-known Cattle Authority.'

"Read that," he said.

"We regret to announce," Noel read, "the death of Mr. Jos Mallow, for many years in charge of the famous herd of dairy cows at Rising Castle. He had for some months been under the care of the well-known local medico Dr. Ford, but was in excellent health till last Tuesday when he complained of a feeling of oppression, and almost immediately passed away. The funeral will take place on Friday, details to be announced later. Lord Stoke when approached by our representative said, 'Mallow was a fine cowman and will be deeply regretted by all.' His widow survives him."

"Do you realize what that means?" said Mr. Wickham, and before Noel could say whether he did or not, the agent eagerly continued, "It means that our chances with Northbridge Verena have gone up fifty per cent. Mallow could show a cow better than anyone in the county. Lord Bond has a good man, so has Mr. Palmer at Worsted, but Bunce is as good as they are. I had a double whisky when I read it. Well, good night. I thought you'd like to know."

Noel thanked him and he went away.

"Oh, Lydia," said Colin in an off-hand way. "I've got to make a trunk call. If you don't mind I'll do it from the pantry, then it won't disturb you." He went off to the pantry.

Noel and Lydia looked at each other.

"I am sure," said Lydia, "that I shall like her very much. I've just jolly well got to. But I still like you better than anyone in the world, Noel."

In proof of which she kissed her husband very affectionately and they went upstairs, first turning out the lights.

CHAPTER 3

Next day Colin went back to London, where he was able to make and receive trunk calls from his own little flat. One of these trunk calls was to his sister Lydia. After rather perfunctory inquiries as to the health of his niece and nephew he said that Mrs. Arbuthnot was most anxious to see Editha Cottage as soon as possible; that she wanted her sister-in-law who was going to live with her to see it too; that Kate only had the little bedroom available at the moment and how awkward it was. He then stopped talking.

"I say, are you cut off?" said Lydia.

Colin's voice said he wasn't.

"Why did you stop talking then?" said Lydia.

Colin said he wondered, he meant he was just wondering, he meant he rather wondered, if it wouldn't be a bother——

"All right," said Lydia. "I'll have them both here. They can spend the night, see the house next day, talk to Kate and go back after lunch. Will that do? Let me know which day and I'll meet them at Northbridge Halt."

There was a brief silence, after which Colin's voice said it was most awfully nice of Lydia and it would be so nice if she could possibly manage to meet them at Barchester Central, as they would have had a cross-country journey and might be tired. Lydia, who had determined to do the thing handsomely, suppressed a feeling of annoyance and said all right, and to let her know which day they could come as soon as possible.

"Friday then," said Colin's voice. "Thanks most awfully, Lydia. They get to Barchester Central at 7.15. I say, are you cut off?"

But his voice spoke to the unresonant air, for Lydia, really annoyed with her brother Colin for the first time in her life, had hung the receiver up. Not only was 7.15 a preposterous hour to expect people to be met, but Friday was the night she and Noel were engaged to dine at the Deanery. She would have to see if someone from Northbridge could drive her and Noel to the station and pick up the guests, when they would have themselves dropped at the Deanery, send the Arbuthnots back to the Manor with an apology, and get whoever it was to come back to fetch them from Barchester, or else get a Barchester taxi to do it. Permutations and combinations on this theme pursued each other through her mind, and the more she thought of the muddle it would make, the less she felt that she could ever really like Mrs. Arbuthnot. Which was a very unjust thought, for the whole thing was really Colin's fault. At last she felt so addled that she rang up the Deanery in what was, for her, a very bad temper and told Mrs. Crawley exactly what had happened.

"The only way out of it I can see is for me to bring these friends of Colin's back to the Manor and give them dinner," said Lydia, "and you keep Noel. I am furious with Colin, but I'll have to do the civil to these Arbuthnots. You can easily got another woman."

To which Mrs. Crawley replied that Lydia had better bring her guests to the Deanery as an old friend of her husband's, a clergyman, and a young theological student were coming to dinner, and she was at her wits' end to collect two women to make up their numbers.

"It is an extraordinary thing," she said, "considering the number of superfluous women in any cathedral town that I was absolutely in despair. Not a spinster to be had and even the widows of the higher clergy, and heaven knows there are enough of them in Barchester, are all away or engaged. We aren't dressing. Mrs. and Miss Arbuthnot, you said? I am sure they will be charming."

Lydia, feeling that she had now become so involved in the machinery that struggling would be quite useless, thanked Mrs. Crawley and accepted the invitation. She then wrote a postcard to Colin, for she still felt too cross to talk to him, asking him to prepare the Arbuthnots for a dinner-party, and put the whole thing out of her mind till Noel came down on Friday at tea-time. He was rather amused by the story, said young men in love were a great bore, and then talked about really important subjects such as a new gate for the three-acre field and having the septic tank at Nanny Twicker's cottage cleaned.

As they drove towards Barchester Lydia confessed to Noel that she was rather nervous at the idea of meeting what was probably her future sister-in-law and did hope she would be nice, to which Noel heartlessly answered that if she couldn't believe Colin who had told her at least twenty times that she would like Mrs. Arbuthnot, she would never believe anything.

The 7.15 was punctual. Lydia stood outside the exit trying to decide which passengers might be her guests, her heart sinking at the aspect of most of them. A tall, rather bigly made woman, not very young, with harsh features, unmistakably a lady, dressed in good tweeds which had seen much service, paused at the sight of Lydia and came towards her.

"Excuse me," she said in a rather deep but agreeable voice, "but are you Mrs. Noel Merton? It is very kind of you to meet us. My sister-in-law is just coming. A dog got its lead wrapped round her feet. Here she is."

The sister-in-law now appeared. She was of middle height with an elegant figure, a pretty face, fair hair beautifully waved and an appealing expression. Lydia shook hands, apologized for dragging them straight into a dinner-party and led them to the car. In a few minutes they were at the Deanery, where Mrs.

Crawley had kindly given orders that Mrs. Merton and her guests were to be taken to one of the spare bedrooms, as the travellers would want to wash and tidy themselves.

While the strangers were thus occupied Lydia began to collect her thoughts. If Colin really cared for this tall woman then she would like her as hard as she could. She looked capable and she looked kind, though rather rugged. The sister-in-law was undoubtedly by far the more attractive of the two and had very pretty hands and a charming way of speaking and was full of expressions of gratitude to Lydia. Doubtless Colin knew his own business best, but Lydia was a little perplexed. The two ladies gave themselves a final shake and they all went down to the Dean's study where the little dinner-party was assembling.

"This is Mrs. Arbuthnot," said Lydia, introducing the tall woman to Mrs. Crawley.

"I'm so sorry, but I'm not," said the tall woman. "I'm only Peggy's sister-in-law."

Lydia said she was dreadfully sorry to have been so stupid, but when Miss Arbuthnot had said her sister-in-law was just coming she had thought she meant that Mrs. Arbuthnot was the sister-in-law, and then became so confused in trying to explain that she had to give up. But Miss Arbuthnot took it like a good fellow and said it was entirely her fault for not explaining properly who she was at once. Lydia felt much relieved that Mrs. Arbuthnot was the pretty one and quite understood Colin's admiration for her, though she liked Miss Arbuthnot very much too.

This matter having been adjusted, Mrs. Crawley expressed her pleasure at meeting both Arbuthnots.

"Francis Brandon you do know," said Mrs. Crawley to Lydia. "And this is Susan Dean who is living with us at present."

A very pale thin young man with a nervous expression was then introduced as Mr. Parkinson.

"We will give Crofts five minutes," said the Dean, looking at his watch. "No more. I hear," he continued, turning to Miss Arbuthnot, "that you are thinking of taking a house in Wiple

Terrace. A charming piece of early nineteenth-century building. Are you interested in architecture?"

"Not really," said his guest. "I like gardening and birds. Not
dogs, though. And I'm very keen on farming, but we can't afford
to farm."

A tall middle-aged man in dark clothes, with a moustache
and beard and very blue eyes under shaggy eyebrows, then came
in and was introduced to the company in general as Colonel
Crofts, upon which they went in to dinner. Lydia found herself
between the Dean and the pale thin young man who was so
obviously the candidate for ordination that she felt quite sorry
for him, particularly as he appeared to be very nervous and gave
her the impression of not knowing where or who he was, or who
any of the people in the room were. Having but the haziest idea
what candidates for ordination were supposed to do, she asked
him if he was working very hard.

"Beg pardon?" said the young man, his face twitching with
shyness.

Lydia said it again.

"I'm used to hard work," said Mr. Parkinson. "I wasn't at one
of the posh schools you know. I had to work to get scholarships."

Lydia, with the best intentions in the world, said how nice to
get scholarships and both her brothers had got through school
and college on scholarships and so had her husband and quite a
lot of her friends.

"Ah, but mine were State-aided," said Mr. Parkinson. "Not
for rich men's sons."

"A friend of mine, Mrs. Morland," said Lydia, "has a son who
got a very useful State grant to help him to go back to Oxford
after the war, because his scholarship wasn't big enough."

Mr. Parkinson looked at her as fiercely as his pale bony
countenance would allow and said his mother worked herself to
skin and bone to get him properly educated.

"That must be awful for you," said Lydia sympathetically.

"Mrs. Morland works very hard, too. She has to write a book every year and quite a lot of short stories."

"You don't mean Mrs. Morland that writes the Madame Koska stories, Mrs. Er——" said Mr. Parkinson, suddenly becoming human. "The young lady that's my fiancée reads every one that comes out. I'm going to give her the new one for her birthday."

Encouraged by this Lydia did her best to please Mr. Parkinson, who confided to her that they were to be married as soon as he had a curacy and how his first sermon was to be a tribute to his future father-in-law who had been very kind to him. Lydia asked what the text was to be.

"Mavis chose it," said Mr. Parkinson. "That's her name; Mavis Welk. Mr. Welk is a very hospitable man and I have supper at his house three nights a week. So she said it reminded her of St. Paul's Second Epistle to Timothy and I ought to take the words 'The Lord give mercy unto the house of Oneasyforus, for he often refreshed me'."

While Lydia's social self applauded the choice of text, her subconscious self told her that something was very wrong. Her classical education had been strictly limited by the poor teaching at the Barchester High School and her dislike of the mistress who taught Latin, but she felt quite certain that Mr. Parkinson was making a mistake for which, at what he called a posh school, he would have had to write out at least five hundred lines. Nor was she left long in doubt, for the Dean whose scholar's ear had caught and transmitted to his brain Mr. Parkinson's rash words, turned from Mrs. Arbuthnot and asked Mr. Parkinson if he would repeat the text. Mr. Parkinson, flattered, did so.

"Hum," said the Dean, looking steadily at Mr. Parkinson, his heavy eyebrows, in which were several hairs of incredible length, bent fiercely upon the anaemic candidate for ordination.

This awful pronouncement struck that end of the table dumb, and no one would have been surprised if he had added, "and I will see you in my study after dinner." Lydia bravely flung herself into the breach and asked the Dean about his youngest daughter Octavia, an old friend of hers happily married to a neighbouring Vicar formerly an army chaplain. The wretched Mr. Parkinson was thus left solitary for the time being, for Mrs. Arbuthnot on his other side was getting on very well with Noel Merton.

Noel had not enjoyed himself so much for some time. The very pretty woman next to him was charming and quite sufficiently intelligent and reminded him in many ways of Mrs. Brandon as she used to be; or rather as she must have been, for Noel did not know Mrs. Brandon when she was in her middle twenties as, at a guess, Mrs. Arbuthnot must be. An acquisition, he thought, to the county, and quite sympathized with Colin's admiration for her.

"Colin Keith is your wife's brother, isn't he?" said Mrs. Arbuthnot. "He has been so kind. I do so want to get settled and somewhere in the country so that my sister-in-law can have a garden and study birds. She adores birds. Have you any in these parts?"

Noel, such is the natural silliness of men, found this idiotic question from a pretty creature with appealing eyes very reasonable. He said he believed there were some quite rare birds in the neighbourhood, and he had heard of a golden-crested mippet on Fish Hill, but hadn't the faintest idea what a golden-crested mippet was.

"I must tell my sister-in-law," said his neighbour. "I do think birds are so dreadful, don't you?"

She looked up at Noel much as Mrs. Brandon would have looked, giving him a conspiratorial glance which Lydia intercepted and was pleased to see, for it meant that Noel was enjoying himself. Then she had to give her attention to the Dean who was very unfairly enjoying the attentions of two women at once, for while giving Lydia the news of Octavia Needham he had managed to keep a firm hold on his other neighbour.

"I believe, Miss Arbuthnot," he said, "that you will find

several bird-enthusiasts in this neighbourhood. Mr. Downing, whose scholarly works on Provençal poetry are doubtless known to you, is also a keen student of bird life."

His guest looked interested, but before she could speak her host went on with what he had determined to say.

How lucky was this country, said the Dean, in that bird and beast could be studied with no danger. Venomous snakes, he said, were practically unknown; the last wolf had been killed many centuries ago; no large birds of prey seized sleeping children in their cradles or pecked the livers out of defenceless sheep.

"India's the place for birds," said Miss Arbuthnot. "When Fred was in India I spent a year up country near the regiment and did some splendid bird work. I found a stengah's nest once, the whisky-soda bird, you know, and the female got a bit out of my hand. I nearly lost a finger."

In proof of which she held out a strong, well-shaped hand with the mark of a deep scar across the knuckles.

"I suppose the Fred you talked about was Captain Arbuthnot?" said Noel.

"The nicest brother anyone ever had," said Miss Arbuthnot. "Partly why I liked your wife's brother was that he is so fond of her. It reminded me of Fred."

Then her other partner, Colonel Crofts, seized the opportunity of talking to her about India where he had served for many years, which left Mr. Francis Brandon and Miss Susan Dean free to continue a conversation which had been going on through most of the meal. Francis, who had come to the Deanery as a duty rather than for fun, found Susan very pleasant and easy to talk to, as a member of a large family usually is. The Brandons and Deans had known each other on and off for a number of years, but Francis had not met Susan at close quarters since the war. He found her most sympathetic to his love of dancing and gramophone records and so well in fact did they get on that Mrs. Crawley congratulated herself on having made the meeting and arranged in her mind for them to be engaged in the autumn and have a spring wedding. Not that she was a matchmaker in any meddling sense, but having married off her own large family of sons and daughters very successfully and being the past-proprietor of a large number of first-rate grandchildren, she felt from time to time a desire to keep her hand in for the benefit of the second generation, some of whom would soon be grown up. Francis had a good war record and a good peace-time job in Barchester. Susan Dean had done excellent work for prisoners of war and was now holding the responsible position of librarian to the Barsetshire Red Cross Hospital Libraries. There was money in the background in both cases. Nothing could be nicer, and it was most gratifying to see them getting on so well.

Up till this moment Mrs. Crawley had merely looked upon her unknown guests as presentable dinner-table birds of passage and had not given much thought to them. But when she heard that they were thinking of settling in Barsetshire and possibly in Southbridge, she became more interested, said she should certainly call on Mrs. Arbuthnot at Editha Cottage if she would permit it, and approved Miss Arbuthnot, who was being a great success with Colonel Crofts.

"We have known Colonel Crofts for many years," she said. "He and Josiah were at school together. Colonel Crofts did think of entering the church, but his people are all army and he went into the Indian service. Now he is retired and to our great pleasure and I must say surprise—what is it, Verger?" she said to the butler, who was really called Verger, though difficult to believe.

"Excuse me, madam, but it is Miss Octavia," said the butler, who prided himself on calling all his employers' married daughters by their maiden names. "She thought you would like to know that Mrs. Winter has a little boy and both are doing well. And she sent her love, madam, and will come to lunch on Monday."

"I am delighted," said Mrs. Crawley, who somehow looked upon all babies, especially first babies, as a personal tribute to herself. "You know the Winters, Noel, don't you? Philip and Leslie?"

"Of course I do," said Noel. "I wasn't thinking and the name didn't click or register or whatever names do. When I first came to Northbridge Manor, long before the war, Philip Winters was engaged to Rose Birkett. And then Lydia and I met him again at Beliers during the war. He and I were both on hush-hush work at the Dower House. Lydia was very good to Leslie Waring, as she was then. But she is good to everyone," he added, looking at his Lydia with an affection that made the Dean's wife think of Coventry Patmore, though nothing could have been more different. And then the party went upstairs to the handsome drawing-room that looked out of its six large windows onto the Close.

In former days the drawing-room, as Verger often said, had been a drawing-room. But what with the war and what with growing grandchildren, the far end of it, which could be made into a separate room by folding doors, had become almost a playroom. Here, when the nurseries were too full of young grandchildren, the elder grandchildren could read, or paint, or make model railways, and were allowed to leave their various employments in place instead of having to put them away every night. Here, rather to the Dean's annoyance, a radio-gramophone had been installed, gift of a wealthy arch-deacon son-in-law, and the young people danced a good deal. Hither Susan Dean led Francis Brandon to hear a new dance record. Francis was a very good dancer, Susan was not so good, but they enjoyed themselves and wished there were another couple or two for company.

Mrs. Crawley, having made all suitable apologies to the Arbuthnots, went to do her duty by the increasingly wretched Mr. Parkinson. Lydia and Mrs. Arbuthnot talked about Colin till Colonel Crofts joined them, saying that he believed Mrs. Arbuthnot's husband had been in the Indian Army and though he was retired he had two sons in it; one of whom Mrs. Arbuthnot thought she had met. But this subject showed signs of becoming exhausted, which gave Lydia a chance to ask a question that she had for some time been pondering.

"Colonel Crofts," she said, looking round to see that the Crawleys were not within hearing, "when Mrs. Crawley said I might bring Mrs. Arbuthnot and her sister-in-law, she said she was expecting a friend who was a clergyman. Did she mean Mr. Parkinson? I thought he wasn't ordained yet," she added, looking towards the sofa where Mrs. Crawley was trying to make that depressed young man feel at home. "He was next to me at dinner and pronounced a name out of the Bible all wrong and Dr. Crawley glared."

"No, he isn't ordained yet," said Colonel Crofts. "Mrs. Crawley meant myself, I expect."

"But you are a Colonel," said Lydia.

"I know I am," said Colonel Crofts, "and I'm rather proud of it. At least I am proud of having been the Colonel of my old regiment. Your husband would have known it, Mrs. Arbuthnot."

"But a Colonel can't be a clergyman," said Lydia; not rudely, but seeking enlightenment.

"A retired Colonel can," said Colonel Crofts, "if he really wants to and is willing to work hard enough. I have commanded men all my life and I know how to do it. So when I retired I thought the best thing I could do would be to command them in another way."

"So he went to his Bishop, not this old Puss-in-Petticoats," said the Dean, who had overheard the Colonel's last words and joined the group, "and the Bishop said he would get him off the Latin considering his age, and Crofts said he had been at a good school and thought he knew more Latin, and Greek too, than the curates they are turning out now. It reminded me of the day you caught the Head out in a geography lesson, Crofts. Do you remember?"

"It was all a piece of luck," said Colonel Crofts. "I was born in India and lived there till I went to school and my people had served there for four generations and I had been on survey expeditions with my father and knew the maps by heart. Always be accurate, I used to say to my subalterns, and you won't be wrong."

"So Crofts was ordained in due course," said the Dean, who was more human with his old friend than Lydia had ever known him to be. "Not by this Pompous Prelate, I am thankful to say, but by a Gentleman. He is in priest's orders now and I think we have very good news about a living which you will hear in due course. And I devoutly wish that we were getting a few more like him."

With which words he cast a withering glance at Mr. Parkinson and went away.

"It's all because of your beard and because of your clothes not being very clergymanish," said Lydia the outspoken. "One can't exactly stare at people's beards to see if they are clergymen underneath. But I think you are perfectly splendid. Don't you, Mrs. Arbuthnot?"

"I do. I think it is wonderful," said Mrs. Arbuthnot. "Perhaps Fred might have become a clergyman if he hadn't been killed and lived long enough to be retired. He would have done it splendidly. I wish you had known him, Colonel Crofts. He was the best polo player in the regiment."

Her eyes became misty and Lydia felt compassionately towards her, but didn't know what to say.

"I admit that my beard is rather unfair," said Colonel Crofts, addressing Lydia so that Mrs. Arbuthnot might recover herself in peace. "But my moustache looked rather worldly with a clerical collar and I thought if I grew a beard it would look more reverend. I am afraid I must go now. I am trying to knock a little Latin into that poor fellow over there in my spare time, but it's pretty hopeless work."

"I hope you will be able to come and see us at Northbridge

when you aren't so busy," said Lydia, who had been much taken by the retired Colonel and his practical religion.

"I should like it of all things," said Colonel Crofts, taking her hand. "If you are kind enough to write to me I am Lieutenant-Colonel the Reverend E. F. Crofts. It sounds well, don't you think?"

Lydia said it sounded very well and she hoped he wouldn't be puffed up by it.

"I hope not," said Colonel Crofts. "Fear God and Honour the King, and you can't go wrong. Good-bye, Mrs. Merton. Good-bye, Mrs. Arbuthnot and God bless you."

He made his farewells to the Crawleys and punctiliously to Miss Arbuthnot because he had sat by her at dinner and she knew India, and so went away.

"You look tired," said Lydia to Mrs. Arbuthnot. "We will get your sister and go home. I'm afraid it's been a long day for you."

Mrs. Arbuthnot said she wasn't tired, but Colonel Crofts had reminded her of India and Fred, so Lydia thought they had better say good-bye. They found Mrs. Crawley and Noel in the small drawing-room, watching Francis and Susan Dean dance.

"I simply can't get that step," said Susan. "Show me once more." Francis performed the step. Susan tried again, but not very successfully.

"It's like this," said Mrs. Arbuthnot and performed it very prettily. Francis, sliding towards her, took her in his arms and they gave an exhibition which would have done credit to any Palais de Dance Finals. Susan, entirely without envy, admired her supplanter wholeheartedly and put on another record.

"Thank you so much," said Mrs. Arbuthnot to Susan after some ten minutes of perfect teamwork with Francis. "If I get a cottage down here you must come and see me and I'll show you some steps."

Susan flushed with pleasure. Miss Arbuthnot was torn from the Dean who was giving her a résumé of the People at the Palace as he irreverently called the Bishop and his wife. For no

one, he said, ought to come and live in the diocese unless they
had been warned. Why the present holder of the see had been
appointed, he said, he had never been able to understand, except
that an all-merciful Providence thought fit to try us.

Miss Arbuthnot said that if it came to trying people Providence seemed to know its job pretty well. It had made her
brother be killed in Burma and not even in a battle, just by an
idiot native who had stolen a gun and was shooting at random.
Her eyes did not grow misty as her sister-in-law's had done, but
her face became very hard.

The Dean, who had taken a liking to Miss Arbuthnot although his preference was generally for pretty women, said
something kind, and realizing that she did not wish to make a
show of her grief he continued as if there had been no interruption. Who, he said, the next Bishop would be, it was impossible
to guess, but seeing the sort of people that were in power now,
he thought it very probable that provided the present Bishop
lived for another ten years, which it would be just like him to do,
Mr. Parkinson, he said bitterly, for the affair of Oneasyforus still
rankled in his mind, was exactly the kind of man a Government
like the present Government would appoint. He was uneducated, without a background, was marrying young and would
undoubtedly have a large family of ailing, spindle-shanked
children with vicious tendencies and entirely undisciplined, who
would all be born, fed, clothed, insured, schooled, given holidays, glutted with milk which they would waste, and generally
pampered by the rulers whom the vote, so lamentably given to
the ignorant and the unthinking, nay, revolutionary, among
whom he comprehended everyone who was not of his way of
thinking, had put over us to chastise us with scorpions.

Mrs. Crawley who was a model of wifely obedience in public
knew her husband without his gaiters and though fond of him
had few illusions, said he must really let the Mertons and their
guests go, as Mrs. Arbuthnot must be very tired. Mrs. Arbuthnot said very bravely that it was nothing; her sister-in-law

looked at her with affectionate amusement, knowing that she was almost incapable of fatigue, and they all went away. When they got back to Northbridge Lydia packed her guests off to bed at once and offered them breakfast in bed. Mrs. Arbuthnot accepted, but Miss Arbuthnot said she would come down if it weren't a trouble to anyone.

"It's not a trouble," said Lydia to Noel when they were safely in their bedroom, "but I do wish people wouldn't come down to breakfast. I like having just you at breakfast, Noel, and of course Colin when he is here."

Noel told her she was a goose.

When Lydia came down to breakfast next morning there was no sign of Miss Arbuthnot, so she rather hoped she had over-slept herself. But just as she and Noel were in the middle of a really interesting talk about Nanny Twicker's septic tank, Miss Arbuthnot appeared on the terrace outside. Noel got up and opened the french window which the English summer had kept almost permanently closed, and in came their guest in that state of glowing freshness so annoying to those who are not early risers. Lydia hoped she had slept well.

"Splendidly, thank you," said Miss Arbuthnot.

She was sitting with her face to the light and Lydia was able from her own place with her back to the window to scrutinize her guest's face. By daylight her features were more marked, even rugged, than they had appeared on the previous night, and her eyes looked dark and tired. A poor sleeper and a polite liar, thought Lydia, who had not nursed during the war for nothing and had a kind heart; and she pressed food upon Miss Arbuth-not.

Noel, who unlike many husbands was always willing to be agreeable at breakfast, said he and his wife had been discussing a subject most unsuitable for the breakfast-table, namely a septic tank at their gardener's cottage, but as he believed Miss Arbuthnot liked birds he would do his best to talk about them; adding that the rooks were a perfect pest.

"Oh, I don't count rooks as birds," said Miss Arbuthnot. "Rook pie isn't bad when they are young, but otherwise they are simply black-coated workers. You don't know if there are any lesser clodhoppers about here, do you?"

Noel apologized for his ignorance.

"Let's talk about the tank then," said Miss Arbuthnot. "I was talking to your gardener's wife before breakfast. What a nice woman she is. She reminded me of Fred's and my old Nanny."

"But she is an old Nanny," said Lydia. "Not mine, but she was my elder brother's and sister's Nanny. That's the sister who lives at Southbridge and has found the cottage for you. I do hope you'll like it. I am so sorry for your sister-in-law, and you too. About Captain Arbuthnot I mean."

And so often happens, Lydia's plunge into the middle of the matter did no harm. In fact Miss Arbuthnot seemed rather glad than otherwise to talk about her brother.

"Peggy was heartbroken," she said. "She simply adored him. But she would adore any husband, bless her. I shall never have another brother."

From most sisters-in-law this might have sounded unkind, but the Mertons felt certain that it was merely Miss Arbuthnot's way of facing facts.

"I know what you mean," said Lydia. "If I hadn't married Noel I might have married someone else, though I'm sure he would have been horrible. But Colin was always there and there couldn't be anyone else."

Noel said if that was the way he was going to be treated, and at breakfast too, he was going to see Mr. Wickham.

"In case I don't see you again, Miss Arbuthnot," he said, "I'll say good-bye now. I hope you will like the cottage and that we shall have you both as neighbors." And he went off to see the agent.

Lydia then explained the plans for the day. At about eleven

o'clock she proposed to drive the Arbuthnots over to South-bridge. Here Kate Carter would show them the cottage, the Vicar's aunt would discuss fixtures with them, there would be lunch at the Carters' House and they would be driven to Barchester to catch the 2.45.

"Someone had better go and tell your sister-in-law," said Lydia, "or she might forget to get up. She looks that sort. I mean I think she is frightfully pretty and nice, but I expect you do all the work, don't you?"

Miss Arbuthnot laughed and said she was sure Peggy would love a visit from Mrs. Merton, and she wished Mrs. Merton would remember to call her Effie, because sometimes there was so much Arbuthnoting about that she and Peggy got quite confused. Lydia said all right, only Miss Arbuthnot must do it too; which confused manner of speech is so clear to all female readers where Christian names are involved that we will not expatiate upon it.

So Lydia went up to Mrs. Arbuthnot's bedroom, knocked at the door and went in. Mrs. Arbuthnot was sitting up in bed looking as pretty as ever. Her hair, where many women's would have been tousled, was merely in an admired disorder, making a charming frame for her face which was already made up in just the right way for a day in the country and a lunch party. She was wearing a most becoming little jacket. Her breakfast tray was on a table by the bed and she was at the moment engaged in polishing her nails. Lydia noticed with one quick glance that though the room was strewn with undergarments and the dressing-table covered with bottles and jars, somehow nothing looked frowsy; at which her Puritan mind was pleased.

"Oh, I say, I'm most awfully sorry," said Lydia. "I never put any cigarettes in your room."

Mrs. Arbuthnot, polishing her nails a little harder, said she never smoked in her bedroom because Fred hadn't liked it and she had rather got out of the habit altogether. Lydia was afraid her guest might cry, so she put the tray outside, sat down by the bed, and told her the plans for the day.

"And don't bother to pack," she said. "Palmer will do it. She has been here for ages and tries to bully me, but I don't let her."

Mrs. Arbuthnot looked at her nails and then looked up at Lydia.

"I'd simply love to be packed for," she said. "Fred used to pack for me. He did it quite beautifully with oceans of tissue paper."

"I had a letter from Colin this morning," said Lydia, "and he sent you his love and was so sorry he couldn't get down this weekend, but I expect you know that."

There was no kind of jealousy or suspicion in Lydia's words and Mrs. Arbuthnot appeared to find them quite natural.

"I had a letter too," she said. "I can't tell you how charming Colin has been. He was such a help when Effie and I were moving into the beastly little furnished house where we are now. Really like a brother, only brothers aren't always helpful. Fred wasn't exactly helpful either except about things like packing my clothes or choosing hats for me, but he was such fun to have in the house. Effie always did the housekeeping."

Lydia listened with interest, and after a little further talk with Mrs. Arbuthnot she went away to her household duties. But all the time she was wondering what Mrs. Arbuthnot was really like. She might be a pretty, helpless butterfly, she might really be a quite sensible, competent woman, who between an adoring husband and a practical sister-in-law had resigned herself to doing nothing in particular—and doing it very well, thought Lydia.

By eleven o'clock Mrs. Arbuthnot was dressed, packed for, and ready to start. Miss Arbuthnot was a few minutes late, excusing herself for the delay because she had found what looked like a red nitwit's nest in the water-meadow, but it turned out to be only a lesser clawhammer. The journey to Southbridge was soon accomplished. By previous arrangement they went straight to Wiple Terrace where Kate met them.

"The Vicar's aunt is bringing the key herself," said Kate when the introductions had been made. "She said she particularly wished to explain about it to Mrs. Arbuthnot. But she is always very punctual."

And even as she spoke the Vicar's aunt came down the lane that ran by the side of Editha Cottage. She was a tall gaunt woman with a long well-bred face and bony ankles, wearing an unfashionable long dress which dipped on one side. Her black straw hat with a purple ribbon, her old but obviously handmade shoes, her mauve scarf, her worn black crocodile handbag, were highly depressing and left no doubt that she was an English Gentlewoman and would be exactly the same at the North Pole, the Equator, Buckingham Palace, Monte Carlo, or Mngangaland.

"I must apologize," said the Vicar's aunt, "if I am late. I was doing the flowers for Sunday."

"You know my sister Lydia," said Kate. "And Mrs. Arbuthnot and Miss Arbuthnot. The Vicar's aunt does the flowers quite beautifully, Mrs. Arbuthnot."

"I believe in colours," said the Vicar's aunt, who was hunting in her bag for something. "They say something definite to me. Last Sunday seemed so definitely green that I only used branches and leaves for the church, except of course on the altar where arum lilies were indicated. For tomorrow I feel psychically sure that white is needed. This inclement summer is no help, but I was lucky enough to get some white lilac and some syringa. And for the altar, of course, arums."

Lydia said it must look splendid.

"Some people," said the Vicar's aunt, still grabbling in her bag, "consider syringa unsuitable for a church. I do not. When white is the key-note I have used camellias and gardenias, besides Mrs. Sinkin and white phlox. Also Madonna lilies, or Mary lilies if you prefer to call them so," she added darkly, leaving her hearers under the impression that she suspected them of Arianism, or Pelagianism at the very least.

Miss Arbuthnot, with great presence of mind, said she liked
white owls. As for white peacocks they were, she added, a fraud,
being mostly a dirty grey.

"Ah," said the Vicar's aunt. "Off-white. It stains the white
radiance of eternity," which statement reduced her hearers to
silence until Kate, who as a house-master's wife had attained the
art of keeping parents to the point, said she thought they had
better see the house at once as Mrs. Arbuthnot had to catch a
train.

"I have it at last," said the Vicar's aunt, drawing the door-key
from her bag. "This key has an unfortunate habit of getting lost
very easily, Mrs. Arbuthnot."

Mrs. Arbuthnot, impressed by this sign of individuality on
the part of a large old-fashioned door-key, asked if all the keys of
the house were like that.

"No, they are absolutely normal," said the Vicar's aunt, as she
opened the front door. "It is a curious fact that whenever I use
this key I have a very distinct impression of gamboge, a colour
which has definitely evil colours in the psychic colour scale. Now
your colour, Mrs. Arbuthnot, is pale yellow, like a primrose, and
you will be very happy in Editha Cottage."

Miss Arbuthnot said to Lydia that until they knew about the
rent and the fixtures they couldn't say if they would live there or
not, so being happy hardly came into the question.

"You will live here," said the Vicar's aunt. "I see you as deep
crimson, very suitable to the cottage. But neither of you will live
here long."

"Do you mean they will die or anything?" said Lydia, who
liked to get everything clear.

"Not death, but a new life," said the Vicar's aunt. "And what
I particularly want to show you," she continued, leading the
party to the kitchen, "is where everything is kept. I shall leave
you the coal and coke, and you can have these stores if you like.
They were all sent to me by my nieces and nephews overseas."

She opened a cupboard which contained a number of tins of

food, including tinned fruit of every kind, at which her visitors'
eyes gleamed, for tinned pineapples, peaches, pears, and indeed
any form of fruit had long been absent from the shops. She then
showed Mrs. Arbuthnot where the logs, the kindling wood, the
shoe polish, the plate polish, the brass polish, the knife polish
and all the aids to cleaning were kept. She did not exactly order
the future tenant to keep everything exactly as it was, but all the
party had a strong impression that she was capable of haunting
the cottage in an aura of whatever she thought suitable if Mrs.
Arbuthnot's pail and scrubbing-brush were not kept in the
identical place under the scullery sink where she kept her own.
Apart however from these innocent if exhausting peculiarities
she showed herself of a very accommodating spirit about all
fixtures, and Mrs. Arbuthnot and her sister-in-law were delighted with the cottage, both being intelligent enough to see
the rooms as they might be when the Vicar's aunt's furniture had
been removed. The Vicar's aunt was moving to the Vicarage
within the week. The Bursar of Paul's had already been unoffi-
cially approached by Everard Carter, and it appeared that Mrs.
Arbuthnot would have no difficulty in getting possession of the
house within a fortnight.

All these preliminaries having been very amicably arranged,
the Vicar's aunt took them round the garden. At the side of the
house was a little lawn. Behind the house there was a small
paved terrace, then another little lawn, and beyond it a well-kept
vegetable garden. The great advantage of Editha Cottage, so the
Vicar's aunt pointed out, was that coals and tradesmen could
approach from the lane at the side, as was also the case with
Adelina, whereas at Maria and Louisa all kitchen and garden
visitors had to come in by the front door; for the long narrow
gardens of the terrace abutted on a field to which there was no
exit.

"And now," said the Vicar's aunt, "I shall give you a cup of tea
before you go."

As it was already a quarter past twelve no one much wanted

cups of tea, but it seemed ungracious to refuse so the Arbuthnots, Kate and Lydia sat in the already overcrowded drawing-
room while their hostess brought the kettle, which had been
simmering over a low flame in anticipation of the feast, to the
boil. While the kettle finally made up its mind during those last
moments when the water is obviously red hot but will not
bubble, the Vicar's aunt came in several times with supplemen-
tary advice and information all of a practical and helpful nature.
Mr. Brown at the Red Lion, she said, could be relied upon to
provide such beer as was available and occasionally spirits. Mrs.
Dingle, a respectable widow who worked at Adelina Cottage
three days a week would oblige with help on three other mornings and really understood turning a room out. The man who
did Miss Hampton's garden on Wednesday afternoons, Maria
on Monday and Tuesday, Louisa on Thursday and Friday,
would continue to do Editha on Saturday afternoons. The
laundry called on Monday once a fortnight and Mrs. Dingle
would take home any personal washing once a week and she was
quite a good laundress and always managed to get a little starch
when no one else had so much as seen the ghost of any for more
than a year.

The kettle then boiled over with loud hissings onto the
Vicar's aunt's little semolina pudding which was sitting under
the grill waiting to have a sprinkling of sugar on its surface
browned, and the Vicar's aunt brought in the tea. Through the
open window, for though it was a bitterly cold May morning
English usage had caused the Vicar's aunt to have the windows
open top and bottom, the click of a latch and the noise of a
wooden gate shutting, noises familiar to all the inhabitants of
Wiple Terrace, were heard and there was a knock at the door.

"My nephew," said the Vicar's aunt. "I asked him to join us."

She opened the front door and brought her nephew in. To
Kate who went to the village church during the School holidays,
preferring the School chapel in term-time, to Lydia who had
often been to the church with the Carters, the Vicar seemed a

quite natural phenomenon. But to the Arbuthnots, who had not unnaturally expected the nephew to be if not a young man at least a young middle-aged man, the entrance of a tall, elderly, bony clergymen with a kind of ecclesiastical grizzled side-whiskers and rather stooping shoulders, was distinctly surprising.

"My nephew Dunstan," said the Vicar's aunt. "Dunstan, Mrs. and Miss Arbuthnot," whom she indicated with two separate waves of her hand, "are going to be excellent tenants. Their colours are most harmonious. Mrs. Arbuthnot's husband was in the Indian Army."

"Ha," said the Vicar, shaking hands with the ladies and addressing Miss Arbuthnot. "Captain Arbuthnot, probably knows the Suffragan Bishop of Kedgeree, an old pupil of mine, a man well known in the mission field."

"If you listened to what I said, Dunstan," said the Vicar's aunt, though without heat, "you would do better. Miss Arbuthnot is not Mrs. Arbuthnot and in any case Mrs. Arbuthnot's husband has joined the majority, as I told you."

"Ha," said the Vicar, more interested than abashed by his aunt's rebuke. "You cannot have made yourself clear, Aunt Monica. I understand you to say that Mrs. Arbuthnot's husband was a Captain."

"Gamboge, Dunstan," said the Vicar's aunt, looking at her nephew through half-closed eyes, her head tilted back, as if he were a specimen of something. "I suppose you have been worrying over tomorrow's sermon. If you remembered the words, 'Sufficient unto the day is the evil thereof,' and didn't worry so much, you would find yourself primrose yellow like Mrs. Arbuthnot and not talk so much about indigestion."

"You know perfectly well, Aunt Monica," said the Vicar, "that indigestion is purely mental strain. And as for gamboge, a curious word whose provenance I must inquire into with the aid of the dictionary, I shall believe it when I see it."

To Kate and Lydia, who were used to the Vicar, and his aunt,

these friendly bickerings were a matter of course. Mrs. Arbuthnot looked slightly alarmed. Miss Arbuthnot, taking charge of
the situation, said in a clear patient voice such as one keeps for
children and idiots, "I am Miss Arbuthnot. This is my sister-in-
law Mrs. Arbuthnot. My brother, who was her husband, was
killed in Burma. We do like the cottage so much."

The Vicar appeared to be sincerely shocked by what she said.
He apologized for having possibly, owing to his own stupidity,
given pain and said how delightful it was to think that Editha
Cottage would have such charming tenants. If any poor words
of his, he added, could be of avail in their grief, it would be not
only his duty but his privilege——

"No, Dunstan. Not prayers for the dead," said the Vicar's aunt
in a piercing aside. "Un-English."

"You know quite well, Aunt Monica," said the Vicar, "that the
Bishop does not approve of them. Of course if you are on his
side there is no more to be said."

He folded his long bony hands, finger-tip to finger-tip, and
gently beat the air with his right leg which was crossed over his
left leg. There was a short uncomfortable silence which even
Kate's gentle tact found it difficult to break.

"You are right, Dunstan," said the Vicar's aunt. "And now,"
she added, in what Lydia felt to be a primrose yellow if not a
crimson voice, "we must not keep Mrs. Carter and her guests."

Good-byes were said. Mrs. Arbuthnot, raising her fine eyes
to the Vicar, said she was looking forward very much to coming
to his church. The Vicar, who appeared gratified, said he hoped
she would use the Vicarage pew as Wiple Terrace had no settled
abiding place in the church.

"I fear," he added, "that I shall not be here much longer. But
for such time as I am, it will be a privilege to exercise hospitality
to my Aunt's successors."

"Are you really leaving us?" said Kate. "I heard something of
the sort, but I didn't like to ask. We shall be so sorry."

"It is practically settled," said the Vicar. "You and your

husband shall be among the first to know and I shall hope not to lose touch with my valued parishioners. Good-bye, Aunt Monica."

"Now sleeps the crimson petal," said the Vicar's aunt as her elderly nephew went away, from which Miss Arbuthnot gathered that the Vicar's colour was once more satisfactory, and felt relieved.

Lydia then drove her party to the Carters' House where they had lunch and Kate explained that the Vicar's grandfather had married twice and had two large families, by which means several of his grandchildren, among them the Vicar, were slightly older than their uncles and aunts. The Vicar was the eldest grandson of the first marriage, his aunt the youngest daughter of the second marriage, and five or six years his junior. Everard said there was good clerical precedent for such relationships, but nothing would ever make them clear to the laity. There was then some pleasant general conversation. Both the Carters liked the new tenants of Editha Cottage very much and when it transpired that a certain Major Thomas Oldmeadow, famous at Southbridge for having been Captain of Games and having had measles twice in one term, was a connection by marriage of the late Captain Arbuthnot, both ladies were taken onto the strength, so to speak. Kate, after a short telegraphic conversation with Everard conducted mostly with their eyebrows, begged the Arbuthnots to use the House as an hotel while settling into Editha, as the mattress had promised to come back next week. This offer was gratefully accepted. Then it was time to go to the station.

"I think we are lucky," said Everard to his wife when Lydia had taken the guests away. For though Wiple Terrace had really nothing to do with the School, being entirely the property of Paul's College, the School had always taken an interest in it. The old cricket coach had lived in Louisa which, together with Maria, was now tenanted as we know by two of the School staff. Miss Hampton and Miss Bent, though not officially linked with the School, had been very useful during the war and continued to be friends during the peace and were almost looked upon as honorary members, while the Vicar's aunt was persona grata in virtue of her clerical connections. "We might have had people like those dreadful Warburys who were at Louisa in the beginning of the war. I wonder where they are now. Poor Geraldine."

But the subject was not pursued, for the Warburys, a very unpleasant family connected with the films, had only passed across the life of Southbridge, cordially disliked by high and low, especially when the Headmaster's younger daughter had imagined herself in love with young Mr. Warbury who was a nasty piece of work. The Warburys amid universal dislike had gone to America to escape the war and Geraldine was now safely married to an old Southbridgian and had two nice dull children.

"But what I was really thinking," said Kate earnestly, "was that if Colin does marry Mrs. Arbuthnot, it will be so nice for him to have Editha. So many people who get married now have to live with their in-laws. And he must have a house in Barsetshire as well as his flat."

Everard pointed out that as both Colin's parents were dead and neither Lydia nor Colin had mentioned any parent or parents of Mrs. Arbuthnot, this danger was negligible.

"That is exactly what I meant," said Kate with feminine logic. "But I wonder where Miss Arbuthnot will go. There isn't room for three at Editha and I don't know of anything else vacant except those dreadful furnished rooms that Mrs. Dingle's sister-in-law lets. Of course we could manage her here for a bit while she looks round."

Her mild forehead was so puckered with anxiety that Everard felt quite concerned and he told her not to worry because there was, as far as any of them knew, no talk of an engagement at all.

"I do hope Colin will get married," said Kate, who was so happily married that she wished all her friends and relations to follow her example. "I don't think he has ever been really in love. Do you think he is really in love this time, Everard?"

"How can I tell, my darling goose?" said Everard. "I have only seen Mrs. Arbuthnot for the first time today, and though I found her very pleasant that is no guide to Colin's feelings. I daresay he is only being kind. He is kind, you know."

"Dear Colin," said Kate. "Do you remember how good he was when Bobbie had earache and he brought him a toy engine and Bobbie broke it next day? And he took Angela to the Flower Show and bought her a mug with A on it. And when Philip fell out of the pram, Colin picked him up and he stopped crying at once."

By this time Mrs. Everard Carter was almost crying herself at the thought of so much kindness to her adored children, and Mr. Everard Carter, who was on the domestic side nearly as silly as his wife, felt a surge of manly emotion over Uncle Colin's noble behaviour.

"There is only one thing," said Kate, looking round to see that no one was listening, though no one was near. "I do secretly wish that Colin weren't going to marry a widow. I know it isn't Mrs. Arbuthnot's fault that her husband was killed, but I have always thought of Colin marrying some very nice girl; someone we know in the county or the Close, like Delia Brandon or that nice Anne Fielding that Robin Dale is engaged to."

"As Delia has been married to her cousin Hilary Grant for several years and Anne Fielding is going to marry Robin, I don't think much of your choice, my love," said Everard.

But Kate said he knew quite well what she meant and Everard admitted that he did, after while he went over to the Headmaster's House to talk business while Kate went up to the nursery. On the landing she was waylaid by Matron.

"Now, I said to myself when I saw you coming upstairs, Mrs. Carter," said Matron, "it's a shame to trouble Mrs. Carter on a Saturday afternoon, but Jessie is starting one of those nasty colds and I wondered if you would mind my sending her to bed, because, 'Jessie,' I said to her, 'it will be far more worry to Mrs.

Carter if you get one of your nasty colds and it goes through the
House and as likely as not the nursery too,' I said, 'than if you go
to bed and have some aspirin,' and I can take her up some nice
hot tea later on."

Kate, almost becoming pale at the thought of one of Jessie's
colds going through the nursery, also of Nurse's reactions to the
same, said Matron had done quite the right thing.

"And just the one more thing, Mrs. Carter," said Matron, "if
I'm not keeping you. I've quite run out of Bronko-Kure. It did
wonders when Anderson minor had that dreadful cold and I've
used it ever since, and I wondered if you had any. I could ask
Nurse of course, but some people, well you know, Mrs. Carter,
some people are what one might call difficult and I thought I'd
better just mention it to you."

Kate said she would see if there was some Bronko-Kure in the
medicine cupboard and if not Nurse could get some when she
took Philip down to the village in his perambulator.

"Thank you very much, Mrs. Carter," said Matron. "It does
seem a shame this Government doesn't let us have some lemons.
There's nothing like a nice hot lemon drink for a cold. What a
sweet face Mrs. Arbuthnot has, Mrs. Carter. I was just happening to pass through the hall when she and the other young lady
arrived and I said to Jessie, because I heard her sneezing and
went straight to the sewing-room to send her to bed, 'Jessie,' I
said, 'Mr. Colin Keith's friend is a sweetly pretty lady. The other
young lady looks a very nice lady,' I said, 'but Mr. Keith's friend
is really what you would call glamour,' meaning in a nice way of
course. 'I hope she will come here again,' I said to Jessie, 'because
she is really so sweetly pretty and such a change from the poor
Vicar's aunt in Editha Cottage.'"

Kate, marvelling as she often had occasion to do upon Matron's astounding knowledge of what was going on in the School
and the village, said in her Housemaster's Wife's manner that
Mrs. Arbuthnot had had a great shock when her husband was

killed and hoped to get a complete rest at Editha Cottage and so passed on to the nursery quarters. But she did not attempt to hoodwink herself. She quite well knew that Matron, and therefore the whole School staff and most of the village, had already married Colin to Mrs. Arbuthnot, found another cottage for Miss Arbuthnot, and probably settled the ages and sexes of all Colin's progeny.

In the nursery she found her young family being got ready to go and look at the Saturday afternoon cricket on the playing-field.

"Oh, Nurse, have we any Bronko-Kure?" she said. "Matron wants some for Jessie. She is starting one of her nasty colds."

"Bronko-Kure, madam? Oh *no*," said Nurse pityingly. "We didn't find it any use at all. We did try it, madam, if you remember, just to please Matron, when Bobbie started that nasty chest cough, but really it seemed to make him worse if anything. If Jessie really has a cold," said Nurse, who evidently suspected Matron and her head housemaid of a conspiracy to defraud, "I have some of that Kuro-Bronk. When Angela had that sore throat and we thought it might go to her chest, we gave her Kuro-Bronk, if you remember, madam, and it turned to a lovely loose cough."

Kate, with unruffled placidity, said she was sure Kuro-Bronk would be splendid. Nurse gave her the bottle.

"There isn't much left," said Kate. "Will you go down to the chemist when you have Philip in the perambulator, Nurse, and get a new bottle? And you might get some Bronko-Kure too. Matron will like it."

Nurse said some people did, leaving Kate to infer from the mere inflexion of her voice that such people were not only congenital idiots, but probably potential murderers. Kate said she would take Bobbie and Angela to the playing-field and Nurse could join them when she had got the medicine.

"That young Mrs. Arbuthnot, madam, what a sad affair," said

Nurse. "To be a widow and not even one baby. How long had she been married, madam?"

Kate said she didn't know. Not very long she thought.

"Poor young lady," said Nurse. "It's nice for her that Mr. Keith takes such an interest. But he always was a kind gentleman. I just happened to be in the garden with Angela when Mrs. Merton arrived and I thought poor Mrs. Arbuthnot had a really charming expression, hardly like a widow at all."

Without inquiring into the definition, Kate said that she and Mr. Carter were so pleased that Editha Cottage would have good tenants and she believed Mrs. Arbuthnot was interested in gardening, and Angela had better bring her pullover as there was rather a wind. She then walked with the two elder children towards the playing-field where a cricket match was going on between two elevens from the Junior School, the two small batsmen looking heavily overweighted by their pads. As the afternoon was chilly she went to the pavilion, so called by courtesy though really a kind of large wooden staircase with a tin roof over it. Here she found Robin Dale who was keeping the score.

"How did the Arbuthnots' visit go?" he asked. "All right, Bobbie, I'll show you how to score in a minute."

Kate said very well and they were going to move into Editha as soon as possible, adding, "Good gracious!" in a startled tone unusual in her.

"Can I draw?" said Miss Angela Carter.

Robin gave her a blue pencil and some scoring-sheets.

"It never occurred to me before," said Kate, "that there isn't a telephone at Editha."

"That," said Robin, "—just wait a minute, Bobbie, and I'll tell you what to do—will be highly inconvenient for long-distance calls. Or for local calls, say from Northbridge."

Kate, who had not usually much sense of humour, suddenly saw what Robin meant and began to laugh which made Miss

Angela Carter laugh too. Master Bobbie Carter said could he score.

"All right, Bobbie, in a moment," said Kate. "Really, Robin, if one more person talks about Mrs. Arbuthnot, I shall go to bed."

And she described to Robin her interviews with Matron and Nurse.

"If Colin doesn't marry Mrs. Arbuthnot," she said, "Matron and Nurse will never forgive me. And now I suppose you won't either."

"Of course I shan't," said Robin. "Just wait till this side is out, Bobbie. They'll all be out in a few moments and then we can start fair. But, as we have mentioned the subject, is it serious?"

"I don't know," said Kate. "She is perfectly charming and her sister-in-law is very nice too. But it does sound rather depressing somehow to marry a widow."

Robin said there were widows and widows, which seemed to cheer Kate a good deal. The small boy who was batting hit a ball gently into the air and an even smaller boy just caught it.

"Out," said Robin. "Now, Bobbie, I'll show you how to score. Every time anyone makes a run you put it down here. Now, suppose someone has made a run, what do you do?"

Bobbie, breathing heavily and with concentration, marked the scoring-paper.

"Right," said Robin. "And if——"

But Master Bobbie Carter, who like all little boys had to show off to someone, was demonstrating his first essay in scoring to Miss Angela Carter.

"By the way," said Robin, "Miss Hampton and Miss Bent were coming back from the Red Lion when Mrs. Merton came out of Editha with the Arbuthnots. They were going to call."

"Will they ask about Colin too?" said Kate.

Robin said the didn't see why they should.

"Well," said Kate, as patiently as she could, "Colin had that long call from Mrs. Arbuthnot the night he dined here. You remember. And he asked the exchange to charge the call to us, and our operator is a niece of Mrs. Dingle who does for the whole of Wiple Terrace."

At which she and Robin simply had to laugh, and then eleven white-clad shrimps came onto the field and two more shrimps took their places at the wickets and Master Bobbie Carter settled down in earnest to learn scoring from Mr. Robin Dale.

CHAPTER 4

K ate Carter's fears were fully realized. At Northbridge, at Pomfret Madrigal, at High and Low Rising, at Worsted, Winter Overcotes and Skeynes, society was increasingly interested in Mrs. Arbuthnot and her sister-in-law who had taken the cottage at Southbridge. The Close was interested because the Deanery (taking as the Palace thought an unfair advantage) had had them to dinner and Mrs. Crawley had said she was going to call upon them as soon as they were settled. This was partly curiosity on Mrs. Crawley's part because she had never seen the inside of Editha Cottage; partly her natural kindness to two newcomers whom she and her husband had liked; partly a quite groundless idea that Colonel Crofts might marry Miss Arbuthnot; and also a challenge to the Palace, whose unsocial habit was to ask accredited newcomers to a nasty tea-party about twice a year and not take much trouble to remember who they were. And as the newcomers having only been to tea at the Palace rather naturally did not call afterwards, the Bishop's wife felt there was no need to take any further trouble.

If anyone wonders why so small an event should have made such a stir, we can only say that the boringness of public events, which had got entirely out of hand, left really nothing to talk about except food, a subject which did but exacerbate the already inflamed feelings of all housewives, and that Colin's chivalrous interest in Mrs. Arbuthnot and his frequent telephone calls (broadcast by courtesy of the local operator) were a welcome change. There was no malice, but everyone scented romance and in a Rose Dartle-ish way Wanted to Know.

"I think," said Mrs. Brandon to her son Francis, "that considering you met Mrs. Arbuthnot at the Deanery, we ought to do something about it."

Francis said it was too late. His mother looked at him in mild bewilderment.

"Bless your heart, my sweet mamma," he said. "I never knew any woman who had so much charm and so little intelligence."

Mrs. Brandon said Mrs. Arbuthnot sounded very nice.

"I didn't mean Mrs. Arbuthnot, mamma, I meant you," said Francis, at which his mother appeared pleased.

"If you mean we ought to do something about my having met her, we can't," Francis pursued. "I have met her and that's that, and very pretty too. If you mean we ought to call, I am all with you. But not until she is settled. I shall make inquiries. And the Deans are having a tennis-party the week after next and Susan says Mrs. Dean does so hope you will come too. It's the same day that the gardens at Pomfret Towers are being shown for the Nursing Association, but as the gardens now consist of two or three hayfields and a very fine set of allotments and were never much at the best of times except a few lawns and a shrubbery, I don't think we need go. You will like Mrs. Dean, mamma. She is rather like you, only a little more intelligent because her husband is alive."

"You must not say things like that," said his mother with great dignity. "I was just as intelligent before your father died as I am now. And," added Mrs. Brandon with great spirit, "I am sure your father would not have liked you to say things like that."

"I am sure he wouldn't," said Francis cheerfully. "I expect he'd have disinherited me. Miss Arbuthnot looked a very good sort too. Rather grenadierish and no beauty, but quite the gentleman."

Mrs. Brandon gave it as her considered opinion that Miss

Arbuthnot must be very nice, reserving judgment on Mrs. Dean. In which we fear she was influenced by the feeling any woman has who is told she is like another woman, were that other woman Helen of Troy.

There was a tap at the door.

"If that woman knocks at my sitting-room door once more, I shall scream," said Mrs. Brandon. "How can one explain to people that they needn't knock unless it's a bedroom?"

"You can't, my love," said Francis. "But one thing I can and will do for you, which is to say Come in."

Miss Feilding, the teacher in charge of the remains of the nursery school, then entered the room in tears, holding a letter.

"Oh, how are you, Miss Feilding?" said Francis. "I go, I go, see how I go, for I am sure you and my mamma have secrets to talk. Now I am invisible," he addded, as he shut Miss Feilding into the room and himself out of it, and so to his office at Barchester where he rang up the Red Cross Hospital Library and told Susan Dean that his mother would love to come to the tennis party; after which their talk became irrelevant and the girl who worked in Susan's room said she would make some tea.

"Do come and sit down, Miss Feilding," said Mrs. Brandon with a cheerfulness she did not feel.

Miss Feilding came in and sat down. Her swollen eyes, her inflamed nose and the damp handkerchief clutched in her hand showed Mrs. Brandon all too clearly that it was no use being cheerful.

"I do hope," she said, "that none of the babies are giving you trouble. They all looked so well last night."

"That's just it, Mrs. Brandon," said Miss Feilding, her articulation (which we will not attempt to reproduce) much impeded and thickened by her sobs. "It's all of them."

Mrs. Brandon's first impulse was to say "Thank heaven it isn't Nurse," for a clash between that worthy and domineering creature and Miss Feilding was the one thing she feared, being otherwise, despite her apparent fragility, a very brave woman.

But realizing that this was not the way to treat a crisis that to Miss Feilding at any rate was of supreme agony, she said she did hope it wasn't anything infectious.

"No, no, much worse than that," said Miss Feilding. "Oh, haven't you heard from Matron, Mrs. Brandon? She said in her letter that she had written to you."

"Then I am *sure* she has," said Mrs. Brandon soothingly, "and when her letter comes I shall *quite* understand. Not an accident?" She added, suddenly wondering if one of the babies had been squashed in a door or fallen out of a window.

"We've all got to go," wailed Miss Feilding. "I was in the garden and when the postman came he gave me the letters. Matron and the whole school are moving to a lovely house in Sussex with milk and vegetables and eggs and a lovely view of Chanctonbury Ring, and we are all to go there at the end of August. I really don't know what to do," upon which she wept afresh in a most unbecoming way.

Mrs. Brandon was in a dilemma. What she wanted to do was to get at Nurse, who was slavishly adored by Miss Feilding. If she rang Rose would come, and if she asked Rose to ask Nurse to come to the sitting-room Rose would have the sulks for at least three days. She might go and find Nurse herself, but it seemed cruel to leave Miss Feilding crying her heart and every drop of moisture in her body out in the sitting-room. Most luckily Nurse, by the direct intervention of Providence, or by chance, which seems to be about the same thing, had run out of the green cotton with which she was machining the green knickers extracted from Mrs. Brandon's green tweed skirt and had come down to ask her mistress if she had a spare reel to save her having to run down to the village on her bike.

"Oh, Nurse, poor Miss Feilding is quite upset," said Mrs. Brandon, using what she felt to be the correct wording for the situation. "She must tell you all about it. Sit down for a moment."

This was very clever of Mrs. Brandon. Had she attempted to

tell Nurse what had happened, Miss Feilding would have cried more loudly than ever and probably had hysterics. But as you cannot tell a story with real effect if you are quite inaudible with choking and nose-blowing, Miss Feilding had to pull herself together to a certain extent.

"Now tell me all about it," said Nurse, just as she used to say to a yelling Francis or a sobbing Delia, 'Now, tell Nurse what's the matter.' And as her nursishness used to calm the young Brandons, so did it calm Miss Feilding, who gave a fairly coherent account of the misfortune hanging over her.

"We must wait till Matron's letter comes," said Nurse, "and then we'll talk it all over nicely. The posts are really quite dreadful now, madam. Not like when we had Mr. Churchill."

Misfortunes rarely come alone. The belated post had come that morning by way of the back door and a cup of tea, and Rose now came into the room with Mrs. Brandon's letters. If there was one thing that Mrs. Brandon did not want, it was for Rose to find Nurse in the sitting-room closeted with her mistress and the nursery-school teacher. Heartily did Mrs. Brandon wish that she had taken the bull by the horns and rung for Rose to fetch Nurse. At the worst she could have died a soldier's death, sword in hand. Now she was caught like a rat in a trap, a red-handed conspirator, and she knew that Rose would put out her dinner-gown (for evening dress one could not call it now when it was just that awful old frock one was so sick of) and turn on her bath with an awful display of patient merit taking slights from the unworthy; and that under this terrific provocation, the worst ever given though through no fault of Mrs. Brandon's, the sulks would probably last for a week. Action was necessary, and prompt action. Miss Feilding, though she knew one should never show one's feelings before servants, was unable to control her tears, now however flowing less violently. Nurse, saying, "If you don't mind, madam, I will just look," searched busily in Mrs. Brandon's large workbox for green cotton.

"Thank you, Rose. Has the post only just come?" said Mrs.

Brandon. "Nurse, will you get a clean handkerchief for Miss Feilding, one of Mr. Francis's big ones?"

"Just a few minutes ago, madam," said Rose, while nurse, with a serene and composed demeanor, left the room. "Cook was just giving him a cup of tea, madam," she added, impelled by the malign deity who makes us talk more than is necessary to our own undoing.

"I would like to have the letters as soon as they come," said Mrs. Brandon, who had put on her spectacles and seen a letter with the nursery school's name printed on it. "Miss Feilding was in the garden and the postman gave her a letter. It had some very upsetting news about the babies and I was just going to telephone to Matron about it. If you had brought the letters at once, there would have been no need for Miss Feilding to be upset, as there is a letter for me and everything is all right," said Mrs. Brandon, opening the letter and pretending to read it on the spot.

"I'm sure I'm sorry, madam," said Rose, for the first time in her life transgressing the servants' code of honour of never admitting a mistake or apologizing.

"Don't let it happen again," said Mrs. Brandon.

Rose returned to the kitchen where she reported that madam was in a real temper, all because the letters weren't brought in at once, as if one could be all over the place at the same time. Cook, who felt that the postman when he came to the back door was a kitchen perquisite, said that elevenses were *at* eleven and if she chose to give the postman a cup of tea that was still in the teapot from breakfast that was her business and not Rose's and no wonder madam was put out. So Rose said she had the silver to do and hadn't time to waste like some people and went away to her pantry.

Nurse had by now come back with one of Francis's large handkerchiefs which was of great assistance to Miss Feilding. Mrs. Brandon, having read Matron's letter, imparted its contents to Nurse. She was a little afraid that Nurse might give notice if the babies were to be removed, but Nurse, much elevated by her triumph over Rose, was in a particularly gracious mood.

"Really, madam, a Home Farm and their own garden produce and all," said Nurse. "I'm sure Miss Feilding will be very happy, though of course we shall miss the babies and her."

If Miss Feilding felt any slight at being placed second to the babies, she did not show it; nor was she indeed by now capable of showing anything except a blotched and swollen countenance.

"We shall miss you and the babies very much," said Mrs. Brandon, "but it will be very nice for you to be all together in such a lovely place."

"Matron says the house is quite a dream," said Miss Feilding, who had evidently determined to make the best of things. "And such a lovely view of Chanctonbury Ring."

Nurse politely asked, though it was quite evident that she did not in the least wish to know, what Chanctonbury Ring was.

Mrs. Brandon, her delicate features assuming an expression of faint distaste, said it was a dreadful bore, because wherever you went in Sussex you could see it from, and people would tell you that you could see it, when you could see with your own eyes that it was there.

"And looking exactly the same, whichever way round it is," said Mrs. Brandon severely, "owing to being round."

This explanation cannot have afforded much enlightenment to Nurse, but as she had only asked from a sense of noblesse oblige, it made very little difference.

"So thank you for letting me know at once, Miss Feilding," said Mrs. Brandon, rising as an indication that the audience was terminated. "In any case you are not leaving us till the end of August, so we will forget all about it for the present. And now I expect you will want to get back to the babies."

"Thank you so much, Mrs. Brandon," said Miss Feilding. "It's really quite a weight off my mind now we have talked it over. Perhaps Miss Vance will come and pay us a visit when we are settled.

So startled was Mrs. Brandon by hearing Nurse spoken of by her name that she almost lost her self-possession, for Nurse, ever since she had come to Stories when Francis was six weeks old, had been Nurse, and her family name was known to very few people.

Nurse said in a condescending way that it would be very nice and she'd think about it, and Miss Feilding went back to her young charges who were quite safe with an inferior attendant.

"That's all very sad, madam," said Nurses when Miss Feilding had gone. "But I was thinking perhaps it is all for the best, because with Miss Delia and her two babies and one never knows, madam, what else may happen, we can really do with the two extra rooms. And now Mr. Francis is at home again it will be nice to have the drawing-room if he wants to have a few friends. And we hope, madam, that Mr. Francis will find some very nice young lady and then the nurseries will feel quite like old times."

"By the way, Nurse," said Mrs. Brandon, whose chain of ideas may easily be followed. "Mrs. Crawley tells me that Mrs. Merton's brother's friend, Mrs. Arbuthnot, has found a cottage at Southbridge."

"So I did hear, madam," said Nurse. "They did say after the last war that it was the widows with houses got married first. A gentleman does want a house. Of course, madam, if Mr. Francis did find a nice young lady and they couldn't find a house, we should always have plenty of room here when the babies have gone. Well, I had better get on with those knickers."

Nurse went upstairs with the reel of green cotton, leaving Mrs. Brandon to ponder upon her words. That Nurse intended Delia's children, born and unborn, to spend the greater part of the year at Stories, Mrs. Brandon had fully realized; but this new and ingenious plan for co-opting Francis's babies, who were still entirely motherless, was a slight shock. She was never a meddler in her children's affairs and accepted with a kind of affectionate tolerance every young friend that they had brought to the house. Delia had married young and was securely anchored, but Francis's loves had come and gone for a good many years now. They had all been charming, all good dancers, she had liked them all, but Francis had never stayed long with one partner, and gradually his partners had turned into other people's wives. What was going to happen? Mrs. Brandon was very fond of her only son, but she had not the faintest wish to keep him at her apronstrings and sometimes had horrid thoughts of herself as a very old widow with false teeth and Francis, a middle-aged bachelor devoted to his mother, always about the house. She did not in the least want him to grow old along with her. At such periods of gloomy foreboding she had occasionally pressed this or that young lady of the county upon her son, who had kindly feigned an interest he did not feel and slipped lightly away. Susan Dean, of whom she had heard a good deal lately, had seemed to her another highly eligible daughter-in-law, of good if not quite county family, handsome, with well-to-do parents. For Mrs. Brandon, though charmingly affected and apparently helpless, was capable of seeing facts as they were. The Brandons were not quite county and Francis would probably do well to marry within his own sphere. He was one of the lucky ones who could make money and was doing very well in his business; so a wife with some money of her own would be a very suitable partner. All of which may sound prosaic, but is really quite sensible. She determined to go to the Deans' tennis-party and see what was happening. But even while she was arranging a wedding in the cathedral and herself in the right-hand front pew outshining with her own mild lustre the Deans across the aisle, supported perhaps by Sir Edmund Pridham as a deputy father for Francis, Nurse's words came into her mind with a sudden horrid pang. Houses were difficult, were very difficult to find. If Francis and Susan could not find a home they might have to start by living with one of the in-laws. The Deans were a large family with recurring grandchildren and could hardly be expected to find room for a married daughter and her husband. Stories would be rather empty when the nursery school had gone. What more natural, her friends would think, than for Francis to bring his bride back to his mother's very comfortable home and carry on as usual.

"It is not," said Mrs. Brandon aloud to herself with great firmness, "that I would mind a daughter-in-law in the house, because I'd rather like it. But I cannot and will not have Francis being a devoted son."

And to her own great surprise she nearly began to cry, a thing she had hardly ever done in her life. She knew it was silly, she knew she was anticipating all kinds of uncomfortable things which would probably never happen, and she was ashamed. There was no reason for shame. All over England women of all ages, battered for six years by foreign enemies and increasing discomfort, far worse battered for the last year by discomfort and tyranny beyond what they had yet felt, mostly inflicted upon them by their own countrymen, feeling, when they allowed themselves to think, very hopeless about the future, were in a state of nerves where only a touch was needed to make them break down. Very few of them would or could afford this luxury: one does not break down while one has duties to do. So Mrs. Brandon denied herself the luxury of a good cry and concentrated on the various village jobs she had taken on. So successful was she that when Francis came home that evening he had to ask his mother if anything was wrong, as she looked so tired.

"I was only thinking," said Mrs. Brandon, "how dreadful it would be if you always lived at home and had to look after me when I was old."

"Really, mamma, you shouldn't say such things," said Francis indignantly. "You know quite well that I am looking out for a woolly-haired mulatto from St. Kitts whom I shall at once marry and live on her money at The Cedars, Muswell Hill. And till that auspicious day, I hope you will look after me, not I after you."

At which piece of good news Mrs. Brandon laughed and stopped feeling morbid and they passed a very pleasant evening, only interrupted by a twenty-minute conversation between Francis and Susan Dean.

The Deans' tennis-party was on the following Sunday. The weather, inspired thereto perhaps by the state of affairs it saw going on all over England, was outdoing itself in nastiness. The cuckoo, in the words of Miss Anne Fielding's favourite poet Lord Tennyson, of a sunless June was singing in the rain. Days ebbed and flowed in a grey tide and everyone disliked everyone else a little more and tempers became more brittle, especially the grocer's, where a fine display of tinned pilchards on every shelf mocked the customers who asked for cornflour, washing-soda, cereals of any kind, matches, or any of life's common needs, in vain. All the Deans' large circle of acquaintance looked forward to the party, for there, during a few hours, they would be in a semblance of the world of their lost inheritance. Being a Sunday the shops wouldn't be open and one would not have to think about food, the Deans kept very good company, one would probably meet a lot of old friends. Also there was a hard court which could be used if the grass court was too soft, so unless it poured the whole time the tennis players would be assured of some games.

Providence in a grudging way had so far favoured the Deans that the rain had stopped and a very unpleasant wind had blown steadily for twenty-four hours, drying the grass and mangling most of the flowers. By lunch-time the wind had dropped and an uninteresting sun, giving enough light but not much heat, was sulkily doing its daily round. So that considering the state of the world and the way the Government was going on the Deans might be congratulated on a very fine day.

"I cannot think, said Mr. Fanshawe, the Dean of Paul's College, who had married the Deans' eldest daughter before the war, "why we are taught in our impressionable youth that the sun is millions of times larger than the earth and extremely hot. The result is that we go on believing it, whereas if we used our developed intelligence and looked at the sun without bias, we should see that it was a nasty pale little thing about the size of a football, the round sort I mean," said Mr. Fanshawe, who prided himself on being a classical man, in complete ignorance of all games, "giving out grudgingly a minimum of warmth."

Mrs. Dean, the still lovely mother of a large, handsome, prosperous family of children and grandchildren, said she was sure it was doing its best.

"No," said her son-in-law, who was nearly her age and lived in the greatest harmony with his wife Helen, almost twenty years his junior. "Certainly not. I am still," said Mr. Fanshawe with an affected ingenuousness that deceived no one, "a devout believer in Holy Writ. What does the Psalmist say? He says the sun comes out of his chamber like a bridegroom. What the Bible says is always right. I have been, before I was married," said Mr. Fanshawe, casting an affectionate look at his wife who was helping one of her children to cut up a piece of chicken, "best man to more than one of my friends and I may add that their appearance before the ceremony, while I was plying them with brandy and seeing that their waistcoats were buttoned properly—it is astonishing how many bridegrooms put the top button into the second buttonhole and so get wrong all the way down—was remarkably like that of our present sun: pale, staggering and entirely useless."

Mr. Dean said he thought it meant a bridegroom on the following—but before he could finish his sentence his youngest daughter Jessica, at home for a short weekend to rest from her theatrical labours said, "no, darling," in a very firm voice, and Mr. Dean stopped.

"It is quite right to believe everything in the Bible," said Jessica, in the voice which had won the heart of practically every woman between seventeen and seventy, for of the men we do not speak, as they are well known to have little box-office value except for non-stop revue at which the dwindling male population of England may be found every afternoon in masses under the erroneous impression that it is being shocked. "But it's no use discussing it, because no one knows what it really means."

Mr. Fanshawe, who was very fond in a scholarly way of his brilliant young sister-in-law, said that he had always been under the impression that discussion helped to clarify the ideas.

"Not if you haven't got any, Charles," said Jessica Dean. "I don't mean you; you've got heaps. But when you hear most people talking about things—oh, Lord!"

Mr. Fanshawe said she was probably right. On the other hand, he said, people who had ideas were often even more pestilent than people without ideas, because their ideas were so confoundedly silly.

"Please, grandmamma, can I have the wishbone?" Said the elder Miss Fanshawe. She was the oldest of the grandchildren, in fact almost too old at eight to want wishbones except that she felt, quite rightly, that her juniors were not worthy of it.

"Yes, darling," said Mrs. Dean. "Pass your plate and I will give it to you."

Mrs. Dean had always been a little vague, and there were now so many grandchildren that she had given up trying to remember their names when more than three of them were about and usually called them indiscriminately darling. If, she had said to her husband, they would all stay the same age she could remember, but they would keep on getting older and looking different. Her husband who was very fond of her and would not for the world have had her improved said if she would make up her mind which age she wanted them all to be, he would see what could be done. Gin, he understood, stunted the growth, but what with Laurence's four and Helen's three and Gerald's one and Robin's twins and Betty's three in America who would soon be coming over he hoped, and the possibility of Susan and Jessica and the other twin marrying and having families, it would be very difficult to choose an age that would include everybody. Mrs. Dean had said not to be silly and he knew what she meant, so nothing else was done about the children's ages.

Three other visiting grandchildren put in impassioned pleas for the wishbone.

"Ray can have it today because she asked first," said Mrs. Dean, suddenly remembering the name of her eldest grand-child, called Rachel after her. "And you can have the next three wishbones the next three times we have chicken, darlings."

"Then can I pull it with Ray?" said the next eldest grandchild.

The two younger grandchildren said could they pull it too.

"You can all pull it," said Jessica, amused and bored by the scene. "I've thought of a surprise way. But the surprise won't work unless you go on eating your dinner."

The three younger grandchildren were still immature enough to believe in a kind of magic and fell to again. Ray looked at her Aunt Jessica with a kind of affectionate mistrust. Jessica winked at her, with the famous wink of Mrs. Carvel had given to Lord Malkin in the second act of Aubrey Clover's *Attitude to Life*. All four grandchildren immediately began to wink too.

"I refuse," said Mr. Fanshawe, "to be sidetracked by wish-bones. When I mentioned people with silly ideas, I was thinking of the Master of Lazarus. Have you heard his latest folly, Dean?"

Mr. Dean, whose life as a very busy and distinguished engi-neer had not brought him much into contact with the gossip of the older Universities, said he hadn't.

"You know he had been academically red for a long time," said Mr. Fanshawe. "In fact Lazarus is ruined for the next twenty years or so. He has salted it thoroughly with young red dons; those very depressing academic reds who come of good enough families to know better. He got into Parliament during the war as a Socialist, though if I had my way it would be illegal for heads of Colleges to stand for Parliament. It swells their heads and puts far too much power into the hands of the Bursar. But be that as it may, he has now taken a Labour peerage, a depth to which no head of a college had previously descended, and calls himself Lord Skinner."

He paused for his audience to show their horror.

Mrs. Dean asked why.

"Why, Rachel? It is his name," said Mr. Fanshawe.

"But a person can be a lord with the same name that they had before," said Mrs. Dean, with the earnestness of a beautiful and slightly stupid woman.

"I didn't say he couldn't," said Mr. Fanshawe. "But Lord Skinner is a very silly name when you reflect that he is Master of Lazarus, a noble title in itself. What old Henryson would have said," Mr. Fanshawe continued, alluding to a mid-nineteenth-century Master of legendary fame for learning, discipline and rudeness, "I cannot think. And Lady Skinner, who rides about on a bicycle in a mackintosh looking as if she had no clothes under it like Lady Godiva, has told all her friends that she wishes to be known as Mrs. Skinner."

Had Miss Anne Fielding, Robin Dale's affianced bride whose favourite poet was Lord Tennyson, been present, she might have questioned the accuracy of Mr. Fanshawe's words about Lady Godiva, but all the Deans were splendidly illiterate and beyond a general impression that Lady Godiva rode a horse in a pageant, as indeed she too often does with neck-to-ankle tights under her false hair, they knew little or nothing of her.

"That," said Mrs. Dean, "is very foolish. I might as well say I wanted to be called Lady Dean when I am really Mrs. And that reminds me that the Crawleys can't come this afternoon, but I am rather glad, because two Mr. and Mrs. Deans is so confusing. Say your grace now, darlings, and then you can get down."

The four grandchildren suddenly became angels, folded their hands, thanked God for their good dinner and relapsed to normal, clamouring to their Aunt Jessica for their surprise.

Jessica made a face at her sister Helen, implying that having promised a surprise she had not the faintest idea what it was to be. Susan Dean, who had been eating her lunch steadily and keeping an eye on the two youngest grandchildren, suggested that the wishbone ought to be thoroughly dried first, as a damp wishbone was practically unbreakable, and what about putting in the airing cupboard till after tea. Jessica quite agreed and warmly thanked her sister for the suggestion. And then, said Susan, she would tie four bits of ribbon to the wishbone and they could each pull one.

"Francis Brandon told me about putting them in the airing-cupboard," she said. "He said his and Delia's nurse used to do it."

"I don't think I know Francis Brandon." Said Jessica. "Is he a new one?"

"Don't be silly, Jessica," said Susan. "You know Mrs. Brandon who lives at Pomfret Madrigal. She's rather like mother, pretty and soft. I don't mean silly. I mean she looks as if your finger might go right in if you poked her, and her hair is like mother's, a kind of shadowy hair."

"That's a good word," said Jessica approvingly. "May I have it for Aubrey Clover? He collects words. Is Francis in love with you, Sue?"

"I haven't the faintest idea," said Susan though showing no surprise at her younger sister's question for she was apt, as was the rest of the family, still to consider Jessica as the fat little girl who fell off the Tebbens' donkey when Lord Bond's bull came down the lane, the petted youngest who need not be taken seriously. "I shouldn't think so. You can have a go at him if you like."

"Angel!" Said Jessica, giving her sister a hug and pressing her cheek against Susan's, a technique which she had perfected to avoid trouble with lipstick, and which had become so famous in theatrical circles as Jessica's Kiss, that a well-known firm of perfumers were approaching Jessica, or rather her excellent lawyers, on the subject of a new scent with that name, with pecuniary advantage therefrom for all parties concerned. "Angel! But I don't want to a bit. I shall have a good look at him and see if he is good enough for you."

"He's awfully nice," said Susan. "We've danced a lot, only he is really too good for me. He's got an awfully nice sister called Delia Grant."

Jessica with sisterly kindness made further inquiries and heard that Francis lived with his mother and was quite well off and had got an M.C. in the war and loved going to theatres. It all sounded very nice and dull and goodness knew what all those boys and girls really thought about each other, said Jessica to herself from her vast experience of life, for being a servant of the public she was wise in her generation, watched the world, and had never been in love. They played together as if they were in a kindergarten, she thought, and most of them didn't seem to have the wits to know if Harry was nicer than Bill, or Mary than Jane. Susan ought to marry, thought the popular actress who was barely in her twenties, streamlined and enamelled to the eyes, but with a warm and tender heart for her family. And it must be the right man; for the Susans of this world, honest and good, suffer too much if they hazard their heart on an unlucky number.

The sun had now come out in a depressed way and the tennis-party began to accumulate. The hard court had a doubles at once. The grass court was examined by Mr. Fanshawe, himself a good player of the old-fashioned style with a deceptive, slow, underhand service that slid away from many an opponent who would easily have taken a smashing overhand ball. He pronounced it good enough to use so long as it didn't rain again and the two sets were soon in action. Mrs. Dean had established herself in an angle of the house just outside the drawing-room, where she could enjoy such warmth as there was and talk to her friends. Jessica, who by some freak of Providence in a quiet family had the stage in her bones, was studying the role of the quiet little youngest daughter of the house and playing it very well. In this she was ably seconded by the rest of the cast, for the county as a whole remained provincial, in the best sense of the word, and though it had heard of and even seen Jessica Dean whose name was in neon lights in Shaftesbury Avenue, it thought of that shining young star as the youngest girl of the Deans who had gone on the stage and took very little interest in London's opinion of her.

Although Susan had disclaimed any special interest in Francis Brandon, Jessica thought that she looked at each group of newcomers with more than usual interest and made several rather unconvincing excuses for not playing. Presently there came through the french window of the drawing-room a charming middle-aged woman with a tall, good-looking young man. Jessica was observing Susan closely. Susan did not colour, flutter, cast down her eyes, simper, or even faint. But her face, nearly always a happy one, looked faintly radiant as she went up to Mrs. Brandon, shook hands, smiled at Francis, and took Mrs. Brandon to where Mrs. Dean was sitting. Mrs. Dean got up and welcomed her guest, and both ladies then confounded themselves in apologies for not having called on one another before. Strictly speaking it had been Mrs. Brandon's duty to call on Mrs. Dean who had only been in Barsetshire for a dozen years or so, while Mrs. Brandon had lived at Stories ever since her marriage. But Pomfret Madrigal and Winter Overcotes had never been in close relation, each lady had been much occupied, the war had cut off intercourse almost altogether, the peace had on the whole made things more difficult still. Each lady knew about the other, each scented in the other a possible rival in her own brand of good looks. Velvet glove met velvet glove. It appeared to the quiet little youngest daughter of the Deans that this scene might be worth watching.

"We have heard so much about you from Susan, Mr. Brandon," said Mrs. Dean, looking up at Francis in exactly the way Mrs. Brandon was looking up at Mr. Dean. The quiet little youngest daughter observed that Mrs. Brandon here had the advantage, for she was not so tall as Mrs. Dean and hence, to

men at any rate, the soft gobbins, thought Jessica, more appealing. "Fifteen, love," she remarked to herself.

"Do come and sit with me, Mrs. Brandon," said Mrs. Dean.
"I'm not supposed to stand much. *So* stupid to have a heart."

"And that," remarked Jessica aloud to herself, "is fifteen all."

Susan then brought Francis to talk to Jessica with a very
agreeable pride in her friend and her sister.

"May one allude to Miss Dean of the Cockspur Theatre?"
said Francis, "or are you strictly incog.?"

Jessica said she was just Susan's little sister today and favoured
Francis with Mrs. Carvel's wink, after which they got on extremely
well, discussing with considerable amusement the unadmitted
rivalry between their respective mothers.

"Of course," said Jessica, "mine has a very unfair advantage in
having a heart. As a matter of fact she hasn't. She used to have,
but it got all right, so she keeps it in reserve and brings it up
when necessary."

"Mine has very robust health, I am glad to say," said Francis,
"but she has never stopped being a widow whenever it suited her.
My respected papa died when I was about four and I really don't
think mamma minded after the unpleasant surprise had worn
off. But it is a useful weapon."

"On the other hand," said Jessica, "mine has my father to fall
back upon. If she doesn't want to do anything she can always say
he forbids her to."

Francis admitted that this was an asset.

"Mine is rather stupid, though I adore her," said Jessica.

Francis said his was a deceptive character as she looked a
charming fool and was quite intelligent inside. In fact, he said,
he was willing to back his mother for the Afternoon Stakes for
at least sixpence.

By this time the quiet little youngest Dean girl had summed
Francis up, liked him, and turned him over to Susan with a look
of approval. Whether she thought Francis was a stayer we
cannot say, but she felt pretty sure that Susan would come to no

harm with him. Francis may have been slightly disconcerted at being so coolly dismissed, but he was pleased to be with his nice, handsome Susan and they went off happily to the tennis courts.

The next irruption of guests was the Warings from Beliers Priory with their niece's husband Philip Winter, who ran a small preparatory school chiefly for the sons of naval men in the huge and otherwise unusable Priory. Mrs. Brandon with her uplifted eyes and her deceptive appearance of interest made an immediate conquest of Sir Harry; Lady Waring was claimed by Mr. Dean; Philip Winter went off to play tennis. Apart from Sir Harry's well-worn anecdotes of the Boer War conversation rather languished. The sun had slipped away while no one was looking, an uneasy wind was rising, both games of tennis had come to an end, and when Jessica came to say that tea was ready everyone was glad to get into the drawing-room.

Here the noise rose to a pleasant hubbub in the middle of which Mr. and Mrs. Carter and Mrs. Arbottle were announced by the elderly butler.

"I took the liberty," said Kate Carter to Mrs. Dean, "of bringing a friend who is staying with me, Mrs. Arbuthnot. I would have telephoned, but we weren't quite sure if she would arrive in time."

Mrs. Dean, whose husband was an Old Southbridgian, liked the Carters and was pleased to meet any friends of theirs. Mrs. Arbuthnot, looking very elegant and pretty, was made welcome in the usual English tennis-party way. That is, her hostess shook hands, said a few words expressing her pleasure that Mrs. Arbuthnot had come to live among them, added, having thereto been primed by Susan in a stage aside, that her daughter had so much enjoyed meeting her at the Deanery, introduced her to the first person at hand and felt she had done all that could be required. Mrs. Arbuthnot had not particularly wanted to come to a tennis-party in a strange land on her first day at Southbridge and would much have preferred to visit Editha Cottage, but her sister-in-law with mistaken kindness had said if it was only to measure the front windows to see if their old curtains could be made to fit she could easily do it herself and of course Peggy must go. So Mrs. Arbuthnot who was the soul of good nature had left Miss Arbuthnot happily engaged with note book and yard measure and advanced with the Carters into the middle of a country strange and possibly hostile. For being of minor county stock herself, though from another part of England unknown to or ignored by Barsetshire, she fully realized that any newcomer would have to run the gauntlet in the ranks of the local society. Not that anyone would be unkind or malicious, but just as her father a retired Indian judge and her mother an Admiral's daughter would have considered any newcomer to the part of Devonshire where they had lived, so, she knew, would Barsetshire take stock of herself.

While she talked to the acquaintance upon whom Mrs. Dean had bestowed her, a nice dull woman who lived in an ugly red-brick house called Bolton Abbey and had working parties during the war, she was quite conscious of looks in her direction, of the question, "Who is she?", of scrutinizing though not unfriendly glances. And she thought, as she often did, how much nicer it was in many ways when Fred was alive and they lived in India with the safe walls of the regiment about them. But Fred was dead. She and her sister-in-law had found it best to pool their small incomes and live together and she must do her best to fit into the new society. Though she was used to meeting people and felt certain that with tact and goodwill she could reconcile her future neighbours to her presence, she would at the moment have given anything to be in India, even if Mrs. Colonel Matcham had been of the company, flirting with Fred on the verandah as she too often did.

However of all this the lady who lived at Bolton Abbey knew nothing and finding that Mrs. Arbuthnot was a newcomer she kindly gave her a good deal of not particularly correct information about some of the guests, and Mrs. Arbuthnot, who knew without being told that her mentor was not of the world she was discussing and had probably been asked because one must be civil and a tennis-party doesn't really commit one to anything, made the right replies, put the right amount of interested civility into her voice, and though our readers may hardly believe this, did not allow her eyes to rove once during a detailed account of how many sets of underclothes the Bolton Abbey working party had made for evacuated children during the war.

Jessica Dean, that nice quiet youngest daughter of the Deans, talking to Sir Harry Waring, suddenly stopped dead, stared, answered Sir Harry, stared again, pushed Kate Carter almost into Sir Harry's arms, and went straight to the place where Mrs. Arbuthnot was hearing about the way some of the working-party members would never remember to bring their milk with them.

"Peggy!" Jessica almost screamed.

Mrs. Arbuthnot looked up and gasped in a ladylike way.

"Jessica!" She cried. "My dear!"

"You will excuse me, I know," said Jessica, turning upon the tenant of Bolton Abbey the smile which caused middle-aged female secretaries and school-teachers to go three times to every play Miss Dean appeared in, "but I haven't seen Mrs. Arbuthnot for ages, and I have to rush back to London almost at once. Do tell me, *how* is Milly?"

The tenant of Bolton Abbey, too innocent or too taken by surprise to remember that Miss Dean's theatre did not open on Mondays, said of course Miss Dean must have a chat with her friend and Milly had just had six lovely kittens.

"We know all about the father, of course," said the tenant of Bolton Abbey archly. "I would never dream of letting Milly go out at those times and meet just any gentleman cat. The kittens' father lives at Kitty's Kat-Kennels and I hope to get first prizes with some of the kittens. Nearly all his kitty-boys and kitty-girls do very well at the Cat Shows."

Even Jessica, belonging to the theatre world and officially a rogue and vagabond, was almost appalled by this mixture of

prudery and full-blooded Dame Quicklyism. She thanked the
tenant of Bolton Abbey, apologized again, and took Mrs. Arbuthnot to a corner of the drawing-room.

"My *dear*!" said Jessica, giving Mrs. Arbuthnot a most affectionate embrace, though remembering not to print lipstick upon
her face. "I didn't know you were here. How lovely! Where are
you?"

Mrs. Arbuthnot, disentangling with great skill these apparently contradictory remarks, said she was at Southbridge with
the Carters who were kindly putting her up while she moved
into a little cottage.

"Lovely," said Jessica. "My dear, it is too heavenly to see you
again. Oh dear, what fun it was. Mother," she called to Mrs.
Dean who was passing them as she moved on her social round,
"Peggy Arbuthnot was at Umbrella when I was there last year
with Aubrey's party entertaining the troops, God help them.
She came to our rescue when that awful Sonia girl went down
with a hangover and played Mrs. Lupton to my Mrs. Carvel in
Aubrey's play. I don't know what we'd have done without her.
You must come and see me in Aubrey's new play, Peggy."

Mrs. Dean smiled full-blooded approval upon the newcomer
who had helped Jessica, said she would like to come and call
when she was settled, and continued her progress.

"And your charming husband," Jessica continued. "How he
flirted with that odious woman——" she paused.

"Mrs. Colonel Matcham," said Mrs. Arbuthnot obligingly.

"That's the one," said Jessica. "Brazen piece she was. How is
he?"

Mrs. Arbuthnot, whose curiously practical mind saw no sense
in beating about the bush, said he was killed. Up-country, she
added, politely wishing to minimize her misfortune.

"My DEAR," said Jessica, the country girl part of her horrified
at her indiscreet question. But luckily the actress got the upper
hand almost at once; the quick and quite real sympathy, the
feeling that every play even one of Mr. Bernard Shaw's must

come to an end, the facing of the facts of private life and subordinating them to being a servant of the public. Her genuine sorrow and sympathy were expressed, but already she was recasting Mrs. Arbuthnot in her mind. A woman who could play Mrs. Lupton at twenty-four hours' notice, with the added handicap of having played the part in private regimental theatricals of which the youngest daughter of the Deans had no opinion at all, must not be left to moulder in a cottage in Southbridge. The right people must at once be enlisted upon Peggy's side. A changing in the groups brought Lady Waring into view.

"I do so want to introduce an old friend of mine to you, Lady Waring," said the quiet little youngest Dean girl. "She was very kind to me when I was touring in India last year. Her husband was killed and she has come home to Southbridge."

The last statement, strictly true in the letter, as whatever place one settles in is one's home in a way, was a masterpiece of red-herring strategy, leading Lady Waring as it did to see Mrs. Arbuthnot as a child of Southbridge who had returned to the nest, there to nurse a broken wing.

"I am very sorry indeed," said Lady Waring. "We lost our only boy in 1918. What was your husband's regiment?"

Mrs. Arbuthnot named it.

"Harry," Lady Waring called to her husband. "I want you to meet a new neighbour of ours who has come to Southbridge. Mrs. Arbuthnot's husband was in the Four Hundred and Sixty-second. He was killed last year."

This was not said with any want of sympathy, simply as the orderly-room sergeant might set out certain facts before the officer of the day.

"The fortunes of war can be very hard," said Sir Harry, as he shook hands and looked down approvingly upon a charming woman who would have been a credit to any regiment. "I was attached to them in 'ninety-three. I remember the Colonel then was a man called Bear. Curious name. The regiment was known as the Polar Bears. A kind of nickname, you know, because they were so good at polo."

Mrs. Arbuthnot said her husband adored polo and was in the regimental team, which made Sir Harry look on her with added approval. Pity Arbuthnot had been killed. Mrs. Arbuthnot as the Colonel's wife would have adorned any regiment.

"Who is the Colonel now?" he asked.

Mrs. Arbuthnot mentioned the name of Matcham. Sir Harry had never heard the name, which somehow pleased her.

"His wife was a nasty piece of work," said Jessica, who had a memory of Peggy Arbuthnot's face when Captain Arbuthnot and Mrs. Matcham disappeared onto the verandah for the rest of the evening at a regimental dance after the play. "She was a sister under her skin to half Piccadilly Circus."

Sir Harry took her allusion but a feeling of chivalry towards ladies forbade him to recognize it publicly. However Jessica's outburst had done its work and enlisted Sir Harry's sympathy and interest for one so charming a young widow. He had seen more than one man-eating Colonel's wife in his early army career and had watched junior officers' wives trying to put a brave face on it while their husbands spun for the Omphale of the day; and having had but one devotion in his life and that an enduring one, he had judged such women heavily in his own mind.

Lady Waring said very kindly that she would like to come and call on Mrs. Arbuthnot when she was settled. Mrs. Arbuthnot expressed her pleasure at the offer. Somehow the whole room knew that Mrs. Arbuthnot was now approved. A gentle stream of invitations flowed over her. Nothing very exciting, for it was increasingly difficult to offer hospitality unless one had one's own hens and vegetables and even better a cow and a bee, but all showing good will. The ranks of Barsetshire had opened and Mrs. Arbuthnot was safely inside them.

"Mrs. Arbuthnot looks even prettier than she did at the Crawleys," said Susan to Francis.

"She does," said Francis. "She is rather my mamma's type and as is well known I adore my mamma, but quite this side idolatry, bless her. Come on, let's see them meet."

At this moment Mrs. Arbuthnot, wafted from power to power, had just been introduced by Mrs. Needham, wife of the Vicar at Lambton and youngest daughter of the Dean of Barchester, to Mrs. Brandon.

"My son Francis and I were talking about you only the other day," said Mrs. Brandon. "He did so enjoy meeting you at the Deanery. There he is with Susan only you can't see him because of Mrs. Palmer's hat."

Mrs. Arbuthnot looked dutifully in the direction indicated, saw the top of a male head appear above Mrs. Palmer's massive black straw hat with a large purple bow on it, and murmured her appreciation.

"He is very nice," said Mrs. Brandon, "and really very kind and we get on very well. The only drawbacks is that his old nurse who lives with me and is quite wonderful at things like making an old tweed skirt into knickerbockers for the nursery school I have in my house though only for the present, is always wanting him to be married."

"All nurses do," said Mrs. Arbuthnot. "Fred's old nurse practically drove us into getting engaged. We were really only finding out if we were fond of each other and I went to stay at his grandmother's house because his mother died when he was small, and Nurse drove us into rooms alone and made us go into the rose-garden by moonlight when we wanted to put the gramophone on and dance, and finally she told the cook we were engaged, so of course we had to be. We couldn't disappoint her."

"It was the same with me," said Mrs. Brandon, assuming the air of a virgin martyr, though she had married her quite nice dull husband because he asked her to and she thought it would be nice.

Her son Francis, who was always pleased to see what his

mother was up to, observed her assuming what he called her mysterious mischief face and moved nearer to her.

"I was too young to know what marriage meant," said Mrs. Brandon, enjoying herself enormously. "Then Henry died, abroad, so I was left with Francis and Delia."

This was, on the face of it, a perfectly truthful statement of what had occurred; for if your husband dies of pneumonia while on a holiday at Cannes, it is certainly abroad; and if you have two small children you are perfectly within your rights to say so, even if you adore them and are left very comfortably off.

"How do you do?" said Francis to Mrs. Arbuthnot. "But what my mamma has not told you is that the little son, sole relic of her wifehood, for we will not count my sister Delia, grew up to be the tall, not-so-young, debonair man of the world that you see before you, a crutch to his mother's declining years."

Mrs. Brandon said Francis shouldn't say things like that.

"It's too late, mamma, I have said them," said her son.

"You have no children," said Mrs. Brandon to Mrs. Arbutnnot in a muted voice with a question in it, but a question so delicately hinted, as Francis observed, that only an artist could appreciate it.

Mrs. Arbuthnot, evidently not an artist, simply said Yes; adding No. At least, she said, she meant she hadn't any.

Francis felt so certain that his mother was going to ask why, that he prodded Susan and told her to introduce the Vicar of Lambton to his mother. But before Mrs. Brandon had publicly disgraced her son, or the Vicar had been torn from Sir Harry to whom he was talking, there was a stir in the party as of a torpedo cleaving its way under water with a betraying ripple above (if that is what it does) and Colin Keith came into view, looking rather hot.

"I do apologize," he said to Mrs. Dean in a very swivel-eyed way, half his attention being fixed on Mrs. Arbuthnot, the other half directed by good manners towards his hostess. "I only came down to Northbridge for the day and Lydia didn't give me your message till nearly tea-time."

Mrs. Dean said she quite understood and was so glad Mr. Keith could come and there would be more tennis after tea.

"Lydia didn't tell me it was tennis," said Colin "At least she did, but I was in such a hurry to get here I forgot to change."

Mrs. Dean said they could easily lend him some flannels as the boys always left a lot of clothes in the house to save bringing luggage. But this was not at all what Colin his further eye still glued on Mrs. Arbuthnot meant, and he mumbled some kind of excuse.

"Charles will look after you," said Mrs. Dean, beckoning her son-in-law. "Charles, here is Colin Keith, Mrs. Merton's brother. Can you find some flannels for him?"

Mr. Fanshawe appeared perfectly willing.

"Thanks awfully," said Colin. "Excuse me just one moment, I see Mrs. Brandon," and escaping from his well-meaning friend he greeted her with a warmth only belied by his talking rather incoherently and casting quick looks at Mrs. Arbuthnot in a perfectly giddifying way; all of which Francis noted with amusement.

"Do you know Mr. Keith?" said Mrs. Brandon to Mrs. Arbuthnot. "But of course you do, because Lydia told me he was looking for a house for you. Listen, Mrs. Arbuthnot, I have just had a very good idea. I think I have twelve yards of very good curtain material put away that I got just after the war began, but Nurse wouldn't let me use it. It you are short of curtains, I would love to give it to you."

"But that is most kind of you," said Mrs. Arbuthnot. "As a matter of fact my sister-in-law and I were wondering what on earth we would do about curtains. I didn't realize when I came back from India how difficult things were here. If only Effie and I were a newly married couple we could get a priority docket, I understand. But we aren't. Are you sure you can spare so much?"

"I'd simply love to. Nurse doesn't like them," said Mrs.

Brandon with great candour, "and I don't either. They are rather blue and that isn't one of my colours."

"Mamma's colours are pinks and mauves and all the sweet-pea colours," said Francis.

Mrs. Arbuthnot said she adored blue, and the two ladies plunged into a discussion of lengths and breadths while Colin hung on the edge of the conversation unable to get a footing. It was finally decided that on an early date Mrs. Brandon would get herself driven over to Southbridge with the material, bringing Francis if it were a weekend, and then Mrs. Arbuthnot must say exactly what she felt about it.

"And you must come to Stories when you are not so busy," said Mrs. Brandon. "Come for a night. If you could get to Barchester on a Saturday morning, Francis would meet you when he has finished work and drive you out, and then he could drive you back on Monday morning, or on Sunday evening if it suits you better."

She shook hands warmly with Mrs. Arbuthnot and went to bid farewell to her host and hostess.

"It's wonderful to see you," said Colin reverently to Mrs. Arbuthnot, when at last he was able to claim her attention. "I didn't bother about the tennis-party when Lydia told me, because I didn't know you were coming, and then Kate rang up and said she was bringing you, so I had to come, but I couldn't get the car till Noel came back from going round with the agent. I thought I'd never get here."

"But you did, you see," said Mrs. Arbuthnot.

This simple and beautiful statement deprived Colin of the power of speech and before he had regained it he was gently taken possession of by his sister Kate, who looked upon parties favourably or unfavourably according as she was or was not able to meet members of her own family at them. To complete his misery, Francis Brandon slipped into his mother's empty place and pursued what Colin full of righteous indignation could only regard as a flirtatious conversation, while Susan sat by and admired. So divided was his attention, so earnestly did he struggle to hear what Francis was saying to Mrs. Arbuthnot with one ear and try to answer his sister Kate's questions with the other, if we may be permitted so to express ourselves, that kind Kate wondered if he was sickening for influenza and resolved to ring Lydia up as soon as she got home and tell her to take his temperature.

A quiet dark girl with an air of being excessively smart, though only a woman could have explained why, so simply was she dressed, now came and joined the group, speaking familiarly to Mrs. Arbuthnot and calling her Peggy. It was apparent to Colin's more attentive ear that she and Mrs. Arbuthnot had known each other in India and he longed to tell them that he had been in a military hospital at Poona for three weeks under suspicion of jaundice, but could think of no pretext.

"I am so sorry," said Kate Carter to Mrs. Arbuthnot, "but we shall have to go now. Everard is taking chapel this evening. How are you, Jessica? You know Colin, don't you?"

"I'd like to," said the quiet dark girl. "I'm working very hard just now, but we might have lunch in town one day."

Colin, whose one thought was to snatch a brief moment with Mrs. Arbuthnot before Kate took her away, hastily said a few perfunctory and not very grateful words. The dark quiet girl looked amused.

"Susan will tell you where to find me," said the dark quiet girl. "Bring Peggy and I'll get Aubrey to come. He'd love to see her again."

This invasion of Colin's rights was intolerable. He had come to a party simply to express devotion to Mrs. Arbuthnot and at considerable inconvenience to his brother-in-law who had lent him the car from sheer kindness. And what had happened? He had found her very much at home, surrounded by friends, in no need of devotion. Francis Brandon, whose slight advantage in height Colin was beginning to look upon as a personal insult, appeared to be on far too good terms with her. An unknown girl called Jessica, a silly name, probably with some kind of Government job, had given herself airs and practically demanded a lunch the sole purpose of which appeared to be that a bounder called Aubrey wanted to meet Peggy again, blast his impudence. And how dare the girl say Peggy? Peggy was a very beautiful, nay, sacred name; a word which caused one to feel slightly mad and have spots before one's eyes.

Mrs. Brandon and Francis had gone. Kate and Everard took Mrs. Arbuthnot away. Colin got into Noel's car and drove back to Northbridge.

Mr. Wickham according to custom was at Sunday supper and the talk was largely of estate matters in which Colin could not help being interested, for it was his old home and he knew every inch of it. After supper Noel went to his room to do some work while Lydia asked Colin about the party and if Mrs. Arbuthnot had enjoyed it. Colin said he supposed so. Mr. Wickham, not very sensitive to atmosphere, said there was a fellow called Arbuthnot that he knew in the last war whose mother was still a damn good-looking woman; nearer eighty than seventy, he said, but every inch a winner; made one think of one of those old French Marquises, what? "I wonder if it was Mrs. Arbuthnot's husband," he added.

Lydia said it couldn't be, because Captain Arbuthnot couldn't have been more than about Colin's age and anyway he had been killed in this war, not the last, which Colin said was a non sequitur.

"And a post hoc ergo propter hoc too, old fellow," said Mr. Wickham, "and many of them. But there's a fellow that writes about birds in *Country Life*—F. E. Arbuthnot. He knows his stuff. Wonder if he's a relation. I'd like to meet him. I must ask this pretty lady."

If Colin had known how to fight a duel he would have called Mr. Wickham out at once for his profane allusion to a goddess. Lydia asked who else was at the party.

"Oh, lots of people," said Colin. And then repenting this

want of courtesy to his youngest sister of whom he was particularly fond he exerted himself to be a little less disagreeable and consequently felt more agreeable to himself.

"Who would a quiet dark girl have been?" he asked. "She works in London, I think. Kate called her Jessica."

"That was Jessica, of course," said Lydia.

"I know that," said Colin, "but who is she? She seemed to be staying in the house and knew Peggy in India."

"I told you," said Lydia patiently. "Jessica Dean."

"Jessica Dean!" Colin repeated, with every possible inflexion of surprise, horror and remorse. "Lord! she asked me to give her lunch and I thought she was a typist or something. What a fool she must have thought me."

Mr. Wickham, a man so Colin considered with no fine feelings at all, roared with laughter at this unfortunate social gaffe. Lydia looked concerned, for she wanted her brother Colin to have his heart's desire in everything and could not bear him to be disappointed.

"Little Jessica won't bear malice," said Mr. Wickham. "If I know her she'll make a good story of it."

This statement gave Colin no comfort at all. Lydia, interested in this sidelight on their agent, asked if he know her well. Mr. Wickham, with a wink that revolted Colin's very soul, said not as well as he would like.

"I got to know her through Aubrey Clover," he said. "There was I in the old *Irresponsible*, trying to salvage some of the poor devils on the beach, and there was Clover in the *Seaford Belle*, one of those little paddleboats that used to run about between piers in the South Coast, trying to salvage a few more of them. Anyway, the *Seaford Belle* was bombed and Clover managed to get most of his lot over to us before she sank. He got a bit of shrapnel in his tummy and that was that. Farewell to arms and all that. So he went back to the stage and entertained the troops all over the place. We used to meet and have a drink sometimes, and when little Jessica came along, quite a kid she was, we got very friendly. She's a fine girl and no flies on her at all. Well, Mrs. Merton, I'm going home to have a drink."

To the outsider this might have sounded like a reproach to the Manor for want of hospitality, but, as we know, Mr. Wickham had his own sources of supply and it was understood that he would only drink the Mertons' drink as an act of friendliness. Colin took him to the door, refused an invitation to come back to the agent's cottage and polish off a bottle of whisky that needed polishing, began to say something, stuttered, and said it didn't matter.

"Now," said Mr. Wickham, looking at Colin with the authority of an older man who had been a sailor, "don't worry about little Jessica. She won't have given it another thought," which Colin considered a tactless way of putting it, though grateful for Mr. Wickham's reassurance. "Ring her up next week and take her out. And she can bring Clover along and you bring the pretty widow. Good-night."

Mr. Wickham walked away into the cold light evening. When Colin returned to the drawing-room Lydia was just going to bed.

"Good-night, Colin," she said, hugging him in her old impetuous way. "I'll see you before you go tomorrow morning and I've switched the telephone to the pantry."

Annoyed as Colin was by this piece of sisterly meddling, he had to admit on consideration that it was well meant. While not exactly meaning to do so, he found himself going down the passage to the pantry. Mrs. Dingle's niece at the exchange volunteered the information that Mrs. Arbuthnot had just been talking to young Mr. Brandon on the 'phone, so she probably wouldn't have gone to bed yet. So angry did her kind interest in Francis make Colin that he nearly slammed down the receiver, but while making up his mind to do so, Mrs. Arbuthnot's voice came charmingly to him, and the merest courtesy to a female made him listen to what she had to say.

"I think," said Noel Merton to his wife Lydia some half-hour later when he came up to bed, "that Colin must try to get a higher retaining fee on his briefs."

Lydia, gratified, said that she knew Colin would be a success.

"It is not so much that," said Noel. "But if all his calls to and from Mrs. Arbuthnot are coming on our telephone bill at weekends, I must do a little quiet blackmail. What it is to be a bachelor. But much nicer," he added, "to be a dull married man."

CHAPTER 5

Mrs. and Miss Arbuthnot were now temporarily installed with the Carters. The Vicar's aunt, a man of her word, had already moved her furniture to the Vicarage, and Editha Cottage looked as depressing as all houses do when the walls and floors are patchworked with the shapes of departed pictures, furniture and carpets. After considerable difficulty a permit had been obtained to have ten pounds' worth of painting and repairing done, a concession which might conceivably have got the little scullery and half the kitchen into habitable condition. At this point, when the new tenants were beginning to wish they had never taken Editha, private enterprise intervened in various forms. The odd-man at the Carters' House, known to many generations of boys as Edward and apparently possessing no surname, had a genius and a passion for painting and distempering. Mr. Brown at the Red Lion had become possessed, by means into which no one liked to inquire and which were popularly supposed to include six dozen beer and three bottles of whiskey, of various odd lots of almost pre-war paint which the sergeant of the camp had no business to dispose of. The School carpenter had managed to extract from the local representatives of the Ministry of Works who was his wife's cousin rather more wood than was really needed to repair the dry-rot in the chapel, and was prepared to dispose of it at a reasonable figure to anyone whose idea of a reasonable figure corresponded with his own.

Matron's eldest nephew, the one who was her married sister's son and was now wireless operator on the newest and largest Atlantic liner, happened to be on leave and spending ten days with his aunt. Like many first-class professionals his one idea of a holiday was to perform variations upon his normal work and he threw himself into the matter of electricity at Editha Cottage with such enthusiasm that the Arbuthnots were almost ungrateful. At whatever hour they visited their new home to see how Edward was getting on with distempering the drawingroom, or whether Snow, the carpenter, could repair the coal-shed when he had finished fitting the best bedroom bookshelf, or to try the length of the curtains that Mrs. Arbuthnot had been running up on Matron's machine out of the stuff Mrs. Brandon had sent that she didn't like, a description that our female readers will fully understand, they were bound to be waylaid and detained by Matron's eldest nephew, a conscientious young man who liked his clients to know exactly what he was doing and why, with the appalling verbosity of the trained scientific mind.

So wearing did his kind explanations become that Mrs. Arbuthnot and her sister-in-law were reduced to very mortifying ruses, such as going round quietly to the back door, taking off their shoes and fitting the kitchen curtains by signs and whispers if Matron's eldest nephew was in the drawing-room; or climbing into the drawing-room by the window if he was fitting a plug for the electric iron in the kitchen, so that he would not hear the front door. Miss Arbuthnot, who was strong and active as well as on a large scale, had once gone so far as to get out of the back-bedroom window onto the top of the little coal-shed and so to the ground when she heard him coming upstairs and realized that she was cornered. Of all of which he was quite unaware and continued to impart useful information which his hearers did not understand nor, being proper women, wished to understand. For to all women except the rare ones who can put in a new fuse wire without the certain conviction that one will get a shock and be killed even if the current is turned off, electricity is still rather like an animal of savage instincts reared in captivity, which may turn and rend its keeper at any moment and for no reasons.

On the Saturday morning at which we have now arrived, a dull, cold, unpleasant product of mid-June, Mrs. and Miss Arbuthnot were to spend the day at their new house taking a sandwich lunch with them, partly so that they could work on without stopping, partly to leave Kate in peace with her husband. Their plan was to clean the two bedrooms, now distempered and painted by Edward, and if time permitted also to clean the stairs. Their furniture was to come at the beginning of the following week and by the time it came they hoped, with Mrs. Dingle's help, to have the whole house clean.

The relationship between the sisters-in-law had always been a happy one. The wife had realized the peculiar devotion of the brother and sister and had managed, being a kind and intelligent woman, to leave this devotion undisturbed. Having at first valued Miss Arbuthnot for her sisterly feelings towards Captain Arbuthnot, she had come to value and then to love her for her own sake. Miss Arbuthnot, accepting generously her adored brother's wife, had come to be very fond of her and silently took her side whenever Captain Arbuthnot strayed, as he far too frequently did, towards the siren of the moment. So that by degrees the two women had entered into a kind of tacit conspiracy to go on loving Captain Arbuthnot because he was himself and to pretend that all was well when all was ill, by which the regiment was not in the least put off the scent though it admired the ladies' gallant show of indifference.

Both were very capable, though Mrs. Arbuthnot to most people's surprise was on the whole the more capable of the two. Like Mrs. Brandon her efficiency was masked by an air of charming helplessness, while Miss Arbuthnot's tall, strong figure and heavy almost masculine face concealed a more tender heart. Not that Mrs. Arbuthnot was hard-hearted, but Captain Arbuthnot's roving hands had made her take life lightly on the surface because her heart felt too deeply. Several men had fallen in love with her before and after her widowhood. None had touched her heart and she used them all; not unscrupulously, but treating them just as they invited her to treat them, as useful and willing fetchers and carriers. Colin Keith had been more than useful since she had been in England, and as she liked him very much she saw no reason why he should not go on being useful, to which end she only had to go on being herself.

What Colin felt, for thought is hardly the right expression for his slightly demented frame of mind, about it all, we cannot exactly say. Had he been a little younger his feelings might have expressed themselves by the rapturous words, "Oh! Mrs. Arbuthnot!" repeated aloud to himself when in vacant or in pensive mood. He was now, after five years in the army, past the age of calf-love, but he had never before been seriously affected by the tender passion and was floundering among emotions that he should have experienced earlier. His sister Lydia in the days of her violent and outspoken hobbledehoyhood had expressed the opinion that Colin was born to be an uncle, and so far an uncle he had been, spending most of his vacations and spare time at his old home with Lydia and Noel, or with his elder sister Kate, adored by his nieces and nephews at Northbridge and Southbridge and by his nice dull elder brother Robert's children now living on the Hallbury side of Barchester. Such affairs of the heart as he had experienced had been pleasant rather than searing, in no way interfering with his work, until with Mrs. Arbuthnot Cupid's dart had pierced his heart and if not splitting it quite in twain had lacerated it considerably, causing him as we know to spend a great deal of other people's money on trunk calls and be rather a bore to his friends. We regret to have to say it of a rising young barrister whom we have known and liked for a good many years, but Colin Keith was being as silly as he ought to have been ten years ago, and being like all lovers of an ostrich-like nature, would have been much surprised and annoyed if he had realized that most of his Barsetshire friends were discussing his affairs with interest and amusement.

"I think," said Miss Arbuthnot to her sister-in-law, after they had entered their house by the back door, listened and looked cautiously and found silence and emptiness, "that we can really get those curtains up in the bedrooms. Then when the furniture comes we can sleep in the house and get things straight downstairs a bit at a time."

Mrs. Arbuthnot agreed. Though both ladies were happy with the Carters, their natural longing to be in their own home grew every day as they saw Editha Cottage in its fresh paint and distemper, the little kitchen well scrubbed and cleaned by Mrs. Dingle, the little garden blooming with vegetables and a few luxury flowers.

"How lucky we were to find it," Miss Arbuthnot continued.

Mrs. Arbuthnot said it was Mrs. Carter who had found it. Miss Arbuthnot said it was really Colin Keith, who had suggested Barsetshire and asked all his friends to look out for a house. Mrs. Arbuthnot said would Effie be an angel and get the hammer from the kitchen drawer so that she could get that valance above the window done while she was on the steps. Miss Arbuthnot obligingly fetched the hammer and Mrs. Arbuthnot drove in the nails with considerable accuracy and skill.

"I wonder why I said valance?" said Mrs. Arbuthnot. But as her mouth was full of nails her sister-in-law had to ask her what she had said. Mrs. Arbuthnot repeated it, adding that people always said pelmet now, which was a silly word except that it gave one a rhyme for helmet, which led the ladies to a consideration of the rhymeless words in the English language, notably silver. Miss Arbuthnot said if people could think of a word like pelmet to rhyme with helmet, they could easily think of a word to rhyme with silver, and she for her part was going to invent a word. A discussion of this word and what its meaning should be made both ladies have the giggles till Mrs. Arbuthnot, having nailed the valance or pelmet neatly into place, came down from the step-ladder and looked at her handiwork.

"How Fred would have loathed this place," she said in an abstracted way.

Miss Arbuthnot did not answer at once, for she was considering the implications of the remark. As usual, Peggy was right. To Fred, a lover of crowds, of gaiety, of women, of horses, of social life in all its aspects, a small country village near a public school, a village where most of the women were at the most favorite analysis young middle-aged and all occupied by household or various good works from morning to night, with no male society to speak of except school-masters mostly married, the doctor, the Vicar, and a few retired service people, in a damp neighbourhood near the river, with the everlasting grey pall of England's summer sky sitting like lead on their heads, the life would have been insupportable.

"Of course there would have been Eileen," said Mrs. Arbuthnot, alluding to the perfect barmaid at the Red Lion, whose Victorian black satin bust and increasingly golden hair, as well as her kind heart and the way she stood no nonsense, were the admiration of all Southbridge.

"I would rather like to see Fred with Eileen," said Miss Arbuthnot, thinking with grim impartiality of her beloved brother and his weaknesses. "It would have been an eye-opener for him."

"I would like," said Mrs. Arbuthnot, not in malice towards the deal but in a spirit of scientific inquiry, "to see Eileen dealing with Mrs. Matcham if she and Fred tried to get a drink after hours."

Both ladies were silent, both with a pang of regret for the Fred they had loved, both facing the fact that life with Fred would have been for his wife increasingly and humiliatingly unhappy and for his sister a long, fruitless attempt to change his unchangeable faults, and perhaps coming to discount his undeniable qualities and charm. The cuckoo of a joyless June sang a few hollow notes from a tree in the field, the garden and everything felt damp and depressing. Without a word being spoken the ladies applied themselves violently to the curtains in the back bedroom and the bathroom.

"There," said Mrs. Arbuthnot triumphantly. "Now the furniture can come when it likes and it will meet its match!"

From below the sound of footsteps came to the upper floor; gentle footsteps as of one who habitually wore rubber soles on his boots.

"Lord!" said Mrs. Arbuthnot. "I'd forgotten the bedside lamps. That must be Matron's nephew."

With one accord the ladies went to the back-bedroom window, but it was too late. The gentle footsteps were mounting the stairs. Miss Arbuthnot with her long legs could have escaped as she had done before by the coal-shed roof, but her sister-in-law, smaller and less acrobatic, would have been trapped.

"Oh, well," said Mrs. Arbuthnot philosophically and went onto the little landing.

"Good morning, Mrs. Arbuthnot," said the cheerful voice of Matron's eldest nephew. "Good morning, Miss Arbuthnot," he added as that lady appeared. "I see you ladies are busy, but I thought I'd just get those reading-lamps fixed. It's been a bit of a job, but I've got you a couple of standard sockets and plenty of flex. One would hardly credit the way this house is wired. Three different gauges of socket, ladies, and not one of them standard size. Old Methusalem must have done the original wiring, and if he knew A.C. from D.C. that's about all he knew, and he didn't know that properly. You'll hardly believe me, ladies, when I tell you that the front bedroom's on the same circuit as the scullery and the bathroom, and the back bedroom's the same as the dining-room, and as for the drawing room and hall and the back lobby, they have got me completely guessing for the moment. And how whoever it was that put that socket in the kitchen for the electric iron to plug in got away with all that flex without a casing, I can't imagine. And no power. Not a single power plug in the house. How the lady that was here, the Vicar's aunt, got the ironing done, I don't rightly know."

Miss Arbuthnot said it was quite simple if you had an iron like hers that ran off the light.

"That's what all you ladies say," said Matron's eldest nephew, "but that kind of iron is a regular death-trap. Just look at the kitchen. A wire down the kitchen wall spliced onto the wire from the central light and a plug-in. I ask you. It's simply asking for trouble."

Mrs. Arbuthnot said she had not had any trouble with the iron, except that she was rather frightened when sparks came out of the holes you put the spikes in, and sometimes it all got very hot.

"There," said Matron's eldest nephew with a satisfied air, "you have it in a nutshell. Insufficient protection, against the rules, a wire tacked onto the wall with staples and there you have the lay-out. And what comes next?"

Mrs. Arbuthnot said if the iron got too hot she pulled the plug out of the holes till it got cooler.

"It's not the iron that matters," said Matron's eldest nephew, "though probably the element will burn out one of these fine days and then where will you be? It's the plug I'm thinking of. If that plug's getting overheated the next thing you'll have is a short. Does either of you ladies know how to put a fuse wire in?"

"I don't," said Miss Arbuthnot. "I should be simply terrified."

"Well, I won't say you're wrong," said Matron's eldest nephew. "It's ladies trying to put fuse wires in that keep the electric industry going."

Mrs. Arbuthnot said she knew where to turn the light off at the main, but she never knew which of the little things was which.

"Like Auntie," said Matron's eldest nephew. "Well, I daresay you are right. With a house wired like this anything might happen. I can't think why the electric people haven't noticed that wire for the iron, considering the meter's just above it. If I let a job like that pass in the wireless room I'd lose my job good and quick and not get another in a hurry. Ill tell you what I'll do. I'll insulate that wire for the iron and put the proper switch at the bottom and a socket for a red lamp. If I can't get a red lamp, I'll get some paint from Snow and paint a plain bulb. Then, when you use the iron the red light goes on — see?"

Miss Arbuthnot asked rather anxiously if that would mean that it was dangerous to use the iron.

Matron's eldest nephew, concealing with some difficulty his contempt for such ignorance, said it was only a signal that the iron was on. Like the red traffic light, he said.

"Then there ought to be a green one to show when it's off," said Miss Arbuthnot frowning with the effort to concentrate.

Matron's eldest nephew, realizing that his comparison had but further confused the issue, patiently explained that the red light would only be in the nature of a warning that the iron was on. Anyone, he added, who came into the kitchen and found the red light on would know that the iron was hot and turn it off.

"Oh, you have to turn it off," said Mrs. Arbuthnot, much disappointed. "I thought if you had a red light the iron couldn't burn things. You remember the awful burn I made when I tried to iron Fred's pajamas at Exeter," she added, addressing her sister-in-law. "But of course that iron hadn't a red light. It was one of those ones you heat with things like aspirin."

At this point Matron's nephew felt that the electricity was on the whole a subject unfitted for females and said he thought he could get for them on this next trip, through a friend in New York, an iron with a thermostat which would stop any risk of burning, for which suggestions Mrs. Arbuthnot was very grateful. Matron's eldest nephew then asked permission to go into the bedrooms and see about the bedside lamps. The permission was freely given and the sisters-in-law went downstairs, feeling a little dizzy from so much science, and began to tackle the drawing-room curtains.

One of the advantages of Editha Cottage was that the Vicar's aunt had caused to put up those awful curtain rods on which hooks run about with great ease and celerity on a kind of overhead railway and the curtains are pulled by cords. Mrs. Arbuthnot had installed her sewing-machine in the drawing-room, the Vicar's aunt had obligingly lent her a plain deal table which she did not at the moment require, Kate had lent two chairs, and as the weather was not much colder than an ordinary June day she was able to work in the empty room as much as she liked. The curtains had been finished on the previous day. All that remained was to hook them onto the rings, pull the draw-strings to the requisite degree of tightness, and all would be finished.

"Oh Lord!" said Miss Arbuthnot. "The steps are upstairs."

"If Matron's nephew tells me once more about the kitchen iron I shall go mad," said Mrs. Arbuthnot. "Perhaps we could manage with the chair. I'll hold it for you."

So Mrs. Arbuthnot very bravely held the chair, which was a good solid one with a wooden seat, and Miss Arbuthnot mounted it and tried to fasten the curtains, but even she was just not tall enough to reach the rings. The sisters-in-law looked at each other.

"We'll have to go up and get it, that's all," said Mrs. Arbuth-not with the courage of despair. "He can't kill us."

Miss Arbuthnot said she thought he could, but there was no other way of getting the ladder, so they went upstairs. On the landing they met Matron's eldest nephew holding a reading-lamp.

"I ask you, ladies, look at this," he said, holding the lamp towards them in an accusing way. "How many amps do you think you're on?"

As neither lady had the faintest idea what he was talking about, nor would either have known an amp even if she had seen one, though Miss Arbuthnot had a vague idea that it was something to do with that engaging by-product of the Gas

Light and Coke Company, Mr. Therm, they very wisely held their tongues.

"You've only got to look," said Matron's eldest nephew kindly but firmly, as he took the bulb out of the lamp and offered it to Mrs. Arbuthnot, who accepted it gratefully but gingerly, rather fearing after his threatening words that it might explode in her hand.

"Voltage," said Matron's eldest nephew, evidently thinking that this would explain all. "It's all on the bulb."

Comprehension slowly dawned on Mrs. Arbuthnot's pretty face.

"*I* know," she said. "You mean those things on the top of the light that you can't read unless you turn the light on and then it shines in your eyes so that you can't see anything."

"Some of you ladies don't *want* to see anything and that's a fact," said Matron's eldest nephew, but not ungallantly, so that his words almost became a tribute to the sex. "You hold it up, like this, and you'll read it quite easily."

Mrs. Arbuthnot, much impressed by this assurance, said she must go and get her spectacles and wherever could she have left them because she was sure she had them a few minutes ago. But Miss Arbuthnot, whose eyes could tell a gallowsbird from a broad-tailed mippet at a hundred yards, or count the spots on the mother whisky-soda bird's breast without its suspecting her presence, took the bulb and read aloud, "One hundred and ten V sixty W."

"That's it," said Matron's eldest nephew, pleased with his pupil's success. "And Southbridge is on two-thirty. Well, what happens then?"

Mrs. Arbuthnot, goaded by this Pumblechookian dialectic, said she didn't know and had Matron's nephew seen the steps anywhere, because she wanted them.

"Then I'll tell you," said Matron's eldest nephew. "If you plug that lamp in and turn it on you'll have a short. And a short in the bedroom will put the bathroom and the scullery out of action.

You'll need new bulbs in all your reading-lamps. I'll see about that for you. I'll take the old ones away with me or one of you ladies is bound to forget and turn the light on."

Mrs. Arbuthnot thanked him and said it did seem a pity that they couldn't use up the old bulbs before they started on the new ones, as we were asked not to waste anything.

"You *can't* use them," said Matron's eldest nephew, almost despairing of female intellect. "And where on earth they still run on a hundred and ten beats me."

But Mrs. Arbuthnot, taking advantage of his despair, had seized the steps and was already half-way down the stairs with them, followed by her sister-in-law. Her persecutor removed the bulbs from the bedside lamps and continued his work on the front bedroom, with a running commentary of a disparaging nature on the fellow or fellows responsible for the wiring of Editha Cottage.

It did not take long to put up the drawing-room curtains and the sisters-in-law felt great satisfaction as they surveyed the room. The walls were newly distempered a very pale yellow, the paintwork had had what the School carpenter called a lick, but it was an honest lick with good paint; the windows had been cleaned by Mrs. Dingle, the floor which was not very good wood but that could not be helped had been stained by Miss Arbuthnot. All was ready for the furniture, and the ladies could look forward to being properly installed before the end of the following week.

"I think lunch, Effie," said Mrs. Arbuthnot, eyeing longingly the basket in which kind Kate had packed food and a large thermos of coffee. Miss Arbuthnot said it was only half-past twelve, but she felt as if she had been working for seventeen hours and wanted coffee more than anything else in the world. So they unpacked the basket, spread on the table the cloth which Kate's forethought had provided, and sat down to their meal; Miss Arbuthnot on a chair, Mrs. Arbuthnot who was smaller and folded up more easily on a suitcase. Just as Miss Arbuthnot was pouring out the coffee steps were heard on the staircase. The ladies looked at each other with apprehension and despair. Matron's eldest nephew appeared at the door.

"Sorry to intrude," he said, "but I just looked in to say I was going. Auntie has dinner at half-past twelve and I'll catch it for being late, so I thought I'd have a look round and see that everything was O.K. You haven't any more of those reading-lamps, have you?"

The ladies assured him that the two bedside lamps were all they had brought with them and faithfully promised to remember to remove the bulbs from any other lamps that came with the furniture. Matron's eldest nephew said if they would excuse him he would just like to give a look at that socket in the corner by the fire. Miss Arbuthnot poured the coffee back into the thermos, corked it firmly, and exchanged looks of resignation with her sister-in-law. It is quite probable that Matron's eldest nephew would have spent the rest of the afternoon there, oblivious of lunch and what his aunt might say, had not the Vicar's aunt appeared at the side window, taken a comprehensive look at the room, walked round to the front door and rung the bell. Mrs. Arbuthnot opened the door and brought her visitor into the drawing-room.

"A picnic," said the Vicar's aunt, looking benignly upon the thermos and the sandwiches. "Quite in keeping. Is Empson here?"

"I don't know," said Mrs. Arbuthnot. "I haven't seen anyone. Who is he?"

"Oh, there you are, Empson," said the Vicar's aunt, looking over her spectacles at Matron's eldest nephew, who was behaving rather like the Quangle-Wangle with his head in a slipper in his efforts to use a screwdriver on a plug in a dark corner. "Mrs. Carter rang me up just now. Your aunt's wireless is out of order and you are to go back at once and see to it. She thought you might be here and I was in any case coming down to see Mrs. Arbuthnot, so I said I would take the message."

On hearing of his aunt's summons the head wireless operator of the newest and largest Atlantic liner sprang to his feet, assured the owners of the house that he would see about some two-thirty-forties and two-thirty-sixties at once, and left the house. So impressed were the Arbuthnots by his swift departure and the sudden revelation of his name, that they looked with almost superstitious reverence upon the Vicar's aunt who had so quickly exorcized him.

"We never knew he had a name," said Miss Arbuthnot. "Matron always speaks of him as her oldest nephew and we couldn't quite call him that, so we had to say just you. If it comes to that we don't know Matron's name either, because everyone calls her Matron."

"Dudley," said the Vicar's aunt.

"Like Morton's Fork," said Mrs. Arbuthnot, in whom the conjuncture of names in Matron and her eldest nephew had induced a surge of historical memories, and then she remembered that she was a hostess in her own house, gave the Vicar's aunt the other chair and offered her some coffee.

"No thank you," said the Vicar's aunt. "Never before lunch. Rarely after lunch. Occasionally after dinner. Yes, your walls are quite your colour. So are the curtains, though unexpected."

Mrs. Arbuthnot explained that the material was a gift from Mrs. Brandon who didn't like blue, but it was very generous of her to give them the material all the same, because she could have had it dyed.

The Vicar's aunt said that explained everything.

"But be of good cheer," she added, which injunction frightened her hearers a good deal as they were feeling quite cheerful already in an unesoteric way. "Blue is not harmful. You can live with blue. And you will not live with blue for long. But what I really wanted to say was two things. The first is my nephew's new appointment which I feel that you both, as my successors in Editha Cottage, ought to be among the first to hear. He has been appointed Principal of St. Aella's Home for Stiffnecked

Clergy. It is a fine Elizabethan house on the Omnium Estate with a very good stipend. I shall continue to keep house for him and hope to do some helpful work among the inmates by means of intensive coloured thinking. We shall of course regret leaving Southbridge and our many friends. Did you ever find the little poker with the bent end for taking the lid off the Ideal boiler?"

This transition from religious to practical affairs was so sudden that the Arbuthnots were rather taken aback till Miss Arbuthnot luckily remembered that she had discovered, while digging up a flower bed under the scully window, what must be the implement in question and had wondered what it was.

"All then is well," said the Vicar's aunt. "The second thing I wished to mention is that the future incumbent of Southbridge is spending a day with us and I would like to bring him to call upon you."

Mrs. Arbuthnot said she would love it, but she was afraid she couldn't very well offer the Vicar designate any tea, as they had no crockery or provisions in the house and no furniture. But the Vicar's aunt said it would only be a brief courtesy call early in the afternoon, and as it was obviously impossible to prevent her bringing whomever she wished to bring, Mrs. Arbuthnot said she would be delighted. So the Vicar's aunt went away to preside over Vicarage lunch and the ladies finished their picnic.

"How like Mrs. Carter to have a thermos with a proper pouring-out thing," said Miss Arbuthnot. And if her remark is obscure, we defy anyone to explain more clearly what she meant.

Her sister-in-law agreed, admiring the thermos's classical beak and added that all Mrs. Carter's family were kind. The Mertons, she said, had been very kind indeed. And Colin, said Miss Arbuthnot, Mrs. Arbuthnot looked a little self-conscious and said yes, Colin had been extraordinarily kind.

"Only I sometimes feel, Effie," she said, "as if he thinks I am just what an Indian Army widow ought to be. A dear little woman who needs protecting. And it is most embarrassing when he makes his relations pay for my telephone calls. If he weren't an idiot he'd know I wouldn't make trunk calls if I couldn't afford them."

Miss Arbuthnot said perhaps he was an idiot; one never knew. But he was very nice and now they had better get on with the dining-room curtains in case Matron's eldest nephew came back again. So they took Kate's cups to the scullery and washed them and were just going back to the dining-room when Snow, the School carpenter, came in at the back door with his bag full of tools and his white apron folded on top of them.

"Good afternoon, mum," he said, addressing either or both the ladies, they were never quite sure which. "I thought I'd find you about. I saw that young George coming back from his dinner and he said, 'You'll find those ladies up at Editha, Jim,' 'All right, George,' I said to him, 'that'll just suit me down to the ground, because I've got a free afternoon and I want to fix those shelves for the front bedroom and there's a pane broken in the scullery I'd like to mend, seeing I've got the measurements and cut the glass, and I daresay there'll be some other little odd jobs." So when I'd had my dinner I got my tools and I came along."

Mrs. Arbuthnot thanked him warmly, though she secretly rather dreaded another kind, talkative man about the house. Still, Snow's was an easier kind of loquacity to bear than Matron's eldest nephew's, for his was the true Barsetshire mind, very sound, very shrewd, given to do all its slow thinking aloud, but on the whole far more restful than the wireless operator and his jargon. The ladies left Snow in the kitchen, slowly putting on his apron of office, and went to the dining-room where they had a long though amicable argument about what you did with the yards of white string that hung down at each end of the tops of the curtains when you had pulled the ruffled top to the requisite shortness; for we really cannot make them, or ourselves, any clearer than this. Mrs. Arbuthnot was in favour of tying the ends into a long, gigantic bow, retying this bow into another bow, and so on till it got quite small and very large, if Effie saw what she meant, and trusting to luck that it would stay behind the curtain. Miss Arbuthnot favoured winding the ends round her hand just loosely enough to be able to slip the skein off when it was finished, tying it round the middle with a piece of string and pinning one end to the back of the curtain. So each of them did one curtain in her own way and as the curtains looked exactly alike when finished, nobody had won or lost. Just as Miss Arbuthnot was on the steps for the last time, rehooking a hook that had viciously worked itself loose owing to not having been put right through the ring on the overhead railway, Snow appeared at the door.

"It's about those shelves," he said slowly. "I'd like you ladies to come up and look at them. Of course if you want them four foot three you can have them four foot three, but seeing as how I've got four nice bits of wood, good wood too, four six and a half, what I say is, why not *have* four six and a half?"

If Miss Arbuthnot, by saying with an air of having considered the whole matter profoundly that she thought four six and a half would be splendid, thought she could put Snow off his employers' scent, she was mistaken. The ladies, said Snow, never seemed to understand like that an inch was an inch and it stood to reason six and a half inches was six and a half inches and to cut wood would break his heart and he would like the ladies to come up and look for themselves, for an inch, he said, was as good a mile, which version of an old saying his hearers took to be a Baretshire folk-proverb and perhaps they were right, for after all, said Miss Arbuthnot to her sister-in-law as they unwillingly went upstairs in Snow's magnetic wake, an inch might easily be a miss. As it had been plain from the beginning that Snow was going to make the shelves as he thought fit, the Arbuthnots would have preferred to be allowed to stay downstairs and get on with their own work, but Snow was a merciless craftsman, demanding to the last drop of blood the full weight of his employers' attention, whether at the School, or when obliging friends of the School. It was useless for Mrs. Arbuthnot to say that the wood looked beautiful and she didn't mind a bit how long the shelves were. This was a Latitudinarianism, a falling sway, not to be tolerated, and a real disappointment to Snow, who enjoyed what he called arguing people down. Seeing his disappointment, Miss Arbuthnot very kindly took up the cause of the four-foot-three bookshelves and gradually allowed herself to be converted to four six and a half.

"It's just as you like, mum," said Snow, savouring his triumph and very meanly pretending it was a defeat. "If you want four six and a half, four six and a half it's got to be. Study the employer is my motto and Mr. Carter and Mr. Birkett or any of the gentlemen at the School will tell you the same. I'll get onto those shelves straight away, and then I'll have a look at the scullery window."

"I didn't think you had so much low cunning," said Mrs. Arbuthnot to her sister-in-law when they at last escaped.

"I hadn't," said Miss Arbuthnot. "It was simply the instinct of the cornered beast. I say, Peggy, do you think we shall ever have a moment's peace in this house? I thought we were going to vegetate and put our feet up, but it's far worse than the Regimental Polo Week. I do want to get the curtains finished because it's Sunday tomorrow and the furniture has promised itself for Tuesday. Do you think if we did the kitchen now we could hide before Snow comes down?"

This seemed a good plan. The ladies took the steps into the kitchen. Here the curtains, being purely domestic, did not have overhead railways but a plain curtain rod. The curtains had been run up on the sewing-machine from pre-war dustsheets presented by Kate, who disliked to see her beds sheeted in white when the family went away for its holidays and provided cheerful red and white check bed covers. The rings were already sewn onto the curtains and it merely remained to slip the rings over the rod. Miss Arbuthnot mounted the steps, lifted one end of the rod off its support, slid one curtain onto it and was just sliding the other when there was a loud knock at the back door. Mrs. Arbuthnot, who was holding the curtain up in her arms

while her sister-in-law put the rings on the rod, let it fall and
went to the door. The slight extra weight pulled the end of the
rod downwards and both curtains slid quietly off onto the floor.
Miss Arbuthnot knew when she was beaten. She let the unat-
tached end of the rod rest on the kitchen window-sill and
descended the steps to meet two strangers. One was a tall
good-looking elderly woman in old but smart tweeds, a well-cut
shirt with a tie to match the tweeds, sensible shoes and a very
dashing felt hat on her neat, short, wavy grey hair. Her compan-
ions was a kind of peasant art variation, being baggy and untidy,
with what Miss Arbuthnot respectfully recognized as a Liberty
scarf wilting round her neck.

"We are Adelina," said the first woman, removing an amber
cigarette-holder from her mouth. "Your sister, or is it your
sister-in-law, let us in very kindly. We are neighbours, you
know."

"Do you mean you are neighbours of each other or of us?"
asked Mrs. Arbuthnot, who was used to entertaining people and
enjoyed it. "This is my sister-in-law," she added, introducing
Miss Arbuthnot.

"Bent," said the taller visitor, extending her hand in a glove,
which though war-worn bore the unmistakable look of real
hogskin from a good glover, "I was right. It is Miss Arbuthnot
who is the sister-in-law."

"We both are," said Mrs. Arbuthnot. "At least Effie is my
sister-in-law and I'm hers. Do sit down, if you don't mind a bit
of a mess."

"Not in the least," said the taller visitor. "Show me a mess and
I'll clear it up. My name is Hampton. This is Bent. She is the
muddler, but a good sort," which doubtful compliment seemed
to please Miss Bent. "Do you mind if I bring the dog in?"

In spite of her manly appearance and off-hand manner, it was
clear that Miss Hampton was considerate of other people's
feelings. Mrs. Arbuthnot hastened to assure her that though
they hadn't got a dog they would be pleased to see any dog of a

friend, so Miss Bent got up and opened the back door to a short-legged dog with shaggy black hair, a head far too large for his body, and mournful eyes, who at once sat by Miss Bent's side and looked miserably about him. Miss Arbuthnot, having patted his head, asked what his name was.

"Gallant," said Miss Hampton.

Mrs. Arbuthnot said what a nice and unusual name.

"We used to call him after anyone who was being gallant in the war," said Miss Bent, looking nostalgically into the past. "All sorts of people like Benes and Schuschnigg and Zog and Smigly-Rydz and Mannerheim. But nobody's gallant now, so we just call him Gallant."

A silence fell upon the little party. It was all too true. Ever since peace had broken out brightness had fallen from the air. Gallantry had faded away, melting in the light of politics. The great names had receded, had taken peerages, had retired to the Quantocks, gone back to their private lives, died when the need to use themselves for their country ceased. The Little Man was having his little day and trampling all to his own mean level.

"I do see your difficulty," said Miss Arbuthnot.

"Hampton did meet a woman who knew someone who knew Mr. Attlee's sister-in-law and said she is quite nice," said Miss Bent. "We talked it over, but it wouldn't do."

Mrs. Arbuthnot said rather diffidently, what about Churchill?

"We did consider it," said Miss Hampton. "But when we thought of all Mr. Churchill has done for us and the way England has treated him, we felt that even calling our dog Churchill wasn't enough. Bent agreed with me."

By this time all the ladies were feeling rather tearful, reflecting on dead glories and present drab hopelessness, and it was perhaps lucky that Snow chose that moment to come downstairs to see if he had left those one-and-a-half-inch nails in the jacket he had hung behind the scullery door. He greeted Miss Hampton and Miss Bent as old acquaintances and said he'd like the ladies to come up and look at those shelves. They could, he said, then see for themselves that six four and a half was just what was wanted for a lady's bedroom. The Arbuthnots were once more conscious of the mesmeric power of a craftsman who is far too aware of his own worth, but Miss Hampton had no intention that her neighbourly call upon Editha should be interrupted. Miss Arbuthnot had already got up.

"Sit down," said Miss Hampton, though quite kindly. "When you have finished those shelves, Snow, and anything else Editha wants, you can come to Adelina. The sitting-room window needs a new sash-cord. Nearly fell on me after lunch. Don't be late."

The Arbuthnots expected the French Revolution to begin, but Snow, with a sheepish smile, said he'd be round by teatime and took his one-and-a-half-inch nails and went away.

"Good workman, but give him an inch and he'll take an ell," said Miss Hampton. "Have you any more jobs for him?"

Mrs. Arbuthnot said he had promised to mend the scullery window and the coal-shed, but of course if Miss Hampton wanted him——

"Want him, dear woman? We all want him," said Miss Hampton. "But fairdooze. Your job comes before mine."

"I am so sorry, I don't quite understand," said Mrs. Arbuthnot. "Oh, I see. Fair does. Thank you very much. Would you think us too dreadful if we finished putting the curtains up? We had nearly got them on and then they all fell off."

"I know them," said Miss Hampton darkly. "They need handling. You talk to Bent and I'll see to the curtains. You can give me a hand," she added to Miss Arbuthnot, beginning at the same time to thread the curtain rings onto the rod with incredible rapidity.

Mrs. Arbuthnot fetched the chairs from the drawing-room and obediently sat down by Miss Bent.

"Have you read Hampton's last book?" said Miss Bent.

Mrs. Arbuthnot said she was very sorry she hadn't and what was it called.

"*Chariots of Desire*," said Miss Bent reverently. "It is about the sex life of lorry drivers. All from nature. It sold thirty-three thousand copies here and could have sold three times as many if it weren't for the paper and the printers and the binders. Hampton puts every ounce of herself into her books. She never spares herself," said Miss Bent, gazing with affectionate concern at her friend, who had mounted the steps, put the rod onto its support, dusted her hands together in a manly way and gone with Miss Arbuthnot into the scullery to continue operation on the window curtain there.

Mrs. Arbuthnot said she had read Miss Hampton's public-school novel, *Temptation at St. Anthony's*, and enjoyed it frightfully.

"People do enjoy it," said Miss Bent tolerantly. "But vice goes much deeper than mere enjoyment. It is scientific. She is writing a new book now, about co-educational schools. It will be strong meat, but England can take it. She is going to call it *A Gentle Girl and Boy*. Keats of course."

Mrs. Arbuthnot said she looked forward to reading it and had often noticed how nice and gentle boys from co-educational schools were, but the girls seemed to stay just the same. Miss Bent congratulated her on her perspicacity and was obviously going to enlarge on the subject when, rather to Mrs. Arbuthnot's relief, her sister-in-law and Miss Hampton came back from the scullery, having hung the curtains and discussed the gas-cooker of which Miss Hampton approved.

"I like your sister-in-law," she said to Mrs. Arbuthnot, looking with approval upon Miss Arbuthnot's tall, strong figure and her rather masculine face. "Not one of Ours, but a Good Fellow," which appeared to be the highest compliment she could pay.

A figure passed the scullery window, paused and moved on.

"Oh Lord!" said Mrs. Arbuthnot. "It's the Vicar's aunt. She said she was bringing the new Vicar, at least the man that's going to be the new Vicar, to call. I do wish she wouldn't always look

in at the window first like people in Maeterlinck. Hadn't we
better go to the drawing-room?"

But it was too late. The Vicar's aunt had seen them and came
in by the back door, followed by her nephew and another
middle-aged clergyman with a striking face and a well-trimmed
beard and moustache, whom the Arbuthnots at once recognized
as Colonel Crofts and greeted warmly. There was a general
hubbub of voices, the ladies from Adelina were introduced,
apologies were made for the lack of seats. The Vicar's aunt and
Miss Hampton as senior visitors were given the two chairs, Miss
Arbuthnot sat on the dresser which was a fixture, and the rest of
the party perched on the kitchen window-sill which was tiled
and fairly wide, and on the kitchen table. Snow was by now
making a quite deafening noise with his hammer upstairs and
the Arbuthnots did not like to go and ask him to shut the
bedroom door for fear of being drawn into an endless conversation, so everyone had to talk rather loudly.

"I had no idea I was going to meet you again," said Colonel
Crofts to Miss Arbuthnot. "I was only told that we were going
to call on some new parishioners. I call this an excellent beginning"

"We didn't know either," said Miss Arbuthnot. "The Vicar's
aunt only said the clergyman who was going to be the new Vicar
was at the Vicarage and she would bring him to see us. Somehow one doesn't think of a new Vicar as being a friend. I thought
of something like Mr. Parkinson."

"Poor Parkinson," said Colonel Crofts. "I fear he won't pass
his examination, though the standard of Latin and Greek is
deplorably low. But if he doesn't his future father-in-law, who is
an undertaker, has promised to take him into the firm, so he will
be connected with the church."

Miss Arbuthnot said he might put "Failed Theological Examination" on his professional cards, like a Babu, and they
laughed a good deal about it in a very unclerical way.

"But one thing I do want to ask you," said Miss Arbuthnot,

suddenly becoming serious, "if you will promise not to think it impertinent. Is it all right to go on calling you Colonel? I mean I know you are really a Colonel, but then you are really a clergyman too. What would be right?"

Colonel Crofts said he had rather wondered himself, but he had had it out with the Bishop—not that arch-fiend at Barchester but a real Bishop—and decided that as he had the honour to hold a commission in His Majesty's Army, the title of Colonel was his for ever, but he would also be Reverend.

"I expect what will happen," he said, "is that my old friends will go on calling me Colonel and my new friends, for I do hope to make new friends here, will call me Mr. I shall answer to both. But on letters I shall be Colonel the Reverend and that I shall insist on. So far I have only had business letters here, but when my friends begin to write to me I hope they will address me correctly."

"I like the address immensely," said Miss Arbuthnot. "May I write you a letter? I should like to be the first person here to use your proper titles."

"And I should like you to be the first friend to use them," said Colonel Crofts, slightly altering the form of her words. And then they talked about the Crawleys and about Southbridge Vicarage, which the Arbuthnots had not yet visited.

Meanwhile the Vicar's aunt was telling the ladies from Adelina about her nephew's new position.

"Splendid!" said Miss Hampton. "A fine job. I'd like to see the Home."

The Vicar, who was in charity with all the world when he thought of the handsome house and the good income, even with his Aunt Monica with whom he was often on sparring terms, said the house was pure late sixteenth century and the plumbing and central heating, which had been carried out under the auspices of the Society for the Prevention of Cruelty to Ancient Buildings, very efficient. And, he added, the Government Office which had occupied it from 1940 to 1944 had left so much coal and coke in the cellars that they were safe for at least two winters.

"That's all very nice, dear man," said Miss Hampton, "but it's the Stiffnecked Clergy I'm interested in. All bachelors or widowers, I suppose. I'd like to come up for a week-end and study their inhibitions."

The Vicar, who was used to Miss Hampton's methods, crossed his legs, put his long hands together finger-tip to finger-tip, and gently rocking his unsupported foot said it would be a great pleasure to entertain Miss Hampton as a friend, but he feared the Bishop might object to his Stiffnecked Clergy being used, if he might borrow a phrase all too familiar to us during the recent trials at Nuremberg, as guinea-pigs. At this Miss Hampton laughed in a loud but gentlemanly way and told the Vicar he had spiked her guns, after which they fell into a delightful conversation about what they would like to do to the Germans, in which the Vicar displayed splendidly un-Christian sentiments, thus earning Miss Hampton's high approval. Miss Arbuthnot was still comfortably engaged with Colonel Crofts, Mrs. Arbuthnot was discussing with the Vicar's aunt and Miss Bent the question of getting some fruit locally to make jam, when Matron's eldest nephew came in by the back door and made a kind of naval salute to the party.

"Nice to see some company," he said approvingly. "If you haven't a radio friends are the next best. By the way, Mrs. Arbuthnot, what about your radio? You'd better let me fix it for you. I wouldn't be surprised if it was A.C. and you ladies just plugged in on D.C., and then what?"

Mrs. Arbuthnot, ignoring this last statement which meant nothing at all to her, said she hadn't got a wireless.

Matron's eldest nephew, horrified at this state of abysmal destitution, said she mustn't listen to what people said about radio sets being hard to get. There were plenty, he said, if you knew where to look, and he could without the faintest difficulty get her a nice super-het three-valve anodyne with combination breakdown and a three-play cutout; or at least this was what it sounded like to Mrs. Arbuthnot.

Mrs. Arbuthnot thanked him very much and said she didn't want one.

"Now, if it's a question of terms," said Matron's eldest nephew, "don't you worry, Mrs. Arbuthnot. I'll arrange all that," and in the warmness of his heart he was apparently ready to go straight to Barchester, knock up his radio supplier on a Saturday afternoon, bring a machine back and install it on the spot.

"But I don't want one," said Mrs. Arbuthnot. "I *hate* it."

This was the most extraordinary experience that Matron's eldest nephew had ever had. Even more extraordinary than the Indian prince who had had a special sound-proof suite for his wives with four gold-encased radios performing from four different stations all through the twenty-four hours. Not even when the sixty-foot wave crashed over the bridge of the R.M.S. *Vomitorium* and the whole wireless installation was smashed to smithereens had the wireless operator received so severe a shock. Nor was his confusion lessened by the remarks which followed.

"So do I," said Miss Hampton. "Why should I have to hear a voice coming out of a box, or believe it? It is part of the present general plan for teaching people not to think."

The Vicar's aunt said it was all very well for bedridden or very aged persons, a class of whom she seemed to have the lowest opinion, but wireless was one of the minor factors in the decay of Christianity, and if people thought that turning a knob was the same as going to church they would discover their error when it was Too Late, a statement which struck terror into her hearers.

"My Stiffnecked Clergy," said the Vicar, still rocking his foot and rearranging his hands, "needs the wireless. They need it. But we shall have to be careful, Aunt Monica. I understand from the Bishop that one or two of the less afflicted among them have already broken three sets through which was being transmitted a performance known in some circles, I will not say in some idolatrous or Ultra-montane circles, as the English Mass, or

Marss. Poor fellows! Even in their ashes live their wonted fires."

"The B.B.C. cut Hampton off in the middle of her talk on Capri," said Miss Bent, her voice shaken by friendship. "So I burnt my new licence and dismantled the set."

Mrs. Arbuthnot asked how one dismantled a set. She had often seen notices about it and wondered.

"I simply pulled the plug out of the wall and have never put it in again," said Miss Bent, dramatically raising two of her painted wooden bead necklaces and letting them fall upon her bosom.

"And if you have a servant," said Mrs. Arbuthnot, "she'll want it on all day and most of the night. Not good enough. And anyway a pound is far too much to spend on something you don't want to have."

"Away with such a fellow from the earth," said Colonel Crofts.

If the whole company had turned into snakes and rushed up and down ladders before his eyes, the wireless operator could not have been more astonished. Heresy upon heresy poured down on him, and what was worse he had, not being well acquainted with the works of Gray or Bunyan, or the acrimony caused by a difference in ritual, a strong feeling that they were either talking nonsense or laughing at him, probably both. On more familiar ground he would have argued the matter, but it was always the same with the first-class passengers; they hadn't the brains to argue.

Mrs. Arbuthnot saw his confusion and annoyance and was very sorry for him, so she suggested that he should do the rewiring for the electric iron if he would be so kind and she would take all her friends into the drawing-room where they wouldn't be in his way. It was then obvious that he was going to take their departure as an insult, but that couldn't be helped, and probably half an hour's happy work on wires and plugs would soothe him. So the whole party transferred itself, with the two chairs, to the drawing-room where after a few minutes' talk the Vicar's aunt said good-bye and took her nephew and her clerical guest away.

"I like our future Vicar," said Miss Hampton. "Soldier and priest. Interesting combination. Pity he wasn't in the Guards. I could have picked his brains then. The artillery isn't so much use. Still, it can't be helped. Good-bye. And remember if you want a drink at any time, Adelina is always open. If we are out, just walk in. The gin and lime are in the corner cupboard and there is plenty of whisky and a syphon. Beer we're a bit short on at the moment."

The Arbuthnots came to the door with them, and even as they were saying good-bye, a car drew up and Colin Keith got out of it.

"Oh," said Colin. "I was down at Northbridge for the week-end and I thought it would be nice to see Kate, so I borrowed Lydia's car and came over, and I thought I'd just come round by the cottages. I mean I thought if you happened to be at Editha I could drive you up to the Schoolhouse."

"Young blood," said Miss Hampton, in quite a friendly way, for Colin had become on excellent terms with Adelina during the term he had taught classics at Southbridge before the war and the ladies were always pleased to see him. "How is your sister?"

Colin said she was quite well.

"Remarkable woman," said Miss Hampton. "Absolutely normal. Come along, Gallant."

The short-legged black dog, who had behaved so well that the Arbuthnots had quite forgotten his presence, came padding down the passage and took his owners away.

Much as Mrs. Arbuthnot liked Colin, she could at the moment well have dispensed with another visitor. Matron's nephew and Snow still had to be dealt with, she wanted to put clean paper in the kitchen drawers and the little linen cupboard, and in general be free to fuss about the house. But her innate hospitality got the upper hand and she welcomed Colin warmly, as did Miss Arbuthnot, and took him to the drawing-room, asking him how he liked it.

"Oh, it's splendid," said Colin. "I love those blue curtains. They are exactly like you."

Miss Arbuthnot said Mrs. Brandon had given them the material, which somehow seemed to Colin a soulless remark. It would, he felt, have been more tactful in Miss Arbuthnot to say she had business at the bank, or must go and write letters, so that he could have a quiet talk with Mrs. Arbuthnot on interesting topics such as taking her for a drive on Sunday if Lydia would let him have the car again, or telling her all about the book he was writing. But his hostess, though kind and charming, had a horrid way of talking over his head as though he were a school-boy about things like curtains and reading-lamps and kitchen drawers; things which Colin, who lived in a service flat in London and spent his weekends with one of his sisters or with friends, found very unreal and boring, not realizing that to the servantless housewives of England, who have never had a sit-down strike (most of them having in fact practically never rested since 1939 and being by now too tired and nervous to sit down at all except to eat or work) or asked for or obtained any help or amelioration in their lot, and who have done their often dull and exhausting duty without flinching, such subjects as kitchen drawers and curtains are of interest and importance, and of far more value than political or economical speculations which are good enough for men. So he gently sulked, unnoticed, and affairs might have gone on like this for ever, had not Matron's eldest nephew appeared at the door with a displeased face.

"Have you finished?" said Mrs. Arbuthnot. "How kind of you."

Matron's eldest nephew said he was making a tidy job of it, but he couldn't find his screwdriver and wondered if anyone had taken it.

"You had it this morning when you were on the floor in the corner," said Miss Arbuthnot. "Perhaps it is there."

Matron's eldest nephew said he wasn't a one to leave tools about. That, he said, was a job for the ladies. He then smiled to show that his remark was merely gallantry, but it was evident that he suspected them both. Mrs. Arbuthnot suggested that he might look in the corner, which he did in a sulky and perfunctory way, appearing rather gratified than otherwise that the screwdriver was not there. Footsteps were heard on the stair, there was a tap at the door, and Snow came in carrying his bag of tools. The shelves, he said, were now finished and he would like the ladies to look at them. Four six and a half they were, just like the ladies had said, and if they did prefer four foot three, it was all on account of what they said that he had made them four six and a half. His eye then lighted on Matron's eldest nephew.

"This yours, my lad?" he said, pulling a screwdriver from his apron pocket. "On the floor it was, over in the corner there. I come down to fasten that loose board and there I seed a screwdriver in the corner and I said to myself, 'That's young George's, that is.' You hadn't ought to leave your tools laying about, my lad. Here you are."

This awful triumph so terrified Mrs. Arbuthnot that she said she would love to come and look at the shelves and beat a hasty retreat upstairs, followed by Miss Arbuthnot and Colin. The shelves were admired, but only in a half-hearted way as they were all listening for the sounds of mortal combat. But all was silent, so when they had stayed upstairs long enough to pretend they had been looking at the shelves they all came down again. The drawing-room was empty. From the kitchen came the sound of voices. Colin volunteered to reconnoitre and came back with the news that Snow and Matron's eldest nephew were amicably working on the wire for the iron together.

"I do wish they would go," said Mrs. Arbuthnot almost impatiently. "Men do talk so much."

"I feel guilty," said Colin. "But my profession is talking. Do I talk too much to you?"

"Oh, that's quite different," said Mrs. Arbuthnot, giving him what Noel Merton would have called a Mrs. Brandon look. "It's people like those men, who will tell one what they are doing. I enjoy it so much when you talk and Mr. Carter and Mr. Merton and Francis Brandon. One doesn't have to pretend to understand."

Her simplicity, Colin felt, was very beautiful, but why the dickens she should call young Brandon by his Christian name he did not know and thought poorly of women as a whole. He then noticed, so keen are the eyes of love, that she looked tired. Women, he remembered, needed tea when fatigued; touching creatures.

"I say, Peggy," he said. "Let me drive you back to the School-house. Kate is expecting you both for tea and it's nearly four o'clock."

This seemed a good plan. The ladies packed the remains of their lunch into the basket and took their aprons off. Colin with true gallantry again volunteered for the dangerous task of telling Snow and Matron's eldest nephew that Mrs. Arbuthnot was going and asking them to lock the back door and leave the key at the Schoolhouse. While he was doing this, Mrs. Arbuthnot went into the side-garden to see what the dining-room curtains looked like from outside. They looked very nice. She cast her eye over her little domain and saw that it was good. In the side-garden some rose were blooming. As she looked down the back-garden towards the field, her little lawn and the vegetables beyond made a pleasing contrast in greens. From among the pea-sticks a form in shirt-sleeves and corduroy trousers slowly rose, straightened itself, and came towards her.

"Dull day, missus," said the jobbing gardener who, as she had unfortunately forgotten, came every Saturday afternoon to look after the garden.

Mrs. Arbuthnot would have liked to say, "So are you and please go away," but one cannot afford to offend a respectable free-lance labourer with a genius for vegetables who comes regularly on Saturdays.

"You come and look at the peas, lady," said the gardener, a

large, loose-limbed, kindly middle-aged man with a wife who took most of his wages and spent them at the Red Lion, and a large family of girls, most of whom had been in trouble with the military or the Red Cross Convalescent Home during the war and were now earning large wages as servants with free board and lodging for their children of shame who were, we must say to their mothers' credit, a very fine lot. "You won't see peas like that at the Vicarage, nor at the School, nor at the other cottages. Adelina hasn't no old peas like that, nor hasn't Louisa, nor Maria. Ah. You come along and look at them."

Mrs. Arbuthnot sighed as one who needed her tea but obeyed as an employer, which was why Miss Arbuthnot, who had heard a car stop at the door and come out to see who it was, received Mrs. Brandon and Francis who had driven over from Pomfret Madrigal with some red and white check American oilcloth and an old pair of kitchen scales that Mrs. Brandon had found when turning out a cupboard with Rose.

"I know it seems like visiting the poor," said Mrs. Brandon apologetically, "but one is so thankful to get anything now. The scales weigh quite well, but somehow the one ounce was missing. I expect it has been lost. But Nurse found some of those lead weights that one used to have in the bottom of one's skirts, and we got the chemist to weigh one of them and it was a quarter of an ounce, so she sewed four of them into a little parcel. Shall Francis put the scales somewhere?"

"If he doesn't put them down almost at once, he will faint," said Francis. "It isn't only the weight of these confounded things, but their abominable clumsiness. Miss Arbuthnot, my mamma has very little savoir vivre. Mamma, you have not yet met Miss Arbuthnot, you know. I shall first put the scales down on the door-step and then introduce you. Miss Arbuthnot: my adored mamma, who is calculated to drive anyone to the asylum in three minutes."

Mrs. Brandon said Francis shouldn't say things like that,

shook hands with Miss Arbuthnot, looked intently at her, and suddenly coming to, asked where her sister-in-law was.

"I don't know," said Miss Arbuthnot. "I was putting the sewing-machine away. She may be in the garden. Shall we go and look?"

Mrs. Brandon appeared delighted. Miss Arbuthnot, disregarding Francis's attempts to help her, carried the scales and the oilcloth into the house.

"People do trip over things so much when one leaves them on the door-step," she said, rejoining the Brandons and leading them towards the back of the house.

"I accept the rebuke," said Francis. "Maladroit. That's what it was."

Miss Arbuthnot said that was an awfully good word and how glad she and her sister-in-law would be to have red and white check oilcloth because the kitchen curtains, which were really Mrs. Carter's dustsheets, were red check too and they hadn't been able to get oilcloth anywhere, when suddenly she stopped dead.

"Oh dear," she said, looking towards the peas. "It's Chives. He has got Peggy."

"Bring him here, whoever he is and I'll chuck him out of winder," said Francis. "Is he a dog or a mad bull?"

"Even worse," said Miss Arbuthnot. "He is our jobbing gardener. At least he jobs for all the cottages and does us on Saturday afternoons and he is frightfully good with vegetables, but he does talk so much and we daren't offend him, because he is almost a kind of half-wit and they are very valuable."

Francis said sympathetically that she was perfectly right and England would still be England as long as there were half-wits who were good with vegetables.

"So we have to pay by letting him talk to us," said Miss Arbuthnot. "Last Saturday when we were trying to tidy the mess a bit he kept us in a drizzle of rain for half an hour, and I did hope we might escape this week, because he doesn't come till four in summer. But we are just too late."

"The fault," said Francis magnanimously, "is mine, which sounds like a quotation, though I don't know what. Let me make amends. Chives shall talk to me while you rescue your sister. And if I die, mamma will wear the most becoming mourning, and don't tell me not to say things like that, mamma, because I've said it."

"You are very kind," said Miss Arbuthnot, "but you haven't a chance. You don't know Chives."

"But I shall," said Francis. "Come along, mamma."

Mrs. Arbuthnot had by now seen the visitors and with an abject apology to Chives turned to leave him.

"Now don't you go, missus," said Chives. "If the ladies and the gentleman want to see a nice old crop of peas, they couldn't see a nicer. I worked at Pomfret Towers, I did, when I was a lad, and they had some nice peas in that there old vegetable garden—all walls round it there were and we lads worked proper hours, we did. Six in the morning in summer and seven in the winter, till six at night; no, five it were in winter-time. Old Chives he worked with the best of them. Five shillings a week old Chives got, till his lordship give him a rise. And now he's glad to get two shillings an hour."

"I'm sure he is," said Francis, determined to shelter the females and bear the brunt of Chives's conversation, "though his reasoning seems to me a bit illogical."

"Ah," said Chives. "I don't hold with them perishing new-fangled names. If a flower has a name, as in a name, use it. That's what Chives says. Now, sir, just you look here. Take them grannybonnets."

"I do," said Francis. "But what are they?"

"Grannybonnets, sir," said Chives. "You had ought to know a grannybonnet when you see one," he added reproachfully. "Pretty little old flowers they are."

He pointed at the little flower border.

"Sorry," said Francis. "I call them columbines."

"That's all right, sir," said Chives. "Columbines is a pretty kind of name, though grannybonnet is the right one. But if a man as calls himself a gardener goes and calls them aquigeelias. I say he's a fool. And if it wasn't for the ladies, sir, I'd say what I *do* think of him, for it stands to reason aquigeelias doesn't mean a thing, not a mucky mortal thing."

"You are quite right," said Francis. "Absolutely right. If a man said aquigeelias to me I should put him down as an illiterate ignoramus."

"And you'd be right, sir," said Chives with an appreciative chuckle. "Old Chives would put him down too, sir. Good and proper. Now, I want you ladies to have a good look at those old peas. You won't find finer, not in the Duke's vegetable garden. What you want, ladies, is to have a good look at them."

Mrs. Arbuthnot said in a rebellious undertone that she didn't. Mrs. Brandon put her large horn spectacles on, looked vaguely in the direction of the peas, and expressed an admiration which almost satisfied the vegetable-loving Chives, who as a reward gave her a dissertation on the use and abuse of chicken-dung well matured and dug in. So that when Colin, who had mislaid his hostesses, at last discovered their whereabouts, no one took any notice of him and he was able to torture himself by imagining that Francis Brandon had deliberately abducted Mrs. Arbuthnot to the vegetable plot, there to poison her mind against him. His better or legal self did go so far as to admit that Francis had appeared to be addressing himself exclusively to Chives, but this consoling thought he dismissed as partaking of self-deception and wilful blindness, and gave himself the pleasure of sulking unnoticed; a malady most incident to love. Chives, intoxicated by so large and fashionable an audience, was quite prepared to talk until his hearers took root or dropped down dead, which they would undoubtedly have done had not Mrs. Brandon, a woman of decision and resource for all her appearance of fragile uselessness, thanked Chives with the utmost courtesy and driven the rest of the party towards the house.

"Now that's a lady as *is* a lady," said Chives, trying to detain Francis as an audience. "Pity she's in a hurry. The ladies they don't seem to understand that you can't hurry a garden. You can't hurry gardens no more than you can't hurry old Feeby," said Chives, looking up at the pale, tepid orb which represented that summer's sun. "I'd have given her a nice old picking of peas, I would."

Francis, enchanted by this rustic echo of Phibbus' car, pressed half a crown into the gardener's ready and willing hand, hoping to shake him off, but Chives, picking up a basket of freshly gathered peas, accompanied him to the front of the house where the French Revolution was apparently going on, led by Snow and Matron's eldest nephew, who were favouring the company with a long and very boring dissertation upon the work they had done that day, with a certain amount of mutual recrimination on such subjects as leaving screwdrivers laying about and people that used other people's foot-rule without so much as if you please, and demanding justice from Mrs. Arbuthnot and her guests. It is a great hardship to the gentry under such circumstances that a long tradition of tolerance to their inferiors forbids them, except in the case of favoured people like Sir Edmund Pridham whose explosions of temper were the pride of his part of the county, to disperse the rabble with horse-whips. Even Mrs. Brandon could not ride the whirlwind or direct the storm, and as for Mrs. Arbuthnot, when she saw Chives add himself to the talkers with his basket of peas, her property, which he insisted on offering to Mrs. Brandon who didn't want them, her pretty face looked peaked with fatigue.

Kate Carter, who had been to leave a book at Louisa Cottage, saw the tumult, walked calmly to the gate, and in virtue of her status as Housemaster's wife at once took charge.

"Your aunt is asking for you," she said to Matron's eldest

nephew. "She says you are taking her to the Barchester Odeon, so you had better make haste."

Matron's eldest nephew hurried guiltily away, while Kate greeted the Brandons.

"Can you save me?" said Mrs. Brandon. "The gardener will try to give me peas without asking Mrs. Arbuthnot's leave and I really don't want them. Cook will make us have green-pea soup because we have so many at home, and putting them through the sieve always inflames her temper."

Kate with her usual mild firmness took the basket from Chives, said they were just what she wanted for supper at the Schoolhouse and she hoped he would have a lot more as her own peas were so behind hand, and that would do nicely, thank you. All of which she said very kindly, managing somehow to make Chives feel that the future of the Schoolhouse depended on him, so that he went back with the true gardener's unhurried step to his work, determined to show the Schoolhouse gardeners a thing or two about how to grow peas properly. Kate then asked everyone to come back to tea. The Brandons accepted with pleasure.

"I think, mamma," said Francis, "that it would but be civil to drive Mrs. Arbuthnot to Mrs. Carter's house, considering that we came without an invitation."

Kate said that would be very nice and Colin could drive Miss Arbuthnot and herself, which made Colin entertain feelings towards his dear eldest sister little short of murderous.

"Just one moment, madam, if you don't mind," said Snow, approaching Mrs. Arbuthnot. "Before you go I'd like you to have a look at that plug in the kitchen. It's foolproof now, if you see what I mean in a manner of speaking, and when I've painted the bulb red you won't know it. George is all right on the wiring, but when it comes to paint, well that's not an electrician's job," said Snow pityingly.

"Mrs. Arbuthnot hasn't time now," said Kate in her usual gentle way. "Next week we shall all come and see the paint and bring the children. Get in, and we will take you up to the School."

Snow knew when he was beaten and got into the back seat. Miss Arbuthnot restored his self-esteem by inquiring about some nesting-boxes and listening to his views on their construction, while Colin sulkily drove the car, being so short with his elder sister that she seriously considered getting Matron and Nurse to take his temperature. At the Schoolhouse Everard was waiting for them. Tea passed very pleasantly. Colin did his best to appear cheerful by maintaining an aloof attitude which nobody noticed. Mrs. Brandon and Mrs. Arbuthnot, developed the friendly feelings which they had experienced at Mrs. Dean's tennis-party and a date was fixed for Mrs. Arbuthnot to visit Stories.

"I shall look forward to it very much," said Mrs. Brandon, giving Mrs. Arbuthnot a soft kiss, "and I hope you will let me call you Peggy," to which Mrs. Arbuthnot, very grateful for the friendship extended to her by so kind and charming an elder woman, said of course it must be Peggy and she knew she would love Stories.

"They call me Francis, people say, because it is my name," said Francis Brandon impersonally, to which Mrs. Arbuthnot, to his surprise and pleasure, said she thought even a simple Rum-ti-Foozleite could remember that, and both laughed; and then Everard and the Arbuthnots and even Colin quoted from the *Bab Ballads* till Mrs. Brandon pulled her son away to drive her home. The Carters and their guests talked about nothing in particular till Kate offered to take them to the nursery. At the same moment the telephone rang.

"Wait a moment," said Everard, "it's for you, Colin."

Colin took the receiver, his expression of reserved displeasure deepening as he listened.

"It's Noel," he said. "He wants me to bring the car back, so that he can go somewhere in it."

This very reasonable request on the part of the car's owner

appeared to give Colin great offence. He bade a perfunctory farewell to the Carters and Miss Arbuthnot and stood over Mrs. Arbuthnot in a minatory way, holding her hand longer than she found really convenient and gazing his whole soul into her eyes. At least that was, we presume, what he felt he was doing, though to his friends and relations he appeared to have taken a temporary leave of his sense.

"Well, good-bye," said Mrs. Arbuthnot, with great skill extricating her hand from Colin's. "And I can't tell you, though I know I have said this before, how grateful I am to you for helping us to find Editha. When we are really settled you must come to lunch one Sunday."

"I suppose," said Colin, his face unbecomingly dark with emotion, "that means you don't want to see me till you send for me."

"Oh, dear me, no," said Mrs. Arbuthnot. "Come whenever you like. You are sure to be coming over to see Kate before long. My love to your sister, please, and your nice brother-in-law."

Colin gave her such a look as a soul in Hell might have given to Dante when it saw him walking comfortably about on a personally-conducted tour of the nether regions, and abruptly left the room. If he hoped he had made an effect, he was mistaken. The waters at once closed over his head and the Carters and Arbuthnots spent a quiet evening and all went to bed early. Colin also went to bed early, rather to the relief of the Mertons, and so far derogated from his own standard of acute misery as to go to sleep almost at once.

CHAPTER 6

Colin's sulks, refreshed by a good night's rest, were nursed by him during the whole of Sunday. His sister Lydia, who had never seen him in such a condition before, was almost alarmed. As he managed to eat an excellent breakfast and a very large lunch she was not concerned for his bodily health and had no desire to take his temperature, but something was evidently wrong. So when Colin had gone down to pay his usual weekend call on Nanny Twicker, she consulted Noel about it.

"Poor Colin," said Noel the married man. "The charming widow has broken his heart. It will do him a lot of good," he added in what Lydia thought rather a callous way, "only I do wish it wouldn't make him borrow the car without asking."

"I suppose that's it," said Lydia. "I never was in love except marrying you, so I do hope he will propose quickly and then he wouldn't be so cross. There is room for two people in his flat and they will have Editha for week-ends. But then there is Effie. There wouldn't be room for three in Editha."

Noel told her not to count Colin's chickens before they were hatched. "Besides," he added, "there is no reason why a nice sensible girl like Effie, or woman if you prefer, shouldn't get married too. The county is swarming with nice middle-aged men."

So they amused themselves by marrying Miss Arbuthnot to Sir Edmund Pridham, Bishop Joram of Mngangaland now a

Canon of Barchester, Lord Stoke and various other highly unsuitable gentlemen, till Lydia suddenly thought of their agent.

"Why not Mr. Wickham?" she said. "His cottage is big enough for a family. After all, we lived there ourselves before we got back into the Manor. They both like birds, so it would be perfect."

"I expect all their children would be born with beaks," said Noel. "Still, it's quite a good idea. Only don't be rash, my precious love. Your idea of matchmaking would be to lock them up in a room till they came out engaged. I can't imagine them falling in love somehow."

Lydia said perhaps it would be a bit middle aged, though as a matter of fact she knew that Effie was only thirty-seven.

"You surprise me," said Noel. "Though why I say surprise, I don't know, for I can't say that I had ever thought about her age. With her big body and her manly face one doesn't consider it. How old is her sister-in-law?"

"Twenty-seven. I know," said Lydia laughing, "because Colin told me. He thought it was rather beautiful that she was seven years younger than he is."

"If this boy and girl affair is going to develop your sense of humour, my dear love," said Noel, "it will be worth watching. But if Colin is going to be a Despairing Lover all over Northbridge every weekend, something must be done. I shall fall in love with Peggy myself and that will learn him."

"You must tell her that she is the millionth person you've been in love with," said Lydia, for it was an old joke between the Mertons that Noel's pre-marital career as a heart-breaker had rivalled Don Juan's. He had never attempted to conceal from his Lydia the number of drawing-room flirtations he had had as a bachelor; she had never asked whether they had been more than flirtations, having a well-founded confidence in her Noel's word. For her own part she had treated Noel as a good sort of elder brother from when she was an ungraceful sixteen to the spring of Dunkirk when her heart had suddenly told her what it really wanted. Noel, hardly able to believe that his brusque, competent, independent Lydia had found a heart's haven in his arms, had never stopped thinking her the most delightful and satisfactory woman in the world. Not that he eschewed the society of women by any means, and women continued to find him very attractive, but somehow they all became Lydia's friends as much as his; perhaps a little more her friends than his, which all goes to show what nice women Noel knew. So he said he would certainly warn Mrs. Arbuthnot of his intentions and Lydia rubbed her face against his shoulder while he kissed the top of her head, a proceeding apparently satisfactory to both parties.

"I suppose," said Noel, "that your brother Colin will now spend most of the Long Vacation here. He did talk about Switzerland but I feel that the lure of Editha will be too strong, unless of course he proposes and is turned down and goes to the Engadine to throw himself over a precipice and so cure a broken heart."

"You wouldn't mind his being here, would you?" said Lydia.

"Bless your heart, my sweet chuck, I wouldn't mind having the whole Government here for the Long Vacation if it would give you pleasure," said Noel, "though I might draw the line at their female secretaries. And I daresay he will find it convenient to stay with Kate for part of the time, unless she is taking the children away. I wonder what Mrs. Arbuthnot thinks about it all. I should like to see Colin settled. I remember, years ago, when I was staying here with your people and you were a most unrefined schoolgirl—no, I mean unconfined, though you were unrefined too—we had a conversation about people getting married and you said you thought Colin was an uncle. I sometimes think you were right."

Lydia said so long as he, Noel, wasn't her uncle, she didn't mind who was and the conversation came to an end.

*   *   *

Meanwhile Colin, paying his Sunday call at the gardener's cottage, had been forced by Nanny Twicker to sit down and have a large cup of cocoa and some cold apple-pie. In vain had he protested that he had only just made a very good lunch. Gentlemen, said Nanny severely, could always do with a bit of something in the afternoon, and Mr. Colin mustn't judge her pastry by the colour, because that was the Government's fault with that nasty flour they gave us.

"They do say, Mr. Colin," said Nanny, "that the Government's going to ration bread. Really, we might as well be foreigners like those nasty Mixo-Lydians. You mark my words, Mr. Colin. The more the bread is rationed the nastier it will be. It's just as well I always bake at home. All my young gentlemen liked my bread. I remember the summer Mr. Eric and Mr. Tony and Mr. Percy were here they ate one of my two-pound loaves and a pound of my own butter at breakfast one morning besides two pounds of sausages and an egg each and a pot of my strawberry jam. That was what I call rations. Not this nasty flour they give us now and skimps of butter you can't see. Still, Miss Lydia always sends me my milk regular and I make my bit of butter."

While his old nurse ran on, Colin's thoughts went back to the summer when he had taught classics at Southbridge and three of his boys had spent an ecstatic weekend in Nanny's cottage and Rose Fairweather, Rose Birkett as she was then, had thrown the engagement ring that Philip Winter could so ill afford into the stream. If his sister Lydia had been there she would have reminded him that it was Philip who dropped the ring into the stream on purpose, after Rose had hurled it at him and missed her mark; but so is history written. Now Rose was married with three children. Philip was married. Noel, Lydia, Everard, Kate, Delia Brandon, Geraldine Birkett, Octavia Crawley youngest daughter of the Deanery; all the relations and friends of his youth, all were married. He was left alone and palely wandering. A wave of self-pity surged over him. Then he pulled himself together and thought how lucky he was with an increasingly large practice at the bar and two delightful married sisters with nice husbands and children to stay with, not to speak of his elder brother Robert and his wife and family. And there was the book he was writing, a book which might in times to come be quoted by lawyers as yet unborn. "I submit, m'lud," they would say, "that in *Keith on Lemon*, page one hundred and three, the case now before the court is fully provided for." And so absorbed did the pining bachelor become in these professional daydreams that Nanny filled his large cup to the brim again with very hot, strong cocoa.

"Oh, I say, Nanny, I really can't," said Colin.

"Oh yes, you can, Mr. Colin," said Nanny, just as she would have said it to Master Colin more than twenty-five years ago; much more than twenty-five, almost thirty. "What nice ladies those ladies were that Miss Lydia brought to see me, Mrs. Arbuthnot and her sister-in-law. Poor thing, it seemed quite dreadful her being a widow with that lovely hair and such a sweet expression. I hear they are at Southbridge. That Jessie of Miss Kate's came over to tea with me last Sunday and she said Mrs. Arbuthnot was such a nice lady and Miss Kate's house-maid told her she had all her nightgowns and things handmade. I expect she'll be marrying again, poor young lady."

Colin's mind, suddenly diverted from its reflections upon *Keith's Commentaries upon Lemon on Running Powers*, for such was the proposed name of the book on points of railway law which he was re-editing, fell into a confused state of crossness. How dared Jessie, that hideous spectacled housemaid of Matron's, talk to Kate's housemaid about Mrs. Arbuthnot's nightgowns and retail the gossip. One did not consider nightgowns, hand-made or otherwise, in connection with a goddess. She rose in mysterious splendour in the morn and sank to repose on roseate clouds at night, like a lovely picture by Boucher. And then Colin, who had quite a pleasant sense of humour when not under the spell of the tender passion, suddenly reflected that Boucher's divinities were far too apt to go to bed and rise at morn wearing nothing but a necklace of impossibly large pearls;

at which he began to laugh, and then had to explain to Nanny that he had thought of something funny.

"You were always a one for jokes, Mr. Colin," said Nanny and proceeded to relate several rather pointless stories of nursery humour which made Colin blush for his former self, but his old nurse enjoyed them so much that he tried to pretend they amused him.

"Such a dear little boy you were," said Nanny Twicker. "Mr. Robert's eldest is just like you. Miss Kate's boys have a look of old Mrs. Keith and Miss Lydia's Master Harry is just like old Mr. Keith. When are you going to marry some nice young lady, Mr. Colin? It's high time you did and have some dear little children of your own."

This was too much. One thought of a goddess and one was told one ought to have dear little children. Colin could willingly have stamped like Rumpelstilzkin till his foot went right through the floor. With a tremendous effort he kept his temper, kissed Nanny, and went for a long walk, resolutely turning his back on the direction of Southbridge. But all in vain, for wherever he might tell his legs to go he could not command his thoughts, and among them was the thought of Francis Brandon talking to Mrs. Arbuthnot in far too familiar a way. Francis had not found a house for Mrs. Arbuthnot. If it came to that, neither had Colin, but it was through his sister Kate that Editha Cottage had been found. Let Francis beware. If he trifled with Mrs. Arbuthnot's affections he would have to reckon with that rising young barrister Mr. Colin Keith. And as Colin walked faster and faster, moving with the increasing speed of his own thoughts, he had involved Francis in some rather shady affairs connected with his business, got him into the dock, thrown up the most important brief of his career to defend his rival, got him triumphantly acquitted without a stain on his character, accompanied him from the court to Mrs. Arbuthnot's house (conveniently and imaginatively situated in Chelsea or Belgravia), left him there, paced Hyde Park till closing time, except that there wasn't any closing time now that there were no railings to keep people out, returned to Mrs. Arbuthnot's house, gone in to say farewell before leaving for New Zealand next morning, heard from those lovely lips the words "I have sent Francis away. *You* will not leave me, Colin. I am so lonely," and pressed her to his heart, his for ever. And by the time he had elaborated this exquisite idyll to his own satisfaction, he had walked four or five miles and got back only just in time for tea, his temper distinctly improved by the exercise he had taken.

"Good Sunday," said Lydia. "I mean it's Nurse's Sunday in. The alternate Sundays are Black Sundays. Do you mind nursery tea, Noel? One of Nurse's old children is coming to tea, that nice Susan Dean, so I thought it would please Nurse if we all had tea upstairs. You know her, don't you, Colin?"

Colin did remember her at the tennis party and was quite pleased at the thought of meeting her again, though he would have preferred it to be her sister Jessica, to whom he had not yet made amends for his gaucheness about the lunch.

Accordingly Colin went up to the nursery where the tea-table was laid for seven or eight people. Master Harry Merton was already in his tall chair and Miss Lavinia Merton was having her face and hands washed in the bathroom.

"I hope I'm not too early, Nurse," said Colin, as she came into the room with a shiningly clean Lavinia.

Nurse graciously said that we were always pleased to see Uncle Colin, weren't we? And perhaps Mr. Keith would stay with the children while she put the kettle on the ring.

"You haven't such a thing as a match, or a lighter, have you, sir?" said Nurse.

Colin handed her his cigarette lighter. Nurse lighted the gas and returned the lighter to its owner.

"It's really quite shocking the way one cannot get matches nowadays," said Nurse, for the moment at leisure to converse. "Mrs. Merton hasn't been able to get more than two boxes a week for ever so long, and what is the use of one box, sir? Not that I grudge Cook her box, for Mrs. Merton who is always so thoughtful got these utility lighters for us all—very useful they are when they haven't run dry, or need a new wick or a flint. Really, sir, as I was saying to Mrs. Merton the other day, it is all just one thing after another and if Cook refuses to use the lighter and will use the matches, I said to Mrs. Merton, well this is hardly a free country where some people won't use the utility lighter and don't seem to consider other people at all. And I happen to know quite well that Cook gets five or six boxes of matches whenever she wants them, because her brother works at a tobacconist's in Barchester. Lavinia, leave baby alone."

Lavinia, who had been trying to tie her feeder over her brother's face, looked at Colin for sympathy, evidently saw signs of it and embraced one of his legs with great violence, clinging to it like a limpet.

"Really, Lavinia, what goings-on," said Nurse, scandalized. "Oh, if you don't mind sir, that is all right. And of course, as I was saying to Mrs. Merton, smoking is a really most unpleasant habit particularly when there is food about and when I think of the way Cook smokes, well of course she uses a lot of matches, but the idea of cigarette ash on the nursery food is quite upsetting. I never allowed any smoking in my nurseries, unless it was the gentleman of the house. That sounds like someone coming upstairs. I'll just go and look at my kettle if you'll excuse me, sir."

She went into the next room. Steps were heard on the landing outside and in came Susan and Jessica Dean.

"Hullo, Nursie," said Susan. "Jessica is down for the week-end so I brought her with me. Hullo, Colin."

Colin made to go and greet the ladies, but found movement impossible owing to his niece Lavinia's apparently permanent embrace, which made him feel as if he had his leg in a splint and a heavy weight attached to his foot.

"I do apologize," said Colin, shuffling forward as best he could, "but Lavinia has somehow got attached to me and I cannot prise her off."

"Hullo, Lavinia," said Jessica.

The voice, velvet soft and as smooth as the finest liqueur, had an immediate effect. Lavinia stopped kissing her uncle's trouser leg, looked round at Jessica and relaxed her hold.

"Now, Jessica," said Nurse, "how often have I told you not to use that word. Lavinia picks up everything."

"Hullo," said Lavinia, looking shyly at Jessica.

"Say how do you do nicely to Jessica," said Nurse, wisely ignoring Lavinia's greeting, "and to Susan."

The brilliant young star of the Cockspur Theatre, unruffled by Nurse's autocratic air, embraced her heartily, as did the very competent young librarian of the Barsetshire Red Cross Hospital Libraries; and it was just as well that they did, for to their ex-Nurse they were simply Susan and Jessica, and Jessica being the youngest had always been rather spoilt and needed, so Nurse considered, keeping in her place; though if any outsider had tried to repress Miss Jessica Dean, it is probable that Nurse would have sent such a one to bed without any supper.

Mr. and Mrs. Noel Merton, who were by courtesy of Nurse admitted to tea in their own nursery, now made their appearance. Nurse brought in the teapot, Lavinia was hoisted onto a chair with a fat cushion on it, Master Harry Merton was girded with a large feeder and Nurse asked Lydia if she would pour out, to which Lydia replied that she would be so glad if Nurse would do it. This was of course a mere matter of form, for Nurse had no intention of letting anyone pour out in her nursery while she was there and even the fearless Lydia would have preferred not to raise the question.

"No milk for me, Nursie," said Jessica.

Nurse said that might be all very well for London, but they had plenty of their own milk at Northbridge, and poured it with a lavish hand. Jessica made a face at Colin expressive of her feelings. Lavinia, who had with the fickleness of a charming woman transferred her devotion from her uncle to the newcomer, at once copied the face. Nurse, who was cutting the crusts off bread and butter for Master Harry Merton, realized with a nurse's sixth sense that there was mischief afoot, looked up and saw Lavinia.

"Don't make faces, Lavinia, and eat your bread and butter," said Nurse, but Lavinia, flown with the excitement of a party made the face again, adding, "I'm Hullo Jessica."

The corner was obviously the only place for Lavinia, and if the room had had a hundred corners Nurse would willingly have stood her in them all. But a public occasion such as a nursery tea with one's parents, one's uncle and two guests present, gives great latitude to offenders. Lavinia knew quite well that Nurse would not visit her wrath upon her in the presence of the public; she also knew that Nurse would probably pass a general Act of Indulgence after tea and talk, so she stopped making a face and put a large piece of bread and butter rather carefully into her mouth so that a good deal of it stuck on her face. Her Uncle Colin who was next to her tried to wipe it off with her feeder and got some of it onto his coat sleeve.

"That's not the way, sir," said Nurse pityingly, as Colin got his handkerchief out. "You'll only rub it in."

"Here, let me," said Susan, and with the blade of a knife she deftly removed the sticky mess.

Colin could not but be grateful.

"Thanks awfully," he said. "I knew Nurse was longing to take me into the bathroom and sponge my face and hands. I'm terrified of that woman."

"Oh, Nursie's all right," said Susan just as, Colin thought, a professional lion-tamer might say that his lion was as gentle as a lamb, and then she and Colin compared notes about their nursery days and got on very well. One side of Colin would have preferred to be talking brilliantly to Miss Jessica Dean of the Cockspur Theatre thus, he hoped, obliterating the unfavourable impression he must have made at her parents' tennis-party. But the other side, the side that was now in action so to speak, found something very friendly and safe in a conversation about cribs and rocking-horses and fairy stories, in the course of which he gathered that Susan Dean had something to do with books.

"You ought to write a book," said Susan Dean. "One of those childhood-recollected-in-tranquillity books, like Mr. Percy Lubbock's *Earlham*. People simply adore them."

Colin said he was writing a book, or trying to write a book, but rather a dull one. Susan said that there were heaps of people who loved really dull books and what kind of dullness was it.

"It was rather affected of me to say dull," said Colin, "because I don't think it's dull at all. A man called Lemon wrote a standard book on the running powers of railways on each other's lines, and I am trying to bring it up to date."

"I know exactly," said Susan. "Like the bit between London and Princes Risborough where the Paddington trains and the Marylebone trains get in each other's way and Coke upon Littleton."

Even Colin's quick trained mind did not take in at once the full meaning of the remark, but during a few seconds while he paused to reply it dawned upon him that Susan Dean was not only well educated but also, which is not always the same thing, very intelligent. Her description of the G.W.R. and L.N.E.R. joint line was to the point; her comparison of himself with Coke highly flattering, showing also a fine appreciation of Lemon's status.

"How do you know all those things?" he asked.

Susan looked surprised. A member of a large clever family with engineering in the blood and brought up among books, an allusive conversation like the one they were having was her normal element. So it was for Colin among his London friends; friends who belonged mostly to legal circles; not so much with his family, for Kate and Lydia were splendidly uneducated in the best sense of the word. Kate could be relied on for quick and eternal comprehension of one's domestic needs and a placid acceptance of subjects which she considered suitable for men, such as the classics, among whom Everard and Colin still browsed. As for Lydia, she had an exhaustive knowledge of Shakespeare's plays and her mind was clear of cant in a way that would have satisfied Dr. Johnson. Everard Carter had gone so far as to try his hand at an imaginary conversation between Dr. Johnson and Lydia, himself writing as Boswell, and came to the conclusion that short of absolute rudeness, for Lydia would not have knocked an opponent down with the butt-end of her pistol, they would have been pretty evenly matched, adding that when he went to heaven, the first treat he would demand would be a philosophical discussion between those two great minds.

"I don't exactly know if I do know them," said Susan. "I mean I haven't really read Coke upon Littleton, because I don't suppose anyone would unless they had to. But one gets to know a fair amount about books in the Library, because people want every kind of book. We have quite a lot of demands for law books."

The Library? Colin felt he must be careful. Was it Boots or Smith? Or one of those rather precious libraries run by efficient women? Susan didn't seem like an efficient woman; not in the chintz-and-raffia sense at any rate. He did not quite know how to steer his course.

"I expect you find your subscribers very trying sometimes," he hazarded.

"Do you mean the librarians?" said Susan. "They are mostly extremely nice and helpful."

Librarians. What the dickens was the girl talking about?

"Lady Pomfret is our new County Organizer," said Susan, "and I work under her. I'm the Depot Librarian."

This, felt Colin, should have been the clue. There was something he ought to know, ought to guess, and it eluded him like something in a nightmare.

"She worked for the Red Cross and St. John all through the war," said Susan, "as well as a million other things, and it's perfectly splendid to have her as our chairman. We're going to have an exhibition in Barchester next month of voluntary book-binding for our Hospital Libraries. I'll send you a card."

Colin gasped inwardly with relief. So that was what Susan was. And he looked on her with considerable respect. No longer was she the elder sister of the brilliant Jessica. She was the Depot Librarian of an important county organization, which almost meant its head. And very nice she must look in a well-tailored Red Cross uniform with dashing white gloves and her fair hair curling neatly under her cap.

"I'm in London all the week, being a barrister," he said. "But if your exhibition is open on Saturdays perhaps you would have lunch with me in Barchester and show me what I ought to admire."

"As a matter of fact we are opening on Saturday week," said Susan, "but I've promised to lunch with Francis Brandon. He goes to business in Barchester every day and I stay at the Deanery and go home for week-ends, so we quite often meet for lunch. Isn't his mother nice?"

Luckily the last sentence was one to which Colin could make a suitable reply, for like everyone else, except possibly old Lady Norton and Miss Pettinger the loathed Headmistress of the Barchester High School, he found Mrs. Brandon perfectly delightful. As for Francis——but one must be fair, a lawyer must be able to look on both sides of a case even if he inclines professionally to the side he is paid to represent. Francis Brandon was very pleasant, very easy-tempered, a good dancer, doubtless extremely successful in whatever his business was in Barchester, good-looking if one liked that sort of looks: but per contra a libertine, a roué, a trespasser upon other people's property, a man who would think nothing of flirting with a charming if credulous woman who was alone and helpless, probably also a professional seducer of widows if the truth were known; a man who would use his mother and his mother's car to cloak his intrigues and force wealthier men than he to drive their elder sister and the School carpenter and Mrs. Arbuthnot's sister-in-law from Editha Cottage to the Schoolhouse when they might have been driving the adored object; a man, as he had just discovered, who not content with trifling with widows' affections also took girls out to lunch on the day one wanted to take them oneself. But one must be calm; this way madness lies if one reflects upon the wrongs one has suffered at a rival's hands.

"Yes, she is quite delightful," he said. "And Francis is a very good sort of fellow."

And that wasn't the way to put it, to be so deucedly condescending; but it would have to stand, thought Colin.

"He's awfully nice," said Susan, "and he dances divinely. I'm not good enough for him really. But Mrs. Arbuthnot is quite perfect with him. Lydia," she called across the table, "do you remember how beautifully Francis and Mrs. Arbuthnot danced that night at the Deanery? It was like feathers being blown across the floor."

Lydia added her praise to Susan's. Noel, who had been talking London talk with Jessica, joined their conversation and expressed his admiration of the dancers. Lavinia and her brother were taken away, cleaned, and returned to the nursery with injunctions from Nurse to be good while she washed up the tea-things. Susan volunteered to help her so that she could give her the latest news of the various Dean grandchildren, most of whose fathers and mothers Nurse had had under her care, for Nannies are also Grandnannies and like to follow the lives of succeeding generations. So the Mertons and Colin were left with Jessica Dean, and Colin apologized for not having made a lunch engagement with her before and begged to be allowed to settle a date with her.

"I'd love it," said Jessica, quite truthfully, "and we'll get Peggy Arbuthnot. But it must be my party. At least it shall be Aubrey Clover's. He is longing to meet Peggy again and he simply doesn't know what to do with his royalties. I'll ring you up in town and fix a day. You didn't seem so keen when we met before,

or I'd have fixed it long ago." She then favoured him with Mrs.
Carvel's wink and Colin went red in the face.

"Dear me, you are the man I would really like to flirt with,"
said Jessica to Noel. "I am sure your technique is perfect."

"It was," said Noel. "In fact I was well known as the Lothario
of the Inner Temple. But marriage has ruined me."

"I don't wonder," said Jessica, looking at Lydia. And at the
sight of a married couple of some seven years' standing, so
evidently and peacefully in love, the facile tears of the real actress
brimmed in her dark eyes. "Too, too Darby and Joan," she said.
And as she spoke, the tears which with any other woman would
have brimmed over, spoilt her make-up and made her nose red
and shining, quietly sank again like the water running out of a
bath thought Noel to himself, much interested by the phenomenon, only without all the gurgles.

"How on earth do you do it?" he said admiringly.

Jessica said it was just a gift. "And if Noel ever gives you any
trouble," she said to Lydia, "ring me up and I'll come to the
rescue. Cockspur 1313 is my number: two unluckies make one
lucky. It's been a heavenly party. I wish Aubrey had been here.
He is writing a new play with a Nanny in it and he could have
got marvellous local colour. He is simply longing to meet Peggy,
so we will have our lunch as soon as I can arrange it and he and
Peggy can hold hands. I suppose I ought to take Susan home."

But Susan, who came back from the washing-up in time to
hear her younger sister's remark, said she simply must stay and
see baby and Lavinia have their bath, so Lydia said they had
better stay to supper as it was cold and only Mr. Wickham,
which cannibalistic menu did not appear to surprise her guests at
all. Colin remained in the nursery. Noel went to his study, and
Lydia and Jessica had a good gossip about Colin and his passion
for Mrs. Arbuthnot. Jessica spoke with such authority of men
and love that Lydia felt very young and callow in spite of having
a husband and two children; yet at the same time she felt almost
middle aged and protective towards the precocious child.

"I suppose," said Lydia, who had been thinking so hard that she hardly heard Jessica's last words, "that you must always be thinking about acting. I mean, you said you wished Mr. Clover could be at nursery tea because he is writing a play with a nurse in it, and I expect you were getting some hints for him."

"Not Mr. Clover, darling," said Jessica, "it sounds too, too unkind. Aubrey. Yes, I was and wasn't."

Lydia said she didn't think she wanted to call Mr. Clover Aubrey if she didn't know him, and how did Jessica mean that she was and she wasn't.

"Everyone calls him Aubrey," said Jessica indifferently. "It's not his name really."

Lydia inquired what his name was.

"Caleb Lover," said Jessica. "He always signed letters C. Lover because he didn't like the name Caleb, and no wonder, poor lamb, but his parents were frightfully religious, so they called him that, and his writing is quite ghastly, so people thought it was Clover and then he thought it was a good name, so he stuck to it and of course he needed a Christian name, though why he chose Aubrey I don't know. One must be called something. All I meant was that I knew Nursie inside out because she was with us when I was a little girl, but I wanted to rub up the part a bit."

"I say," said Mrs. Noel Merton, blurting out her thoughts just as Miss Lydia Keith might have done, "were you learning any other parts?"

"Since you ask," said Jessica, "I was."

"I suppose it was Colin," said Lydia. "I must say being in love makes him rather cross and liable to take offence, but he is really very, very nice and I am frightfully fond of him, next to Noel."

"Oh, Colin," said Jessica, lightly dismissing him. "Just like all not quite young men in love. No use for Aubrey. I was thinking about you and Noel."

"Me and Noel?" exclaimed Lydia. "But we are ordinary."

Jessica laughed.

"That's what makes it so damn difficult," she said. "If Aubrey could put over a husband and wife like you and Noel, he'd be simply ruined by super-tax and go to the workhouse. You are both quite divine and that's that. Even Aubrey isn't clever enough; or else he's too clever. I don't know."

Lydia, though she found Jessica's analysis of herself and her husband rather silly, quite realized that Jessica was talking in terms of a world to which she had no clue and stoutly said that she didn't understand in the least.

"You wouldn't, darling," said Jessica. "And you needn't. And I'm going to say something else you won't understand. I adore your husband, but I'm on your side. Just like that."

Jessica was quite right. Lydia did not understand in the least, nor did she try to. People who were actresses were not like ordinary people, she very rightly considered, and not really accountable for their words or their actions. So there was a short silence. Not of embarrassment, for Lydia and Jessica liked and trusted each other; more of reflection on Jessica's side and on Lydia's of wondering whether the opened bottle of sherry would go round, and then Colin and Susan came down, full of admiration for Lavinia's handling of her sponge and her young brother's real gift for splashing the bath water with both hands. Noel came in with the opened bottle of sherry, followed by Mr. Wickham.

"Well, well, well, if it isn't little Jessica," said Mr. Wickham. "One moment, old girl, while I discharge the cargo."

He pulled a bottle out of each pocket of his old shooting-jacket, put them on the table and folded Jessica in a hearty embrace, to which she responded with equal abandon.

"Lipstick all over my face as usual," said Mr. Wickham most ungallantly, looking at himself in the mirror. "How you girls can put all that stuff on your faces I don't know."

"We'd look perfect frights if we didn't," said Jessica, neatly repairing the damage as she spoke. "This is too divine, darling

Wicks. Aubrey will be livid when he hears I've seen you. What about lunch in town?"

Mr. Wickham rapidly and skillfully uncorking a bottle of sherry and a bottle of rum, said he was always one for a free lunch if his bloated employers would give him a day off. A real day off, he meant; not the day he had to go to London next week for the Amalgamated Countries Pure Jersey Maintenance dinner. Noel said it went to his heart to pay a man wages and then let him have a holiday, but he would be generous for once and why shouldn't Wickham spend two nights in town and then he could go to Jessica's play and have lunch with her as well.

"Ah, if they'd all been like that we'd never have had the French Revolution," said Mr. Wickham, and then Lydia herded them all in to supper, taking the sherry and rum in with them. Lydia and Jessica each had some rum and orange juice; Noel, Colin and Susan had each a glass of sherry; while Mr. Wickham disposed of most of the rum unaided, refusing to contaminate it with orange which he said was only a lady's drink. He and Jessica did most of the talking, the rest of the party being quite pleased to sit back and be entertained by a pair of brilliant cross-talk comedians.

"And now," said Mr. Wickham when supper was over, "I must regretfully do what is known in refined circles as leaving from the table, as I have a great hideous heap of Milk Marketing Board stuff to get through."

"Always take your exits before they boo you," said Jessica. "Look here, Wicks. Aubrey is giving Colin and me lunch next week and Peggy Arbuthnot is coming. You'll adore her."

"Keith's pretty widow?" said Mr. Wickham in a way that revolted every finer sentiment that Colin possessed. For several hours Colin had so far forgotten himself, or it might be more truthful to say had so much enjoyed himself, that it had not occurred to him to be a baffled and ardent lover. Mr. Wickham's coarse and unfeeling words about Mrs. Arbuthnot brought him back to his better self and he at once fell a prey to hatred and jealousy, combined with determination to go to the lunch at whatever cost to himself and protect his sweet, innocent friend against such men as Wickham and (probably) Aubrey Clover; though as Aubrey Clover was paying for the lunch the cost to Colin would appear to be negligible. The date was fixed and Mr. Wickham, forgetfully taking the remains of the rum with him, went back to work.

Jessica then said that she and Susan must get back to Winter Overcotes as they both had to be at work next day.

"Good-bye, and thank you for a divine party," said Jessica, giving Lydia an affectionate but careful kiss. "If you were the London sort I'd ask you to lunch, but I think it would bore you. We are rather bores, you know, unless you are in the gang or quite stage-struck. But may I come and see you again?"

It seemed to Lydia very flattering that a stage-star, even if she was really only the Dean's youngest daughter, should ask permission to come and see her, and it did not occur to her in honest simplicity that Jessica wanted to come because she truly admired her in every respect. However, Lydia believed Jessica when she said that she could never make stage copy from Northbridge Manor, so she said she would love to see her again and Noel seconded her invitation.

Were we the London sort, we would describe at great length the lunch which Aubrey Clover, incited thereto by Jessica Dean, gave to Mrs. Arbuthnot, Colin Keith, Mr. Wickham and Mrs. David Leslie, the smartest of the not quite so young marrieds in London. But our muse does not sing of London, which is in any case a land of lost delights since to the destruction of war were added the horrors of peace. Suffice it to say that the lunch-party did take place, that everyone except Colin was delighted to see everyone else, and even Colin forgot that he was in love owing to the delightful discovery that he and Aubrey Clover had been at one point in the war only fifty miles distant from each other, which led them to fraternize with complete disregard of the rest of the party. Mrs. David Leslie and Jessica Dean found an enormous number of common friends in London and Barset-shire about whom they said extravagantly unkind things; while Mr. Wickham and Mrs. Arbuthnot talked about the changes in India since Mr. Wickham had been on the East India Station during the 1914 war; so that as far as any glamour or excitement was concerned, they might well have been lunching at the Cross Keys in Barchester, except that the food was slightly worse and the drink even more expensive. After this Colin was week-ending with friends in other parts of England for a time and life simmered down to its normal round.

CHAPTER 7

Two very important events were to take place in Barsetshire towards the end of July. The first was the formal opening of the exhibition of the Red Cross Hospital bookbinding which Susan had mentioned to Colin. The second was Speech Day at Southbridge School. And this was more than usually important because it marked the end of an era. Mr. Birkett would say his last words as Headmaster to the School where he had served since he was an assistant master in the Junior School. To him and his wife it had fallen to guide the School through the years of war, to receive the Hosiers' Boys' Foundation School evacuated from London, to send boys year after year into some form of armed or civil service, each carrying with it its own dangers; to pacify the elder boys who were afraid that the war would stop before they could get to it, to reassure the physically unfit that they were not damned as renegades because their eyesight or a weak heart made fighting out of the question, to tolerate the parents who insisted on sending their younger boys to America, regretfully as the war came to an end to have to refuse boys whose American schooling was inadequate for any school entrance examination; to deal with catering, blackout, the handing on of clothing more especially sports outfits from older to younger boys as the clothing coupons made purchases for growing boys increasingly difficult and there was less and less to buy; to bear with mistresses in the place of junior masters, though we are glad to be able to say that Miss Banks who mistaught Latin in the Lower School had been got rid of at the end of the previous term and was now safely in a highly lucrative job in Paris with Unesco (whatever that may be) and a secretary of her own, whom she bullied dreadfully and who had a slavish adoration for her. And these were only a few among the thousand jobs that Mr. Birkett had quietly and determinedly done.

So there was to be a very special Speech Day with nearly all the Governors of the School present, which unfortunately had to include the Bishop. But, as Mr. Birkett philosophically remarked, it was the office rather than the man that they must consider, and if the Founders of the School had known the sort of man the present Bishop was going to be, they certainly would not have laid it down that each successive Bishop of Barchester was to be by right a Governor, and at any rate the Bishopess could not sit on the platform. A presentation was to be made, which was a dead secret except to many Governors, parents and old boys who had subscribed to it. The School Carmen, a quite dreadful affair written as everyone knows by the Rev. J. J. Damper, Headmaster from 1849 to 1856 and author of several hymns including the favourite hymn of the great Duke of Omnium, 'Each morn we humbly bow the face, Before the coming of Thy Grace,' was to be sung, with a new verse specially written by P. Hacker of Lazarus College, the best classical scholar Southbridge had ever produced, now reader in New-Platonism and Aristotelian Ethics to the University of Oxford and rapidly becoming celebrated as a crusted character with a tame chameleon as his best friend. Mrs. Birkett said she was afraid she would cry. Mr. Birkett said there was no doubt that she would and he would probably have a stroke and be a gaping idiot for the rest of his life. It would also fall to Mr. Birkett to welcome, in a few well-chosen words, his successor Everard Carter and then, said Mr. Birkett with gloomy relish, everyone would cry.

But this ceremony was still some weeks away and for the

moment the exhibition of bookbinding for the Red Cross Hospital Libraries had pride of place. Mrs. Arbuthnot and her sister-in-law, both very neat with their hands, had already enrolled themselves as volunteer workers and were going to help at the exhibition. So Mrs. Brandon suggested that Mrs. Arbuthnot should be driven back to Stories by Francis and spend the week-end. Miss Arbuthnot was invited by Lydia to come back to Northbridge with her after the exhibition and stay till Monday, and Mrs. Dingle was to sleep at Editha for two nights in case of burglars, though as she was rather deaf and a heavy sleeper it is doubtful whether she would be much use.

On the opening day of the Red Cross Exhibition Francis Brandon, as he often did, gave lunch to Susan Dean at the Cross Keys. Had Colin been present he would have been pleased to recognize the correctness of his judgment about Susan Dean in uniform. Expense being luckily no particular object with the Dean family, Mrs. Dean, who lived almost entirely on her pre-war wardrobe as so many of us do, was able to help with clothing coupons, so Susan's uniform was a paragon of tailoring and completeness. Her London tailor, a refugee from Vienna before 1914, who was a consummate artist and a frightful bully, considered this work to be one of his masterpieces, though deprecating the Red Cross pattern.

"Eef you weesh to be smart you cannot arve pockets like that," he expostulated, almost in tears. "'Ow often arve I tell to you, Miss Dean, a jacket weeth many pockets is a dah-oody jacket."

Susan admitted the generalization, but said it was the Red Cross regulation and she couldn't do anything about it, so Mr. Klobber had to give in, begging her with tears in his eyes never to put anything in any of the pockets.

"But look here," said Susan, "what's the use of pockets if you don't put anything in them? I must have handkerchiefs and things."

"You can arve your 'ankerchief in your bag, Miss Dean," said Mr. Klobber, who was on his knees putting pins into the skirt.

"And do not forget what I say to you. When you seet down, ollways pull the skirt up behind a little, and so you will not stretch the seat. For," said Mr. Klobber, passing his hands lightly and reverently down the skirt, "eet ees a beautiful fit, Miss Dean. Eet ees as if moulded to the figure."

"But I can't hitch my skirt up behind every time I want to sit on a chair," said Susan. "It wouldn't look well in the office and Lady Pomfret wouldn't like it."

"Ach! Lady Pomfret!" exclaimed Mr. Klobber, by now almost crying. "A most beautiful figure, English naturally, but I make suits for her like an angel, beautiful tweeds, and what does she do? She stoffs the pockets fool of rubbish, and as for the skirts they are like an old peasant woman. I break my heart over the skirts. And you, Miss Dean, eet ees the same thing. Never shall I teach my English ladies how to treat my beautiful suits. Eet ees ollways: 'Oh, Mr. Klobber, please to press my skirt, eet ees all baggy behind,' and 'Oh, Mr. Klobber, please to press my jacket, the pockets are oll bolgy.' Now in Vienna, the ladies put on their suits that I make them and go for a little walk, or go to a party where they stand, and talk, and look elegant. Never do they sit in my suits, and as for pockets, ollways empty."

Susan said she was awfully sorry, but she hadn't any parties in Barchester and had to sit nearly all the time in the office, but she would try to remember. So Mr. Klobber took eighteen coupons and twenty-seven guineas and went on to the next job, and Susan filled her pockets with handkerchiefs and notebooks and at once forgot to hitch up her skirt, but nevertheless looked very well turned-out and attractive.

"It's very few women that can wear a shirt and a tie and get away with it," said Francis approvingly as they sat down to lunch. "Lady Pomfret can and so can young Lady Norton, though I loathe her just one degree less than the Dreadful Dowager," for so Victoria, Lady Norton, was known to many of her friends. "When I think what my divine mamma would look like in a shirt——"

"Or mine," said Susan. "The older she gets the more she wears things that trail. I daresay I'll trail when I get old. Anyway, I'm awfully glad to get out of uniform in the evenings. I'll tell you another one that couldn't wear a shirt: that's Mrs. Arbuthnot. She'd look awfully pretty but not quite real; like someone in a play."

"She is coming to Stories for the week-end," said Francis, "My mamma has cottoned to her like anything. I shall be quite out of it."

So Susan said he had better come to Winter Overcotes on Sunday and play tennis and then they talked about nothing in particular and laughed and found one another very good company till it was time for Susan to be at the Freemasons' Hall where the exhibition was taking place. We cannot exactly say that Susan Dean had even a faint pang of jealousy at the thought of Mrs. Arbuthnot being at Stories for the week-end. After all Francis was at liberty to have as many friends as he liked and she didn't care for him as much as all that, and evidently he realized that Mrs. Arbuthnot was a more suitable companion for his mother than for himself. This last thought gave her considerable comfort, though if she had stopped to reflect she might have realized that she and Mrs. Arbuthnot were about the same age.

Barchester was not well off for public halls. The Town Hall had one very large room, but it was at present occupied by the Food Office. No one quite knew what was being done there, but there was a strong feeling that when the new ration books were issued there would be something nasty to do with bread and *that*, of course, my dear, simply means hell, as if we hadn't enough to do standing in the grocer queue, the butcher queue, the fish queue, the shoe queue and believe it or not four times have I stood outside Goodfits' to try to get shoes for Mary and Tommy and if they get deformed feet blame this Government not me, for stop children's feet growing you cannot. The Athenaeum, founded about the time of the Chartists as a counterblast to the Mechanics' Institute, had so far sunk in the intellectual and social scale as to refuse to let its room to anybody who could not produce a signed application from the Friends of the Soviets' Society; though as its room, owing to the march of science, now looked onto a twenty-foot railway embankment with arches under it where Government Balancer Meal for chickens and Artificial Fish Manure were stored, it did not really matter.

So it was regretfully decided that the Freemasons' Hall, a fine example of West Kensington Gothic, was the only possible place for the St. John and Red Cross Exhibition. This venerable building had a considerable frontage onto the High Street which was narrow and usually blocked with slow-moving traffic except between noon and two o'clock, when all traffic became practically stationary owing to its drivers having their dinner; so that the agonized hoots of cars trying to get through never ceased. By rights there should have been no parking in this section of the High Street, but the police, sharing the general passion for making things more difficult for everybody, had shown their zeal by prohibiting parking on alternate sides of the road on alternate days, thus making parking permissible on the same sides of the road on the other alternate days: this is quite clear, we hope. As most of the traffic was large and obscured the parking notices and there was a universal confusion about which day of the week, or alternatively which side of the road was which, the result was that no one in the Freemasons' Hall could hear themselves or anyone else speak, except before 10 a.m. and after 6 p.m., which made it peculiarly unsuitable for any function taking place between those hours. Furthermore, the entrance, being modelled on that of a Doge's Palace (un-specified, but generally considered to be Desdemona's father's), was approached by a steep and narrow flight of stone steps leading to a small lobby, at the farther end of which a circular stone staircase led to the hall, so that all visitors ran considerable risk of being first pushed backwards and trampled to death outside, then squashed and asphyxiated in the lobby under the eyes of a large engraving of the late Duke of Connaught, and finally getting onto the thin end of the circular steps and either falling down backwards or being squeezed through the cast-iron banisters like toothpaste. Since the nasty accident on King George VI's Jubilee Day, when a Past Grand Hierarchical Triangular Memphian Master had had one leg squeezed between the banisters and could not get it out till two men had worked on the railing with hacksaws for forty minutes, a stout wire-netting had been fastened to the inside of the banisters, but even so the Mayoress had got her umbrella through the mesh, where it had been snapped in two by the upward surge of the lower orders of Masons' wives.

However, there it was, and one must make the best of things, as Lady Pomfret so truly said when the choice of a hall was being considered; so there the exhibition was to be held. Luckily the Freemasons, who were considered to do themselves pretty well, had a number of stout trestle tables which could be stacked against the wall and set up when wanted and on these the examples of bookbinding were set out. The opening was to be quite informal, so apart from a few chairs on the platform no other furnishings were required, and the Committee voted unanimously against tea, an action almost unprecedented in the history of the Library Committee which in spite of doing excellent work was apt to be rent by social or personal differences and contained some very good examples of the jealousies which do not exactly help voluntary organizations to run smoothly.

"Well, I must say," said young Lady Norton, who was only called young to distinguish her from her mother-in-law the Dowager, "that though Sally Pomfret has her name on a lot of committees one simply *cannot* do justice to more than one or two public objects, but I suppose it was the only way of being made a Lady of Grace." For the Countess of Pomfret, who had worked indefatigably for the Joint Committee of the Red Cross and St. John all through the war, was really a St. John and had been rightly rewarded by a rise in rank.

"If I had thought about my appearance," said young Lady

Norton, "I might have gone into St. John, but I felt I would do
just as useful work for our splendid men in the Red Cross
without wearing a hat with a bottle-brush in it," which was an
unkind and extremely untruthful way of describing Lady Pomfret's neat hat with its black and white cockade. "And as for that
girl Susan Dean being a paid librarian when her people are very
well off, it seems to me against all the finer traditions of the Red
Cross." To which Mrs. Villars, wife of the Rector of Northbridge and chairman of that particular sub-committee, had
quietly said she thought it would be better not to introduce
personalities into the discussion and would Miss Hopgood
kindly read the minutes of the last meeting, which Miss Hopgood always had some difficulty in doing owing to her own
handwriting which was a painstaking form of script with a
specious appearance of legibility totally belied by its effect upon
the reader. But before she could get under way her aunt, widow
of the astronomer and a woman of uncompromising manners,
said to young Lady Norton that for women of a certain age it
didn't matter in the least what one wore and that if she for her
part looked a fool in the Red Cross uniform at her age and size,
it did not disturb her in the least, nor did she see why it should
disturb other people, which remark young Lady Norton who
was of a bulgy build and never bothered to have her uniform
pressed took as directed against herself, which indeed it was, and
Mrs. Villars had to ring her bell, after which the meeting proceeded on more conventional lines; but the story got about, and
though Lady Pomfret could afford to disregard such pinpricks
and mostly did, it was one more small horridness added to the
horridnesses great and small which now seem to make most of
one's life and she almost wished she were not a countess. And
then she looked at her husband whom she had married when he
was plain Mr. Foster and thought how much harder his life was
than hers, having to go to London which he loathed and sit in
the House of Lords, which like most clubs had swollen to
unmanageable proportions owing to the number of new and

unknown members; and her tireless watchful affection felt it was really a good thing that she was a countess and could take some of Gillie's burdens on her shoulders.

As it was a Saturday, Barchester had hoped that Lord Pomfret would come to the Red Cross exhibition, but his countess had set her face against it and packed him off to spend the afternoon with her brother Roddy Wicklow, who was also the agent and even more silent than his employer, by which means they got through a lot of business in a very efficient way.

By the time Francis and Susan had finished their lunch and walked from Canal Street to the High Street, the Freemasons' Hall was already pretty full. At each of the tables sat two or three ladies, mostly in rather faded, patched, flowery aprons, some giving a demonstration of how the binding was done, some explaining to the onlookers how the books were collected, stored, sent out to the Red Cross and other hospitals and there distributed. On the platform were a number of women in uniform, and Susan Dean was now unobtrusively shepherding the guests of honour to their right places, being agreeable to the Press and keeping an eye on people like Miss Pettinger who felt that every platform was her stamping-ground. What most struck Francis among the workers, the demonstrators and the various St. John and Red Cross notabilities, was that not only were they nearly all ladies, however poor, plain, or dowdy, but that such of them as were obviously not ladies in the narrower social sense were of the stuff from which ladies are made; true as Mr. Churchill, solid as a peace-time cake and wholly reliable. After the faces of any crowd at any theatre, cinema, concert, race-meeting, political meeting, consisting as they mostly do of gawks, oafs, lumps, foreigners, talking and eating through whatever is being acted, shown on the screen, played, sung, run, or spoken, the sight of so many English women of breeding, totally unconscious of themselves or their looks, carrying off the most shapeless uniform by sheer force of personality, or looking, as in the case of Lady Pomfret and Susan Dean, of a neat smartness that only the Royal Navy as a rule attains, made Francis vaguely wonder if he was seeing true. But there was no doubt about it. Here at last was England Found again, and Francis, who was something of a dab at French, compared himself (though not in all respects) with the late M. Proust when he went to his last party and found again the years he had lost.

His attention was then called to a table at which Mrs. Arbuthnot and her sister-in-law were busy with scissors, paste, cretonne and cardboard, so that the public could see exactly how paper-bound books were turned into new books for the libraries.

"Regarded as a worker, you look remarkably like Gainsborough's Mrs. Graham as a housemaid," said Francis to Mrs. Arbuthnot admiringly, "only a good deal more capable. If I had written a paper-bound book I would at once ask you to bind it for me and wear it next my heart, where it would infallibly deflect an enemy's bullet and save my life."

Miss Arbuthnot asked what kind of enemy. Francis said probably Uncle Joe, or even more probably, as Wicked Uncles begin at home, one of the Uncles on the Government benches.

"As a matter of fact," said Miss Arbuthnot, "if you had written a book we would probably be binding it. We are making a speciality of books by Barsetshire authors. Really the list isn't bad."

She pointed to a row of books in front of her, some being cheap paper editions neatly bound in boards, some pre-war with their covers stiffened and refurbished. Francis looked at them. Barsetshire might indeed be proud. Old Lord Pomfret's *A Landowner in Five Reigns*, his mother's novel *A Step Too Far*, which had shocked Mr. Gladstone, biographical works by George Knox, a pile of Mrs. Morland's best-sellers about Madame Koska, the late and Rev. J. J. Damper's *Peregrinations in Palestine*, Mr. Downing's scholarly edition of an early twelfth-century *Tenso* by Peire de Baruelh on a dispute between two troubadours as to the relative merits of a mole upon their respective ladies' respective cheek and bosom regarded as a powerful incentive to *amour par amictiez*, Philip Winter's little book on Horace which still brought to him and the Oxbridge University Press a regular income of something under three pounds, Mrs. Barton's Renaissance novels, her husband's *Minor Domestic Architecture of East Barsetshire*, a copy of the sixth Earl of Pomfret's translation of an ode of Ronsard privately printed, Miss Hampton's powerful novels most of which had been banned in Manchester and the Vatican City, a book on the French romantic poet Jehan le Capet alias Eugène Duval by Hilary Grant who had married Delia Brandon, and others too numerous to catalogue, especially as we have not yet invented them.

"That heap by itself is Mrs. Rivers's novels," said Miss Arbuthnot. "She isn't exactly Barsetshire, but her husband is a cousin of Lord Pomfret's so we thought we could include them. They are all in cheap editions."

Francis, who had with joy read several of Mrs. Rivers's novels, said anyone who concentrated on the theme of Middle-aged Woman has Comeback was bound to succeed, though he wasn't sure if the Delayed Seduction theme as demonstrated by that man that went meandering on for ever in the Lit. Supp. and then in the *Sunday Times* wasn't even better selling.

A kind of simmering which had been going on in the hall for some moments now rose to boiling point, as Lady Pomfret came onto the platform wearing her St. John uniform like an elegant Amazon.

"Diane Chasseresse, four children or not," said Francis aloud to himself, while the librarian, Miss Dean, cast a competent eye over the platform, saw that all her charges were in their places and took her seat near the exit, her neat legs crossed at the ankle, her white-gloved hands lightly clasped upon her lap, ready for anything at any moment.

Lady Pomfret spoke a few words about the work the Hospital Libraries had done and were doing. A delegate from Loamshire spoke briefly and to the point. A Hospital Librarian spoke of his own experiences in hospital and how he would never have got through *Gone With the Wind* if he hadn't been in bed for three weeks owing to being funny in a bomber. Lady Pomfret collected these and one or two other speakers into a bundle, docketed them, and declared the exhibition open. The librarian then shepherded her flock off the platform and people went on looking at the exhibits just as they had been doing before they were officially visible. Francis was still lingering at Mrs. Arbutnot's table when Mr. Wickham came up and said he had been detained by lunch at the Barsetshire Agricultural Committee. Not but what, he said, he could have lunched better at any pub in Barsetshire, but one often heard things at the Agricultural and he had heard several useful things.

"Just forget about heifers for a moment," said Francis, "and look at those books, all beautifully bound by Mrs. and Miss Arbuthnot."

Mr. Wickham said books weren't much in his line, except books about the navy and naval history or——and here his voice trailed away as he took up a book which was lying at the back of the others.

"By Jove," he said reverently.

Francis looked. The book was called *Coot and Hern*, the author F. E. Arbuthnot.

"That's a book I've been trying to get for ages," said Mr. Wickham. "I read those articles when they came out in *Country Life* and whoever wrote them knows what he's writing about. I wonder if he's any relation of yours?"

His question was addressed to the Arbuthnot ladies in general. Mrs. Arbuthnot said it was a relation of hers but not of her sister-in-law's, at least she thought not; and then began to laugh in a way which in any less attractive woman would have been giggling. Francis, glancing at Miss Arbuthnot, saw that her large masculine face was bright red and wondered idly if the author was her illegitimate brother.

"I wrote to him when I was in the Atlantic, the winter before Dunkirk," said Mr. Wickham, "but he never answered."

"I *did*," said Miss Arbuthnot indignantly. "I wrote to the address you gave and told you that the lesser clodhopper has been seen as far north as Aberdeathly. In fact, I saw one there myself when I was visiting Christopher and Elsa Hornby."

"We lost a lot of our mail that winter," said Mr. Wickham absently. "But you aren't F. E. Arbuthnot. You're a woman."

"I *am* F. E. Arbuthnot," said Miss Arbuthnot crossly. "It's my name. Florence Edith Arbuthnot."

"But your name is Effie," said Francis, throwing himself into the detective work.

"Of course it is Effie," said Mrs. Arbuthnot, who was laughing in a very kind way. "Florence is an awful name, so Fred always called her F. E. and the name stuck."

"Well, well, well, I apologize," said Mr. Wickham. "F. E. Effie. It's a jolly good idea and I was absolutely taken in. I say, those articles of yours are first-rate. I always thought the lesser clodhopper petered out round about the Clyde. Live and learn. Do you know that there is a golden-crested mippet over near Fish Hill? Betty Topham that used to live with her aunt Mrs. Turner at Northbridge found its nest."

"Not Betty Topham who lives at Hacken's Fen?" said Miss Arbuthnot. "I stayed with them last spring and we sat up all night in a leaky punt to hear the common flygobbler coming back from the Riviera. It was heavenly. I'd never heard their homing cry before. They say, 'Too-pee-terrip-pip-a-rip-squee.'"

"Now that is where you are wrong," said Mr. Wickham, bending over the table with a serious expression. "What they do say is 'Too-pee-*pirret*-pip-a-rip-squee,' or sometimes just 'quee.'"

Miss Arbuthnot's face grew lowering and it appeared to Francis that there were the makings of a very good quarrel which he was prepared to find amusing, when his mother emerged from the crowd at his elbow. She looked intently at Miss

Arbuthnot with a rather puzzled expression, interpreted by Francis naturally enough as surprise at seeing her in such a temper. Then Miss Arbuthnot remembered that she was supposed to be showing books to the public and rousing their interest in the Red Cross and asked Mrs. Brandon if she would like to see how nice her son-in-law's book looked in its new cretonne coat.

"We'll thrash this out," said Mr. Wickham. "I'll drive you up to Fish Hill to see the golden-crested mippet to-morrow it you like."

Miss Arbuthnot, who had got over her temper, thanked him and they made plans for a great bird expedition and Mr. Wickham went away.

Mrs. Arbuthnot had for some time been conscious of an uneasy pain in her right shoulder, which now resolved itself into Colin Keith, looking as if his feelings would boil over at any moment.

"You are busy," he said in an accusing voice.

Mrs. Arbuthnot was really fond of Colin, also truly grateful to him for making all his family and friends take so much trouble on her behalf, but she did wish he had not chosen that particular afternoon to come and glower; a manifestation of the tender passion which was but too well known to her among the more serious subalterns of her late husband's regiment.

"Oh, Colin! How nice," she said. "I wish you had written a book, then we could put it with the Barsetshire authors. Don't they look nice?"

On hearing these words Colin arranged to emigrate on the spot. Not once, nor twice, had he mentioned carelessly to Mrs. Arbuthnot that he was at work on a commentary on *Lemon on Running Powers*. He had sometimes wondered if, in her angelic and childlike innocence (a description of Mrs. Arbuthnot which would have amused that lady very much) she had quite understood what he was talking about. It was now all too clear that she had neither understood nor cared. Pah! Women all over. Still, this was no reason to deprive himself of the pleasure of being gloomy, to which social feeling he gave himself up in a whole-hearted way, lingering near Mrs. Arbuthnot's table and hating anyone who came to talk to her; and a great many people did come, for the news had spread that her table was exhibiting Barsetshire books and local patriotism was roused, not to mention such of the authors themselves as were present. Of these some came suspiciously to see whether their books had pride of place and if not, which of their rivals had ousted them; one, namely Mrs. Rivers, came to patronize anyone who was in charge of the table; others who were less conceited were genuinely surprised and flattered to see their work in such good company.

Mrs. Rivers, whose novels of passion in women who though intellectual, well dressed, and well read are quite sex-starved with a nice husband with a good job and several children, was a cousin by marriage of the late Lord Pomfret through her husband the Honourable George Rivers. Her novels are well known to all library subscribers who know that they need only ask for Hermione Rivers's new book to have hours of pure escapism. As nothing would drag the Honourable George from his farming and country interests his wife was far too apt to invite herself to stay with his titled relations, especially with the Pomfrets. Both Lord and Lady Pomfret, who had never forgotten how rude and unpleasant she and her son Julian had been at the Towers in old Lord Pomfret's time, disliked her as much as they had time to dislike anyone in their busy lives, but both felt the sacredness of family ties and never refused her when she invited herself. Owing to the growing discomfort at the Towers during the war Mrs. Rivers had not troubled them much, but she had turned up again as one of the major horrors of peace and afflicted them very much indeed. On this occasion she had insisted on accompanying Lady Pomfret to the exhibition with the firm intention of tacking herself onto the official party, but Susan Dean with great courtesy and firmness had introduced Mrs. Rivers to Miss

Pettinger, who had treated Mrs. Rivers as though she had failed
to pass the School Certificate for the second time. Mrs. Rivers
had been as rude in return as her warmest admirer could wish,
but Miss Pettinger, who was impervious to every shade of manners,
only laughed and said she must read one of Mrs. Rivers's books as
soon as she had a little leisure, so that by the time the exhibition was
open Mrs. Rivers was in a very bad temper.

It was peculiarly unfortunate that Mrs. Rivers chose that
particular moment to patronize Mrs. Arbuthnot, for a galaxy of
Barsetshire authors had gathered at the table and were getting
on very nicely. It is true that George Knox, the celebrated
biographer, was booming in a very overbearing way, but none of
his friends minded and his adoring wife was always ready to
deflate him, as was his old and valued friend Mrs. Morland.

"How are you, Mr. Knox?" said Mrs. Rivers, ignoring his wife
and the rest of the company. "It is quite amusing to see one's
books here. The Red Cross is really quite enterprising. I sent a
copy of my last novel, *Autumn Passion Flower*, the Middle-Aged
Women's Book Guild choice you know, to Sally for her Red
Cross. One must do all one can for those poor men, though one
wonders sometimes what exactly one's books mean to them
and——"

"Ah, dear lady," said George Knox, who had not the faintest
idea who Mrs. Rivers was, but had no intention of letting her do
the talking, "you are indeed right. When I reflect upon what
those men—mere children so many of them—have done, I feel
honoured, yes, greatly honoured, that they should even finger
any poor book of mine. For example, my biography of Lord
Stanhope, one of the Two Sta's, though the allusion will mean
nothing to you, the other, of course, being Starhemberg, plung-
ing the reader as it does into the mazes of international politics,
bringing vividly before him the Archduke Charles, the reverse of
Alamanzo, the victory of Port Mahon, the skilful negotiation
with Dubois, the Septennial Act, the whole pageant of European history during the last years of the Grand Monarque, the

tortuous course of English politics under our fist Hanoverian king, this biography, I say," said George Knox, who had obviously lost the thread of his argument but was not going to be stopped by anyone—"this biography, I say, what can it mean to an unlettered yokel, a pale clerk whose interest had been his counting-house stool, a rude mechanic," said George Knox, who was apparently living in the eighteenth century, "what, I ask, can it mean? Nothing, you will say," he continued, though his hearers even with the best will in the world could not have got a word in against his billows of speech. "But, who knows, the seed may germinate, and the sower of the seed, though he may never see the harvest," said George Knox, suddenly becoming a doddering old man, "will have earned his meed in ways we wot not of."

"Not 'wot,' George," said Mrs. Morland. "'Know.'"

"I have always felt in writing My Books," said Mrs. Rivers, seizing her chance and overriding the company in the high-pitched dictatorial voice which makes so many educated Englishwomen so cordially disliked, "that it is a great privilege to be read by all sorts and conditions. I had a delightful letter from a sergeant in the British Army of Occupation in Germany the other day, showing an understanding of *Esthonian Equinox*, my last book but one, which one does not expect."

There appeared to be so many answers to this statement that no one spoke till Mrs. Arbuthnot, who felt herself to be a kind of unofficial hostess, said so many unexpected things happened now and they were always horrid. She then wished she had not spoken, and with good reason, for Mrs. Rivers who always suspected offence where none was intended was just going to make an arrogant reply when a large, healthy-looking, young middle-aged man, who had obviously been on Active Service within the last year, burst through the crowd with purpose in his eye.

"I'm the librarian of the Barchester General," he said, shaking hands with Mrs. Rivers a good deal harder than she liked. "I can

assure you, Mrs. Rivers, that our men are practically omnivo-
rous, or I might say omnilegerous. It's not only fiction, though
of course a good deal of fiction is read and I must say at once that
I've not had the pleasure of reading any of your books though my
brother who is in the Army of the Rhine says the last one kept
the mess in a roar, but every kind of book. It would surprise you
to know," said the librarian, opening a despatch-box and looking over some papers, "how varied their interests are. Now, just
look at this list of books read during the last three months. Not
counting fiction, you will see books on practically every subject
from Aaron to Zwingli. You must come and visit us. Mrs.
Morland is giving us a talk on The Art of the Thriller next
month. I'll send you card. And we're always awfully grateful for
books. It would be very generous of you to send us a few copies
of your next book, because a good laugh does our patients more
good than all the doctors and clean light fiction is always in
demand. Send them to Miss Dean at the depot and she will
acknowledge them. I shall make a point of reading your book,
something like *Autumn Crocus*, isn't it? And I look forward to a
real good laugh. You'd like my brother, Mrs. Rivers. He has a
very keen sense of humour."

He then dashed away to catch the chairman. Everyone felt
uncomfortable for Mrs. Rivers, though this was really unnecessary, when luckily Mrs. Morland changed the subject by suddenly catching sight of one of her own books and being so
overcome by the honour that she had to thank the Arbuthnots
almost with tears in her eyes.

"For somehow," she explained, "one doesn't think of books
one earns one's living by as *real* books. When Tony was in
Burma a friend of mine in the Red Cross used to send him a lot
of books which he adored, but they were what I call real books.
I mean by people whose names one knows," said Mrs. Morland,
who was totally unable to realize that her own name was almost
famous, "who can write dull books that one feels one ought to

read. I don't suppose you met Tony, my youngest son, in India, Mrs. Arbuthnot?"

Mrs. Arbuthnot, who was quite used to this comprehensive question, said she was afraid she hadn't, very charmingly making it sound as if the fault were hers; and what was Mrs. Morland's son doing now?

"Well, he had a nasty kind of Breaking-out which I attribute entirely to Gandhi," said Mrs. Morland, "because everything was so dirty in India and so many insects. But it is much better now and luckily on his shoulder where it doesn't show and he is engaged which is really most satisfactory besides having got into the Tape and Sealing-wax Office, so I suppose I'll have to go on writing books for ever, as this Government pays him practically nothing and then takes most of it away with the other hand."

She looked so unhappy at the prospect that her friends hastened to assure her that the public would like her to go on writing the same kind of book for ever, which surprised and pleased her. And then the knot of friends broke up and drifted away and a number of strangers came to look and admire, and Mrs. Arbuthnot was so pleasant and Miss Arbuthnot explained everything so well that several women asked if they might come and learn voluntary binding, and we may say that three or four of them, including Miss Dunsford and Miss Dolly Talbot from Northbridge, who were finding the peace both dull and dispiriting, became very useful helpers and could always be relied upon to come on their appointed days and at the appointed time.

Lady Pomfret, who had been to every table, saying the right things to everyone and wondering all the time if Lord Mellings had fallen off his pony, or Lady Emily Foster had been teasing the Honourable Giles Foster and Lady Agnes or her husband had stood about too much and got tired, had now come to the end of her journey at the Arbuthnots' table. Susan Dean introduced them to Lady Pomfret and stood at ease, erect, handsome, watchful, ready to do any of a librarian's million duties at a moment's notice, while the ladies talked. Lady Pomfret, who had heard satisfactory reports of the newcomers from the Deanery and Beliers Priory, was prepared to find them agreeable and when it came out in the course of conversation that the little villa she had taken for a summer at Cap Martin before the war had belonged to an uncle of Mrs. Arbuthnot, she invited them to come to tea at the Towers, thinking, for on those lines her thoughts always ran, that they would be a nice change for Gillie, who worked so hard and had so few treats. All of which was observed by Colin, who had found himself irresistibly drawn back to the Arbuthnots' table just as one bites on an aching tooth.

"I expect they'll find it pretty dull at the Towers," he said to Susan Dean.

Susan said no duller than anywhere else and Lady Pomfret was perfectly splendid and anyway some tennis would do Colin good and to be sure to come in plenty of time tomorrow. To be neglected by the woman of one's heart and then on top of that to be told not to be late by Susan Dean, whom one had taken for a more sympathetic kind of fellow, was almost more than Colin could bear. For twopence he would have shed tears of rage. Had he been dark, with a pale skin and a finely chiselled nose, he would have assumed an ostentatious Byronic gloom; but being an ordinary young man, though with a very pleasant face when not ravaged by the blind god, he merely looked sulky, of which manifestation of the true love no one took the slightest notice.

The exhibition was to remain open till six o'clock, but fresh relays of workers were to relieve the present demonstrators at half-time, so Mrs. Arbuthnot seeing that it was almost four o'clock asked Colin if he could find Mrs. Brandon and tell her that she was ready whenever wanted. Miss Hampton and Miss Bent then appeared to take over. Miss Bent was wearing a floral apron only differing from all the other patched and faded floral aprons in being even more depressed and wilted. Miss Hampton, scorning such femininities, was strikingly attired in a French manservant's large apron, and with a dashing wine-coloured beret and a tailored wine-coloured shirt made a very striking feature of the exhibition.

"Now, girls, off you go and enjoy yourselves," said Miss Hampton to the Arbuthnots for whom she had taken a great liking. "You are alone over the weekend, Miss Arbuthnot, aren't you? Come to tea at Adelina to-morrow. Any time after six. We've just got some Benedictine from Brown and a bottle of Cointreau that a friend brought back from Germany."

Miss Arbuthnot, concealing her feelings about tea-parties that began at six with liqueurs, said she would have loved it, but Mr. Wickham was going to take her to Fish Hill to look at birds and she was going back to tea with him.

"That's all right," said Miss Hampton. "Wickham knows a bottle when he sees one. I've no use for people who put water in the whisky. A neat whisky for me. A chaser to follow if you like, but I don't hold with mixing drinks. Tie Gallant to the leg of the table, Bent. Dogs aren't allowed in here. Sit still, Gallant."

The unfortunate Gallant, who with the humanitarian view of preventing his being trampled on had been held on so tight a lead that he had to walk up the room on his hind legs, was only thankful to sit in peace under the table where he gave no trouble at all, well knowing, with a dog's wonderful instinct, that he had no business to be in the Freemasons' Hall under any circumstances.

Colin now came sulkily back with Mrs. Brandon and Francis. Mrs. Brandon metaphorically fluffed out her feathers like a very nice hen all over the party, cut Mrs. Arbuthnot out from the other chickens as it were and took her under her wing. Francis took the opportunity of saying to Susan that he wished she were coming too, as he knew his dear mamma and Mrs. Arbuthnot would have womanly secrets all the time and make him feel out of it. Susan said she wished she were, but as Mrs. Brandon hadn't asked her she didn't quite see how she could, and anyway she had to go home for the weekend because there was tennis, inviting Francis to come if he felt too deserted at Stories.

"I rather think I might," said Francis.

"It would be a help," said Susan, looking towards Colin who was exhibiting melancholy to an uninterested world. "Colin is coming and he isn't exactly a cheerful person at the moment."

Francis, taking a good look at Colin, said he certainly looked like an overboiled suet pudding, and what was it.

"I think it's Mrs. Arbuthnot," said Susan in a low voice, which however did not prevent Colin, with the fatal instinct that makes us know when we are being discussed, turn his head and look suspiciously in their direction.

"All right, we'll have a conspiracy," said Francis. "I'll come to Winter Overcotes and you and I will beat Colin and whoever his partner is, and then I'll tell him I think Mrs. Arbuthnot is in love with Bishop Joram," which seemed rather brilliant and funny to Susan and they both laughed.

"Mamma is looking to me for succour," said Francis. "I must fly. Tomorrow then."

He patted Susan's shoulder and left her. The very competent Depot Librarian of the Barsetshire Red Cross Hospital Libraries stood erect, handsome, watchful, ready for any of the million duties that might be required until the exhibition closed. But she did not stand at ease, for Francis's kindly pat had seriously disturbed her. Never before had her equanimity been assailed. Today, quite suddenly a conspiracy against Colin Keith, a few light words, a light touch, had made her feel slightly giddy. That the conspiracy was not a very kind one her own kindly self knew, and her own self hinted to her that Francis might find amusement in teasing others besides Colin, possibly in teasing herself. Yet, such is the contrariness of women, she could not stop thinking of Francis, because he had touched her shoulder perhaps, or perhaps because his careless affection had by degrees charmed her. The good, hard-working girls who went through the war in civilian jobs were often too tired to be amused by men,

even if they met them. Susan's work had been among other
women, old and young. What men she had met had mostly been
of the donnish type like her brother-in-law Mr. Fanshawe, and
in any case her height and her unemotional good looks made
men think of her as a good sort, an attitude not conducive to
love. Since she had spent all her weeks in Barchester with the
Red Cross she had, as we know, seen a good deal of Francis. The
subject of dancing had tacitly been dropped, for Susan would
never make a good dancer, but the meetings which were inevitable between people who lived in much the same circles, the
lunches, the walks they had had together, had gradually led to
what seemed a flowery slope. And now Susan wondered if the
flowers were fading, if the slope was a little too steep, if Francis
were just amusing himself. There was no way of finding out
except to go on. It was all a little frightening and Susan wished
she could ask advice. Her younger sister Jessica would probably
know exactly what one ought to do, but somehow one doesn't
consult one's much younger sister, even if she is far more
grown-up than oneself. Francis's touch was still on her blue
serge shoulder-strap like a caress and Susan was a thousand
miles away. Then the Librarian of the Barchester General came
up with his attaché case of papers to ask her advice, and the very
competent librarian at once gave her undivided attention to the
matter in hand, and by the time it was settled the Brandons and
Mrs. Arbuthnot had gone.

Mrs. Brandon was now able to use her car again within the
petrol limits. Her chauffeur Curwen had returned from an
aero-engine works with an enhanced opinion of himself and a
lower opinion of his employer and everyone else, but secretly
glad to get back to civilian life and pretend he was master in his
own cottage, where his wife, who had taken in ripe middle age to
lipstick, cigarettes and a cheap permanent wave, thought but
poorly of him and was not at any pains to conceal the fact.

"Home, please," said Mrs. Brandon when they were all three
in the car, "and we'll go by Brandon Abbey. And it is dreadful,"

she added when the glass screen between employer and employed was safely closed, "how much expression Curwen can put into the back of his neck. When he is displeased, it is exactly like a German's."

And indeed, Curwen's stout back, rigid with anger at his mistress's presumption, every bristle on his stout neck standing on end, bore a striking resemblance to the well-fed and underworked German prisoners of war who still drove about the country-side in lorries while their conquerors bicycled or walked to work in all weathers.

Mrs. Arbuthnot said perhaps he had had some German ancestors, and Francis with great agility invented and developed a theory that in his name, Al, or Alfred Curwen, was merely Kurwenal in another guise, at which he and Mrs. Arbuthnot had the giggles, while Mrs. Brandon looked upon them much as Julia Mills had looked upon David and Dora, recalling the ancient days when she and earth had anything in common, a pose not unobserved by her son and not unappreciated.

As they drove in that horrid damp chilly afternoon which was all that the summer could manage, Mrs. Brandon's thoughts went back to summers before the war when the sun had shone and the wind had been still and the rich, green Barsetshire country had lain warm and peaceful in the golden light. Now everything was grey, and uneasy wind ruffled every leaf, every blade, every stream and pond, and Mrs. Brandon felt chilly and grown old. But this was not the way to treat a charming guest, so she roused herself from her depression and told Mrs. Arbuthnot that the wall along the side of the road was Brandon Abbey.

"That's where Aunt Sissie used to live," said Francis. "She was awfully rich and very rude and always in bed. It's the most hideous house in the county."

"She was my husband's aunt, not mine," said Mrs. Brandon, "and it was most uncomfortable, for she was always holding it over us that she would disinherit Francis and it wouldn't have been polite to explain that he never expected to have the Abbey and wouldn't have known what to do with it. She used to threaten to leave it to Hilary Grant, who was another nephew and married my daughter Delia, but very luckily she left it all to some kind of charity. She gave me this ring."

And Mrs. Brandon, taking off her glove, showed a fine diamond upon the beautiful hand that war and peace had not succeeded in spoiling. Mrs. Arbuthnot's admiration was deep and real.

"I saw a lot of diamonds in India," she said, "when Fred was in one of the royal states, but I never saw a more beautiful single stone."

Mrs. Brandon said it came from India and had been a present to old Miss Brandon from a soldier brother who died out there, and then Francis suggested that they might drive up, and rather down to the Abbey which lay in a hollow, and see what was happening.

"The charity never got it, because the Ministry of General Interference took it over," he said to Mrs. Arbuthnot, "but Sir Edmund Pridham, who knows everything, says they will probably be out by Christmas. Shall I tell Curwen to stop at the lodge, mamma?"

But Mrs. Brandon said she thought it would be hardly worth offending him twice in one afternoon and Mrs. Arbuthnot was not particularly interested in seeing an ugly house full of typists, so they drove on to Pomfret Madrigal.

In spite of a reduced staff and rationing the household at Stories was always delighted to see a guest, as it gave opportunity for fussing. Cook, even without a kitchen-maid, was still glad to show her art and had a woman from Grumper's End to help with the washing-up. Ethel, even without a second housemaid, was enchanted to put the Pink Room into commission, while Rose had kept her spirits up since the peace by having daily tiffs with Nurse and Ethel, who disapproved of the parlourmaid giving a hand with the housework. All these cross-currents became rather a bore to Mrs. Brandon at times, but she knew that her guests would be well looked after and not notice the cracking ice, and held her peace.

Ethel was giving the last touches to the Pink Room when Nurse and Rose almost collided in the doorway, Nurse with two special padded dress-hangers from the cupboard upstairs, Rose with a little satin-covered cushion from Mrs. Brandon's drawer where she kept things she wasn't using.

"Now, I don't want no fussing in the room after all the trouble I've had turning it out," said Ethel, whose first quality, as with every good servant, was ingratitude mixed with rudeness.

"Well, Ethel," said Nurse, with the graciousness that she knew Ethel particularly disliked, "I'm sure I'm not one for fussing, but really if madam knew there was only those painted wooden hangers in the wardrobe, I'm sure she'd be quite upset. Hasn't Ethel got the room nice, Rose?"

"Well, I'm sure, Nurse," said Rose, who though Nurse's dearest foe was always capable of almost sycophantic friendship if it was a question of a combination against Cook or Ethel, "the room couldn't be nicer, but I was just thinking the poor lady would want a little pillow if she has a nice lay-down before dinner. It just makes all the difference a little pillow under the neck and madam never uses it."

"Well, I don't mind, seeing as you've brought them," said Ethel, "but I dessay the poor lady won't notice. Dreadful her losing her husband and all."

"And no children," said Nurse. "Now madam had the two dear little children, though Mr. Brandon did die before miss Delia was born. Dear me, what a dreadful time that was. You wouldn't remember it, Ethel, but I can assure you I never slept a wink till Miss Delia had safely arrived. I used to look at Mr. Francis — Baby he was then — in his cot and wonder if he'd have a little brother or a little sister. You remember, Rose."

It was all very well to call Rose in as an ally against Ethel who had only come to Stories when both children were older, but one can pay too dearly for help. Rose had been Mr. Brandon's parlourmaid before his marriage and was a little older than her mistress and altogether senior in every way.

"If you'd been here before Mr. Francis was born, Nurse," she said, "you'd have had something to remember. Poor Mr. Brandon. I never see a gentleman in such a state. 'Oh, dear, Rose,' he would say to me when I was shutting up at night, 'I do hope all will be well.' You never saw him before he cut off his moustache, Nurse."

This was a blow that Nurse who had not entered the household till Francis was six weeks old was unable to counter, but fate was on her side, as indeed it usually was. Looking carelessly out of the window as if she had not heard Rose's words she saw the car coming up the drive and was able to say There was madam and Mrs. Arbuthnot, poor lady, so that Rose had to hurry downstairs to open the front door.

"Small but apt," said Francis, gallantly handing Mrs. Arbuthnot into the hall. "Mrs. Arbuthnot, this is Rose. She remembers me before I was born and takes every advantage of it."

Mrs. Arbuthnot showed perfect tact. Even up to 1939 Francis would not, she was certain, have made a personal introduction between guest and parlourmaid. Guest, if a stranger to the house, would have ignored parlourmaid or at the most slightly inclined her head in recognition of her presence, and parlourmaid would have taken deep offence if any more marked familiarity had been attempted. At any time during the war, while barriers were temporarily down, parlourmaid if an old retainer might have tolerated a few words or a handshake from guest, if an old friend of the family. Now the war was nominally over all the really good pre-war parlourmaids had reverted more or less to type. Some of these new girls, as Rose scornfully remarked, why they didn't know their places at all, calling the mistress Mrs. Brown instead of Madam and not wearing uniform and letting ladies shake hands with them. Not but what it was the ladies' fault too, Rose had to admit. There was that Mrs. Grant, Mr. Hilary's mother that married Miss Delia, she used to try to shake hands with Curwen and with her, Rose; but she and Curwen had known their places and of course the poor lady had lived with those Eyetalians who haven't any idea of how to behave. And as for the young married ladies who have girls that aren't no better than they ought to be as maids, with their children and all playing with the young ladies and gentlemen just as if they knew who their fathers were and more than likely the girls didn't know neither, really, Rose considered, you'd think they'd never been told what was proper. From which reflections we may assume that the good cap-and-apron class still remains one of the staunchest supporters of the old order and will batten upon it and defend its rights till the last really well-trained servant is dead.

Mrs. Arbuthnot had a very good social sense. After Francis's introduction she could not ignore Rose as, she knew, Rose would prefer to be ignored. She also realized at once that to attempt any familiarity with Rose would bring down upon her the chill disapproval of the perfect parlourmaid. With great presence of mind and skill she steered a middle course, saying, as Rose held the drawing-room door open, "Mrs. Brandon told me you had been such a help during the war," and passing on. Rose then shut the drawing-room door and went away to invent errands which would take her to the kitchen and the sewing-room, there to proclaim to Cook and Ethel over their endless tea and Nurse busy with making something of Mrs. Brandon's into something for one of the babies, that Mrs. Arbuthnot was a real lady and it did seem a shame her losing her husband, and no babies neither.

"I read a piece in the paper," said Cook, "as said there's more widows marry than single women when there's a war on. I dessay she'll have another chance. Somebody nice and quiet, poor lady." Not that Cook had heard any rumours about the late Captain Arbuthnot's divagations, but a nice quiet husband seemed to her a suitable end for a war widow. Ethel agreed on principle, but said there were some that preferred to Live with

Memories, a piece which she had also got out of the paper, namely "Aunt Martha's Column" in her favourite Sunday journal.

As for Nurse, she was rewinding the bobbin with pink sewing-cotton and couldn't hardly hear herself speak, she said, though it didn't prevent her hearing Rose and saying if all one heard was true there might be some news about Mrs. Arbuthnot and Mrs. Merton's brother. After which she quickly reinserted the bobbin and began to machine so violently that Rose went downstairs to unpack Mrs. Arbuthnot's things.

In the sitting-room Francis watched with lazy complacence his charming mother and their charming visitor getting on like a house on fire. To give pleasure to people he was fond of was one of Francis's chief amusements. He was very fond of his mamma, he liked Mrs. Arbuthnot very much; and here were these two delightful women performing for his benefit. The whole scene, he felt, was almost Edwardian, except for the length of the ladies' skirts. A tea-party à trois in a country house, polite and even witty remarks passing over the teapot, everything touched with a light hand, all profane things far removed. He rather wished he had a top-hat with a pair of grey gloves laid on it on the floor by his side, but this would have involved a complete change of attire and he feared the army had absolutely done him in as far as ceremonial clothes were concerned, unless his tailor would consent to try to let them out a bit. So he resigned himself to his usual clothes and the agreeable clucking of his two agreeable hens; for so, irreverently, did he characterize his mother and her guest in his mind; so gentle yet capable, he thought, of a wild squawk on occasion, and giving an impression of infinite softness and fluffiness yet, certainly as far as his mother was concerned and he would say at a venture that the same was true of Mrs. Arbuthnot, highly capable and efficient women.

"You must have a good rest here," said Mrs. Brandon. "We lead a rather quiet, dull life. Our very nice vicar and his wife are

coming to dinner and Dr. Ford who is a very old friend.
Tomorrow an old friend of mine, Sir Edmund Pridham, is
coming to lunch and we are going to Winter Overcotes for tea,
and in the evening I have asked Bishop Joram and a very nice
Colonel Crofts who has turned into a clergyman late in life. He
said he had met you at the Deanery and would like to meet you
again. So you must just be quite quiet and do whatever you like.
Ethel will look after you. She is my old housemaid and has been
with me for years."

If Mrs. Arbuthnot thought that meeting a ceaseless proces-
sion of strangers was not exactly a good rest, she did not say so
and was in fact quite pleased at the prospect, for she loved
company and enjoyed very good health. But a rest in some ways
it would be, for though Mrs. Arbuthnot was young and strong
the period of getting into a house can tire the youngest and
strongest of us. Editha Cottage was now furnished and tenanted, but in one's own home it is difficult to subdue a tendency
to be perpetually on the go. One wants the eyes of Argus, the
legs of Arachne, the arms of Briareus, to do all one would like to
do. Twenty times had Mrs. Arbuthnot and her sister-in-law
told themselves and each other that they had the rest of the lease
of Editha to work in, that they must do one thing at a time and
not too many things in a day and remember to have regular
meals; twenty times a day had they broken every one of their
good resolutions, had eaten hurried meals at all hours, sat up too
late like children who plead for just one minute more, and in
general behaved like women. All of which Mrs. Arbuthnot
described to her hostess with gentle malice towards herself.

"You must take lessons from my mamma," said Francis, "who
can do nothing more busily than any woman I know."

Mrs. Brandon said he should not say things like that. A knock
was heard at the door.

"Oh dear, it must be Miss Feilding," said Mrs. Brandon. "No
one else knocks at the sitting-room door. Come in. This is Mrs.
Arbuthnot, Miss Feilding, who is here for the weekend. Miss

Feilding," she added to her guest, "is in charge of some young children that were here during the war from a nursery school. Do sit down, Miss Feilding. Most of them have gone back and Miss Feilding is looking after the last of them till September when they go to a beautiful home in Sussex with farm produce and a wonderful view of Chanctonbury Ring."

"Eighty-five," said Francis aloud to himself.

Mrs. Brandon had discovered that Miss Feilding, in spite of having passed all requisite examinations with credit, was of the low though affectionate mental calibre that adores what are known as toddlers and extremely susceptible to suggestion. So whenever occasion presented she alluded to the beauty of the home in Sussex, the advantages of cows and hens and vegetables and the omnipresence of that beautiful but most boring of landmarks, and Miss Feilding, in spite of her devotion to Stories and its mistress, was by now quite eagerly looking forward to the move.

"How delightful," said Mrs. Arbuthnot comprehensively.

"Well, I won't sit down, thank you so much, Mrs. Brandon," said Miss Feilding, "but I did just want you to see Baby Parting if you don't mind. He looks such a pet in his little knicks."

An unseen agency then propelled into the room Baby Parting, a stout flaxen-haired, pink-faced little boy between three and four, with a broad smile, wearing a green cotton blouse and green tweed knickerbockers.

"Hullo, Parting," said Francis. "You look very neat."

"Pockets," said Master Parting, thrusting his fat hands with some difficulty into them.

"It's the knickers I made out of that tweed skirt of yours, madam," said Nurse, now appearing as the unseen agency made manifest. "Show Mrs. Brandon what you've got in your pockets, Cyril."

Master Parting, frowning softly with concentration, pulled out of a pocket a glass marble with green whorls inside it.

"What's in the other pocket?" asked Mrs. Arbuthnot.

Master Parting grinned more widely than ever.

"Let me see," said Mrs. Arbuthnot, and her voice and appearance seemed to impress Master Parting favourably, for he came and leant against her knee, giving her a very good view of the nape of his neck.

"I think," said Mrs. Arbuthnot, slipping a few of her fingers into his other pocket, "that-I-can-find-a-HANDKERCHIEF." With which words, she pulled out a small green chiffon square.

"What a nice handkerchief!" she said admiringly.

"Ny squaunkerchuff," said Master Parting.

"A remarkably ny squankerchuff," said Francis. "May I look at it? I didn't know you were a conjuror, Mrs. Arbuthnot."

"I'm a witch," said Mrs. Arbuthnot. "Look at the old woman with the bonnet on, Cyril."

She took off two rings, and wrapping her fist in her scarf produced the toothless crone with jewelled eyes putting her tongue out which so delighted our youth and is probably now a dying art. Master Parting, who appeared to have the root of the matter in him, at once saw the joke, chuckled deeply as the really rather frightening old woman put her tongue out and in while her jewel eyes glistened, and jiggled up and down with pleasure. Encouraged by this success, Mrs. Arbuthnot borrowed Francis's white handkerchief and made a rabbit which darted in and out of the most extraordinary places and was finally put to bed by Master Parting in Francis's pocket, with its head sticking out.

"There, that's enough now, isn't it, Cyril," said Nurse, with the true nursery instinct of seeing what Master Alfred is doing and telling him not to. "Miss Feilding will have quite a tired little boy to put to bed, won't she?"

Miss Feilding, being a highly trained and certificated nursery teacher, ought to have resented this attitude, but Nurse had established the ascendancy that any good Nanny can acquire over anyone she likes, far more over a Miss Feilding, who at once fell in with the suggestion.

"Say nighty-night and shake handy-pandy," said Miss Feilding to her charge.

As the charge seemed rather undecided about this, Mrs. Arbuthnot took a good kiss of the nape of his neck and handed him over to his attendant who took him away. Nurse lingered, to enforce approval of the green knickerbockers.

"You haven't met Nurse yet," said Mrs. Brandon to her guest. "She brought Francis and Delia up and looks after us all."

Nurse graciously shook hands with Mrs. Arbuthnot and said should she take her up to her room as she had heard Ethel running the bath. As Nurse had to be allowed a free innings with the visitor this seemed as good a time as any other, so she was consigned to Nurse and taken upstairs. As they reached the landing Ethel came out of Mrs. Arbuthnot's room carrying two padded coat-hangers and a small satin cushion. This open defiance of Nurse and Rose, who would now certainly come over horse, foot, and impedimenta to Nurse's side as soon as she knew of this treachery, was tantamount to open rebellion. Lesser strategists would have pushed Mrs. Arbuthnot into her room and had it out with Ethel on the landing, but Nurse was a match for any diplomatist. Ignoring Ethel, she said to Mrs. Arbuthnot, "I am sure everything is nicely unpacked for you, madam. I'll just come in and see if everything is as you like it," upon which she wafted Mrs. Arbuthnot into the room and closed the door leaving Ethel, like Ignorance, outside the shut gate.

This was the most signal triumph that Nurse had ever achieved. Had Ethel only removed the padded dress-hangers she could have exulted with Rose over Nurse's defeat. But her ambitious spirit had caused her to remove both Nurse's and Rose's contributions, and Nurse had seen her, red-handed, carrying the booty and would, or at any rate could, betray her to Rose. There was only one thing for it, and that was to replace the hangers and cushion at the earliest opportunity and say nothing about it.

Dinner, with Mr. and Mrs. Miller and Dr. Ford, passed off

agreeably. Mrs. Brandon and Dr. Ford spoke of old Miss Brandon who lived at Brandon Abbey and how ill-tempered she used to be, though Mrs. Miller, who had for a time been companion and little less than slave to Miss Brandon, stood up for her old employer and said she had been companion to old ladies who were far worse.

"After all," said Mrs. Brandon, pensively admiring her hand, "Aunt Sissie did give me this ring. Do you remember all those dreadful photographs in her sitting-room, Mrs. Miller?"

Mrs. Miller said she did, and did Mrs. Brandon remember the black wooden gorillas that stood outside her bedroom door, and then the talk turned to other subjects, notably the horrid feeling in the air that They were going to do something nasty about the bread. Mr. Miller said that indeed, indeed, bread was the staff of life, which somehow put a stopper on that particular conversation, and the party broke up early as Dr. Ford had to go to two cases and Mrs. Miller liked to get her conscientious husband to bed early on Saturday.

"And now," said Francis stretching himself, "what do you say to one small dance, Mrs. Arbuthnot?"

"I do wish," said Mrs. Arbuthnot, addressing herself to Mrs. Brandon, "that you would both call me Peggy. I feel so old with everyone Mississing me. Nearly everyone in the regiment called me Peggy."

"My Peggy's but a young thing, And I am just eighteen," said Francis. "And don't tell me not to say it, mamma, for it is a quotation, as well you would know if you read the *Oxford Book of English Verse*, which is the only poetry book I really like."

Mrs. Arbuthnot put in an impassioned plea for *Lyra Heroica* and Mrs. Brandon, who had settled with her embroidery on the sofa, upheld the *Golden Treasury*. But no one listened, for Francis had put a record on and he and Mrs. Arbuthnot were moving over the floor like blown feathers. Mrs. Brandon fell silent and worked at her tapestry, remembering how often Francis and Delia had danced together before civilization ended, and wondering if she could induce Delia and her husband to come and live at Stories for a time when the nursery school went, to appease Nurse's child-lust. If they wouldn't, it appeared to her just possible that she might have to let Nurse go to Delia for her next baby; not so much on Delia's account as on Nurse's. Still, that event was still a matter of conjecture and it was no good worrying. It had been nice on the whole to have the little nursery school and Master Parting was the nicest of them all. How good Mrs. Arbuthnot, Peggy she must remember to call her, had been with him and how prettily she had played with him, giving him her green chiffon handkerchief.

"Bed, mamma," said Francis, taking the last record off the gramophone. "Off to bed the pets must flock, For it's nearly eight o'clock, though eleven would be more truthful."

The telephone rang from the hall.

"I'll see who it is," said Mrs. Brandon. "It may be Delia."

"Good-night, Francis," said Mrs. Arbuthnot. "Thank you for the lovely dancing. And may I have my handkerchief back?"

So taken aback was Francis that he produced it from a pocket at once.

"I didn't think you saw me," he said. "Lord! what a plague this Foul New World fashion of not dressing for dinner is. Had I but put on my dinner-jacket, a bit tight in the chest now but let that pass, I would have removed the handkerchief reverently and put it in the little box where I keep my best studs."

"I said I was a witch," said Mrs. Arbuthnot, holding out her hand.

"It's Colin Keith," said Mrs. Brandon coming back. "For you, Peggy,"

"Oh dear," said Mrs. Arbuthnot, half-laughing as she moved towards the door. "He does ring up so late."

"Allow me," said Francis, "to make a living rampart of my body. I will pretend I am the butler we haven't got and tell him you have gone to bed. Shall I?"

"It seems a little rude," said Mrs. Arbuthnot, "but it is rather late and might disturb your mother."

"The word mother," said Francis, "causes the finest chords in a man's heart to vibrate. My mamma's rest shall not be disturbed. Good night."

He strode off to the telephone and Mrs. Brandon conducted her guest upstairs, where she took a last look round the bedroom to see that all was comfortable.

"I know what you need," she said, after examining the bed and looking into the wardrobe. "I don't think Ethel has gone to bed yet. I'll see."

She looked out upon the staircase and saw Ethel coming up to bed, followed by Nurse and Rose.

"Please get that little satin cushion out of the drawer in my room, Ethel," said Mrs. Brandon. "You know the one I mean. And will you get some of those padded hangers out of the top cupboard, Nurse. They are nicer for Mrs. Arbuthnot's dresses."

We feel unequal to making any comment on this scene. The awful triumph of Nurse; the less awful though deeply satisfactory triumph of Rose to whom Nurse had confided in strict confidence Ethel's dreadful treachery; the complete overthrow of Ethel before her fellow-servants; these annals are written in letters of blood and not of them can our modest Muse sing.

Mrs. Brandon then kissed her guest affectionately and left her. Not till Mrs. Arbuthnot was undressing did she realize that Francis had not returned her green handkerchief. For a moment she was annoyed; then her sense of fun got the better of her and she couldn't help laughing at the thought of poor Colin being fobbed off by a sham butler, which would not for a moment deceive him, and herself being deliberately robbed of a handkerchief. But it would have been disconcerting to both gentlemen to know that her chief thought as she went to sleep was how very nice and kind Mrs. Brandon was.

Francis knocked at his mother's door when he went to bed and found her as usual in a very becoming pre-war négligé with her large horn spectacles on, reading a thriller called *Wot! No Corpse in the Mortuary?*

"Well, darling," said Mrs. Brandon, taking off her spectacles and putting them in the book to mark her place, "was that all right?"

"Quite all right," said Francis. "Poor Colin has got it very badly. Still, it's not to be surprised at."

"Is that English?" said his mother anxiously.

"I don't know," said Francis, "but it's what I mean. Peggy is a most attractive baggage. And I shall say things like that, mamma, so it's no good your looking at me."

"I was not thinking of that at all," said Mrs. Brandon, resuming her spectacles to make herself look more dignified. "I was thinking that there is a something I simply cannot account for."

Francis said he had often felt like that himself about things, and what was it.

"Miss Arbuthnot," said Mrs. Brandon.

"Now, my good mamma," said Francis, "what do you mean? Why should you account for her? She is Peggy's sister-in-law, sister of the late and I gather not very satisfactory though gallant Captain Arbuthnot. No beauty, I admit, but she seems a good sort of fellow and Peggy is very fond of her."

"You wouldn't understand, Francis," said Mrs. Brandon loftily. "When I saw her at the Red Cross today she reminded me very distinctly of somebody and I cannot think who it is."

Satisfied with this thunderbolt she took her spectacles off again.

Francis said lots of people were like somebody and after all, considering how many millions and squillions of people there had been in the world, it would be practically impossible for anybody not to look like somebody. That, said his mother, was entirely beside the point. The point was, she said, that Miss Arbuthnot reminded her forcibly of someone she had known and it was most annoying not to be able to put a name to it.

"Sleep on it, darling," said Francis. "I say mamma, how nicely

Peggy played with Cyril. I felt quite maudlin with sentiment when I looked at them."

"They were certainly very nice knickerbockers," said Mrs. Brandon, putting on her spectacles and taking up her book, "but perhaps it is a good thing that the children are going. Nurse has taken all my clothes to make things for them and I expect she will begin on yours now."

Francis said he would lock everything up till they went, kissed his mother, put Mrs. Arbuthnot's handkerchief in the little box where he kept his best studs, and went to bed.

CHAPTER 8

The success of the Red Cross Exhibition, the anticipation of Speech Day at Southbridge, the Barchester première (as these things are called) of *Mayflower Madness*, starring Hash Gobbet with a false forehead and a real wart specially grafted onto his face for the filming as Oliver Cromwell and Glamora Tudor as Queen Henrietta Maria with whom Cromwell was in love and nearly sailed on the *Mayflower* to escape a passion incompatible with his political views only John Bunyan would read *The Pilgrim's Progress* in modernized English to him at Ye Charles's Hedde on Plymouth Hoe so that he went to sleep and missed the boat, the gentle interest of that part of Barsetshire in Colin Keith's moonstruck condition, not to speak of the Bishop's broadcast on Sweden entitled "Germans in Human Shape," were now all obscured by Bread. THEY, as everyone had anticipated, had put it on the ration without so much as a by-your-leave, and the British housewife, with death and murder in her heart, set out on yet another series of queues.

In addition to pages in the ration book called "Do Not Fill In Anything In This Space," and "Points" and "Personal Points," and "Do Not Write On This Counterfoil Until Instructed," and large capital T's and K's and little things called Panels whose use nobody knew, and a thing called Grid General which meant absolutely nothing at all, the harassed and overworked housewife was now faced with large capital L's and M's and small capital G's, each of which, so she gathered from the bleating of the wireless if she had time to listen, or the Sunday paper which she hadn't time to read, meant so many B.U.s. And what B.U.s were, nobody knew or cared, except that B seemed an eminently suitable adjective for whatever they were. The net result of this new piece of meddling was longer and better queues, fewer and more unpleasant loaves, and a sudden outburst of very nasty so-called cakes rather like india-rubber bath sponges in colour and consistency. On Saturday mornings all the horrid little children in Barchester and in every town in England, being members of what is called a Cinema Club, an ingenious device invented by the film trade for making the children of England cinema-minded and thus potential cinema-fodder as adults, were sent out early in the morning by their mothers, who were naturally enchanted to get rid of them for several hours, with a shilling and instructions to buy cakes and eat them outside the cinema which opened at half-past nine, which arrangement enabled the mothers not to have to get breakfast. This Children's Crusade, swarming into the buses even if they only lived half a mile away so that grown-ups could not get to their work, stripped the bakers' shops like locusts and then ate, kicked each other, shrieked, yelled, fought and threw paper about till the cinemas opened; during which interval the kind and overworked police were detailed to prevent them deliberately walking under the traffic, which was a perfect godsend to the local underworld who could steal milk bottles and do small burglary with impunity. The housewives, a hopeless minority among these young pests, had to trudge farther afield almost crying with fatigue to find bread, and when their second or third round of shopping was accomplished, for all the shops opened at different times and if one went to the grocer who opened at 8.30 to get a place in his queue one was too early for the fish that didn't open till ten or the second delivery of bread that wasn't in at any specified time, and they wearily trailed home for what they hoped was the last time that day, the dear little children coming yelling and pushing and fighting out of the cinemas stormed the 'buses for a half-mile ride at half-fare, and heavily laden mothers of families had to drag their baskets home as best they could, while each child occupied a grown-up person's seat. And if anyone had known it, there were going to be some further very horrid scenes over things called "G"; but this secret weapon was not yet released.

The net result of this further regimentation of the luckless English was a great increase of boredom and crossness, which made people wonder what use it had been to stand alone against the Powers of Darkness if the reward was to be increasing discomfort and a vast army of half-baked bureaucrats stifling all freedom and ease, while some of the higher clergy preached on Mr. Noel Coward's test of "Don't let's be beastly to the Germans," only they meant it and he didn't. But the tired, patient, bewildered British Lioness continued to shop and cook and work and do without help and submit to insolence, as she has always done and always will do. And if anyone says it was a judgment on her for using her vote to put the Government in, we can only say that for all her goodness and virtue she is not fit to have a vote, for she is not interested in politics, looking upon the, very rightly, as the sort of thing men like to talk about; and the fault lies with those who rashly and foolishly put that weapon into her noble but irresponsible hands.

The increasing depression and exhaustion were of course worst in London, the stepchild of what Empire the politicians have left us, just as England is the stepchild of the world. In Barchester itself things were uncomfortable enough, but on a much smaller scale. In the country things were on the whole easier, for tradesmen still knew their customers, there was a general give and take, vegetables were grown, and in spite of the Government's determined and addle-headed efforts to exterminate cows, poultry and pigs, misguided patriots still managed to get some milk and eggs and bacon, which they usually shared with neighbours less well off. At Northbridge Manor the Mertons were a kind of distributing centre from farm and dairy, and when Noel went to London he usually took some farm produce for friends oppressed by the difficulties of London shopping.

"Though I sometimes wonder," said Mr. Wickham, who had called for Miss Arbuthnot in his clanking little car on Sunday, and was driving her to Fish Hill, "if there is any future at all for the next generation. They can't emigrate because there is no-where left to emigrate to and they wouldn't let you land when you got there. Fancy a world where you can't go and settle in another country unless you can read and write. And what's going to happen to the Royal Navy? God knows."

Miss Arbuthnot said perhaps he would look after it.

"Well, if he doesn't look after the Royal Navy, then God help us," said Mr. Wickham rather illogically. "We get out here. I think we'd better walk the rest of the way. The golden-crested mippet doesn't like cars, and as for motor-bicycles, there is to my certain knowledge a female mippet who has moved three times because motor-bikes try to do speed tests up her hill. And as for hikers——" but at the thought of the Brave New Worlders hiking about the haunts of mippets, Mr. Wickham went quite red in the face in his efforts to suppress his language.

They were now breasting the steep slope of Fish Hill, where the short turf famous for the mutton it feeds is studded with dwarf juniper bushes, assuming at a little distance fantastic shapes of armies or strange animals, with a growth unlike any other shrub. Here one could easily imagine that an enchanter had turned living creatures to green bushes and that at mid-night, or under a full moon, they might resume their normal life and career madly over the downs. The path they followed skirted the edge of a field where sheep were grazing with a pleasing melancholy perpetual sound of gently discordant bells. Hawthorns and stunted trees grew along the other side of the path where the turf had been worn away by centuries of shep-herds and wayfarers, and the chalk lay white underfoot. At the top of the hill the downs stretched away to the right; to the left

was a little wood of the wind-dwarfed trees that flourish on
those heights and in the meadow and river land below lay
Barchester, with the most exquisite spire in England pointing
heavenwards from among the trees of the Cathedral Close.

"I'm a Barsetshire man," said Mr. Wickham suddenly, and
Miss Arbuthnot had the impression that he had forgotten her
presence, or was taking it for granted as part of the landscape.
"Not this part. My people lived near Chaldicotes—that was
another of the fine Barsetshire houses, probably Charles the
Second. But that's all over now. The Government have taken it
for psycho-analysing young men who are going into the Civil
Service. I knew a girl who went there, but they couldn't have
made her worse than she was, so that's all right."

Having uttered what artless thoughts were in his mind, Mr.
Wickham fell silent again and Miss Arbuthnot wondered more
than ever if one could in time be received into a county where
one had not been born. In the dales of the Lake Country
offcomes, she knew, hardly paid or won their footing in a
lifetime; even the second generation was regarded with suspicion by the shepherds and the descendants of the statesmen.
Barsetshire was less remote, less uncompromising, but even so
she felt that one might be in the county but not of it for a very
long time.

As Mr. Wickham's silence was evidently meditative, not
unfriendly, she put this difficulty before him.

"It depends on what you want," said Mr. Wickham. "I spent a
lot of my life at sea and I've knocked about a bit, but I can settle
down here because I belong here. There were Wickhams near
Chaldicotes long before the Sowerbys or even the Omniums
were heard of. Not gentry, you know. Yeoman farmers and that
sort. So we belong. It's rather like the navy. We have our life and
our own interests. Perhaps the navy will come under the steam-
roller and lose its personality. Perhaps Barsetshire will. I hope
not. You can belong to Barsetshire in different ways. You can
belong by birth as my people do, and the Greshams, Thornes,

and lots more. You can work for Barsetshire till it gives you a kind of honorary citizenship. The Crawleys are like that and the Warings, and I may say the Mertons are in a fair way to become part of the county. Or you may marry into it. If you are the right sort they'll take you; first for the man or woman you marry, then for yourself. Then there are a lot of people like the Southbridge lot and Mrs. Brandon and the Deans, who won't ever be Barsetshire. Nothing wrong with them. But they will always be foreigners as far as the real county is concerned. Lord! How I am talking. Sorry to have bored you. We ought to find the mippet at home with any luck. This way."

He led her to the little wood of stunted trees, walking with the quiet tread of the Royal Navy among the gnarled stems. From the depths of the thicket came a gentle call, almost a chuckle.

"You can hear her," said Mr. Wickham in a whisper. "Too-too-quobble-too-quit-quit."

To Miss Arbuthnot it had sounded quite clearly like "Too-whoo-wobble-too-quit-whit," but although she was F. E. Arbuthnot of *Country Life*, it was Mr. Wickham's mippet, not hers, so she held her tongue. Very quietly, inch by inch, they approached the noise and were rewarded by the sight of a fat comfortable matron in a brown dress spotted with yellow fluffed out to twice her size on a nest, for the mippet, being as silly as most other birds or even sillier if that is possible, usually lays in the late summer one or two eggs which are no use either to bird or man and sits upon them with all the besotted affection of a mother, while her husband, although in the main an addle-pated fellow, knows that the eggs will come to nothing and goes off to the club to compare his yellow head-feathers, called by courtesy a crest, with the crest of his fellow mippets.

The mippet looked straight at them, or as straight as anyone can look who can only see her friends out of one eye at a time, and remained perfectly still. It is doubtful whether she saw them at all, for silly as all birds are the golden-crested mippet is easily the silliest; but if she did, she undoubtedly took them for parachutists with horrible designs on the sanctity of the nest. Mr. Wickham and Miss Arbuthnot bore her unwinking stare as long as they could and then cautiously retreated to the edge of the coppice.

"Phew!" said Mr. Wickham, wiping the perspiration from his forehead. "I'd sooner face Cape Horn and an easterly gale than one of those birds. It's a funny thing, but you never know what they are thinking about and sometimes it gets you down. When I was on the India Station I spent some leave up-country and another chap and I went off to look at birds. There's a bird called the stengah, the whisky-soda bird, that's very shy. Well, we waited for her for two days and at last we got a good view of her, but, by Jove, she gave us such a look that we backed out of her garden on all fours—we'd come up that way, you know, not to alarm her. I'll never forget the look in her eye. What the stengah would be like here, I don't like to think. I'd like to let a few loose on the Government when they start messing us all about."

Miss Arbuthnot pulled off her patched washleather gloves and showed him her hand, scarred across the knuckles.

"Stengah," she said.

"By Jove, that's a pretty good job," said Mr. Wickham, taking her hand and examining it. Another man might have shown sympathy with the stengah's victim, he might conceivably have pressed the strong capable hand which had suffered in the cause of philavism, or let it linger for a moment in his own. But Mr. Wickham and Miss Arbuthnot were sensible people who knew that birds were, after doing one's duty and in Mr. Wickham's case seeing there was plenty of drink in the house, the only really important and steadfast thing in a rocking civilization. Mr. Wickham restored Miss Arbuthnot's hand to her as if it were an interesting specimen in spirits, Miss Arbuthnot put her glove on again, and they walked along towards the edge of the thicket looking at the noble view of the plain beneath them, Miss Arbuthnot secretly envying Mr. Wickham because he was a free-born citizen of this noble land, while she was merely an offcome.

"We might just go as far as Mazefield," said Mr. Wickham. "It's only a few hundred yards. And then I know a pub on the Barchester side that gives you beer in a teacup before opening time—that is if they've got any. And then I'll run you back to Southbridge."

Miss Arbuthnot did not much like beer, especially for tea, but it was Mr. Wickham's treat and she thought the pub would probably supply tea in a beer-mug if necessary, so they walked along the crest of the downs, crushing sweet-scented thyme as they went, the air nostalgically melodious with the lin-lan-lone of the sheep-bells. The deep chimes of the Cathedral reached them in five successive beats of the great bell.

"We won't stay long," said Mr. Wickham, "or we'll miss the beer altogether. They always keep some for me at the weekend, or the six o'clock customers would drink it all. Do you know Mazefield?"

Miss Arbuthnot said she didn't and was it a house or a village.

"Just you wait," said Mr. Wickham, striding on with swift loose movements over the springy turf towards a circle of beeches. "It's not a tumulus either, though you can hardly ride anywhere on this part of the downs without your horse putting his foot in one, where people have excavated," which Miss Arbuthnot quite understood to be a deliberate mis-statement, for Mr. Wickham was not ignorant of the antiquities of his county.

Mr. Wickham led the way through the beeches. Before them lay a large circle of green turf, beech-encircled, with a kind of pattern marked by the naked chalk from which the turf had been removed.

"Maze," said Mr. Wickham proudly. "Like Hampton Court only more so. Pilgrims used to come here like anything and walk in, and the old monks made a jolly good thing out of it. you know, sixpence admission and refreshments extra and all that.

Mead and venison and all that sort of thing, I daresay. They say
a lot of the gate-money went to building the cathedral. You have
to cover every inch of ground before you get to the middle and
when you get to the middle there's nothing there, as you can
see."

Miss Arbuthnot not unnaturally inquired why it was a place
of pilgrimage if there was nothing there.

"I couldn't tell you," said Mr. Wickham. "It's probably Saxon,
Thor or Wayland Smith or somebody. Or quite as probably
British, Gog and Magog or something of the sort. Only the
queer thing is that the pattern is exactly the same as a maze on
the floor of one of those old French cathedrals; you know, Notre
Dame and all that sort of thing," said Mr. Wickham, whose
acquaintance with France was confined to the various seaports
he had visited professionally. "It makes you think."

Miss Arbuthnot said she supposed it had been a pagan place
of worship, and being holy had been used by the Church to
attract the sort of people that used to go it in pre-Christian
times. That, said Mr. Wickham, was all right. Look at Rome for
example, all full of pagan things being turned into churches and
what not. But what was rum was the pattern of the maze. Miss
Arbuthnot, who like most women jumped to conclusions rather
than thought (or shall we say at the risk of contradiction from
our male reader thought far more quickly than men and was not
afraid of making a fool of herself by clarifying her thoughts
aloud), and what about the pattern being a heathen pattern and
the church taking it up as a Good Thing. Then, she said, the
French cathedral and the Barsetshire labyrinth could easily be
twins without ever having seen each other.

"I get you," said Mr. Wickham. "It was a kind of stock
pattern. The early British or what not made a maze up here with
the Druids and all that lot, and the early French whoever they
were and as far as I'm concerned they couldn't have been nastier
than the late French had the same labyrinth with French Druids

or whatever they called them. And then they put the labyrinth in the Cathedral just to show."

Miss Arbuthnot, impressed by this theory, said to show what.

"Oh, you know," said Mr. Wickham. "Liberty, Egality, Fraternity and all that. I mean, to give everyone a fair go all round, heathens and Christians and everyone. Then the old fellows that came to church would see the labyrinth and think perhaps the new religion wasn't such a bad show after all. Logical you know, and the French are always supposed to be logical though I'm damned," said Mr. Wickham violently, stung by a recollection of ancient wrongs, "if I see where the logic comes in. They've got all their words wrong. Fancy calling a naval commander a captayn de freggat. No wonder they don't get on, and jabbering away all the time."

As Mr. Wickham was getting red in the face and would evidently have tackled any three Frenchmen with pleasure, Miss Arbuthnot suggested that they should walk the maze, which they did.

"The Barsetshire Archaeological come up here once a year and clear the decks," said Mr. Wickham. "They were a bit shorthanded during the war and it was a sight to see old Lord Stoke doing his bit, and Tebben, that man over at Worsted that knows all about Vikings and Sagas and all those old fellows. I had a couple of fellows from my old ship on leave here, and the British Navy put its back into it, I can tell you. And I'll tell you something else," he continued, as they unwound their steps. "We had half a bottle of navy rum and we passed it round and every one had a swig. Poor old Tebben nearly choked. And we poured the last few drops on the middle of the circle. You never know, you know," said Mr. Wickham half-apologetically. "It's like not looking at the new moon through glass; it can't do any harm. If any of those old fellows were about, it may have given them a bit of a kick."

Miss Arbuthnot was by now a little uncertain whether the old fellows were the Druids, or the monks, or the gods of heathendom, or the unknown architects and builders of Barchester Cathedral, or even, so many subjects had Mr. Wickham twirled kaleidoscopically before her, the Free French. So she said she expected whoever got the drops of rum was quite pleased and anyway the Greek and Roman gods were quite happy with the smell of food on their altars.

"I know exactly what they felt like," said Mr. Wickham sympathetically. "There are times when just the smell of rum seems to put heart into you. Now we'll go and put some heart into ourselves with beer, though goodness knows the stuff we're getting now would hardly make a cockroach drunk. Some fellows from the old *Flatiron* once made some rats drunk. Funniest thing you ever saw, though I must say," he added with a smile of happy reminiscence, "we were all pretty tight ourselves. Get in."

Miss Arbuthnot got into the car and a few minutes brought them to a small village with a little inn called the Bridge Inn, with a very elegant portrait-signboard of the bridge which here spanned a tributary of the Rising. On a bench outside the inn some aged men with Newgate frills were waiting for six o'clock. Mr. Wickham bade them good afternoon and led the way into a cold, damp, neat little parlour, almost entirely occupied by a horsehair sofa, a harmonium, the first edition of the *Encyclopaedia Britannica* and a huge round table with a red chenille cover that touched the ground. On the wall hung blotched engravings of the late John Martin's terrifying biblical scenes, including the Deluge and the Fall of Nineveh.

"Those pictures used to frighten me like anything when I was a kid," said Mr. Wickham. "Hoy! Mrs. Hubback!"

Miss Arbuthnot had always been delightfully terrified by them in her youth when staying with an old and rather mad great-aunt who lived in a moated farmhouse and wore a silk dress and ringlets, and she and Mr. Wickham exchanged reminiscences of Belshazzar's Feast and the Fall of Babylon.

The door opened and a stout middle-aged woman came in.

"Tea for the lady and myself, Mrs. Hubback," said Mr. Wickham embracing the landlady, who took no notice at all, merely inquiring whether the lady wanted hot tea or cold tea.

"Hot for the lady, cold for me," said Mr. Wickham. "Unless, of course, you'd like it cold," he added to Miss Arbuthnot.

Miss Arbuthnot, who by now had a pretty shrewd idea what the cold tea was, said she would like hers hot. Mrs. Hubback waddled away and soon returned with a tea-tray on which were two teapots, one small and one very large, a small and a large teacup, a large jar of creamy milk, bread and butter, jam, honey and home-made cakes.

"Splendid, Mrs. Hubback," said Mr. Wickham. "How's Hubback?"

"He's all right, sir," said Mrs. Hubback, with an accent on the word "he" which seemed to indicate that she thought but poorly of her husband. "He got some young partridges over Nutfield way last night. Do you want any, sir?"

Mr. Wickham said he could do with a brace in the boot. Miss Arbuthnot, feeling that she was being implicated in something queer, hastily pretended she hadn't heard and complimented Mrs. Hubback on the excellent tea, adding that she had not seen so much or such good cakes for ages.

"How *do* you manage, with the rations, Mrs. Hubback?" she said.

"Rations?" said Mrs. Hubback. "They don't bother us, miss, and we don't bother them. I'm not going to eat that nasty marge at my time of life, nor that nasty bacon neither, nor them allocation eggs as they call them. Old-age-pension eggs I call 'em. We manage all right, miss. You see, we all know each other. Ring if you want some more tea, sir."

She removed her bulky form and Miss Arbuthnot poured herself some tea which was hot and fragrant and laced it with the rich milk. Mr. Wickham poured himself a drink from the large teapot into the large cup and drank it off, foam and all.

"That's very ingenious," said Miss Arbuthnot.

"You don't know Mother Hubback," said Mr. Wickham. "You see that coffee urn? Fine old Sheffield plate and all that. I've known that urn full of whisky. One gets a kind of kick out of whisky from a coffee urn. Like those old fellows that used to have parties somewhere near High Wycombe with the girls dressed as monks."

Miss Arbuthnot, recognizing in these words a hazy remembrance of Medmenham Abbey, said people took their pleasures simply in those days.

"By Jove, you are right," said Mr. Wickham, pouring himself another cup of cold tea and making a sandwich of bread and butter liberally plastered with honey. "They were easily pleased then. Well, here's to them," and he drained his cup at a draught and rang the bell.

There was an interval before Mrs. Hubback reappeared.

"There's a reverend gent wants some tea," she said, removing the large teapot and the large cup and wiping the tray with a damp cloth. "The bar will be open in ten minutes, sir, and I'll bring you some fresh tea. This way, sir," she said to what was presumably the reverend gentleman outside the door, and in came Colonel Crofts disguised as a clergyman.

"You won't mind the gentleman having his tea here, miss?" said Mrs. Hubback.

"Colonel Crofts! How very nice. I don't think you and Mr. Wickham have met," said Miss Arbuthnot. "Thank you so much, Mrs. Hubback, we'll all have tea together."

While the fresh tea was making she explained Mr. Wickham and Colonel Crofts to each other who at once found friends in common and some war experiences shared, so that Miss Arbuthnot was rather out of it. But she had lived much in male society before her brother's marriage and quite understood how much nicer it usually is for them to talk to each other than to women, so she poured out the hot tea and pushed the bread and butter and honey and cake within the gentlemen's reach, and they talked away. Mr. Wickham, who was by now on much the same terms with Miss Arbuthnot as Mr. Richard Swiveller was with Miss Sally Brass, took this quite for granted, but Colonel Crofts, much as he enjoyed talking war shop, felt that a lady should not be so ignored and asked Miss Arbuthnot how her sister was, expressing at the same time a respectful hope that they would both come and support him when he conducted his first service at Southbridge. Miss Arbuthnot pledged herself and her sister-in-law for that date.

"And if you are alone at the Vicarage, Colonel Crofts," she said, "do come to supper at Editha Cottage after the evening service. I know Peggy would love it."

The new Vicar thanked her and then said regretfully that he must be getting back, as the Vicar's aunt was packing her china and pictures and he had promised to go and help her. Mr. Wickham offered him a lift.

"Many thanks," said Colonel Crofts, "but I have my bicycle."

Mr. Wickham as delicately as possible expressed his surprise and distress that the new Vicar had not a car.

"I have, you know," said Colonel Crofts with great simplicity. "But I thought it over and I came to the conclusion that a car was in trust, so to speak. One might need it at any moment for one's parishioners; to take someone who was ill or had had an accident into Barchester. And when I see all the German prisoners of war driving about while my people walk or bicycle, I feel I can't use my car with a clear mind. Not for short distances at any rate. And I really like bicycling. Of course I keep the car cleaned and oiled," he added anxiously, lest anyone should think he had laid by treasure for moths and rust to devour. "I do rather wish though that I had it out today and then I could have offered to drive Miss Arbuthnot back to Southbridge."

His hearers couldn't help feeling that Colonel Crofts was very good, a rare quality when entirely unselfconscious, and Mr. Wickham had a momentary impulse to leave his car outside the inn, put peas in his shoes, and walk painfully back to North-bridge. But a moment's reflection showed him that this would be extremely uncomfortable for everybody, including himself, so to salve his conscience he insisted on paying for all three teas, an offer which Colonel Crofts accepted with pleasure, saying that it would give him an excuse for asking Mr. Wickham to dinner at the Vicarage as soon as he was settled.

"I have an old batman of mine as factotum," said Colonel Crofts. "He will do everything for me for the present, including the garden. There is only one difficulty. He has done a lot of bell-ringing, an art of which I am completely ignorant; in fact he is an associate member of the Loyal Band of Old Juvenile Bellboys. His great ambition is to ring the bell at Southbridge, but when I, tactfully as I hoped, touched on the subject with the old sexton, I found he took moral offence at the mere suggestion. It seems hard on Bateman. I pointed out to him that Southbridge does not possess a peal, if that is the correct expression, only that one rather unpleasant-sounding bell, but it made no difference. I think," said Colonel Crofts, trying not to look as proud as he felt, "that it is his way of showing his attachment for me."

Mr. Wickham then paid Mrs. Hubback, who said very politely that she hoped the party had enjoyed their tea and next time Mr. Wickham came he must try the coffee, which remark was accompanied by a hearty wink. Colonel Crofts had luckily gone out to pump up his tyres so Miss Arbuthnot was able to laugh which she would not have done if he had been there. Outside the inn they said good-bye to Colonel Crofts.

"I know one should not remind a lady of her promise," said Colonel Crofts to Miss Arbuthnot with a diffidence which she found very pleasing, "but you did me the honour when I was brought to see you in your new home of saying you would write to me when I came to live at Southbridge. I do not want to trespass upon your time, for you must be very busy, but a word of encouragement from you when I take up my new work next week would be of great help."

"Of course I will," said Miss Arbuthnot, uncomfortably conscious that the promise had slipped her mind, though she liked Colonel Crofts as much as ever.

"I shall count on you," said Colonel Crofts. And then Mr. Wickham and Miss Arbuthnot said good-bye to Colonel Crofts and drove away, their last sight of him being his erect figure on his rather old-fashioned bicycle with wide handles, pedalling steadily up the slope.

"Makes one think of those old fellows," said Mr. Wickham suddenly. "St. Francis and all that. I always thought they'd be a bit dull in private life, but Crofts is a fine fellow. If he asks me to dinner I'll take him a bottle of rum and some sherry. And I'll jolly well see that he doesn't give them to the poor either," he added determinedly.

Miss Arbuthnot warmly applauded his plan and then fell silent thinking rather anxiously, as even the most sensible women are apt to do, that a middle-aged bachelor with many duties and many calls on his time might find himself rather uncomfortable in the gaunt Vicarage which had suited the present Vicar and his aunt so admirably. Then she told herself not to be silly, as a good batman was worth dozens of lazy untrained girls or village women. They were now approaching Southbridge and Miss Arbuthnot found herself faced with a dilemma. She would have liked to ask Mr. Wickham in for a drink as a slight token of gratitude for the delightful afternoon, but owing to Them the liquor supply was in very poor condition and she had nothing in the house but a medicine bottle of brandy half-empty, kept for emergencies. Even Miss Hampton and Miss Bent had gone short that month, which shows that things were very bad indeed. She could hardly offer a gentleman of Mr. Wickham's tastes a teaspoonful of brandy out of a medicine glass and if she apologized for her empty cupboard she felt he was quite capable of driving at eighty miles an hour to Northbridge and bringing her two dozen bottles of every drink imaginable.

So she merely thanked him warmly for the treat and said she

hoped he would come over to dinner with her and her sister at some not to distant time.

"A great pleasure," said Mr. Wickham. "We must have another day with the birds. Fish Hill is a good hunting-ground. I've seen the broad-tailed gallowsbird there once or twice. Do you know they still call him Jack Ketch round here. It's a queer thing, but they will only nest in wych-elms."

"It's a very old superstition," said Miss Arbuthnot, "but I have seen nests more than once in a variegated holly near Turnbridge Wells."

"Then," said Mr. Wickham, "it must have been the lesser gallowsbird."

There was a brief but unpleasant silence. Miss Arbuthnot's heavy face darkened, as it had darkened when Mrs. Brandon noticed her at the Red Cross Exhibition.

"The lesser gallowsbird," said Miss Arbuthnot with awful clarity, "*always* nests in Pocklington's alder. Any bird-student knows that."

"Well," said Mr. Wickham, goaded by his feelings to quite schoolboy rudeness, "all I can say is, it is a fact unknown to *human* students," and he waited for this awful sarcasm to sink in."

Miss Arbuthnot said that if Mr. Wickham thought human was synonymous with intelligent, he was neither. She was then conscious that her voice and her hands were shaking and felt desperately ashamed.

"Of course," said Mr. Wickham, starting his car with a maximum of noise, "I must defer to the gifted contributor to *Country Life*, but even *journalists* may be wrong occasionally," and drove off at top speed to prevent Miss Arbuthnot capping his retort.

Miss Arbuthnot, feeling as sick as grown-up people do when they have demeaned themselves to answering back, one of the nursery's major crimes, went into the house and decided to forget all about it, with the excellent result that she dropped large tears of rage and self-pity into her supper and went to bed leaving the dirty things in the scullery. From the field behind the house the indefatigable cuckoo emitted raucous monotonous cadence.

"In July, Away you don't fly. In August, Away you jolly well must," said Miss Arbuthnot, adding angrily to the world in general, "How I HATE birds."

She then drew the curtains to exclude the cold late daylight, got into bed and applied herself to the *Journal of Philavian Studies.*

Mr. Colin Keith was, not to put too fine a point upon it, becoming a distinct bore, as even his fond sister Lydia Merton had to admit. His plans for spending part of the Long Vacation in Switzerland had gradually melted to nothing. Kind Kate would willingly have had him all the time, but the Schoolhouse was full for weekends up to the end of term and she was taking her whole family to Devonshire for August, so it appeared to the Mertons that Colin would spend his holidays at Northbridge.

"Not that I grudge Colin his bed and board," said Noel sententiously, "for he is the best junior I've ever had and your brother, and I happen to like him very much. But if he is going to be in love all the time he will be very poor company. I wish he would propose to Peggy and get it over."

"I think," said Lydia, "he feels he isn't worthy. At least I don't think he really feels it, but he feels he ought to feel it. But I quite agree he ought to hurry up. I'd like Peggy for an in-law and I'd like Effie for an in-law-in-law. Only I do rather wish," she said a little sadly, "that Peggy wasn't a widow. One always thinks of widows as designing."

Noel said nonsense, she must remember David Copperfield's mother, which made Lydia protest stoutly that Colin would never be a Mr. Murdstone because Mrs. Arbuthnot hadn't any children. She made as though to say something more, checked herself, and looked thoughtful.

"I know exactly what you are thinking, my precious love," said Noel. "You are thinking that if Colin marries Peggy perhaps she won't have any children all over again and how dreadful that will be and how Colin will be very unhappy. But as I am a barrister and very intelligent, I will now expound to you the following: A, there is no reason, at least none that we know of, why Peggy shouldn't have as many children as people on tombstones; B, it won't be at all dreadful if she doesn't; and C, whatever the prayer-book may say Colin does not want to marry her to have a family but because he is in love, or thinks he is which is the same thing. So now do stop worrying about your brother who is quite old enough to look after himself."

Lydia said firmly that he wasn't, or he wouldn't be so silly, and it would be a very good thing if he went over to the Deans for tennis that afternoon and Noel might drive him there as it was Black Sunday and Nurse would be out till supper-time.

So Lydia went away to her nursery duties and about three o'clock Noel drove his brother-in-law to Winter Overcotes. They had both had too much Sunday lunch and were disinclined for talk, so Colin was able to reflect undisturbed upon the joys of seeing Mrs. Arbuthnot for at least an hour. If all the Deans and their guests and Noel too could be dead during that period it would, he thought, be even more joyful, but one cannot make things happen by thinking, which is just as well as one might be sorry afterwards.

If he had hoped to find Mrs. Arbuthnot waiting, her lovely eyes shining favourably upon him, he was the more deceived. Susan was knocking up balls with her brother-in-law Mr. Fanshawe and another nice not-quite-so-young girl and was delighted to see Colin, not only for his own sake, but as a fourth. Noel, who in any case was not going to play, sat with Mrs. Dean who was doing embroidery and quite enjoyed himself, though thinking all the time that Mrs. Brandon did her airs and graces better.

"Jessica is somewhere about," said Mrs. Dean. "She came

down last night and looked so tired that I kept her in bed for lunch. She is rehearsing as well as acting just now. It is very extraordinary to have a daughter on the stage."

Noel said lots of people did now, and what was more instead of sending them to proper schools they sent them to peculiar places where they learnt English-speaking ballet and School Certificate, emerging quite incompetent for either.

"Jessica was at a perfectly ordinary school," said Mrs. Dean, "but it was all in the war, so as she was too young for conscription she went to the Royal Academy of Dramatic Art and somehow made a success. I can't account for it all, except that my great-great-grandmother was once dreadfully frightened by Mrs. Siddons as Lady Macbeth. We nearly called Jessica Sarah, but it was too like Susan. Oh, here you are, darling."

The protean Jessica had come quietly into the room; not as that quiet little youngest daughter of the Deans, but in a perfect smartness of sleek hair and tailor-made, her lips, cheeks and fingernails faintly and exquisitely coloured, so that Noel felt he ought to applaud a studied restraint far more striking than any amount of glamour.

"Hullo, darling," she said, putting her cheek almost against Noel's but carefully not touching him. "I'm a character in search of an author. Aubrey is coming for me after tea. How are you, mummy darling? Being vague and gracious?"

"Baggage!" said Noel, at which the vision of sophistication laughed while Mrs. Dean, apparently taking her youngest daughter's behaviour quite as a manner of course, smiled amiably and settled herself more comfortably with her work.

"That is so nice about mamma," said Jessica to Noel. "She is like a kind comfortable hen with warm feathers and nothing we do upsets her. I think she quite exhausted her affection on daddy and looks on us as strange but friendly animals that have somehow got into the house. She did once come to see me at the Cockspur, and after the curtain we found she had slept right through the last act in a corner of the box. I showed her to

Aubrey, but he said Nature was greater than art and he knew when he was beaten. Tell me about your Lydia whom I adore."

Nothing loth, Noel gave a satisfactory account of Lydia and the children and had a short flirtation with Jessica, conducted with great skill on both sides. Mrs. Brandon with Francis and Mrs. Arbuthnot then came in.

"Divine technique you have," said Jessica. "You can't take me in though. Peggy, my lamb, how divine. And Francis. And dear Mrs. Brandon, how pleased I am to see you."

Upon which a vast amount of kissing took place with soft cheeks just not touching each other. Francis, who was included in the general salutation, much enjoyed Jessica's moth's kiss and made mental notes of it for future use. Mrs. Dean roused herself from a kind of comfortable afternoon trance to greet the new-comers, and the drawing-room was filled with the amiable chit-chat of charming women each of whom appreciated the good points of her friends with unjealous interest. To Noel the whole affair, though pleasant, seemed a slightly muddled interlude. An intelligent and pretty woman was one thing if one had her to oneself, or if there were other men talking to other charmers, but such a mass of femininity was faintly cloying. He looked at Francis, but he was apparently assailed by no such immortal discontent and looked very much at his ease; like the Turk with his doxies around, thought Noel rather crossly.

"I know exactly what you feel like," said Mrs. Arbuthnot who was seated near him. "Fred was the same. He adored women one or two at a time, but he couldn't stand tea-parties."

"Sensible man," said Noel approvingly.

"Well, I don't exactly know," said Mrs. Arbuthnot, thinking how Fred had adored Mrs. Colonel Matcham and many other ladies. She dismissed the thought as quickly as possible, because if one thought of dead sorrows one might be a little sorry for oneself and even ask for a little sympathy and this she had determined never to do. But Noel noticed that her speedwell eyes darkened to deep sapphire and drew his own conclusions, for what little he had heard of the late Captain Arbuthnot had not made him think very highly of that officer. So he exerted himself, using the technique approved by Miss Jessica Dean, and was now in the middle of what can only be called a drawing-room flirtation with Mrs. Arbuthnot whose eyes were again their usual colour. Mrs. Brandon, who in spite of her apparently indolent and even hen-brained mind saw most things pretty clearly, thought with amusement of the excellent drawing-room flirtations she and Noel Merton had conducted before his marriage and approved Mrs. Arbuthnot's handling of the situation, conceding very generously that she couldn't have done it better herself; and she thought with considerable pleasure what fun it was to have Peggy for a weekend, and so nice for Francis.

Tea and the tennis players came in together and what Noel called to himself the dixhuitièmerie of the conversation was drowned in a healthy open-air atmosphere. To put it more bluntly, Susan and the other nice not-quite-so-young girl discussed the afternoon's tennis in a friendly but rather overbearing way, assisted by Colin, whom exercise and fresh air had restored to something more like his normal cheerful self. Mr. Fanshawe who often kept silence when he had nothing to say retired into the tight-lipped Olympian detachment well known at Paul's College to first-year men who were doing that bastard school Modern Greats, though he was perfectly prepared to speak if he found an adversary worthy of his tongue.

It was not till Colin had eaten a good deal of excellent cake and drunk two cups of tea that his higher, or in other words his more trying nature began to reassert itself, the first symptom of this return to grace being a loss of interest in the tennis post-mortem, so that the nice not-quite-so-young girl found it difficult to keep up the conversation and told her mother when she got home that Colin Keith was funny the way he seemed frightfully keen on tennis one minute and all browned-off the next. Not, we are glad to say, that the nice not-quite-so-young girl felt at all neglected, for she belonged to the generation of girls who worked for us in great female hordes and many of whom were so unacquainted with man that they found him on the whole a bore. So she went on talking about tennis to Susan, who would have liked to talk to Colin but felt that one must be polite in one's parents' house.

"What heavenly cake," said Mrs. Brandon to Mrs. Dean, unable, like every other woman in England, to keep away from the recurring subject of food.

Mrs. Dean, who had woken up enough to pour out tea and smile at her guests, said it had come from her daughter Betty in New York.

"I hope that she and her husband may come over and visit us next year," she said to Colin. "Woolcott was on the Peanut Control Board all through the war. They wanted to come this year and bring the children, but we felt it would be a great mistake because they would probably die."

As Colin wasn't quite sure whether it was Mr. and Mrs. Woolcott Jefferson van Dryven or their offspring that were doomed, he made sympathetic sounds.

"We are all used to the food They make us eat here," said Mrs. Dean, becoming almost animated, so strong is grand-maternal love, "but I feel certain that American children who have had enough to eat for all their lives would pick up germs or have scurvy and would certainly have frightful colds. Perhaps next year things will be better."

Mr. Fanshawe, speaking for the first time, said he saw no reason for anything ever to be better. The devil, he remarked, had come among us, having great power.

"I am delighted," said Noel, "to meet a disciple of Mr. Toobad."

This picking-up of his allusion Mr. Fanshawe acknowledged by the tightening of his thin lips that was his way of smiling, and said that the devil of today differed from the devil of Revelations in that, far from knowing that he had but a short time, he was comfortably assured that his reign would be even longer than Queen Victoria's.

"The Dark Ages are upon us, Fanshawe," said Noel, falling into Mr. Fanshawe's vein with considerable gusto. "Humane learning is on her death-bed and we shall never see her revival. Law students will probably be forced to study exclusively commercial law with a left bias and have to eat their dinners at a British Restaurant."

"And we shall all have to spend our holidays in Mr. Butlin's camps," said Colin, "and do everything communally with common Communists."

"And learn Russian," said Susan.

"I always think," said Mrs. Dean, who had been paying a sleepy kind of attention to the conversation as she had got into the straight, so to speak, with her embroidery, filling in bits of background, "that if people are wicked to their Royalty, there is a kind of curse on them."

"Expound, Rachel," said Mr. Fanshawe, who was about the same age as his mother-in-law and very fond of her.

"You know very well, Charles," said Mrs. Dean, "that I can never explain what I mean. I mean people who kill Kings and Queens bring bad luck."

Colin said what about Charles the First.

"That," said Mrs. Dean firmly, "was *entirely* Cromwell's fault and one would not have liked him at all. But we didn't kill Queen Henrietta Maria and her children."

"I know what mother means," said Jessica. "Look at the French guillotining the King and Queen and torturing the Dauphin. They've never had a decent Government since and serve them jolly well right and I hope they never will."

"And the Russians murdering the Imperial Family and all those handsome girls," said Noel, amused to add to the argument. "What is the net result?"

Mrs. Arbuthnot said it would be mortifying to have a president or whatever Stalin was called who always wore a chauffeur's peaked cap; which observation led to the expression from various quarters of good-natured contempt for nations whose rulers had to wear evening dress in broad daylight on ceremonial occasions because they were afraid of looking like kings.

"Whenever I think of the King," said the nice not-quite-so-young girl going red in the face with loyal emotion, "it makes me want to cry."

At this simple statement of faith everyone in the room felt the same prickly feeling behind the eyes and nose that one feels when one sees the Union Jack being broken, whether in real life or at a film.

"Quite right," said Francis approvingly. "And I wish all the Government were boiled in a pudding and the King could rule us and have people's heads cut off."

Several people then expounded their ideas, conceived and elaborated on the spur of the moment, of exactly how the country shall be run.

"To the historian," said Mr. Fanshawe, in his precise academic voice, "the period in which we are now living, or shall I say in whose grip we are struggling to exist, is one of remarkable interest, both absolutely and relatively."

He paused to make an effect.

"I'll be the mug, Charles," said Jessica. "Please, Mr. Fanshawe, could you just explain that last bit again, because Elfrida Dobson and I were taking down what you said and we can't quite read it?"

The imitation of an earnest woman student's manner was so perfect that Mr. Fanshawe had to smile his tight-lipped smile.

"You are perfectly right, Jessica," he said. "In lecturing to women students I have observed that they sit looking at you, their earnest eyes gleaming with lack of intelligence, till you mention a date and then they all write it down and usually ask you to repeat it. The theory I was beginning to develop," said Mr. Fanshawe, looking round his audience with a compelling eye which made Mrs. Dean stop embroidering as if she were doing something guilty, "may be briefly stated. We read in history, and when I say history I mean real books, not two-

penny-halfpenny compendiums of universal knowledge in fort-
nightly parts with coloured illustrations," said Mr. Fanshawe,
the scholar's contempt for Mr. By-Ends, for Ignorance and Vain
Hope, burning in him, "of nations who have suffered under bad
Governments. I need not instance them."

"No don't, darling," said Jessica.

"It would," said Mr. Fanshawe, no whit discomposed, "serve
you right if I did. But what is interesting, though I must say even
to the philosopher damnably galling and uncomfortable, is that
we are living ourselves under a Government as bad as any in
history in its combination of bullying and weakness, its bid for
the mob's suffrages, its fawning upon unfriendly foreigners who
despise it, its effort to crush all personal freedom. The sun will
shortly set upon every corner of the British Empire," said Mr.
Fanshawe with gloomy satisfaction, "and even then they won't
be satisfied. To read of such epochs is one thing, to live in such
an epoch is another. However," said Mr. Fanshawe cheering up,
"the historian of the future may look upon these as the Good
Old Times, living as he will under a total totalitarian State, or in
other words under the unmitigated and petty tyranny of fourth-
rate minds. That is, I think, the substance of what I wished to
convey."

To some of the party these words rang with an ominous
sound, for there appeared to be far too much truth in them. To
others any reference to the Government immediately brought to
mind the question of food rationing, and within five minutes all
the ladies were talking at once about food and the men hopelessly overcrowed. Colin had hoped to get near Mrs. Arbuthnot
and talk to her about himself after the fashion of gentlemen in
love but Noel Merton, by direct inspiration of the devil Colin
considered, chose that moment to draw his chair nearer to hers
and talk about London friends. Mrs. Brandon talked very comfortably with Mr. Fanshawe, who liked pretty women to exist by
their charm and not try to be clever, while Susan and the nice
not-quite-so-young girl fell into Red Cross shop talk. So Colin

was able to have the sulks quite comfortably, and when Jessica found that he was not listening to what she said, she very sensibly stopped talking and practised relaxation till she heard from outside a noise like a siren.

"That's Aubrey, mother darling," she said. "Just wake up for a moment. I'm going back to town with him. He insists on having that hideous siren on his car to show Americans what we had to suffer in the war."

The drawing-room door was opened and the new guest came in. Had each person to whom Aubrey Clover was unknown been asked to give a personal impression of the well-known author and playwriter, the answers would have been strangely different, yet strangely the same. To Noel he looked like a young middle-aged barrister of not very distinguished appearance, to Colin like a man he must have met in the army. Mr. Fanshawe felt that he had seen that face and figure a hundred times in Junior Common Rooms, while the nice not-quite-so-young girl felt great disappointment, for when you know it is Aubrey Clover you expect him to look like what you expect Aubrey Clover to look like, not just like anyone else. Mrs. Dean, who accepted all her children's friends as her children's friends, roused herself to say how do you do and recognized Jessica's friend Mr. Clover. Mrs. Brandon saw the sort of person one sees in other people's houses. Jessica and Mrs. Arbuthnot saw their old friend Aubrey Clover and stage embraces were exchanged, affectionate and ritualistic, full of dears and darlings, signifying nothing.

Mr. Clover accepted rather tepid tea and talked to Mrs. Dean with pleasant but not overdone deference till she more or less went to sleep again and then he said to Jessica he thought they ought to be going.

"And I hope you will have lunch with me again, Peggy," he said to Mrs. Arbuthnot, to which Mrs. Arbuthnot replied, "Of course, Aubrey. I'd love to. Ring me up; we are on the telephone now," and then he took Jessica away.

"I would hate," said Noel to Mrs. Arbuthnot, "to speak ill of any man, but was he making notes?"

"Of you, I expect," said Mrs. Arbuthnot. "I don't think he has done your type yet. Of course he has done ordinary women like me quite devilishly. I'd love to see him have a shot at Mrs. Brandon. She is the most enchanting woman I've ever met."

"It is curious, but you are extraordinarily like her," said Noel. "Or like what she was when I first knew her. What I call a real woman in the old-fashioned sense. Lord! how prettily she did play at flirtation. So could you, I expect."

Mrs. Arbuthnot laughed and said India gave one quite a lot of practice.

"And what was so delightful was that one always felt perfectly safe," said Noel. "She knew the rules quite beautifully."

"I think," said Mrs. Arbuthnot, looking up at Noel from downcast eyes and doing what fifty years ago would have been called dimpling, "that one could feel perfectly safe with me; really almost dull," to which Noel gallantly answered that dull wasn't the word, and then they both laughed and understood each other very well and Mrs. Brandon benignly watched her preotégée's progress and was pleased that she was enjoying herself. The afternoon was wearing on and the party soon broke up, but not before Noel had asked Mrs. Arbuthnot to have lunch with him when next she went to town.

"Good-bye," said Colin to Mrs. Arbuthnot in what he hoped was a reproachful voice. "I have hardly seen anything of you."

"I know," said Mrs. Arbuthnot sympathetically. "But I quite understood. There was the tennis and those two nice girls. How very nice your brother-in-law is. Nearly as nice as Lydia. It is always such fun to meet people who speak one's own language."

"I am sorry I don't speak your language," said Colin, going white.

"I didn't mean you, Colin," said Mrs. Arbuthnot, with a flattering accent on the word you; but the iron had eaten too deeply into Colin's soul. Had he been better read he might have felt that he was accursed, a soul apart, like Manfred or Lara; but Byron was to him (as we regret to say he is to us) mostly a name, and he merely felt he would like to kill Mrs. Arbuthnot and then kill himself. Mrs. Brandon collected her party and took them back to Stories.

"I say, Colin, the Duke's otter-hounds are meeting on Wednesday," said Susan. "I'm taking a day's holiday so will you come with me? I'll borrow one of the cars and we'll take lunch."

Colin, almost forgetting that Mrs. Arbuthnot had misunderstood him, accepted the invitation gratefully and said good-bye. On the way back to Northbridge Noel offended his brother-in-law's finer feelings very much by his praise of Mrs. Arbuthnot, and Colin fell into a remote silence in which he imagined that Mrs. Arbuthnot had come to the hunt and the otter, hard pressed by the hounds, had rushed up the bank and bitten her in the leg. White but courageous, she clung to Colin's arm. "Blood-poisoning," she murmured. Swiftly he bent and sucked—no, that would not do. Not even Queen Philippa would suck a bitten leg. The otter must somehow bite her arm. Could otters rear, if hard pressed? Or would she, all womanly tenderness, have stooped to help the otter; perhaps have taken it in her arms to put the hounds off the scent and been bitten by the poor animal, too wild with terror to know friend from foe? Could one, or rather could one so gentle and delicate as Mrs. Arbuthnot, lift an otter? How much, roughly, did otters weigh? These thoughts and others equally sensible and valuable occupied his mind till they reached Northbridge, where Noel reported to his wife that Colin didn't seem to have enjoyed his outing and was becoming an infernal bore.

By an ingenious conspiracy Noel and Lydia led the conversation that evening to *Lemon on Running Powers*, which was really a godsend, for both Colin and Mr. Wickham were in the morose state induced by brooding upon the harsh words one had said to a woman whom one admires and would even reverence were she not so annoying. Mr. Wickham left early to sample some special triple-brewed stout acquired through a Cambridge friend and reflect upon the obstinacy of women. Colin worked hard at *Lemon* till eleven o'clock, when he retired to fevered dreams of Noel and Aubrey Clover giving Mrs. Arbuthnot lunch in guilty splendour.

How different was the scene at Stories where good humour reigned. Mrs. Brandon was entertaining Canon Joram, formerly Bishop of Mngangaland and Colonel the Reverend E. F. Crofts. No one was in love with anyone and though Mrs. Arbuthnot had felt a little depressed by Colin's determination to be misunderstood, she forgot this contretemps completely in agreeable society. Bishop Joram had fallen in love with Mrs. Brandon at sight during the first winter of the war, but it was his amiable practice to fall in love with every nice English-woman he met, largely, so he said, to make up for living among the Mngangalanders for so long. The Dean, who rather fancied himself as a humorist in a ponderous and clerical way, had gone so far as to suggest that a Friends of the Bishop of Mngagaland Society should be formed on the analogy of the Friends of Barchester Cathedral, to which his wife had replied that he had better be careful, for if Bishop Joram had as much trouble with his friends as the Dean and all right-thinking men had had over the proposal to erect a small chapel in honour of the Rev. Thos. Bohun, M.A., Canon of Barchester from 1657 to 1665 and author of some rather obscure erotic poems, he would probably find himself landed with several breach of promise suits.

It was therefore no surprise to Mrs. Brandon to see Bishop Joram falling in love with Mrs. Arbuthnot over the before-dinner sherry, and by the time they got to the fish (which was the main dish, as the rest of the weekend ration was being kept till Monday) she was pleased to see that his conquest was complete, though being a very sensible man he took his being conquered easily and enjoyed the dinner and the company very much indeed.

"I can give you the latest news of your sister-in-law," said

Colonel Crofts to Mrs. Arbuthnot. "I had the unexpected pleasure of meeting her at an inn, the Bridge Inn I think, where she and Mr. Wickham kindly invited me to have my tea with them. I think they had been bird-watching."

"Effie adores birds," said Mrs. Arbuthnot. "I don't. They look very nice hopping about, but I feel I can't trust them."

This entirely new approach to birds interested Colonel Crofts, who begged to know in what way she found them untrustworthy.

"They never look you straight in the face," said Mrs. Arbuthnot firmly, "and I cannot abide people who don't."

"Be fair, Peggy," said Francis. "If your eyes were on both sides of your head you couldn't look straight at anyone out of both at once."

Mrs. Arbuthnot said owls could; they had sensible eyes. It was birds with small, black, beady eyes she couldn't trust.

"I see your point about owls," said Francis, "not but what they look uncommon silly. My beloved mamma looks very like a kind owl when she puts her embroidery-spectacles on."

Mrs. Brandon said he shouldn't say things like that.

Bishop Joram said there was a bird in Mngagaland called the Mpopo-popo, rather like an owl, he said, except that it squinted and was featherless for the greater part of the year.

Mrs. Brandon said she did not think she would like it.

"It is quite harmless, I assure you, Mrs. Brandon," said the Bishop earnestly. "It is supposed to be the spirit of a great chief called Mpopo. The chiefs there have of course a great many souls, and the very large number of Mpopo-popo birds proves what a powerful chief he was. All children who squint are supposed to be children of Mpopo, so their mothers used to be killed to punish them for entertaining the spirit of Mpopo. When I say entertaining," added Bishop Joram hastily, "I do not wish——"

"We all know perfectly well what you mean, Bishop," said Francis kindly. "You have no idea how biological communications have corrupted good manners while you were in the bush.

And I don't see how one can get out of entertaining people's spirits, which I suppose can materialize anywhere."

Mrs. Arbuthnot, who was afraid she might have the giggles and so distress the Colonial Bishop, quickly asked if they still killed the squinters' mothers.

"I regret to say that I had to put a stop to that," said Bishop Joram. "One must move with the times, though no one regrets the passing of old customs more than I. I happened to have a lantern slide of one of the Easter Island statues and I told them it was Mpopo himself, come to tell them that all mothers of squinters were sacred. It was a shot in the dark, but it convinced them, only unfortunately I had forgotten that women sacred to the gods are buried in a mud hut and starved to death, so it all came to much the same."

Mrs. Arbuthnot said those statues were frightening enough to convince one of anything and that was partly why she never used to go to the British Museum; to which Francis replied that it seemed to work the other way round with the Museum people, because they always kept getting unconvinced about things, like saying that the bust of Caesar really wasn't Caesar when anyone could see it was absolutely like him, and turfing that delightful couple who were sitting up on one elbow—no, his mother could perfectly well understand what he meant if she took the trouble to think—out of the Etruscan room. He was, he said, all for believing things, provided they were old enough.

"Talking of old customs," said Colonel Crofts, who had been burning to discuss the subject of squinting further with Bishop Joram and very unfairly used this excuse—"talking of old customs, Joram, when I was stationed at Suhk Behar in nineteen twenty-one, one of our native troops called Nukkle Dusta, I think, had the most appalling squint I've ever seen, and it is a curious fact, bearing perhaps on what you were saying about your black chief, that he also had a very large family. I believe he became a saint later and all his children went into the Indian Civil Service."

Bishop Joram said, in rather a conceited way, that no chief in Mngagaland would allow any son or daughter of his to enter Government service. An exception was of course made for the many illegitimate children, but the father always insisted on having their salaries paid direct to himself in rum and champagne.

By this time both the clerical gentlemen had almost forgotten the existence of their fellow guests and were obviously prepared to discuss our black and brown brethren in their more repellent aspects till cockcrow, so Mrs. Brandon, assuming a look of angelic interest, inquired from Bishop Joram exactly what the Palace had given them to eat last Friday, though she would not ask what they had drunk, for all Barchester, indeed the whole county, knew the answer to that; while Mrs. Arbuthnot with equal cunning asked Colonel Croft what he was going to do about the verandah outside the Vicarage drawing-room that had always let the rain in.

"I feel quite certain," said Colonel Crofts, "that Bateman—it is confusing to have a batman called Bateman—will tackle it. I have never yet," said Colonel Crofts, with the confident independence of the good officer on the good soldier-servant, "seen the job he couldn't tackle. But what I would really like to do is to pull that verandah down. They are all very well in India, but in England they are no use except to keep the light out of the rooms and make homes for earwigs and spiders."

Mrs. Arbuthnot said she quite agreed and she hoped the Bishop or whoever it was would allow the verandah to come down, as the Vicarage was quite cold and dark and hideous enough without it, and then they both fell into a nostalgia for the warmth of the Indian sun and the dependability of the monsoon as contrasted with England's jig-saw weather and the extreme cold and dark of the summer months.

As there was no port and everyone had forgotten the very name of cigars, the whole party adjourned to the drawing-room where Mrs. Brandon and Mrs. Arbuthnot had a perfectly delightful conversation about the clothes they would like to have only they were all being sent to those horrible foreigners. The two clergymen inevitably fell into clerical shop talk in which Francis kept up his end very well, being accepted as a kind of lay-curate by the other men. Mrs. Arbuthnot, occasionally listening to Mrs. Brandon with her eyes rather than her ears, a social gift which is very useful though it can also land the user in a frightful muddle, was interested and a little surprised to hear how serious and intelligent, if those words were not too depressing, Francis could be and felt a certain respect for him hitherto entirely wanting in their very agreeable intercourse. Mrs. Brandon, doing her tapestry work and wearing her large owl-spectacles, cast a piercing glance at Mrs. Arbuthnot from time to time. It had not escaped her notice that her son's frivolity had a good deal of useful common sense below it and it amused her to watch her guest's dawning recognition of this fact.

Had the occasion been a serious one, say a meeting to discuss some specific point of business, Francis would have remained attentive, but as it was a little party in his mother's drawing-room he presently lost interest in the clergy and came over to the ladies. Mrs. Arbuthnot, who was sitting on a little sofa big enough for one or two according to the feeling of the occupier, looked up and moved enough to make room for Francis.

"How charmingly you smile with your eyes," said Francis. "Anyone can smile with their mouth."

Mrs. Arbuthnot said, unconvincingly, that she didn't quite understand.

"Then why do you do it?" said Francis, enjoying himself immensely.

"The Dean," said Mrs. Brandon, who had been looking at the parsons like the kind owl with which her son had compared her, "has a little sofa just like mine. I remember at the dinner-party they gave in the first winter of the war how I fluffed out my dress till Noel Merton came into the drawing-room, and then I unfluffed it because I wanted him to sit next to me and tell me all about his engagement to Lydia."

"Well, mamma," said Francis, "if you mean that Peggy moved up to make room for me because she wants me to tell her that I am engaged to someone, that is exactly where your toes turn in. I really don't know of anyone I am engaged to at the moment."

"I cannot think," said Mrs. Brandon to no one in particular, "why Francis never did get engaged. Delia was engaged and married before she was twenty-one. So was I," she added, looking reproachfully at her son.

"So was I, if it comes to that," said Mrs. Arbuthnot.

"There, Francis!" said his mother with an air of triumph, but Francis did not pay much attention to her, for he saw Mrs. Arbuthnot's eyes darken and felt that his adored mamma had for once put her foot in it.

"Thinking of the old 'un," he said to himself, but aloud he said, "Would you dance, Peggy, if I put the gramophone on?"

Mrs. Arbuthnot said she would love it if Mrs. Brandon did not mind, but what about Them, looking towards Bishop Joram and Colonel Crofts. Francis said if there was one thing he was good at it was ridding people of pestilent priests and got up.

"Oh, Bishop Joram," he said, "would it frightfully interrupt if Peggy and I put the gramophone on? She seems a bit low and I think it would cheer her up to dance. Would you think it awfully rude, sir?" he added to Colonel Crofts.

Colonel Crofts said he would enjoy it very much and used to waltz a good deal when he was young. Bishop Joram remained silent. Francis, fearing that he might have insulted his cloth, or profaned the Sabbath, said of course it didn't really matter and perhaps it was a bit late.

"Oh dear, I wasn't thinking of that at all," said the Colonel Bishop. "I was only wondering if you would allow me to work the gramophone. It would remind me of old days in Mngangaland. The old head chief had a magnificent radio-gramophone and as he didn't know one note from another he let me order all the records and play them. We had all the Gilbert and Sullivan operas and I looked forward to our musical evenings like anything."

"I quite agree with you about Gilbert and Sullivan, sir," said Francis, "and I don't see why those highbrow people at Glyndebourne shouldn't give us a first-class season of them as soon as the copyright runs out. But I'm afraid I've only got dance records."

"Swing?" said Bishop Joram, his eyes shining with ecstasy. Francis led him to the gramophone and the Colonial Bishop began reverently to examine the record-cabinet.

"You've got 'It's Hev-Hev-Heaven, To Man the pits for Bevin,'" he said admiringly. "I heard it in Aubrey Clover's last revue and I couldn't get a record. May I put it on?"

Francis begged him to play it at once and any other record that took his fancy, and having seen him blissfully established with half a dozen chosen records went back to Mrs. Arbuthnot and with a graceful inclination offered her his hand. Mrs. Arbuthnot, remarking very sweetly, "What an ass you are, Francis," took his hand, rose as lightly as a piece of swans-down and moved into the dance.

"How well those young people dance," said Colonel Crofts, who had taken Mrs. Arbuthnot's seat near his hostess. "My boys are both excellent dancers."

"Three down and four across," said Mrs. Brandon, who was trying to correct a mistake in her tapestry. "Oh dear, I didn't know you were married."

"How could you?" said Colonel Crofts. "My wife died more than twelve years ago. Both my boys are in the Indian Army."

"I am dreadfully sorry," said Mrs. Brandon laying down her work and for once giving her undivided attention to what the speaker was saying. "I truly am. My husband died just before Delia was born and though I didn't really mind very much I minded enough to realize how much one would mind if one really minded. I do feel sure that you minded dreadfully, because you seem so truthful."

Colonel Crofts couldn't help being amused by Mrs. Brandon's description of her own feelings and was touched by her sympathetic voice and look.

"I did mind," he said. "Very much; because I was very, very fond of her and she was very fond of me. More fond than I could ever have deserved. But one does get over most things, you know. And I had the regiment, and my boys have done well and I hope to be of some use to England still."

It did Mrs. Brandon great credit that she did not cap his confidence by telling him how well she had got over her dull husband's death. But there was an earnestness about Colonel Crofts that made her slightly ashamed of her own placid life whose even flow her loss had so slightly disturbed. With an interest so unfeigned that he could not possibly take it for idle curiosity, she asked him if he had ever thought of marrying again.

"Naturally," said Colonel Crofts, "and I think an English clergyman should on the whole be married. If I met the right woman, one who would be willing to be the parson's wife with all that it involves as well as honouring me by accepting me as her husband, I should be much tempted to marry again. You seem to be in difficulties with your work, Mrs. Brandon. Can I help? I am very fond of tapestry work. I made a complete set of seats for six chairs, two armchairs and a settee for my wife while we were in India. Three down and four across," he said, gently taking the work from her. "It ought to be three across and four down. I will unpick it for you if I may. Unpicking is such a disagreeable job."

Mrs. Brandon, watching his neat fingers at work, his head bent in concentration, couldn't help feeling that many women, and very nice women, would be glad of such a husband and wondered vaguely, for women's thoughts always stray from the universal to the particular, if Mrs. Arbuthnot had taken his fancy. Even as this thought came into her mind, Francis and Mrs. Arbuthnot drifted across the floor, singing gently the chorus of Aubrey Clover's popular revue song:

Cheer boys, cheer, a thousand a year,
It keeps you in fags and it keep you in beer.
There may be no houses, there may be no work,
But paying ourselves is a thing we don't shirk,
So cheer boys, cheer, a thousand a year,
So long as we get it, you'll find us all here.

Mrs. Brandon smiled at them and felt that this was not the wife for Colonel Crofts. Someone older and steadier must be found, but for the moment she could think of no eligible woman, spinster or widow. The sound of the telephone bell broke across these speculations.

"Bother!" said Francis. "I'll go. Don't stop the gramophone, Joram."

"It might be for me," said Mrs. Arbuthnot, making a face to express annoyed amusement.

Francis was back in a moment.

"For you, Peggy," he said, "Northbridge," and began to discuss with Bishop Joram the latest recording of Cash Campo and his Symposium Boys, who were still in New York and likely to remain there until the dollar and the pound were on better terms. While they were trying a particularly good record called "Three-star Baby," Mrs. Arbuthnot came back, a little flushed.

"May one, without giving offence, ask how Colin is?" said Francis.

"It wasn't Colin," said Mrs. Arbuthnot, looking amused and slightly guilty, "it was Noel. He only wanted to settle a day for me to lunch in town with him. I've got to go up on business."

Francis felt an annoyance which he knew to be quite unreasonable, and being a very sensible person he squashed the annoyance and finished his dance with Mrs. Arbuthnot. Bishop

Joram then tore himself away from the gramophone and said to Colonel Crofts that he was afraid they must be getting back. As it was the Colonial Bishop's car Colonel Crofts could not protest, though he would have liked to prolong his conversation with that kind, sympathetic Mrs. Brandon. So the clerical gentlemen went back to Barchester.

"I wish Monday didn't always come after Sunday," said Mrs. Brandon, putting her work away. "Are you ready for bed, Peggy?"

And a very pretty picture his mamma and Peggy made going upstairs together, thought Francis, following them at a suitable distance. Mrs. Brandon went with Mrs. Arbuthnot into her room to take the good hostess's last look round and see that all was comfortable.

"I can't tell you how happy I have been here," said Mrs. Arbuthnot.

"Then you must come again," said Mrs. Brandon, kissing her guest good-night very affectionately. "Good-night, dear, and sleep well."

"And good-night, sweet chuck, and pleasant dreams," said Francis undutifully parodying his mamma's manner. Though he would not have minded also kissing Mrs. Arbuthnot, he was afraid of Nurse, who had a habit of hovering about till the last person was safely shut up for the night. So instead he imprinted a light kiss on her hand.

"I do it to mamma sometimes," he explained. "It looks a little eccentric, but what else is there to live for now? Good-night."

"No, darling," he said, looking in at his mother's door, "I am *not* going to discuss who Peggy is to marry. You can arrange it all very nicely without me. You have been an angel to her and she adores you."

He blew his mother a kiss and went to bed.

CHAPTER 9

Colonel Crofts was duly inducted and though he privately agreed with the Deanery that any induction in which the Bishop or his representative took part was practically tantamount to heresy and an interdict, he had to recognize the validity of the ceremony and comfort himself by reflecting that the Bishop was merely an instrument.

This sentiment he confided to a small lunch-party given by the Carters in his honour, at which Sir Robert Fielding, the chancellor of the diocese, with his wife and daughter Anne were present.

> "But Thy most perfect instrument
> In working out a pure intent
> Is man, arrayed for mutual slaughter,
> Yea, Carnage is Thy daughter,"

said Miss Anne Fielding, who had just begun to include Wordsworth among the list of her favourite English poets and had a very good memory.

"An excellent sentiment," said Robin Dale, who had been invited because he was engaged to Anne Fielding, "but how it exactly applies to the Bishop I couldn't say."

The Dean, who had come over to spy out the nakedness of the land, or in other words in the hopes of hearing that the Palace party had made some flagrant omission or commission in the ceremony, said he could well do with some mutual slaughter in the Close, provided the Palace, male and female, were in it and would, though he admitted the enormity of the wish, like nothing better than to knock the Bishop down and jump on him, even if he were hanged for it. It speaks volumes for Colonel Crofts that though he had not as yet publicly declared himself for any party everyone who disliked the Bishop at once felt that he was an ally to be trusted, a man who had the root of the matter in him. Colonel Crofts whose soldier's creed forbade him to speak ill of his commanding officer in any but the most private circles avoided the delicate subject and returning to Anne Fielding's quotation said that he found Wordsworth rather too deep and sometimes wondered if he really knew what he was saying. The talk then wandered off into generalities, but somehow the name stuck to the Bishop and a kind of inner circle who, said Lady Fielding, ought to be called the Society of Dislikers of the Bishop of Barchester, took to calling that prelate the Perfect Instrument, in the certain faith that if his lordship heard the name he would take it at its face value.

"Well, God bless you, Crofts," said the Dean, shaking hands with his old friend. "Let me know if I can help you in any way. Baptisms are a bit awkward sometimes. I have personally christened all my seventeen grandchildren, which is a more ticklish affair than strangers—if one can call a baby a stranger—and I could give you a few hints. There is a particular way of holding a baby when it doubles itself backwards and goes quite stiff and red in the face," said the Dean, picking up a sofa cushion the better to demonstrate his tactics, "which I have never known to fail. As for warming the water in the font, every man must please himself, but babies are far tougher than grown-up people. In fact, Babies Can Take It. Good-bye, my dear fellow, I hope we shall see you in the Close in course of time."

The party then dispersed. Robin Dale and Anne Fielding went to Robin's room to continue the delightful and never-ending subject of how they would improve the Junior House when they were married and Robin was Junior Housemaster, while her parents paid a short call on the Birketts. Colonel Crofts went back to gloat over the Vicarage and talk to Bateman about the little tea-party he was having for his predecessor and his predecessor's aunt, who had stayed on for a few days at the Red Lion from pure friendliness to show their approval of their successor.

It was no good pretending that Southbridge Vicarage was attractive. It was a hideous an example of North Oxford Gothic as the mind of architect could conceive, with quantities of lancet windows ugly to look at and difficult to clean and a kind of Swiss chalet fretwork depending from the various revolting gables and obscuring the light in the top-floor windows, besides the nasty verandah already alluded to which helped to darken the drawing-room, though as the drawing-room faced north into a bank of laurestinus and some horrible and gloomy conifers, such help was hardly necessary. Against these disadvantages it must be owned that the house was well built with good foundations and central heating, and had the great advantage of a back stair. The top floor Colonel Crofts proposed to use as a store-room for a good deal of family furniture, some of which he was keeping for his sons. The first floor contained some good bedrooms where he hoped to see various old friends, and a modern bathroom. On the ground floor there were, besides the large dark drawing-room, a dining-room and a study, both looking south towards the church with a distant prospect of the School. Out of the kitchen premises,now too large for a servantless age, had been made a bedroom for Bateman and a workroom, nominally for the master who was fond of carpentry and all kinds of manual work, but really, as Colonel Crofts well knew, to please Bateman whom the new Vicar frankly admitted to be a better craftsman than himself.

The house had been kept in exquisite order and cleanliness by the ex-Vicar under the eye of his aunt, so that with some unrationed help from the School carpenter and Bateman's all-round skill such distempering and painting as were necessary had quickly been done. The horrid problem of curtains and coverings had not arisen, for Colonel Crofts had large stores of Indian hangings and printed cottons, and within two days from the arrival of his furniture he and Bateman had the house in perfect order. Young Mrs. Propett, so called by courtesy to distinguish her from her aunt-in-law the sexton's wife, a robust grandmother with very sound views on scrubbing and what are called the brights, could come in every morning to help. A very handsome stock of fuel for the kitchen furnace had been taken over from the late occupants. Mr. Brown of the Red Lion whose brother was a coal merchant had said the Colonel needn't worry about another truck load. There was enough wood in the garden to feed the living-room fire for years, and by great good luck the chimneys had all been swept in the late spring.

In fact, no one could have wished or hoped under the present dispensation to be more comfortably installed. The Dean had thoroughly approved. There was no Archdeacon Grantly at Plumstead now to unsettle the new Vicar's mind about throwing out a bow-window, the present Archdeacon being a peaceable man who attended with patience and application to his duties and never lost his temper except when frost stopped the hunt-ing. The only criticism came, as was but natural, from the ex-Vicar who had deprecated the use of cream distemper and paint where he had been used to buff walls and olive-green paintwork. His aunt, if left to herself, might have nourished the same feelings, but the mere fact of her nephew having expressed an opinion was enough to make her wish to give him an auntly setting-down.

"There are some things, Dunstan," she said, "that even you do not understand. You are elephant grey and eau-de-nil, and there it is. These things are beyond our comprehension," to which her nephew had replied rather bitterly that he supposed his aunt's colour was puce, which piece of temper roused in his aunt such a spirit of Christian charity that he wished he had left things alone; for to be forgiven by one's aunt, even if she is younger than oneself, from breakfast-time unto the setting of the sun is not easy to stomach.

When Colonel Crofts, for so most of his friends continued to call him and we should like to count ourselves among the number, got back to the Vicarage he found Bateman in the kitchen, which he kept as neat and shining as the guns he had so tenderly nursed in his artillery days.

"Beg pardon, sir," said Bateman standing to attention, "but there's two things."

"Carry on," said Colonel Crofts.

"There was a lady, sir, a queer sort of lady but quite the lady, sir, brought these bottles," said Bateman, pointing to a bottle of whiskey, a bottle of sherry, a bottle of lime juice, a bottle of rum, and a bottle of gin on the kitchen table, "and she said it was for your housewarming, sir. And the other thing was that there Propett, sir, the sexton."

Colonel Crofts asked what the sexton wanted.

"It's not so much what he does want, sir, as what he doesn't want," said Bateman. "It's them shrubs, sir, outside the drawing-room window and them trees. I happened to pass the remark, sir, that you were thinking of making a clearance there and the old man went right off the handle, sir. He says he planted them trees himself, sir, but it stands to reason they are quite antique," said Bateman, who apparently judged the age of conifers by their size, vaguely thinking of them as slow-growing oaks. "I'd half a mind, sir, to go and cut them trees down at once."

"We'll wait a bit," said Colonel Crofts after a moment's thought. "I don't want to hurt Propett's feelings. He is an old man and probably doesn't like changes. We'll see how things go."

If the Colonel gave an order, it was an order; such was Bateman's simple creed. But this did not prevent his expressing his feelings aloud in the retirement of the scullery and grumbling about people that thought all the timber and all the church belonged to them and the bell too, so that Colonel Crofts had to go to his study and pretend not to hear. Having relieved his feelings by sawing some logs for the fires, Bateman resumed his usual placidity and concentrated on the preparations for the tea-party.

It is idle to deny that Colonel Crofts was disappointed about the trees, for the dismal outlook was abhorrent to him, but he tried very hard to conquer his disappointment and succeeded in making it take a back place. He was also rather exercised about the whisky and the gin. Bateman's description of a lady who was a queer sort of lady but quite the lady would have made it clear that the gift came from Adelina Cottage, without the additional clue that only Miss Hampton could have produced so many bottles, but it was not so much the gift that perplexed him as when to use it. His little tea-party was meant to be a tea-party in the old sense; people sitting in the drawing-room with cups of tea and such cake as the times could afford and presently going home. He had no intention of its dragging on into a cocktail-party, but it was obvious from Bateman's report of the message that Miss Hampton expected the celebration to go on a long time. Colonel Crofts was no killjoy about drink, being very partial to beer with his lunch and some whisky and soda before he went to bed, and in better times would certainly have had good wine for guests who dined with him, but he did not much like the idea of gin. Sherry, yes; though a gentleman should drink it before his dinner, or better still with the soup; not at six o'clock in the afternoon. But gin, no. He could not refuse the bottles and he was afraid that Miss Hampton would think him very ungrateful if he did not produce them after tea, but even at the risk of being thought ungrateful, or even a secret drinker, produce them he would not. Having decided this point in his own mind he set it aside and went to his study to write to his sons in India until the party came.

The party was to be quite small and consist almost entirely of

Southbridgians, the only foreigners being the Noel Mertons if they could get away from their local Flower Show in time. The first to arrive were the ex-Vicar and his aunt, closely followed by the Arbuthnots.

"Now, Colonel Crofts," said the ex-Vicar's aunt, who appeared to have constituted herself hostess in her own right, "we will see over the house and then have tea. As I said to Dunstan, we shall expect to find changes, but we shall greet them in a glad spirit. What did you do with that shelf that always stopped the pantry door opening properly?"

Colonel Crofts said that Bateman had cut a piece of it away and turned the pantry into a kind of gun-room, where fishing-tackle, waders, skis, ski-boots, cricket things and odds and ends could be kept.

"I always told you, Dunstan," said the ex-Vicar's aunt, "that the shelf was a stumbling-block."

"Hardly that, Aunt Monica," said the ex-Vicar. "Only a fool could stumble over a shelf three feet from the ground."

Mrs. Arbuthnot said sotto voce that she didn't think even a fool could do it, but luckily her sister-in-law was the only person to hear her. The ex-Vicar's aunt then began a kind of inquisition into various other fixtures, not in any spirit of criticism of their new owner so much as to put her nephew in the wrong as much as possible, so that the conversation became a kind of indirect duel between them, and Colonel Crofts was relieved when the Birketts and the Carters were announced. The plan of going over the house met with general approval. Colonel Crofts led the way to the top floor. The rooms being unfurnished, if we may use such a word of rooms that are crammed with dust-sheeted furniture and boxes, were not very interesting, but the view from the front rooms looking towards the School was much admired, especially by the Birketts, who could hardly tear themselves away from it.

"It is so lovely," said Mrs. Birkett wistfully, "and it is so dreadful to think that we are leaving. I always thought it would be nice when we retired and Henry could have leisure to see friends and get on with his own work, but now I hate the thought of leaving. I had no idea how fine the School looked from the top bedrooms, if only it weren't for that dreadful woodcarving outside."

"It is hideous, isn't it?" said Colonel Crofts, leaning out of the window and looking at it. "I daresay it would have pleased Mr. Ruskin, but I hate anything that keeps the light out. Hullo, that bit looks as if it had dry-rot."

He pressed upon the wooden frilling. A large piece of it gave way and fell onto a flower-bed.

"Good," said Colonel Crofts. "It is obviously dangerous and I'll get Bateman to take it down."

Kate Carter loudly applauded the resolve, adding that the rooms would make lovely nurseries.

Colonel Crofts said nurseries wouldn't be much use to him at present as his grandchildren were in India, but when his sons next got leave they would probably bring the children and he would be very glad to have Mrs. Carter's advice, which suggestion was so much to Kate's taste that she had arranged both rooms and cut a bathroom off the large room at the back before the party had finished their tour of the top floor.

The first floor was also approved. Colonel Crofts had the large south room and there were two other good bedrooms and a good bathroom.

"You see," said Colonel Crofts, "I would very much like my friends to feel that they could come to the Vicarage for a rest whenever they wished. Bateman would look after them. The house seems large, but everything is so clean here and so easy to manage."

"By the way," said the ex-Vicar, "you'll have to be careful about that woodwork, Crofts. You know this is a Paul's living and they may have something to say if you make alterations. When my Aunt Monica had that window in the small back bedroom enlarged, entirely against my advice I may say, we had some trouble with the Bursar. I just thought I would warn you."

"You may not choose to remember it, Dunstan," said his aunt, "but the affair of the new boiler was very much more serious and entirely your doing."

Her nephew put his long bony hands together, finger-tip to finger-tip and did what we can only describe as a gentle clapping of his fingers expressive of complete abstraction from household affairs and highly galling to his aunt. Mrs. Arbuthnot, fearing a Scene from Clerical Life, said she had met Mr. Fanshawe the Dean of Paul's and thought he seemed very nice and she was sure if one wrote to him about the woodwork he would sympathize. Mr. Birkett and Everard Carter also knew Mr. Fanshawe on his academic side and Mr. Birkett said he would write to him privately. Colonel Crofts thanked him.

"No, I won't," said Mr. Birkett. "You write, Everard. You will be Head here next term and these matters will be in your province, not in mine."

"Nonsense," said Everard, who was used to these rather ostentatious renouncements and if the truth were told was getting a little tired of them. "As long as you are Head you have to do the work. That's only fair."

In this he was strongly supported by both wives so Mr. Birkett, assuming the air of an Elder Statesman recalled to help his country in a crisis, said he supposed he must and was really rather glad to have this loophole, for he considered, though on no grounds at all, that the church and vicarage were part of the patrimony of Southbridge School and under his direct protection.

Colonel Crofts again thanked him.

"But it is really your sister-in-law that I should thank," he said to Miss Arbuthnot as they went downstairs. "She made the original suggestion."

"She would," said Miss Arbuthnot. "She is extraordinarily quick at thinking of useful things and very kind."

"I think," said Colonel Crofts, "that you and she are, if I may

say so, very well matched," a well-turned and heartfelt tribute
which Miss Arbuthnot received calmly but gratefully.

The study was then admired. It was of bad proportions and
the ecclesiastical windows were revolting, but light paint and
distemper and curtains of heavy Indian cotton with rich fantastic designs of architecture mixed up with long-tailed birds and
very improbable beasts of prey gave it a livelier appearance than
it had had since 1849 when the old Vicarage was entirely
remodeled for no reason at all from designs by a pupil of Sir
Gilbert Scott. Mr. Birkett loudly praised the bookshelves, the
ex-Vicar praised and envied the very comfortable writing-table
with a left-hand light, also the comfortable chairs, while Kate
Carter looked at all the photographs on the mantel-piece to see
what the new Vicar's grandchildren were like. Altogether it was
what the whole company considered to be a proper bachelor's
study, combining a certain austerity with practical comfort and
a fender for men to put their feet on. Not that anyone took
Colonel Crofts for a bachelor, but no one had known his wife
and the lapse of years since her death made her husband seem
like an unmarried man, and when he spoke of sons and grandchildren in India it gave the effect of an uncle talking about his
nephews and their children.

"What delightful water-colours," said the ex-Vicar's aunt,
who had been going round the room with a long-handled
eyeglass peering at what was on the walls. "Did you get them in
India? I distinctly recognize the Bay of Jellybolee and the hills of
the Chankly Bore which I once visited on a tour to the Far East."

Colonel Crofts said he had done them at various times and in
various parts of India where he had been stationed. He had
always found, he said, that water-colour drawing was a delightful occupation, even if one never made much progress.

"I have noticed," he added, "that the worse painters are the
happier they seem to be."

"I don't like that remark," said Everard Carter. "If it is true,
you must be very unhappy."

It took Colonel Crofts an appreciable fraction of a moment to catch the compliment, and then he thanked Everard very much and said he must admit that he was on the whole very happy and didn't think very much of his drawings except that they reminded him of the country where he had served. He may have been right, but whatever he thought of the drawings everyone there found pleasure in them. They belonged to the old school of Anglo-Oriental water-colour drawing with meticulous detail to buildings, a conventional treatment of nature, and careful little groups of natives in what were canonically the right spots in the landscape, yet so informed with a loving comprehension of the subject and a very elegant handling of the medium, that they were, even if more topographical than inspired, extremely attractive with a romantic nostalgia of their own.

"Well, that is all of the past," said Colonel Crofts. "My India is thrown to the wolves, and I try not to think about it."

Mr. Birkett added, "By the jackals," from which no one dissented. But a horrid feeling of depression and foreboding had crept into the room, and Bateman's announcement of tea was a welcome change.

The party went into the drawing-room where there was a large wood fire owing to its being July, and very glad they were to sit round it. The room, as in the case of the study, had been much improved by a little redecorating and some handsome curtains which the Arbuthnots praised unreservedly, but for the Birketts and the Carters it was not so easy. The Arbuthnots were newcomers who had not seen the Vicarage before, but the Birketts and the Carters knew it well, and whatever they may have felt it was hardly polite to laud the present incumbent's changes in the presence of his predecessor, so they reserved their admiration for some family portraits in the schools of Raeburn and Lawrence, which looked very handsome on the walls and distracted the eye from the far too high cornice. The tea was excellent and scalding hot, the cakes and sandwiches as good as the peace would allow, and a leisurely satiety descended on the guests.

"I hope," said Colonel Crofts to his predecessor who was in the most comfortable chair from which he could command the dish of hot buttered scones in the fender, "that you do not disapprove my little changes. Everything was left in such excellent condition that there was really very little to do."

The ex-Vicar, wiping a very buttery bit of scone off his mouth, said he was delighted by the appearance of the room. Delighted, he repeated. The drawing-room, he said, had always been his aunt's province and he had not interfered, and he was agreeably surprised to find how pleasant it could look.

His aunt, who was just going to ask for another cup of tea, put her cup down in the saucer with a slight but defiant clash and said that as she had had to furnish the drawing-room from the household belongings of his mother she could not be accountable for its taste, even if his mother was her eldest sister by her poor father's first marriage. This challenge frightened the audience a good deal, but her nephew, softened by tea and the extra butter which Bateman always managed to get in the village, merely replied that whatever his Aunt Monica might think of his mother's taste, he was thankful, devoutly thankful, that they had been spared the peacock-feather fans and blue china of his grandfather's second wife and might he ask for a third cup of tea. Everyone came to the rescue with the first remark that came into their hearts and before they knew where they were they were all back at food and rationing again, and as the tension eased the talk fell into local matters and Colonel Crofts was glad to glean from the Birketts and the Carters various sidelights on his parish that would be very useful to him.

"Admiral Phelps, your churchwarden, is an excellent fellow," said Mr. Birkett, "and kept the whole village going during the war. He commanded the Home Guard and pretty well everything else. Brown of the Red Lion is the other churchwarden, an excellent man too. In fact they are an extremely nice lot of people in Southbridge, and now the Mixo-Lydians have all gone back we can breathe again."

The ex-Vicar's aunt who had quite recovered herself, said she wished all the other foreigners would go home too.

"Oh, the Mixo-Lydians haven't gone back to Mixo-Lydia," said Mrs. Birkett, "only to London, where my niece who lives in Kensington says they are universally loathed. Most of them are applying for naturalization," to which Everard Carter answered that he sometimes thought it was his duty, and never, he said, would duty have been more gladly performed, to write to the Home Secretary every day protesting, simply as a matter of routine, against every application for naturalization that appeared in *The Times*.

"I'm a bit rusty in my classics," said Colonel Crofts, "but there is something in one of the Roman poets about the Orontes flowing into the Tiber which strikes me as peculiarly applicable to the present times."

Mr. Birkett said he thought it was Juvenal, but could not at the moment lay his hand on it.

"Well, it is no use," said Mrs. Birkett stoutly, "I don't like foreigners and I am quite sure that none of them like us except to eat our food and cheat in the queues. I don't know."

And so the talk went on and the summer day outside looked like frozen steel and no one wanted to be the first to leave the warm fire. Presently there was a sound in the hall and Bateman announced, "Admiral Phelps, sir, and Mrs. Phelps and Miss Phelps," and in came a very large woman with a scarf tied round her reddish-grey hair, a younger and very large woman closely resembling her mother, and a small, spare, dry-faced man.

"Well, we seem to be intruders," said Mrs. Phelps, shaking her host's hand vigorously, "but I said to my husband we must really go and call upon the new Vicar. And this is my daughter Margot. Now, don't have fresh tea, because we had ours before we came. It's quite like old times to find you here," she added, shaking the ex-Vicar and his aunt by the hand almost more violently than they could bear.

"Except," said the ex-Vicar, "for the wonderful improvement our friend has made in this room. Indeed, I may say in all the house."

Mrs. Birkett, fearing more trouble between aunt and nephew, hastily introduced the Arbuthnots who were warmly welcomed by the Phelps family and pressed to join or subscribe to the British Legion, the Boy Scouts, the Girl Guides, the Village Institute, the District Nursing Association, the Goat-Keepers' Society, the Royal Apiarian Society, the Additional Curates' Fund, the Cow-Keepers' Union, the Small Poultry-Keepers' Society, the National Rabbit Club, the Empire Society, the Cottage Hospital, the Navy League and five or six other societies, whose united subscriptions, so Everard Carter subsequently calculated, would amount to about thirty pounds a year, a sum which neither of them could well afford. Luckily Mrs. Arbuthnot realized that these invitations were on the whole only a token of good will, so she made an answer of a non-committal nature and got on very well.

Meanwhile Colonel Crofts found himself in an awkward situation. Tea was over. More tea, it is true, could be made so long as there was a kettle to boil, but cakes and scones there were none. An Admiral and his family ought to be suitably enter-tained and there was nothing but beer in the house, for Colonel Crofts in his agitation had quite forgotten Miss Hampton's bottles. He looked for Bateman but his servant, having cleared away the tea-things with incredible rapidity, had left the room. He toyed for a moment with the idea of taking them all to the Red Lion, decided this would be quite unsuitable especially as the Noel Mertons might yet be coming and was about to despair when more sounds were heard in the hall and in came the Mertons and Mr. Wickham, followed by Bateman carrying a large tray upon which were glasses, a syphon, and all Miss Hampton's bottles.

"All correct, sir, I hope," said Bateman to his master, to which

Colonel Crofts gratefully answered that it was quite correct and offered hospitality to the party.

"We're awfully sorry, but we couldn't get here any sooner because there was a raffle and we had to stay to see if we'd won," said Lydia, comprehending everyone in her announcement. "It was a bottle of pre-war Baccardi and of course Mr. Wickham won it, but Noel and I had taken a lot of tickets too so he gave it to us and we all thought we'd better give it to you as it's your first party."

Mr. Wickham showed Colonel Crofts the rum, and moved by some mysterious power went straight to the table where the bottles were and buried himself with their contents.

"You don't mind my doing this, I hope, sir," he said to his reverend host.

Colonel Crofts said not in the least. He liked a glass of sherry before dinner, he said, but he had never been able to acquire the taste for cocktails.

"A word in season," said Mr. Wickham, and quietly put the bottle of sherry behind a chair in a corner of the room. "You keep it for yourself, sir. Anything will do for these people. I've got a pre-war sherry at home, three bottles to be exact. If you will give me the pleasure of your company one evening, sir, we'll knock them back."

Colonel Crofts thanked Mr. Wickham, accepted the invitation, but begged that only one bottle should be opened as far as he was concerned.

"And how is Colin?" Mrs. Arbuthnot asked Noel.

"Nicely, thank you, as this leaves me at present," said Noel. "At least I should say as he left us at the Flower Show. He went back to Winter Overcotes with Susan Dean, and I very meanly didn't tell him that we were coming to Southbridge because I wanted to talk to you myself."

Mrs. Arbuthnot laughed and said she was very fond of Colin, but he did rather expect to have one to himself all the time.

"I am very fond of him," said Noel. "But, if you will allow me to open my heart to you, I find him distinctly less amusing since you and your sister came to Southbridge. He becomes monotonous."

"It's a dreadful thing to say," said Mrs. Arbuthnot, looking at the floor and then looking up at Noel without raising her head, "but I do sometimes feel the same. So many of them get like that. It passes of course, but it can be rather boring while it lasts."

At this frank avowal she raised her head and looked Noel straight in the eyes and they both laughed, with a delightful feeling of being co-conspirators.

"I don't somehow think you would be monotonous," she said.

"If I were in love with you, do you mean?" asked Noel.

"Poor Colin," said Mrs. Arbuthnot with a stage sigh.

"I would hate you to say, 'Poor Noel' like that," he answered.

Mrs. Arbuthnot laughed again and said she didn't think she would have to and how were the children. So the talk fell into commonplaces, but while Noel felt as if he had drunk a small and perfect champagne cocktail, Mrs. Arbuthnot had merely followed her nature and was entirely unaffected. She was also beginning to feel that she had been long enough at the party, but she saw her sister-in-law with Colonel Crofts and Mr. Wickham and thought it would be a shame to interrupt Effie's talk, so she turned to Kate Carter and left Noel to his own devices.

"Mr. Wickham," said Miss Arbuthnot, who had put her last disagreement with that gentleman quite out of her mind, "was in India when he was in the navy and knows a lot about Indian birds."

"I'm not much good at birds myself," said Colonel Crofts, "but there was a fellow out there that painted them beautifully. After my time it was, but my sons sent me one of two of his paintings. I've hung one here, over the little bureau," he said, tilting a reading-lamp so that the light fell on it.

It was indeed a charming drawing, rather stylized, but faithful to nature, with a sympathetic feeling for the glitter of a bird's eye, the rounded harness of its shoulders, the grip of its feet upon the twig, and the delicate shading of its feathers.

"It's the whisky-soda bird," said Colonel Crofts. "You know it, Miss Arbuthnot. You showed me the scar where one bit you. I'd like to know the artist. The initials are F. E. A.; just there in the corner. What do you think of it, Wickham?"

"I knew you were a dark horse, but I never knew you were as dark as that," said Mr. Wickham to Miss Arbuthnot. Their host had just turned off the light and for a moment he could not see her face.

"It was only for fun," said Miss Arbuthnot. "I used to do them when I was up country with Fred, before he married. They went quite well at regimental fetes."

"I don't understand," said Colonel Crofts. "Who *is* F.E.A.?"

"I'm so sorry," said Miss Arbuthnot apologetically, "but I am. At least those are my initials. But it was only for fun. Not real pictures like yours."

"Look here, Miss Arbuthnot," said Mr. Wickham. "I know a publisher called Johns, he's a kind of cousin of mine. If he saw those pictures he'd go mad."

Miss Arbuthnot asked why, rather nervous in case she had unwittingly infringed someone's copyright or something of the sort by selling signed drawings of birds.

"He's doing a whacking great series of books about natural history with illustrations. Awful rubbish they are," said Mr. Wickham with the frankness of a relative, "only fit for Christmas presents. But he pays well and he's looking for someone who will do birds. Not geese flying with their legs hanging down, but proper birds," said Mr. Wickham, who being a sailor himself had a low opinion of water-fowl. "Birds that hop about and perch on branches. You're the man, Miss Arbuthnot." And so infectious was his enthusiasm that Miss Arbuthnot allowed herself to be persuaded into a lunch with Mr. Wickham in London, where she and her sister-in-law were going for a few days on business before long, to meet Mr. Johns.

It was now past six o'clock and the party was breaking up, surprised at the swiftness with which the time had passed. Colonel Crofts vaguely wondered why Miss Hampton and Miss Bent had not turned up, and was also vaguely relieved, for though they were both excellent fellows he did not wish to see too much of them; being indeed a little frightened, as even a holder of His Majesty's commission might well be, of their loud hospitality and their familiarity with the Red Lion, for Colonel Crofts was nearer sixty than fifty and had been brought up among an older generation.

In the hall Mrs. Birkett was the first to say good-bye, again almost in tears when she spoke of the view of the School from the top-floor bedroom.

"I you will allow me," said Colonel Crofts, "I should like to try my hand at a water-colour drawing of that view. The English landscape is very difficult from the Indian, but as I shall pass the rest of my life in England I may as well get used to it. I can't hope to do justice to your School, but if the result is at all pleasing to you I should ask you to accept it as a small thank-offering for your kindness and your husband's. I assure you I have felt I was among friends from the first day I came here."

The Birketts thanked him warmly for his thought and said they would like of all things to have such a remembrance from a friend, and then they and the Carters left. Colonel Crofts took the other guests round the garden to see what improvements he proposed to make and so back again to the front gate, where they met Miss Hampton and Miss Bent dragging the unwilling Gallant on his lead.

"Duty," said Miss Hampton. "Bent and I were coming to you, but Bent said we ought to go to the Red Lion first. Quite right. One mustn't let the side down, and Brown counts on us. So does Eileen. So we did our duty by the Red Lion and came on to pay our respects."

Colonel Crofts could not but ask the ladies to come into the house. The ex-Vicar and his aunt said they would come with them, but the Arbuthnots and the Northbridge party took their leave. Mrs. Arbuthnot said she and her sister would enjoy the service next day all the more for knowing that Colonel Crofts was so comfortable in the Vicarage, with which her sister-in-law heartily concurred, and the new incumbent, though he could hardly consider this point of view as strictly religious, was much touched by it.

The Phelpses also said good-bye, the Admiral expressing the pleasure it would be to serve as churchwarden under a Vicar with such a distinguished record.

"I really ought to be serving under you, Admiral," said Colonel Crofts. "A full Colonel is about equal to a naval Captain as far as I remember. I know I can rely on your help, because I shan't quite know my way about at first."

The Admiral assured him of his support.

"I sometimes envy you fellows," he said in a low voice. "When you have taken the service for so many years you miss it. I don't mean to be irreverent, but I think I can do it as well as a lot of these young men we get now."

Colonel Crofts said he believed it would be quite in order if he asked the Admiral to preach a lay sermon at some future date, which sent the Admiral away speechless with pleasure, and left the new Vicar reflecting how much better was the unqualified sailor than a possible Mr. Parkinson with a theological degree.

"I have to thank you," said Colonel Crofts to Miss Hampton as they went back to the house, "for your very kind present. It was most generous and so much appreciated by my guests. I had no idea they would stay so long and when Admiral and Mrs. Phelps and their daughter came I felt very much embarrassed. I had forgotten for the moment about your gift, but my man, who is an excellent servant, brought the drinks in at once. You will have a drink, I hope," he said, opening the drawing-room door for the guests to pass.

"Not for me," said the ex-Vicar's aunt, who had never been very fond of Miss Hampton, finding her too apt to lay down the law, which she considered her own prerogative as a kind of vice-regent for her nephew, and hoping that her refusal would be understood as a criticism of any beverage supplied by Miss Hampton.

"Now, dear man," said Miss Hampton, a form of address which terrified Colonel Crofts, soldier though he was, "let us understand one another. My father was a parson. He liked his glass of wine, but only at meals. He'd have liked you. You're his sort," said Miss Hampton, giving Colonel Crofts a friendly blow on the back. "Gentleman. I'm not like my father. Put gin or whisky or rum down at any time. So does Bent. You wouldn't think it to look at her, but she does."

And indeed Miss Bent, in a shapeless dress apparently made of coarse oatmeal with some raffia embroidery at the neck and waist, an old panama hat with a kind of green puggaree floating from it, and clanking with wooden beads, was the last person an outsider would have suspected of steady and determined habits of drink.

"But that's all wrong for you," Miss Hampton continued. "Bent and I wanted to give you a present for the housewarming, but we aren't coming to drink at the Vicarage. Tea with you, if you'll ask us. Drink, no. I'm a staunch churchwoman. Can't stand those monkey tricks; bells and what not. I like your service. Got to keep the standard up nowadays. Come on, Bent. Where's Gallant?"

Gallant was nowhere to be seen. Miss Hampton said with a loud and terrifying laugh that he had probably gone back to the Red Lion where Mr. Brown was in the habit of saving a bone for him. But just as she and Miss Bent were saying good-bye the ex-Vicar, who had been listening to the foregoing conversation with the tolerance of one who was no longer responsible for anything that happened in the Vicarage, suddenly remarked, "Something has just occurred to me, Crofts."

Everyone looked anxiously to see if he had sprained his ankle or broken a blood vessel, or even come out in spots.

"It is a most extraordinary thing that I had not thought of it before," the ex-Vicar continued. "Have you been into the second wine-cellar, Crofts?"

Colonel Crofts said he only had a few bottles of claret which he kept in the old pantry.

"Come on, then," said the ex-Vicar, suddenly assuming command of the whole party. "I believe I am right. You haven't the keys, have you?"

"What keys?" said Colonel Crofts, wondering if his predecessor had gone mad.

"The cellar keys. I quite forgot them when we left. They used to hang on a nail over the little fireplace in the pantry. Allow me."

He stalked out of the room, followed by the rest of the party who were by now consumed with curiosity, and went straight to the pantry where Bateman was making Gallant beg for some scraps of cold rabbit.

"There he is, a naughty boy," said Miss Bent. "Here! Gallant! Gallant!"

"He won't come, miss, not till he's finished the rabbit," said Bateman standing smartly to attention. "Clever little dog, that, miss."

"Have you a torch?" said the ex-Vicar, who had taken two keys from a nail above the fireplace."

"Yes, sir, but the battery's run out," said Bateman. "Would a candle do?"

From a cupboard delightfully stocked with every useful odd and end that a household could require, he took a flat candlestick with a stump of candle in it, lighted the candle and handed the candlestick to the ex-Vicar who strode off into the back-kitchen premises saying, "Come on." In one corner of the room was a door which he unlocked.

"I thought it was a cupboard," said Colonel Crofts, "and hadn't tried to open it yet. We haven't had much time to explore."

But his predecessor was already half-way down a steep flight of stone stairs. Colonel Crofts stood aside for the ladies to pass.

"I'm terrified of cellars," said Miss Hampton unexpectedly. "Always was. It's a nasty complex and I've done my best to get over it, but I can't. You go, Bent."

"I am always telling Hampton it isn't a complex," said Miss Bent, whose body was by now invisible so that she looked like the Norn in the *Rheingold*. "It is simply a manifestation. There isn't a complex in her. She wouldn't stand any nonsense from a complex. You'd better go and talk to Colonel Croft's man, Hampton. You might get some material."

With which words her head followed her legs and body down the stairs and the ex-Vicar's aunt and Colonel Crofts came after. At the bottom of the stairs was a large cellar, extending under most of the house, empty except for some wine-bins without any bottles in them, a mangle, two chairs without any seats, and a tall, fluted mahogany pillar with a hideous china bowl on it. The ex-Vicar, ignoring these vanities, went straight across the cellar, unlocked a second door and held the candle aloft to light the interior. It was a small, narrow room with a grating high in the wall at the far end and racks on each side in which were quietly reposing a number of bottles.

"They belonged to the man before me," said the ex-Vicar. "I bought them from him at a valuation when I came here because he had nowhere to put them. Port, claret, sherry," he added, moving the candle among the various bins.

"But these are extremely valuable now," said Colonel Crofts, who had been reverently examining the labels on the bins. "I am so glad you remembered them."

The ex-Vicar said he only drank Marsala by his doctor's orders and his aunt was a teetotaler.

"I wish Hampton had come down," said Miss Bent in a tearful voice. "It would have reminded her of her father. If a bottle was in the least corked he used to empty it out of the window."

Colonel Crofts expressed his admiration of this truly Roman fortitude, though he confessed that he could not quite rise to it.

"Well, Dunstan," said the ex-Vicar's aunt, "all I can say is you might have thought of it before, when we were moving the furniture. But you would choose a Tuesday, though I told you Tuesday is definitely not your colour. We'd better take them upstairs and see about having them sent by rail."

At these awful words both the clergyman uttered an exclamation partly of protest, partly of despair at the female sex in general.

"Dear woman," said Miss Bent, suddenly inspired with her friend's mannerisms as well as her courage, "you're talking nonsense. You can't move bottles about like that. Ruin the whole lot."

"Miss Bent is perfectly correct, Aunt Monica," said the ex-Vicar. "We had better get back as the candle has nearly burned itself out. I will lock up behind you. I'll tell you what, Crofts," he continued, ignoring the ladies entirely, "if you like to take it over, I'll sell it for what I gave."

Colonel Crofts, overcome by this generosity, said it wouldn't be fair.

"It will suit me very well," said the ex-Vicar, waving the objection aside. "As I said, I only drink Marsala and to move that wine would be worse than a crime, it would be very silly," which last words were so obviously directed at his aunt that Colonel Crofts hurried up the stairs lest an explosion might trap them all.

The door was then locked, the keys hung on their nail, and so masterful was the ex-Vicar that before he knew where he was Colonel Crofts had written a cheque and shaken hands with his predecessor.

"Well, God bless you," said the ex-Vicar with a humanity of which Colonel Crofts had hardly thought him capable and which sat well upon his tall bony figure and gaunt face. "May you have a long and happy life here. Come along, Aunt Monica."

His aunt, much shaken by recent events, but bearing no grudge against Colonel Crofts whom she generously recognized to be innocent of any of the trouble, wished him every happiness.

"Your choice is in perfect accord with the house," were her parting words. "If blue comes into it, all will be well. Have a stout heart. God bless you."

She hurried after her nephew and overtook him just outside the gate.

"You are a fool, Dunstan," she said, suddenly impelled after the manner of women to discharge upon the nearest person the annoyance that had been accumulating.

"Yes, Aunt Monica," said her nephew, adding quite audibly, though as if to himself, "and so are you."

But in spite of their differences aunt and nephew quite understood each other. The rest of the walk to the Red Lion was accomplished in silence, the subject of the wine was not mentioned, and next day they left Southbridge on perfectly amicable terms to take up their duties with the Stiffnecked Clergy.

Colonel Crofts then rescued Miss Hampton and Gallant from the pantry, and the ladies went back to Adelina.

"Beg your pardon, sir," said Bateman, "but when I was tidying the drawing-room I found a bottle of sherry in the corner, behind the big chair. Seems as if someone had put it there, sir."

Colonel Crofts, despairing of an adequate truthful explanation, said one of the guests had brought it as a present and told his servant about the wine in the far cellar. At this good news Bateman's eyes shone, for though he considered wine a nasty wishy-washy drink, vastly preferring beer, he had been at one time a mess-waiter and knew what gentlemen ought to drink.

"Nice little dog that is, sir," said Bateman. "Begged for his rabbit like a gentleman. The lady's very nice too, sir. She asked me some funny questions. But what I say is, there's funny people wherever you go, sir, and I think we'll do very nicely here, sir."

Colonel Croft commended Bateman's handling of the party

and went back to the drawing-room, which now looked as if it had never been used, with every chair and table standing to attention. Colonel Crofts walked slowly towards the bureau, took down the picture of the stengah and carried it to the window to get some daylight for though it was only half-past five by real time, the verandah and the shrubs and trees made the room very dark. So F. E. A. was Miss Arbuthnot. A very nice, a very gifted woman. Some people might call her plain, with her heavy face and her rather ungraceful body, but there was something very attractive about her, a kind of steadfastness and simplicity much to the old soldier's taste. He walked back to the bureau, hesitated, and then went to his study, still carrying the picture. Between the view of the Bay of Jellybolee and the prospect of the hills of the Chankly Bore there was a space which, in Colonel Croft's opinion, would look better filled. He got a hammer and a nail from the pantry, carefully measured a middle point between the pictures, neatly drove in the nail, hung the picture and put the hammer back in its place. Then he returned to the study, inspected his work with a gunner's eye for accuracy and rang the bell.

"Sir," said Bateman, appearing almost at once.

"I want you to open that bottle of sherry," said Colonel Crofts, "and bring it here. And a glass."

In a few minutes the bottle and the glass were on a tray beside him. Bateman went back to the kitchen to finish preparing the evening meal. Colonel Crofts slowly drank his sherry and looked at the drawing of the stengah.

"Just what is wanted in a house," he said half-aloud. But to what exactly he was referring, we are unable to say.

Next day, which was Sunday, the Birketts had a tea-party. This gathering was ostensibly a kind of private farewell to some friends before the great final farewell on Speech Day, but everyone recognized that its true end was to discuss the new Vicar. The only drawback to this plan was the Vicar himself could not be asked, but every good deed entails some kind of sacrifice. Mrs. Morland, the well-known novelist, had driven over from High Rising to lunch with the Birketts and talk abut old times, for during the first months of the war she had lived with them as a kind of honorary or supernumerary secretary and made herself extremely useful, being an intelligent and orderly creature in everything except her own personal appearance. With the Birketts she had relived, during and after lunch, the winter of 1939–40 when the Hosiers' Boys' Foundation School had been evacuated to Southbridge and all creeds and classes had united in a gallant and most exhausting effort to understand each other's point of view, with practically no result at all, though much good feeling.

"It was all as useless as the war itself," said Mr. Birkett, who had given himself one of his rare Sunday afternoons off to talk with Mrs. Morland. "We all managed to rub along very well, but the Hosiers were as glad to leave us as we were to get rid of them. You know, Laura, that our Governors, some of whom are quite unmitigated asses, have offered a free place to an approved Hosiers' boy, tenable for four years, which means that in four years from now we shall have four Hosiers here permanently, or rather," added Mr. Birkett, who took a masochistic pleasure in reminding himself that his days as a Head were numbered, "Everard will have them."

Mrs. Morland asked what approved meant exactly.

"It means," said Mr. Birkett, "that the boys must have reached a certain scholastic level, which I may say as far as the exact sciences are concerned will be a high one. As a matter of fact and in strict confidence it means that I, or rather Everard, will have the final decision."

Mrs. Morland said that seemed a very good plan.

"It is," said Mr. Birkett with grim satisfaction. "If we don't like them—I mean if Everard doesn't like them—we shall turn them down. We have also," he said with modest pride, "insisted on a Latin paper. This paper, which any boy in our Junior School

could do, especially since we got rid of a quite dreadful female
we were forced to have as a stopgap last year during which time
she did a great deal of harm, will not count as far as marks go."

He paused meaningly. Mrs. Morland asked why.

"For a very obvious reason, Laura," said Mr. Birkett, justly
irritated by such ignorance. "If we insisted on marking the Latin
paper, the Hosiers would have reasonable cause for annoyance. I
myself, or rather Everard, would be extremely annoyed if, though
this is a supposititious case which would never arise, any boy of ours
applying for entrance to the Hosiers' School were to be marked on
Sinister Economics."

Mrs. Morland asked what they were; specifically, she added,
feeling rather puffed up by her use of the word.

"Left, leftist, red, whatever filthy jargon you like," said Mr.
Birkett impatiently. "I need hardly tell you, Laura, that two
things are and will I hope remain essential in candidates for
Southbridge School. That we should consider a boy suitable,
and that he should at least have heard of mensa. For as to these
new-fangled grammars, these Latin-Without-Tears, these pre-
digested pap for popinjays," said Mr. Birkett, feeding his anger
by alliteration, though inwardly sensible that popinjay was not
except for its initial letter the word he wanted, "which have, I
believe, substituted such words as rosa or puella as archetypes of
the first declension, they make me sick. Mensa is the very rock,
the foundations of the Latin Grammar, even as St. Peter was the
Christian Church. What was I saying? Oh, yes. On this paper,
and on our, or I should say Everard's, personal impression of the
boy he will stand or fall and I think it probable, Laura, that we
shall get some very good boys by this method. Do you remember
a very nice boy called Manners the winter you were here? His
father was a greengrocer and furniture remover in the Isle of
Dogs. We gave him a free place here, after a good deal of trouble
with his parents, and he won an open scholarship in history for
Lazarus."

Mrs. Morland asked what the difficulty with the parents w

"A curious point of honour," said Mr. Birkett. "They had a rooted objection to their boy becoming what they called a charity-boy. As a matter of fact he had also taken a State scholarship which would have seen him through the Hosiers' School, but this they considered as their lawful right, not as charity. I had an interview with them and explained that the original Grammar School here was founded by a Barchester merchant who had done very well during the Reformation out of the spoils of Brandon Abbey, where that hideous house is now, which so convinced them that the whole tendency of the School was anti-clerical that they quite came round. I then," said Mr. Birkett, savouring old emotion in tranquillity, "had the pleasure of inviting them for the night on Foundation Day, with a full-dress service in the Chapel and the Dean—not, thank God, the Bishop—officiating. I gave them the choir seats and it all worked very well."

"It is rather like Tony," said Mrs. Morland, whose thoughts had been rambling off on their own lines, as all our thoughts are apt to do when our friends tell us interesting things about themselves, "when he did his exam for the Tape and Sealing-wax Office. The only thing they seemed to mind about was arithmetic, which is all rubbish and anyone can do it only they teach it all upside-down now so that it doesn't make sense," said Mrs. Morland, proudly conscious of having scored a point. "And then they interviewed him and asked him what he thought of George Knox's books, which I suppose they thought was General Knowledge or Psycho-analysis or something," said Mrs. Morland scornfully, "so he said he knew George, and the woman who was interviewing him had once been a secretary of George's, so they got on splendidly and Tony passed very well."

"The *woman*?" asked Mr. Birkett incredulously.

"I know," said Mrs. Morland. "And I really don't know what use it is for young men to come back from the war if they are to be examined by women, though I must say she was the youngest daughter of a clergyman and had worked very well for George till she got into Government employ."

Mr. Birkett, putting aside such paltering with the right, said his father had, thank God, got into the Board of Tape and Sealing-wax as it was then on a nomination from the Head of his college who had been at Eton with the Minister for Red Tape.

"Well, Henry, it all comes to much the same thing," said Mrs. Morland. "Your father was nominated because his tutor knew a Minister and Tony got in top of the list because the woman who interviewed him knew George Knox. But I daresay it all comes to the same in the end."

Mr. Birkett said with a kind of grim deference that Laura had a remarkable gift for seeing facts as facts.

"Oh, do you think so?" said Mrs. Morland blushing, for in spite of her successful books she continued to have no opinion of herself whatsoever. "I expect it's only that I talk aloud inside myself a great deal about things and I'm always writing them in my head, so I suppose I have to know what I'm thinking about. Not that I mean that in the least," she added, nervously pushing a tortoiseshell pin back into her unfashionable hair, "but it's never any use trying to explain anything to anybody."

Mr. Birkett said he wished the present Government, the Press and the B.B.C. and practically everyone in any kind of power or office would realize this great truth, and then the Carters came in; rather to his relief, for fond as he was of Mrs. Morland, her snipe-flights always left him with a giddy sensation.

Mrs. Birkett welcomed the Carters warmly and said Henry had been telling Laura about the scholarships for the Hosiers' boys.

"A very good thing," said Everard, "and we'll get some excellent boys as long as the Governors don't interfere. But what do you think has happened at Barchester High School?"

As everyone present and indeed pretty well everyone everywhere with the exception of the Palace disliked Miss Pettinger the Headmistress excessively, they were all attention, hopeful of evil tidings.

"I got this from Dr. Sparling," said Everard, alluding to the eminent and sensible Headmistress of the Hosiers' Girls' Foundation School, evacuated during the war first to Barchester and then to Harefield where Miss Sparling, for she had not yet been given her honorary doctorate, had plighted her troth to Mr. Carton, a distinguished fellow of Paul's. "The Barsetshire branch of the Classical Association gave her a dinner in honour of her retirement this month and her marriage with Carton, which will be in August. Miss Pettinger, one supposes by the wish of her Governors, had approached Dr. Sparling on the subject of an exchange of girls between the two schools, and Dr. Sparling, acting on the advice of the Hosiers' Company and on her own strong feelings, managed to turn the whole thing down. Of course she gave some very good reason for public edification, but she tells me that though most of Miss Pettinger's girls are very nice personally and just the type she would like, she couldn't reconcile it with her duty to the Hosiers' Girls' School to take them, as it would set the whole school back in its work by at least a year."

There was a brief silence of pleasurable horror, broken by Mr. Birkett, who said he had always liked and admired Dr. Sparling and would now give her an even more handsome wedding present than he had intended.

"What is it, Henry?" his wife asked. "When last I heard from you it was to be Lemoineau's new book about François Boucher with the lovely illustrations, because you wanted to look at it yourself first."

"Peace, woman," said Mr. Birkett, looking slightly abashed. "I am going to give the future Mrs. Carton all Laura's books, properly bound," at which declaration Mrs. Morland went perfectly crimson and two hairpins fell out of her with sheer emotion. "I happened to drop in at the sale of that dreadful old Mr. Holt's books at Sotheby's where I found a complete set. I had meant to keep them for myself, but they could not be better bestowed."

Most of those present had never heard of Mr. Holt, though the Leslie family and old Lady Norton had known far too much about that very selfish old bore who invited himself from house to house to give advice about gardens and be very rude to young people, governesses, secretaries and other defenceless orders.

"Old Lord Pomfret would never have him at the Towers," said Mr. Birkett, "and quite right too. Will you add to the value of the books by autographing them, my dear Laura?" he added, in high good humour over Everard's story.

It is possible that Mrs. Morland would have burst with over-excitement had not Robin Dale come in, closely followed by the Arbuthnots and the two masters who lived in Wiple Terrace. Conversation became general. And when we say general, we would like it to be understood that it was exclusively about the School, except when it divagated into the subject of food and the iniquity of the present system of bread rationing; on which last subject all the ladies spoke at once, with a ground bass from the masters in Wiple Terrace who were bachelors and either did their own shopping or let their daily woman do it for them, both systems being highly unsatisfactory.

"I saw in the *Barchester Chronicle*," said the master from Louisa, "that all the Bugs or Buxes, or whatever they are, that we haven't used are to be changed into points. I suppose it's a good idea."

"I don't see why you should suppose so, Mr. Feeder," said Kate Carter. "Nothing They have done to us yet has been a good idea."

This spirited attack from the gentle Mrs. Carter took the master from Louisa by surprise and he said he thought the idea was that everyone would get a fair cut at everything, upon which every lady present explained, each at the top of her individual voice, her own peculiar difficulties and wrongs.

"You've put your foot in it all right, Feeder," said the master from Maria.

"What I cannot nor do not understand," said Mrs. Morland in her deepest and most impressive voice, "is why those extraordinary letters."

The master from Maria, a very nice young man recently demobilized, speaking the strange jargon of his contemporaries, said what did Mrs. Morland mean letters.

"I am so sorry," said Mrs. Morland, who liked young men and always wished to be kind to them, "I didn't explain properly, but when I think of a thing and see it in a kind of way in front of me I feel as if everyone else did too," which lucid explanation frightened the master from Maria a good deal and gave Mr. Feeder an opportunity to say he wasn't the only one with big feet.

"My dear Laura," said Mr. Birkett, "you are perfectly capable of explaining what you mean."

"Am I?" said Mrs. Morland, a good deal surprised by this unexpected tribute. "I only meant, why K for soap?"

Mr. Birkett raised his eyes to heaven in protest at women.

"I know what you mean," said Mrs. Birkett. "They put T on the page for tea, so K ought to stand for something beginning with K."

A number of frivolous suggestions such as Kedgeree, Kromeskies and Kissing-crust were put forward.

"No. What They ought to do is to put S for soap," said Mrs. Arbuthnot.

Everyone looked at her with respect and there was a general feeling that she had paid her footing and could now be accepted into the inner circles of the School.

"I suppose," said Mr. Feeder, "that They think the L on the first bread-page stands for Loaf. Fools!"

The master from Maria, burning to make good the ground he had lost, said the M on that next page was probably meant for Muffin, which went down well.

"And then," said Kate, who as the Senior Housemaster's wife held a kind of precedence where food was concerned, "there is a nasty bit called G, right away in the end, after the chocolate."

"Chocolates!" said Robin Dale. "I've been trying to cash my sweet ration for the last fortnight so that I could give it to Anne, and they are out of plain chocolate everywhere."

"And what They think G means," said Kate, kindly but firmly ignoring his divagation, "no one knows. There isn't any kind of bread beginning with G."

"It means absolutely nothing," said the master from Maria suddenly. "There are G's all over those ration books in all sorts of extraordinary places. It would have been much clearer if They had put X. Then we'd have known the whole was an unknown quantity and that They don't know any more about it than we do."

"A good point, Traill," said Mr. Birkett approvingly.

Mr. Feeder from Louisa, returning to his original remark, said that if we were able to change superfluous bread coupons for ordinary points we would get more groceries— "and things," he added nervously, feeling the opinion of the whole room against him.

"Things, doubtless," said Mrs. Morland coldly. "It may be better in Southbridge, but at High Rising practically all we can get on points now is pilchards."

Mrs. Arbuthnot reported that although the Southbridge General Store had no matches, cornflour, custard powder, frying-crumbs, golden syrup, black treacle or biscuits, they had at least a thousand bottles of salad-dressing. Mr. Traill, who sometimes did his shopping in Barchester, said his experience had been much the same, except that instead of pilchards or salad-dressing the whole grocery side of the Barchester Co-op. had been seething with dehydrated mashed potatoes in tins. Filthy stuff, he added. His charwoman had given them to him once, but never again. Kate, who could not bear unkindness to any object, animate or inanimate, said she had heard they were quite good if carefully treated.

Mr. Feeder said if they were as good as all that, why not send them to the Germans who seemed to be getting most of our food anyway, and then wished he hadn't, for his words might seem like calculated rudeness to that nice Mrs. Carter. But Kate, who had very proper feelings about our enemies, said it would really be a kindness to everyone to send them to the Germans as they were so horrid; which words, owing to the ambiguous nature of English pronouns and construction generally, left everyone in doubt as to whether she meant the Germans or the mashed potatoes.

Mrs. Birkett, pouring out tea, now gave a lead to her guests on the subject which was really foremost in their minds by saying that she and Henry had been to tea at the Vicarage and how nice Colonel Crofts had made it, and appealed to her husband to confirm this statement.

"Nothing can improve the proportions of the rooms," said Mr. Birkett, "but Crofts has made a first-rate job with poor material. I feel that Southbridge will be very lucky to have him. So shall we, Smith," he added to the School Chaplain, better known as Holy Joe, who had just come in.

"Sorry to be late, Mrs. Birkett," said the Chaplain sitting down. "Thanks. Just a drop more milk if you can spare it, my little weakness you know. Can you really spare it? Thanks, thanks. It was a boy with a conscience: Leslie Major. One sometimes wishes they wouldn't have consciences, especially on the Day of Rest, and I was just in the middle of a frightfully good thriller."

Several people asked its name.

"*Without my Bones,*" said the Chaplain. "Two demobilized officers down on their luck break into an empty prefabricated house and find six corpses from which all the bones have been removed. There's an awful good description for what they looked like, pretty gruesome. At first they think it's been done by a doctor, but another demobbed man who comes in turns out to be a detective in disguise and he is on the trail of a Russian scientist who has invented something that melts people's bones without affecting the rest of them. Wonderful the way people think of these things."

"Good old Russians," said Mr. Feeder. "Sort of thing they would think up. I can't see what good it would do though."

Mr. Birkett, rather bored by this literary excursion, said it reminded him of Mr. Chadband's description of what happened to you if you didn't eat enough, an allusion gratefully received by such of his audience as were educated enough to take it. And, what he added, was wrong with Leslie Major's conscience?

"I couldn't quite make out," said the Chaplain candidly. "Thanks, I *will* have another bun. He said he often got a peculiar kind of depression after Sunday lunch—no reflection on the food of course—and wondered if it was because he had been late for chapel twice this term. The lad seemed unduly cast down, so I did my best to reassure him and he went off much comforted with some books."

"What sort of books do you give them, padre?" said Mr. Traill. "Mother used to read *The Pilgrim's Progress* to us on Sunday's when we were little and we enjoyed it frightfully because we thought it was true. As a matter of fact I think it's true still. Especially the young woman, her name was Dull. Lord! how often one meets them! It's like Dickens. It's all real life."

Mr. Birkett made no comment but marked Mr. Traill in his mind as a master with a future. He then reminded himself that Mr. Traill's future would be in Everard's hands, not in his, and tried to feel resigned.

"I gave him the book I was reading," said the Chaplain. "He seemed to think it might help him. And a couple of quite good books: *All Corpses Calling* and an American one, *Meet Mr. Murder*. Oh, and an awfully good one about a man that has an operation on his stomach and has a little box put in the hole and keeps secret documents in it, and it has a silver plate over it and the Chinese murder him to get the silver and then the other Chinese murder those ones to get the document, but it had really been stolen by an Englishman in disguise. I mean he was disguised as a lama or something and so the British Embassy got it back. It was awfully ingenious."

"That was kind of you, Smith," said Mr. Birkett. His eyes and Everard's met. No need to tell them that Leslie Major, a dark horse who under a guise of complete dullness had during the past year become a first-class master-baiter, was at the bottom of this. But they had not forgotten how Leslie Major by a well-placed piece of disguised impertinence had managed to expose that dreadful Miss Banks who taught junior Latin so shockingly, and Leslie Major was being given plenty of rope with every hope and a good deal of certainty that he wouldn't hang himself.

"We were just speaking of the new Vicar," said Mr. Birkett, much to the relief of his guests, who were afraid that the red herring of Leslie Major's conscience might deprive them of the treat they were expecting. "I think we are lucky to have him at Southbridge."

"An excellent man," said the Chaplain. "Yes, please, Mrs. Birkett, a third cup of tea, if I may—my weakness, you know. What talk I have had with him impressed me most favourably. We were comparing notes on India," said the Chaplain, who had gone out for six months as secretary to a perambulating bishop. "Of course things have changed since then, but there is something about East of Suez—ah!"

He sighed.

Kate Carter said earnestly that she liked the new Vicar very much indeed and how nice it was that he had grandchildren and the top floor of the Vicarage would make splendid nurseries, especially if he could put a bathroom in, and she thought his service was very nice and not too long for the children.

"He most kindly offered to do a water-colour drawing of the School for us," said Mrs. Birkett. "And I liked his sermon very much indeed."

Mr. Traill had been to early communion on the previous

Wednesday and reported favourably on the new Vicar's kind manner.

"I do like Colonel Crofts so much," said Mrs. Arbuthnot. "He feels almost like a very nice uncle. The only thing is," she added a little nervously, not being quite sure of her ground yet, "that it all seemed a little bare."

"Oh no, Peggy!" said her sister-in-law. "Not bare!"

"I don't mean I want anything as peculiar as that nice Father Fewling of St. Sycorax," said Mrs. Arbuthnot, going pink in her halting efforts to explain the brand of Anglicanism that best suited her. "Only I do like the service just a little bit less austerity."

"I wouldn't call Crofts austerity exactly," said Mr. Traill, who rather prided himself on his knowledge of church matters. "Now, Carson at Nutfield is austerity all right, though I admit it's about all you could be in that tin tabernacle of a church."

"As my father was a clergyman," said Robin Dale, "I suppose I am a little biased, but Colonel Crofts reminds me of my father in more than one way and I can't help liking him for that, even if I didn't like him for anything else. And I think he and papa would have agreed about the services. Austerity doesn't seem to me exactly the right word, though I know what Mrs. Arbuthnot means."

Mr. Feeder suggested utility.

"Oh no! not utility!" said Miss Arbuthnot. "You couldn't call Colonel Crofts utility. I mean not what this Government means by utility. He is very, very useful, I think; which is quite different, and I am sure he would do anything to help people. And his voice is exactly right. And I think he is really good, only it's so difficult to call people that without making them seem priggish and he couldn't ever be a prig."

She stopped, as if she were suddenly frightened of the sound of her own voice, and Mrs. Arbuthnot looked at her with affectionate wonder for it was not like Effie to burst out in this way. Probably as a fellow-artist she felt responsible for Colonel Crofts and thought he was not being properly appreciated. As her sister-in-law's apologia had been followed by a second of silence, appreciable only it is true to the trained social ear, but to such an ear containing some kind of danger signal, she said, again with her unruffled air that she thought Colonel Crofts perfectly delightful, but for her own part she must confess a preference for service like Mr. Villars's at Northbridge, or even better Mr. Miller's at Pomfret Madrigal.

"I enjoyed it frightfully," she said, "when I was staying with Mrs. Brandon. And I liked Mrs. Miller very much too."

This diversion proved to be exactly the right one, leading as it did to the fascinating question of clergymen's wives who are so rarely of the same niceness as their husbands, being either much nicer or by no means so nice. But when, said Mrs. Morland, developing this theory, they were exactly of the same niceness, like the Villarses and the Millers, it was perfect. The School Chaplain being unmarried, the company felt at liberty to analyze the wives of several of the neighbouring clergy, thinking favourably of Mrs. Tompion at Little Misfit who was a Colonel's daughter from Leamington, not taking much interest in Mrs. Carson at Nutfield who had been a well-to-do widow from the Midlands, and uniting in hearty respect for Mrs. Needham at Beliers, youngest daughter of the Deanery, who ran her husband's parish with firmness and efficiency. The higher wives, like Mrs. Crawley and the Bishop's wife, were not discussed.

And this subject having been well thrashed out though in a very kindly spirit, naturally led to the question, a burning one in every parish whose incumbent is unmarried or at liberty to marry again, of Colonel Crofts and his future. Several of the guests did not know he had been married, as indeed how should they, until Kate Carter had mentioned his grandchildren; and the opinion was generally expressed that he ought to marry again.

Kate Carter thought it might be awkward as his children would be younger than his grandchildren and one had seen, in the case of Colonel Croft's predecessor and his aunt, how peculiar such a position might be.

There was a brief silence while the implications of this contribution were considered, broken by Mr. Feeder, who with the temerity of youth put forward the opinion that there would be no need for the new Vicar to have children unless he wanted to. Luckily the School Chaplain was eating the last piece of cake rather quickly and did not hear the remark, or he might have quoted quite embarrassingly from the Marriage Service using, rightly, the very outspoken words consecrated by long usage, which by that long usage have attained a respectability in the best sense of the word that modern variants certainly do not possess.

Robin Dale, who by natural gentleness of nature and by his deep quiet love for Anne Fielding had unusual understanding of that strange and incalculable thing the mind of woman, noticed with concern the rising anger or indignation, he could not tell which it was, in Miss Arbuthnot's face; and being near her, ventured to speak.

"Mrs. Carter thinks of everything in terms of children, bless her heart," he said. "I believe she has already settled the ages, names and complexions of all Anne's and my children and will probably give us orders how many to have. If she saw Methusalem she would at once make plans to marry him to Jessie if no one else was handy." And these words, inane though Robin knew them to be, gave Miss Arbuthnot time to regain her composure and to laugh at the thought of the hideous bespectacled Jessie as Mrs. Methusalem, and even say that Colonel Crofts must be careful not to marry Miss Hampton or he would have to marry Miss Bent as well, so that everything was reduced to a slightly ridiculous level and the anger, or the indignation, melted away.

Then the party began to disperse, some to the School chapel, some to Evening Service at Southbridge and some to their homes. Mr. Feeder and Mr. Traill walked back with the Arbuthnots and were invited to come in and see Editha.

"I like Editha," said Mr. Feeder, after an inspection of the cottage. "She's a bit roomier than Louisa, and you can get your manure in at the side. Anything I want for the garden has to come through the house. Traill is the same."

Mr. Traill said it was frightfully inconvenient, because he had to keep his dustbin in a kind of little kennel he had made in the front garden or have it carried past the sitting-room.

"I like Editha very much," said Mrs. Arbuthnot. "But I do sometimes wish that I could live in bigger rooms. We got rather used to having plenty of space and air in India and I sometimes think I'll go mad if I can't stretch a bit more."

Her sister-in-law agreed, saying that it was very convenient to have everything to one's hand, but if one felt cross a large house was much better because you could get away from people.

"I'm all with you there," said Mr. Traill, "My people have one of those awful houses in South Kensington with a basement as big as Paddington Station and practically no servants, but when I go home I can be as alone in my room as if I were on Dartmoor. Now at Maria I hit the ceiling if I stand up and bark my knuckles on the walls if I stretch, and I hear Miss Hampton shaking cocktails on one side and Feeder's wireless on the other."

"Bad luck, Traill," said Mr. Feeder unsympathetically. "But I do hope it doesn't worry you at Editha," he added, suddenly realizing that if the house on one side heard his wireless, the house on the other side would hear just as well.

"Not in the least, thank you," said Mrs. Arbuthnot. "There's the passage between us on this side. You and Louisa share a wall, I think."

Mr. Feeder said and how, and if Traill played the Bolero again he'd dress up as a toreador and come and break the gramophone. But no malice was intended and the two young masters went back to their cottages to garden, or write letters, or whatever the business of the moment was. The Arbuthnots walked up to the church for the Evening Service and neither of them found any cause to change her opinion of the new Vicar's manner of conducting the service. Mrs. Arbuthnot gently pined for a warmer atmosphere, while her sister-in-law was confirmed in her feeling that Colonel Crofts had exactly the right voice and was essentially good.

While the ladies of Editha were having their supper the telephone rang.

"If it's Colin Keith I have gone to bed," said Mrs. Arbuthnot to her sister-in-law, yawning. But Miss Arbuthnot's voice went on and on in the hall, so she finished her meal alone.

"It was Mr. Wickham," said Miss Arbuthnot, when at last she came back. "The mippet on Fish Hill has given up sitting on her eggs at last. It's the latest due date on record. Oh, bother that telephone," for its discourteous insistent voice was again sounding. "I'll go——It's for you, Peggy," she called, "Northbridge. I'll get on with my supper."

So she finished her meal, while her sister-in-law's voice went on and on in the hall.

"I thought you were in bed if it was Colin," said Miss Arbuthnot; not unkindly though.

"So I was," said Mrs. Arbuthnot, "but it was Noel, about lunch in London."

And if Francis Brandon had been there he might well have said of her, as he was apt to say of his mother, that she had her mysterious mischief face.

CHAPTER 10

The culminating point of that summer, if summer it could be called when everyone was in tweeds and the harvest was already flattened by wind and rain and none of the hens were laying and milk was short, had now arrived, and Mr. Birkett was to preside over his last Speech Day, receive the plaudits and farewells of Governors, parents, old boys and present boys, and say his last public words. It is no good pretending that the Birketts were not in a way glad to lay down their work after so many years, six of which as Mr. Birkett said to Mrs. Morland had counted as about twenty owing to war conditions and the last of which, owing to the horrors of peace, had been ten years of years. They had a comfortable home waiting for them where Mr. Birkett could work on his own subject without interruption, where Mrs. Birkett would be free from entertaining parents, where their daughters and grandchildren could come for the holidays. But it would also be idle not to recognize that they thought at times of their enforced leisure with some apprehension. The Headmaster was going to miss the daily intercourse with his staff, several of whose elder members had been through the war with him; he was going to miss the School chapel where he often took a lay service; no longer would he have a multitude of people depending on the decisions which he had learned to make quickly and justly and had also learned not to be afraid to rescind or modify with the ever-shifting conditions of school life. Never again would he hear the words, "I was looking for you, sir," from a master, or "Please, sir, could I speak to you?" from a boy; words which had so often interrupted his work or curtailed his pleasures yet brought with them the satisfaction of knowing that he could help a master or a boy and in helping them, help to carry on the life and tradition of the School.

"Upon my life, Everard," he said to his Senior Housemaster who was dining with him the night before Speech Day, "when I think of the rest of my life being spent without interruption and having long hours of work with no one knocking at the door, I feel like Julia Mills, benighted in the Desert of Sahara. I think I'll die of it. I have a very good mind to withdraw my resignation."

"I wouldn't if I were you," said Everard Carter. "Not on my account, for I am already gibbering with nerves at the prospect of what I am rashly taking on and would be thankful to be back in my mud hovel like the fisherman's wife, but I think the Governors might object. After all, they are looking forward to tomorrow. It's a kind of Buffaloes' Outing for them."

Mr. Birkett said he would hate of all things to disappoint the Governors, always of course excepting the Bishop. If, he said, by suddenly refusing to resign he could make the Bishop in any way uneasy, he would be willing to take considerable pains. Everard pointed out that once free of the shackles which his present position necessarily laid upon the free public expression of his opinions, he could write letters every day to the *Barchester Chronicle*, or even *The Times*, saying exactly what he thought of the Bishop and this cheered the Headmaster a good deal.

"I am glad the Bissells are coming," said Mr. Birkett, alluding to the Headmaster of the Hosiers' Boys' Foundation School and his wife, who had lived with Southbridge School during most of the war. "It's very good of you and Kate to put them up."

"We look forward to it," said Everard quite truthfully. "By the way, you remember that dreadful science master of theirs, Mr. Hopkins?"

Mr. Birkett said he remembered him very well and how masterfully Mrs. Bissell had kept him in his place at the sherry-party they had in the first winter of the war.

"You know he was locked up later on suspicion of trafficking with the enemy," said Everard. "And now Bissell tells me he is standing as an Independent Communist for Mewlinwillinwodd, the by-election you know, because of their Labour member taking a peerage."

Mr. Birkett said it was interesting to observe that Labour, who had always disliked the Upper House, were doing their best to perpetuate it by creating new peers as fast as the machine could turn them out and, as a rider, that it was time he was dead.

"Time we all were, if it comes to that," said Everard. " 'Time, time the old age were out,' but I haven't very much opinion of the new. When I reflect that I shall never have a houseful of boys behind the green baize door again, I could bang my head against the wall. I can't tell you how dreadful the last week has been. Our hideous Jessie is all blubbered with tears and Matron talks to me in a hushed voice as if I were on my death-bed; as indeed in a way I am."

But this intrusion of his appointed successor's private grief was not to Mr. Birkett's taste, who wished to have full recognition as the principal sufferer in the drama upon which the curtain was about to rise; so he said, with what Everard considered rather offensive cheerfulness, that Shergold who was taking over the Senior House was an excellent fellow.

"I know he is," said Everard crossly. "I know he is an Old Boy and a scholar and a gentleman and was in the navy, but damn the man, I don't want him in My House. When I'm sitting here, in your study, at this table, I shall be worrying about the House. It has always been difficult to get the right House Prefects. Next year's are a good lot, but I shan't be there to start them off. And there's the question of that upper passage and whether we can build out over the maids' quarters. It will worry me all the time."

"Do you think I won't be worried too, and with far more

reason?" said Mr. Birkett, who had not liked Everard's reference to his study and his table. "Shergold will do very well and you must let him make his own mistakes."

"Not on My Boys," said Everard, with an irritation most unlike his usual unperturbed self. "And I really don't see why you should be worried. After all, you'll have retired then."

"Yes, damn it, I shall," said Mr. Birkett. "And there I shall sit in my damned comfortable house, like Cicero in his retirement at Tusculum, working away at the Analects of Procrastinator, and wondering all the time if you are handling the Masters' Common Room properly. It has always been a tricky business and with these men coming back from the Forces it's going to be a sight trickier."

Everard nearly made a jibing retort, but was luckily restrained by his essentially kind and just nature which informed him that he and his Headmaster were both worrying like old women about the same troubles, which existed chiefly in their own imaginations, and he couldn't help laughing. After a second of hurt, suspicious silence, Mr. Birkett began to laugh too.

"I don't know if I'll do it very well, sir," said Everard; falling back into the mode of address he had used as a very young assistant master to the Head, "but I'll have to make my own mistakes."

"You'll make them," said Mr. Birkett, but not unkindly, merely as one stating a fact. "I made frightful howlers in my first term and indeed in most of my first year and I found the only remedy was to carry on as if I hadn't. Of course I had Amy."

"And I've got Kate," said Everard.

And then both schoolmasters shied violently away from this approach to emotion and discussed one or two purely technical matters and agreed that Robin Dale was going to be a very valuable man with the Junior House and what a good thing it was that he was engaged to so nice a girl as Anne Fielding, who although young appeared to both present and future Headmaster to have all the makings of a first-rate Housemaster's wife.

"I'm sorry Rose can't be here," said Everard as he took his leave.

"So am I," said Mr. Birkett, "but the baby is due at any moment now. And to be perfectly truthful, I should be a little nervous if she were here. She is quite capable of getting up in the middle of Speech Day and telling Lord Pomfret it is too meagre that Daddy is going, or adjourning the whole gathering to the Barchester Odeon. I'm very fond of her and this is the fourth baby. She's a good girl, in spite of her looks," which tribute from a much-tried father to a daughter whose silliness was matchless except by her beauty was very high praise.

By this time both schoolmasters were afraid of doing something un-English, something calculated to bring disgrace upon the whole School like clapping the other on the shoulder, so Everard quickly said good-night and went back to the Senior House, where he found his wife Kate knitting a pullover for her eldest son from an old pullover of her husband's which she had unravelled.

"Well, darling," said Kate, taking off her spectacles to be kissed, "did you have a nice time?"

In anyone else's wife Everard would have found this a trite and very unintelligent question. A nice time is a lazy expression and may mean anything from tea with one's old cousin to flying over the Alps; but Everard knew exactly what Kate meant and found the question kind, sympathetic, soothing, understanding; everything a wife should be.

"Very nice," he said. "Birkett is really very generous, because it must be a horrid wrench to leave the School and he must sometimes almost hate us."

"Nonsense, darling," said Kate. "You don't hate Mr. Shergold, which is exactly the same. By the way, he would like to take over that horrid sofa in the big spare room."

Everard asked if they wouldn't want it themselves, but Kate said she had settled with Mrs. Birkett that they would take over the big sofa which wouldn't go into the Birkett's new house, and

Mr. Shergold was most understanding about the upper passage, and she was sure he would get on very well with Matron. Lydia, she said, had rung up about bringing some fruit over on Speech Day.

"Bless her heart," said Everard, who had always been very fond of his young sister-in-law. "How are they all?"

Kate said the children were very well.

And what exactly, said Everard, did Kate mean by that?

"I don't know," said Kate, wrinkling her forehead in a kind of anxious perplexity. "Lydia sounded rather thin. I don't mean that she looks thin, but she sounded thin."

Everard said Kate was getting as bad as Rose Fairweather with her perpetual "meagre" and he hadn't noticed any difference in Lydia.

"You wouldn't, darling," said Kate, with the loving tolerance of any good wife for any good husband. "It's something I can't explain. She sounds rather thin."

Everard suggested that she might be worrying about Colin, whose passion for Mrs. Arbuthnot had temporarily alienated some of his nearest and dearest; not that they disapproved, but it made him such a crashing bore.

"I don't think it's that," said Kate. "But she sounds thin." From which nebulous and hence unassailable position she refused to be moved.

If any reader gradually received the impression that the mild events hitherto chronicled happened during the winter, she is not to be blamed. For though the spring and part of the summer were gone the cold was still quite dreadful, the steely rain almost unceasing, and the winds full of icy venom in every quarter. We would like to be able to pretend that Southbridge Speech Day was the one warm day of the year, but no one who managed to live through that so-called summer would believe us. It is true that the rain held off during the earlier part of the day, but the sky was grey and tempestuous and never could twelve-winded sky have been a fitter epithet, though as Mr. Shergold who had been through part of the war in the little ships remarked, there were four principal points of the compass, so what; an attitude towards poetry which did not in the least impair his efficiency when he took up his new work in the autumn.

If Mr. Birkett and Everard Carter had been asked to give a truthful account of their feelings on that Speech Day, they would probably have agreed that they felt rather sick, had moments of unreasonable elation and moments of equally unreasonable depression not to say despair, combined with a general feeling that they weren't there at all. Their wives, being as wives are of tougher fibre, may have had a small secret pang from time to time, the one for the end of her usefulness as Ma Birky the other for the familiar Senior House, to which was added Kate's private conviction that Master Bobbie Carter would fall down that little step on the nursery landing in the Headmaster's House; but they were quite unconscious of being anyone but themselves or anywhere but where they were and looked after guests with pleasant efficiency.

The Birketts of course had the usual ceremonial lunch of the Dean of Barchester and Mrs. Crawley, various Governors, a few distinguished parents, and the classical scholar and old Southbridge boy Mr. Hacker of Lazarus, an honour which made the Oxford don feel that his boots and his hands were too large and that he was even younger than he was. Very luckily there were fewer women than men and Hacker found himself next on one side to Philip Winter, now the owner of a rising school for little boys at Beliers Priory and formerly Junior Classics Master at Southbridge. This proximity, however, far from assuaging his shyness greatly intensified it, owing to a small point of etiquette. Old habit and a certain respect for old authority caused him automatically to address Philip as sir.

"No need to say sir, Hacker," said Philip. "I'm not correcting your Greek verses now. How's the book on Sophocles getting on?"

Hacker, who had never had a ready command of speech, stuttered and nearly choked with shyness as he said it was practically finished.

"I was going to ask if you would have time, if it isn't a bother, I mean it would be most awfully kind of you if you aren't too busy only of course I wouldn't mention it if you are, but just if you did happen to have a few moments, but only if it isn't a nuisance, just to look at my proofs," said Hacker and then, considerably exercised as to whether he had really said what he wanted to say or expressed himself in any way intelligibly, checked himself, stammered incoherently and added, "sir."

"I shall have to call you sir if you go on calling me sir," said Philip. "That's very nice of you, Hacker, and I'd like very much to look at your proofs. I am rather busy teaching little boys Latin, but I shall certainly make time for your book in the holidays."

"Thank you very much indeed," said Hacker. "It's awfully good of you. I say, sir, which grammar do you use?"

"Look here, say Winter, or Philip if you like," said that gentleman. "I'm still using Lorimer's Grammar. But like all masters I'm writing one myself. I shall return your compliment and ask your advice on it if it ever gets into print. There's one small point about the use of the gerundive," and he briefly outlined his views.

A few moments' conversation on this fascinating subject warmed Hacker's blood, and before he knew where he was he was calling his former classics master Winter quite easily, and together they lamented the late Mr. Lorimer an elderly Scotchman with a genius for coaching who had in the summer before his sudden death crammed Hacker into his Oxford scholarship. And then their talk rambled over old boys and old masters, a good many of whom they would never see again, and Philip asked Hacker about the new verse he had written for the School Carmen, but at this Hacker blushed furiously and began to stammer, so Philip spoke across him and asked Dr. Sparling, the

Headmistress of the Hosiers' Girls' Foundation School, if she knew Mr. Hacker of Lazarus.

"I say," said Hacker, looking to Philip for help. "Not *the* Dr. Sparling that Carton knows?"

But it was the very Dr. Sparling who was shortly going to marry Mr. Carton and whose grandfather's work on Fluvius Minucius had been the basis of Mr. Carton's masterly edition of that neglected author of the Silver Age, and with her Hacker quite forgot his shyness and told her about his chameleon, Gibbon by name, who shared his rooms at Lazarus, so that Philip was able to talk to Lady Fielding on his other side and hear the latest gossip from the Close.

"I see," he said, "that the Member for Barchester has been voting against the Government again."

"Oh, Mr. Adams," said Lady Fielding. "My husband always said he would be a thorn in the side of his party. And how is your wife?"

"Quite well, thank you," Philip said, "but rather tied by the baby at the moment," and then Lady Fielding asked about various friends in Philip's part of the country, including the Deans.

"We rather thought that nice girl of theirs who lives at the Deanery and does Red Cross might have an understanding with Mrs. Brandon's son," said Lady Fielding, "but these young people are so vague. Or was it Colin Keith?"

Philip said he didn't know, but Colin had appeared to be a good deal interested in that pretty Mrs. Arbuthnot who had taken Editha Cottage. Lady Fielding said how amusing and what a pretty creature she was.

"I saw her in town the other day," she said. "She was lunching with that nice Major Merton, or at least one really must say Mr. now, or it will be like the American Civil War. She is most attractive. I hoped to see the Mertons here. I met her in Barchester and I thought she looked rather pale."

Then the talk wandered to other friends, but Philip was left with an uncomfortable feeling. Lydia was an old friend of his and moreover had helped him to woo and win his wife in the desperately short space that twenty-four hours' warning to go abroad gives one, and he had seen with satisfaction her happy married life. Now there seemed to be a chill in the air. Lady Fielding was always amusing about the Close, but she was a discreet woman and a lady and he was quite certain that no remark of hers was meant to be malicious. There was no earthly reason why Noel shouldn't give Mrs. Arbuthnot lunch. Lydia disliked London and was very busy with the estate and the nursery. Noel's work was in London, and though it was the Long Vacation there were plenty of reasons for him to visit his chambers. But why had Lydia looked pale? Then he was annoyed with himself for being annoyed and told himself not to be a fool and joined in a three-cornered conversation with Lady Fielding and the Dean about the lunch-party Bishop Joram had to give for the Head Chief of Mngangaland's eightieth son, now in residence at Balliol where he was reading P.P.E.; and for the benefit of such readers as are too well educated to know these initials we will state, shudderingly, that they stand for Politics, Philosophy, Economics, and if they like to call that a School, they may. But all through the rest of the lunch Lady Fielding's words lay heavy on his mind and he became silent, so that the Dean and Lady Fielding were able to compare notes on the Bishop's new gaiters, considered by the Palace party to be a sign of the Church's growing position in the field of general economic muddle, and by the Dean and the anti-Palace faction a clothing of the episcopal calves in purple and fine linen, highly unsuitable to the times.

"And they do say," said Lady Fielding, "that there is a zip underneath and the buttons are just sewn on for the look of the thing," to which the Dean replied that he hoped the Bishop would get a bit of his leg caught in the zip and serve him right.

After lunch there was some desultory talk in the big drawing-room while the common guests took their places in the School

Hall, and then the Headmaster and his guests walked across the quadrangle with their umbrellas and their coat collars up to take their places.

The School Hall was a large building of no particular character, for the rebuilding of Southbridge School had taken place when English architecture was at one of its many low ebbs. The massive neo-Gothic portal was pure delusion, masking as it did an extraordinarily inconvenient entrance whose swing doors only opened outwards and made it almost impossible for anyone to get up the stairs that led to the balcony. The stairs themselves had vague theological leanings in that they were rather steep, with a great many turns, which had led a previous Headmaster, a persevering reader of Browning's poems, to allude to them as rotten-runged, rat-riddled encumbrances. The balcony with six rows of seats ran round three sides of the hall and was supported by a number of iron pillars painted to resemble an unknown brand of marble, which pillars got frightfully in the way and impeded people's view of the platform. Above the seats, or rather benches, which filled two sides of the gallery was a row of high windows glazed with greenish glass and hygienically provided with ventilators calculated to give a record number of colds and stiff necks, which ventilators it was the joyful and much coveted privilege of the prefects to open or shut, though the opening and shutting was by long and inexplicable custom under the authority of the School gymnasium instructor who also taught boxing. At the far end of the hall was the platform, which was never quite large enough for important occasions and approached by a steep flight of steps with a brass railing. Above the platform the memorial window to the Rev. J. J. Damper, former Headmaster of the School and author of the School Carmen, let in a pallid and unbecoming light, and ever since the land-mine had exploded two miles away in a disused brickfield had let in nearly as much draught as the gallery windows. The central heating was very good in winter for those in the immediate vicinity of the hot-water pipes, and the school cobbler made loud complaints about the cracked and parched leather on the soles of the school boots belonging to boys near the pipes. It was the unspoken nightmare of Mrs. Birkett and Kate Carter that the furnace, which lived in a kind of crypt below the hall and spat and crackled and roared in a terrifying way, would one day char a beam and burn the whole hall and all the boys after the fashion of Bishop Hatto. But so far, owing perhaps to the floor being supported on steel girders, this dreadful event had not occurred.

Before the war plans had been afoot for rebuilding the hall on a larger scale, in a more commodious manner, but the war had stopped everything, and perhaps, said Mr. Birkett to Everard it was just as well, for the architect upon whom the Governors' choice appeared likely to fall was a prey to the word functional and had already submitted designs for a kind of cube with rounded ends, a number of windows about forty feet high and two feet wide, and a bas-relief of Knowledge and Ignorance by Mars Tone, a leading light of the Phallo-Hexagonal Group.

The hall was crowded to bursting point by boys in the galleries and parents and friends downstairs. In the front row were notabilities of the county and the Close, among whom such members of the Birketts' lunch party as were not entitled to seats on the platform took their places. There was a kind of simmering excitement over everything and Mrs. Morland, who was much to her own surprise put in the front row next to Mrs. Birkett, declared that she could see the air quivering as it does on a very hot summer's day.

Prefects now commanded silence in the galleries. The silence spread to the body of the hall and the noisy chatter died away as the roar of London traffic used to die away before Armistice Day was made a fixed and less romantic celebration upon the Sunday immediately preceding itself. Onto the platform came the Dean, Lord Pomfret tired and conscientious as ever, Sir Robert Fielding representing the Bishop who by a special crowning mercy had an engagement in London with the General Council of Interference that day, John Leslie who came of a long-established Barsetshire family and had two boys at the School, the School Chaplain, a famous general and a famous admiral—Old Southbridgians both—various other Governors, no women we are glad to say, Mr. Bissell the Headmaster of the Hosiers' Boys' Foundation School, Everard Carter and Mr. Birkett. And as Mr. Birkett took his seat the pent-up spirits of the boys, which had been suffering severely from their brief and enforced silence, burst out into a roar that could have been heard at the far end of the playing field.

> "But when the face of Sextus
> Was seen among the foes,
> A yell that rent the firmament
> From all the town arose,"

said Anne Fielding in an awestruck voice to Robin Dale at her side.

"Yes, my love, " said Robin. "But wait till he has kissed them all."

Anne smiled at him and Robin thought, not for the first time, how delightful it was to have a wife, at least not really one yet only one felt so safe and comfortable with her that it was almost the same thing, who understood what one said.

"I know I am going to cry," said Mrs. Morland to Mrs. Birkett. "What about you, Amy?"

"I'd like to cry, but I can't," said Mrs. Birkett. "I've got pricking eyes and a lump in my throat, but I can't get any further."

Mrs. Morland, banging each eye fiercely with her handkerchief, said she was frightfully sorry and perhaps Amy would be able to cry later on.

The School Chaplain now gave a short opening prayer. The School organist hit the piano almost as hard as Mrs. Morland had hit her own eyes. The Prefects, by old custom, shouted

"Carmen, Carmen!" across the hall. All the boys in the gallery made a terrific drumming with their feet on the wooden floor. The ceremony was about to begin.

The whole School and most of the audience now burst into the Carmen Southbridgiense, whose music by an unprecedented piece of good luck was an adaptation of an old German chorale. Of the words, by the Rev. J. J. Damper, there is little to say except that they are so bad that they are almost good, having become by lapse of time what is called a period piece, and the refrain to each verse,

> Alma Mater, Alma Mater,
> None than thou shalt e'er be greater,

was roared with enthusiasm from several hundred throats. After Mr. Damper's verses came the special verse composed by Percy Hacker, M.A., lines which we must in fairness admit fitted admirably with the verses which had gone before:

> Last, not least, and most beloved,
> At the parting of the ways,
> We, thy pupils, met together,
> Raise our voices to thy praise,

words which, so Hacker confided to his friends, he could have done much better in Latin or Greek, and indeed it would have been almost impossible to have done them worse.

But after them, instead of the familiar "Alma Mater," the whole School, previously well drilled, sang in deafening unison,

> Mr. Birkett, he can work it,
> Mr. Birkett does not shirk it,
> Mr. Birkett, Mr. Birkett,
> Birkett, Birkett, Birkett, BIRKETT!

the last two lines rising to a combined yell which, so Bishop
Joram said afterwards to the School Chaplain, reminded him of
the Easter celebrations in Mngangaland almost more than he
could bear. By this time the whole School was thoroughly out of
hand. Mrs. Morland was having a good cry, as were several
ex-parents. As ex-Solicitor-General, an Air Vice-Marshal, two
Earls, an Admiral of the Fleet, and an old boy who had been in
prison for fraud on an unprecedented scale, were blowing their
noses and glaring defiantly at anyone who didn't think they had
a cold, and Mr. Birkett felt more than ever Lawk-a-mercy on
me, This is none of I.

> "All Rome sent forth a rapturous cry,
>   And even the ranks of Tuscany
>   Could scarce forbear to cheer,"

said Robin Dale to Anne Fielding, "I got in first that time." At
which Anne laughed and Robin thought again how nice it was
to be going to marry someone who could enjoy being laughed at.

The School Chaplain now damped the general enthusiasm by
praying again, though this was not so much his fault as a
carefully concerted scheme of Everard Carter's who knew that
the boys would be out of hand for the rest of the afternoon
unless strong measures were taken, and the proceedings went on
their appointed way. Mr. Birkett read a brief account of the
School's work during the past years and asked the Very Reverend the Dean of Barchester to address the School, which Dr.
Crawley did at suitable length, though Mrs. Crawley complained that Josiah always gave that little more and how much it
was. Everard Carter read a long list of School successes in
academic and other fields and the prizes were given by Lord
Pomfret, while Lady Pomfret watched him with her ceaseless
almost maternal anxiety and hoped they would be able to get
away early. The cheering and clapping of the prizewinners
enabled the boys to let off steam again, and when the last book

and the last cup had been given and Leslie Minor had gained considerable popularity by falling down the platform steps with a pile of books, the atmosphere was almost normal.

During the prize-giving, which is always dull except to Mrs. Jones when she sees Jones Major get his French prize, most of the audience were able to look about and see what friends were there. Philip Winter, his mind still uneasy about Lydia, suddenly caught sight of Noel, but could not see who was beyond him owing to a parent with a very hideous tall hat which she had bought at a sale in a moment of madness and was unsuccessfully trying to break in. But Noel looked quite normal and amused, so evidently Lydia was all right. He would talk to them afterwards.

"It is very provoking of Lavinia to have measles," said Noel to Mrs. Arbuthnot who was sitting next to him, "but Nurse segregated her from the first moment she began to look measly and we hope Harry won't get them. It is a bore too, because Lydia has to do full-time nursery just now. If I were in London I'd dine at my club, which is about all the help a man can give."

"If only we were nearer I'd love to offer you an evening meal," said Mrs. Arbuthnot, "but it's hardly worth while for you to drive six miles each way for a sardine, which is about all Effie and I have. You wouldn't come to supper tonight, would you? It's only fish, but we cook it quite nicely."

Noel said that was very kind of her and might he ring up Lydia later in the afternoon and see how everything was going, which friendly and harmless conversation was overheard by Colin who was sitting just behind them with the Deans and at once felt cross, a state of mind which had been sadly common with him of late and of which he was ashamed, though unable to conquer it.

"Where's Lydia?" said Susan Dean to Colin.

Colin explained that Miss Lavinia Merton had developed measles and Lydia had taken over the measler while Nurse looked after Harry and carried trays for the nursery and the measle department.

"What a bore," said Susan sympathetically. "I wish I wasn't so busy Red Crossing or I'd go and help her. I suppose she's had it herself."

"I don't remember," said Colin. "I expect so. Everyone has. Of course our old parlourmaid who runs everything is away on her holiday now, so it's a lot for Lydia. I sometimes think I ought to go to London, to my flat, but I do so love Northbridge and London is so dull at this time of year."

"Come back to supper with us," said Susan. "Only I don't know how you'd get back. I'd drive you, only I'm a bit low on petrol near the end of the month."

"As a matter of fact," said Colin, "I bought a little car the other day. I thought I really couldn't go on using theirs."

He did not add, "So I will come to supper with pleasure," for he had a kind of hope, undefined as yet, that something might turn up: the something being closely connected with the possibility of Mrs. Arbuthnot asking him if he would stay to supper at Editha.

But now Mr. Birkett rose to his feet amid thunders of applause and spoke to the School for the last time. He did not speak at great length. He thanked everyone for helping him with his work, thanked Mr. Bissell for his loyal co-operation during the war, touched briefly upon the School Roll of Honour, said that though he could no longer be near the School his thoughts would never be far from it, and any boy, old or young, would be welcomed by his wife and himself in their new home; thanked the Governors for their support, and said he would like to shake hands with the whole School before they all dispersed, upon which the School as one man sang "For he's a jolly good fellow," and practically every member of the audience cried or blew its nose. By this time Mr. Birkett thought he might easily begin to cry himself, so he pulled himself together and said his last act as their Headmaster would be to present to them his successor, Mr. Carter, at which applause broke out more thunderously than ever, partly because the boys liked Everard, partly because anyone introduced by Mr. Birkett would at that moment have been popular, and a great deal for the sheer joy of making a noise.

Everard thanked them all and said he would do his best, but no one would miss Mr. Birkett more than he and he knew they all would miss him, at which the cheers burst out again and the School with one voice shouted "We want Mr. Birkett," till the Headmaster got up and said, "God bless you all. Good-bye," because he could say no more.

"I think," said Everard to the School organist, "we had better have 'God Save the King.'"

This was in a way the first act of his new official life and it was well timed. It was an old tradition at Southbridge to sing the National Anthem in its entirety and anyone who had tried to substitute a verse recommending a universal, mushy and unintelligent love for our enemies in the place of confounding their politics and frustrating their knavish tricks would have had short shrift.

The Chaplain then gave a final blessing and Mr. Birkett came down from the platform and stood with his back to it, while the whole School, masters, boys and outside staff, from Everard Carter and the Head Boy down to the boys at the bottom of the first form and the odd-job man, filed past and shook his head. And by a crowning mercy of Providence he remembered every single name. By previous arrangement, which had been kept a close secret from the Headmaster, the School then sang 'Auld Lang Syne' and quietly dispersed. The Headmaster with his guests and personal friends walked back to his house, while the parents and boys were given tea in the gymnasium.

"I will never retire again," said Mr. Birkett to Everard as they went into the drawing-room together. "Not even for you. I must remember to thank Hacker for that verse in the Carmen."

Everard gravely said that it was well up to the level of the rest of the Carmen.

The emotions of the company were gradually calmed by tea, ough several of them would have liked something stronger.

The Pomfrets were the first to leave, as they very often were with their many and varied duties, but they never forgot to say the right thing and what is more they meant it. The rest of the company wondered if it would be kinder if they followed their example, but when Mrs. Crawley spoke of going Mrs. Birkett begged her not to, because it would do her husband good to be let down gently.

"Henry has been so overworked lately," she said, "that he has forgotten how to rest and if you go he will certainly begin to worry about the School, which isn't his business now. We are dining with the Carters and if I can keep him from working till then perhaps he will go to bed early. We leave tomorrow."

So the Crawleys and Mrs. Morland stayed on with a few other friends and Philip Winter drew Mr. Birkett into a discussion of certain uses of the gerundive and asked him if he would look at the proofs of his Latin Grammar when they were ready. Mr. Birkett said he would be delighted.

"A good Latin grammar is a permanent source of income if properly handled," he said. "We still use Lorimer's, but the School will have to move with the times and I hope we shall use yours, Philip. I mean, I hope the School will use it, for the decision will, of course, no longer rest with me."

There was such a sound of regret in his voice that Everard Carter hastily changed the course of the talk by asking Philip if he knew Mr. Lorimer's theory about Latin grammar.

"He used to say," said Everard, "that his Grammar was used by at least twelve public schools, which meant that some five to seven thousand boys per annum loathed him and wished he had never been born. I hope to see Philip in that enviable position."

At this moment Simnet the butler came in with a telegram for the Headmaster.

"How good people have been," said Mr. Birkett opening it. "Wait a moment, Simnet, there may be an answer. I have had so many telegrams from old parents and boys."

"The Boy," said Simnet, throwing into his voice a contempt

for that species when not of public school standard difficult to express, "did not wait, sir. I called to him to wait, but he did not hear me. On Purpose."

"Never mind," said Mr. Birkett, trying to take in the contents of the telegram, which is made very difficult for us now because it is all typewritten in capitals which are so much less easy to read than ordinary print whatever the Postmaster-General may think, crooked, on nasty strips of paper gummed to the form and usually beginning TXBV and interlarded with similar interjections. "It's signed Bothwell. Amy, do we know anyone called Bothwell?"

Mrs. Birkett came hurriedly across the room to him, for Rose was much in her mind and seeing a telegram she had at once realized with a mother's intuition that her elder daughter had probably given birth to deformed triplets and then died, and was telegraphing to tell her about it. She took the telegram with a beating heart.

"'Rose had a girl this morning both well': not Bothwell, Henry. Thank goodness. I must ring John up after supper."

The whole room buzzed with congratulations and more than one of the Birketts' old friends felt how exactly like Rose it was to produce a baby on such a day and put herself well into the School limelight.

"But I do hope," said Mrs. Birkett who under the stress of the day's emotion was almost nervous, a condition most unusual to her, "that it won't be like Edith Keith," for Rose's husband was a younger brother of Mrs. Robert Keith and though Mrs. Robert Keith was an estimable woman and made her husband very happy, the rest of the family found her very dull. And when we say that as Edith Fairweather she had been Head Girl of the Barchester High School and one of Miss Pettinger's prime favourites, it is easy to understand why Kate, Colin and Lydia were not deeply attached to their sister-in-law though on perfectly good terms with her, nor the Birketts to Rose's sister-in-law.

Everyone who knew Edith Keith sympathized with Mrs.

Birkett and everyone realized that she was overwrought by the long exciting day, and said with great certainty, though no grounds at all, that the baby would be a perfect pet and exactly like Rose, and how nice it would be that Mrs. Birkett could have Rose and the new baby to stay with her now.

"I could have had them just the same if Henry hadn't retired," said Mrs. Birkett, "because it will be the summer holidays," which was quite true, and seemed to put Mr. Birkett in the wrong.

Kate Carter then suggested, though in a very quiet way, for she did not wish to appear too much at home in the house which would next term be her own, that they might drink the baby's health, which was cheerfully and rapidly done while Philip Winter very cunningly held the School Chaplain in leash in case he should feel like praying. Not that the School Chaplain was apt to confound business with pleasure, but he like the rest of the company was flown with excitement and might well have overstepped the mark. But thanks to Philip's efforts he only got as far as saying what a pity it was the baby could not be christened in the School Chapel.

"She might be confirmed here though," said Philip. "Can a girl be confirmed at a boys' school, Dr. Crawley?"

The Dean, who had been listening with amusement to the end of the conversation, said it was unusual but he did not think it was impossible. There was of course, he said, one factor that must be considered—that it was a Bishop who took the Confirmation Service.

He said no more, but all his hearers realized the hideous implication of his words. If Rose Fairweather's latest baby was to be confirmed by the Bishop of Barchester, as would inevitably happen, for his Lordship was tenacious of his rights, she might as well not be confirmed at all. Not that they would have put such a thought into words, but the thought was very near the surface and there was a silence, very brief indeed, but the briefest silence is curious in a party where all are on friendly terms.

"But," said Mrs. Morland, knocking her hat straight and a wisp of hair back behind an ear, "Rose's baby can't be confirmed for about fifteen years. I don't exactly know what the real law is because it only says people who have come to the age of discretion and if the Church took that seriously I suppose some people would never be confirmed at all, would they, Dr. Crawley?"

The Dean, who was obviously thinking that in the case submitted by Mrs. Morland the present Bishop of Barchester would still be waiting for confirmation, smiled grimly and said it would be interesting to submit the question to an Oecumenical Counsel, but the Church of England considered young people from about fourteen years ripe for confirmation and it was better to accept too many than to discourage the weaker brethren.

"Well then," said Mrs. Morland, looking wildly round for sympathy, "you see what I mean. Rose's baby can't be confirmed for the next fifteen years and *anything* might happen before then," from which words it was perfectly clear to her hearers that she had courageously envisaged the beautiful and comforting thought that the present Bishop of Barchester might be dead by that time.

Sir Robert Fielding who had no more love for the Bishop than the rest of the guests but had to be more discreet as Chancellor of the Diocese, remarked with a false air of changing the subject that York and Lambeth had sometimes been filled by men of a very ripe age. Kind Kate Carter said she would be very sorry for the people in Canterbury and York if they had an archbishop they didn't like, because it was so horrid to have someone one didn't like.

"You will pardon me," said Mrs. Bissell, the very nice wife of the Headmaster of the Hosiers' Boys' Foundation School, "but as Mrs. Fairweather's dear wee girl is such a newcomer, one need hardly commence to worry about her confirmation yet. She must be a sweet wee mite, Mrs. Birkett. I wonder what they will call her."

This very practical point of view released the tension, which was really just as well, for as Mrs. Crawley said to Mr. Birkett she was afraid they might all have been had up before Convocation for lése-episcopacy, if there was such a phrase, in which case her husband would probably be ungaitered and turned into a perpetual curate. To which Mrs. Morland, who had been getting her hair tidy again after her ecclesiastical excursion, said it must be exactly like being sent to the galleys for life to be a perpetual curate and she never could understand how the Dean's grandfather, who was perpetual curate of Hogglestock, managed to escape and be Vicar of St. Ewold's. But a judgment fell upon her for such ignorance, for the School Chaplain who had been rather afraid of joining in the foregoing conversation in case the Bishop came to hear of it, made up for his silence by giving Mrs. Morland a great deal of information about the various kinds of living in the Church of England, very little of which that worthy creature could understand, but somehow it all seeped through into the writing part of her mind and was used with great effect in her next but one book where Madame Koska was abducted by a Russian disguised as a commercial traveller for a French silk firm and rescued by a perpetual curate who married one of her beautiful but pure mannequins: and the *Guardian* and the *Church Times* applauded the deep moral lesson of Mrs. Morland's new book and her profound knowledge of church matters, so rare among even the most intelligent of the laity in these troublous times.

A kind of noise like the French Revolution had been rising by degrees from the quadrangle. Philip Winter went to the window and looked out. The motor coaches of the Southbridge United Viator Passenger Company which were to take a large number of the School to Barchester were drawn up in line and crammed with boys and luggage. There were also a good many cars of visiting parents, these also chockful of boys, and from all the buses and cars came a great cheering and loud calls for the Headmaster.

"I can't," said Mr. Birkett, to whom Philip had reported these things. "I really can't. It is more than I can stand."

"You'll have to, sir," said Philip, forgetting that he was now the owner of a flourishing school for little boys and falling back into the old way of addressing the Headmaster when he himself had taught junior classics. "They'll storm the Tuileries if you don't. It's the last time."

So Mr. Birkett went out and stood at the top of the steps with Mrs. Birkett, and their oldest friends clustered behind them. The shouting and the blowing of motor horns died down. The Head Boy, who was quite illegally standing with the Prefects on the roof of one of the motor coaches, called for three cheers for Mr. Birkett, then for three cheers for Ma Birky and then, by what his mother considered direct inspiration though from whom or what she was not clear, for the King. Mr. Birkett's face was set, but he had himself in hand and stood on the steps while the motor coaches and the cars circled the grass of the School quadrangle, drove through the archway and were lost to sight and hearing. Mrs. Birkett and Mrs. Morland were unashamedly crying and enjoying it very much. The rain which had held off for a while began again. In the silence that now filled the quadrangle the voice of the cuckoo who had long outstayed his welcome uttered its hollow, discordant notes.

"And from the deluged park
The cuckoo of a worse July
Is calling through the dark,"

said Anne Fielding softly to Robin Dale, finding that Lord Tennyson, who still remained her favourite poet, had words for all she felt.

"It is," said Robin. "Darling Anne, I love you very much. What fun it will be when you come to live here."

"It will," said Anne. "But it is dreadful to think that we shall have to leave it some day, like Mr. Birkett."

"Now, my love, don't you cry too," said Robin. "You are as bad as the girl who went down to the cellar to draw beer and saw the axe stuck in the beam," at which Anne, who had been properly brought up on Grimms' *Household Tales*, began to laugh. But both of them were penetrated for the moment by a sense of the transitoriness of things and when Lady Fielding called Anne and said they must be getting back to Barchester, Anne kissed Robin in a kind of dream and went away. Robin looked after her, trying to imagine what it would feel like to have reigned over a state for so many years and then to step down, to give the unwieldy sceptre from one's hand, to turn one's helmet to a hive for bees. But the thought was too difficult. He had present duties, one of them being to finish his packing. The guests had now all gone. Mr. and Mrs. Birkett had shut the front door. The Bissells had gone to the Senior House with the Carters. Philip Winter had gone back to his school and his wife, the quadrangle was left to silence and to Robin Dale, who stood lost in reflections upon the world in general till the rain, suddenly taking a deep breath and coming down as it had never come down before, drove him back to his own room. Here he put a few last odds and ends into his suitcase and looked round his little domain. Next term he would be in charge of the Junior House with a Matron of his own and boys of his own, and before next Christmas he and Anne were to be married and there would be a Housemaster's wife. He thought with lofty pity of Mr. Shergold who was taking over Everard's House. A very good fellow with an intelligent active mind; incidentally, though this was an important detail, a gentleman; sufficiently good at cricket, an enthusiast for winter sports, some money of his own one gathered; but not married. Not even engaged as far as anyone knew. And Robin's pity for people who were not engaged was almost as great as his pity for people who were engaged, but not to Anne Fielding. He then shook himself from a dream of Anne, took his bags down to his little car and drove off to Hallbury where he was spending the beginning of the holidays with the Fieldings.

The dinner-party at the Carters was a kind of portmanteau dinner-party serving several purposes. Part of it was the Carter's own farewell to the Senior House, for next day they were taking the children to the sea. Here they intended to leave them with Everard's mother and would come back to Southbridge at the beginning of September, stay at the Red Lion, and thence superintend the move into the Headmaster's House. Part of it was a final farewell to the Birketts, who had already sent most of their furniture to their old home and were going there themselves the next day. Another part was a kind of unofficial welcome from the Carters to their successor Mr. Shergold. The Bissells were honoured guests bound to the School by the ties formed during the war. And last but not least it was an occasion for showing gratitude and affection to Matron who had worked so valiantly, and for her to talk to Mr. Shergold in the neutral territory of the dining-room, for all their previous interviews had been in Everard's study or Matron's own quarters. And this was perhaps the most important part of the evening, for on their relations with each other much of the happiness of the Senior House would depend.

The Carters and the Bissells had only just got back when Noel Merton came in.

"It's all right, Kate," he said to his sister-in-law, "I'm not trying to come to dinner but I want to ring Lydia up. Peggy Arbuthnot asked me to supper at Editha and as Lydia is rather nursery-bound I thought I might as well go. I've never seen the inside of Editha."

Kate couldn't help feeling that if her child were suffering from measles, however lightly, not the demons under the sea would keep her away from its sick-bed, but she also realized with a mild pity that men were not much use and that when Bobbie and Angela had influenza she had occasionally been glad to turn Everard out to dine with the Birketts or Miss Hampton. And after all Miss Hampton wasn't married and Mrs. Arbuthnot was, and it wasn't her fault that her husband was dead, so why shouldn't Noel have supper with her? The Bissells and Everard went upstairs but Kate remained in the study saying she would like to talk to Lydia when Noel had finished.

For the first time in his life Noel felt annoyed with his gentle sister-in-law and all the more so because he knew that his annoyance was quite unreasonable. All he was doing was to ring up and tell Lydia he wouldn't be back to supper, and as Lydia was usually quite ready to go to bed by 9 o'clock after a day of measling she would not miss much of his company and he would certainly be back early. This should have been quite easy to explain on the telephone, but somehow it wasn't, and Noel decided that it was Kate's fault. Lydia seemed quite pleased that he should stay to supper with Peggy Arbuthnot and sent her love to both the ladies and then Noel asked her to wait as Kate wanted to speak to her. As there were no family secrets Noel sat down and waited for Kate to finish her talk, getting rather impatient as it went on.

"I always thought she had had them," said Kate as she replaced the receiver, her mild brow furrowed with anxiety.

"Had what?" said Noel.

"Measles," said Kate. "But she says she hasn't. I know Colin had them and I thought Lydia did too, but it was the year I was in Paris being finished, so I wasn't there. Still, one never gets things from one's children," said Kate with maternal pride. "At least I never have, so I daresay it will be all right. But she sounded pale."

All this was distinctly annoying to Noel and had he been more at ease he might have tried to find out exactly how people sounded pale, just as Everard had tried to find out how they sounded thin, probably with equally poor results. But his conscience remarked in an acid voice that Lydia would be disappointed not to see him after her dull day's measling and to be ordered about by a conscience was intolerable, so he told Kate that Lydia looked quite well but was worrying about Lavinia.

"So she ought," said Kate stoutly. "They are such miseries, poor lambs, when they are ill and don't know why. I worried dreadfully about Bobbie and Angela when they had influenza. I spent most of the day with them and in the evening Everard quite often read aloud to me on the drawing-room sofa, because it was before Phil was born. We enjoyed our evenings so much. He was reading his book about Lord Eldon to me," for Everard, who had read law before he took up schoolmastering, had kept his taste for it and had written in his spare time a book on that eminent lawyer which had won considerable praise in legal circles and even had a certain popular success.

Not for one moment did Kate mean to draw a parallel between her own case and Lydia's, or to imply any criticism of Noel. She was merely remembering with pleasure what appeared to have been a particularly idyllic period in her life, but to her brother-in-law it seemed that criticism was implied in every word. Lydia was not going to have another baby and in any case never reclined upon a sofa, treating such behaviour as sheer laziness and self-indulgence. And she didn't particularly care for being read aloud to and certainly would not have enjoyed the book he was trying to write which was about various knotty points in Equity and would probably have been stigmatized by her, apart from her general approval of everything he did, as rot. But he dissembled his feelings, kissed Kate, and went away to Editha.

"Noel rang Lydia up," said Kate to Everard from her bedroom. "I spoke to her and I felt worried. She didn't sound as alive as usual. I wish Noel would go home to dinner."

Everard, not particularly interested at the moment in Noel's movements, asked if Noel was staying to dinner with them.

"Oh no, he is going to Peggy Arbuthnot," said Kate. "She invited him this afternoon and he rang Lydia up to tell her. I wish Lydia did not sound pale."

But Everard did not understand Kate's feelings and almost offended her by saying that he thought it was a good idea for Noel to go to Editha and then Lydia could go to bed early as she must be tired, and would Kate please stop worrying about Lydia and the measles and where were his grey socks, so the matter dropped for the present and they went downstairs.

Matron was the first of the guests to arrive, for we do not count the Bissells who were staying with the Carters. She was delightfully dressed in pale-blue artificial silk with a little art embroidery round the neck and draped on one side, and startled the Housemaster and his wife by wearing red shoes with a wedge heel and a hole in front of her big toe which was however, thank heaven, as Everard subsequently remarked to Kate, properly dressed in a stocking, for a toe nail would, in Matron, have shocked him very much.

"What a Day of Days, Mrs. Carter," said Matron, shaking hands as if she had come from the other side of the county instead of through the baize door. "How are you, Mr. Carter? And what a pleasure to see Mrs. Bissell again and Mr. Bissell. It seems quite like old times. I was saying to Jessie no later than this morning while we were getting the packing finished and really, Mrs. Carter, boys get untidier and untidier, though whether it is the results of the war or just this dreadful Government we cannot say. Jessie, I said to her, it is quite like old times having Mr. and Mrs. Bissell here, not that you ever stayed in the House, Mrs. Bissell, though as I remember there was quite a talk of your coming here before you took Maria Cottage, it is quite like old times, Jessie, I said, when the war was on and there was the blackout to do every night and morning and what the dirt was is hardly feasible, for you cannot see to sweep and dust properly by electric light in the winter and it was just then that Jessie was being particularly troublesome about not wearing her glasses, so that what with her not seeing where the dust was and the blackout, really, Mrs. Bissell, it was often a case of If you don't at first succeed, Try, try, try again."

Then the Birketts came in, to whom Matron spoke at considerable length about how like old times it was to see Mr. and Mrs. Bissell again till the arrival of Mr. Shergold suddenly put an end to her monologue.

"I am extremely sorry to be late," said Mr. Shergold, who looked exactly like a demobilized naval officer which indeed he was, "but Bellinger's parents rang up to say their car had broken down, so I ran him into Barchester. I hope that was all right, sir," he added to Everard. "He got the 6.57 all right and they will meet him with a taxi."

Everard thanked Mr. Shergold and made no further comment, noting however with approval that his successor was keeping an eye on his future boarders and helping boys out of difficulties, and they went in to dinner. For once the inevitable talk about rations was overlaid by talk about the comparatively happy and peaceful days of the war in which Mr. Shergold, though from a different point of view, was entirely in accord with the civilians.

"When I think——"

"When I remember——"

"What made life so much easier then——"

"When I was having a splendid time off the coast of Tunisia,——" said Mr. Birkett, Mr. Bissell, Everard and Mr. Shergold simultaneously, and begged each other's pardon and stopped dead.

Mrs. Birkett, Mrs. Bissell, Kate and Matron, throwing themselves into the breach of this silence as all good women do, executed simultaneous variations on the theme of how delightful war was compared with peace.

"It was all an extraordinarily interesting adventure," said Mrs. Birkett to Mrs. Bissell, "though how we would have got through it without your help I don't know."

"Mr. Bissell and I feel exactly the same," said Mrs. Bissell. "I can assure you that many a time we pass the remark how happy we were at Southbridge."

Kate said quite truly, though in all good faith, that the School had never been the same since peace broke out and the Hosiers' Boys went back to London, while Matron gave a lengthy account in oratio recta and oratio obliqua distinctly confusing to her hearers of what she and Jessie had said to each other on Thursday, or was it Wednesday, no Thursday it must have been because Thursday was the day she and Jessie were turning that cupboard out and lo! and behold what had they found behind the spare blankets but Bellinger's dormouse curled up fast asleep however he got there she couldn't think and what a mercy Pussy hadn't seen him or it would have been a case of frightening the little mouse under the chair, where was she, oh yes, Jessie had said to her 'It's like the good old days to be turning out the cupboard, Matron,' and she had said, 'Yes, Jessie, we were quite a happy band then," not but what, Mrs. Bissell would understand, everyone wasn't a united family now even with this peace, there now she nearly said United Nations, though it stood to reason that was impossible with people made the way they were, 'but Jessie,' she had said to Jessie, 'we must always remember that nice boy of Mr. Bissell's. Manners his name was, that helped move the furniture for the Children's Party that Christmas,' and lo! and behold there was Manners an Oxford boy now, and Mr. and Mrs. Bissell dining with them as if nothing had happened.'"

As was quite often the case after one of Matron's excursions into what the Carters privately called Jessie-land, everyone felt as if they were sitting under a glass case from which the air was being gradually withdrawn and even Mrs. Bissell appeared unable to think of the correct comment. And there they might have remained, a party in a parlour all silent and all damned said Everard to himself, had not Mr. Shergold remarked that he used to have dormice, jolly little fellows, only they were always asleep or running away, but the best pet he ever had was a jerboa. In the Mediterranean it was, he added.

Well now, said Matron, talk of coincidences, her nephew

used to write to her about his jerboa when he was somewhere in the Mediterranean and it all went to show, though what specifically it showed she did not state.

Mr. Shergold asked if her nephew was a gunner.

Matron said oh *dear* no, he was a wireless operator, her married sister's son, she added.

"I say," said Mr. Shergold, "I wonder if it was Sparks, off the old *Gridiron*. She was bombarding Pantellaria and we had some jerboa races when we got leave. I was in the *Flatiron* then."

Matron, greatly excited, said he was a very good boy and wrote to his mother regularly. Middle height, she added, dark hair and a quiet sort of manner; not exactly *reserved* if Mr. Shergold knew what she meant, but quiet.

Mr. Shergold asked diffidently if he had a name, because he always called him Sparks and couldn't at the moment remember what his name was. Matron said it was Empson.

"Good Lord!" said Mr. Shergold leaning nearly right across the table the better to talk to Matron, "he still owes me five bob on our last race. His jerboa was leading, but when they got into the straight my fellow gave his fellow a whacking great kick with his hind leg and won by three tails. He tried to have it a foul but his captain, Belton his name was, gave it in my fellow's favour."

This fascinating record of North African sport might have gone on for a long time, but Everard judged it time to intervene, though secretly he was delighted that this bond between Matron and the new Housemaster had been discovered, for anyone that had known her nephew had a sure key to Matron's regard and the lucky incident of a jerboa race made Everard feel comfortably certain about Mr. Shergold's future. Kate had also felt that they might have a little general conversation, so very soon, as was inevitable, they were back at rationing.

"I wonder, Mrs. Birkett," said Mr. Bissell, "if you have had the trouble down here we've had in the Isle of Dogs."

Mrs. Birkett asked which special trouble.

"Of course," said Mr. Bissell, "I voted Labour, for in my

position and thinking as I think and knowing what I know a man can do no otherwise, not that I'll ever vote that way again after what has occurred. It is to the change over from B.U.s to Points to which I refer," said Mr. Bissell, clinging desperately to the end of his sentence and hoping for the best.

Mr. Birkett said he had heard a lot about B.U.s but still didn't know what they were.

"Bread Units," said Mrs. Bissell. "A stupid name, but I suppose the people that invented it didn't stop to think."

Mr. Shergold said he didn't know much about them himself, but his mother seemed to get all wrought up about them and anyway what could you expect with this Government. He then begged Mr. Bissell's pardon for interrupting.

"Granted," said Mr. Bissell, smiling tolerantly at this pleasant young master who raced jerboas, reminding him of the days when he, Mr. Bissell, used to race earwigs with a friend at the Isle of Dogs Polytechnic. "Well, Mrs. Birkett, mother here tells me if we have a lot of these B.U.s over we have to change them for food points at the Town Hall. Well, I've nothing against the scheme as such, though I know too much about our Mayor and some of the Council to have much opinion of them. But my point is: say you get the food points, what are you going to do with them? For from what mother tells me, there's so little in the grocers' shops that points are like taking a cup of water from a starving man."

"I know *exactly* what you mean, Mr. Bissell," said Kate Carter. "It's just showing you something you want and then saying you can't have it. What is the use of food points when you can't get cornflour, or sago, or black treacle or rice?"

"All the rice has gone to old Gandhi," said Mr. Shergold. "He ought to read a spot of history. In the Indian Mutiny the sepoys gave the rice to the English and lived on the water it was boiled in, because they said the white men needed it more."

"Well, Mr. Shergold, that's what they said," said Matron, "but I do assure you that when you've boiled the rice, unless of course you boil it *very* quick for curry so that it hasn't time to go really cooked, you get all the goodness in the water. Take boiled chicken and rice, or a broiled knuckle of veal and rice——"

Mrs. Bissell said she wished one could.

Veal, Matron conceded, was quite off the market, but chicken they could still get in the country. Well, she said, of course the stock you got from it was lovely and such lovely jelly when it was cold, but try to eat the rice separately and you would find it tasted of absolutely nothing at all and really not an ounce of nourishment in it.

Mr. Shergold, ignoring the larger aspect of the Indian Mutiny, said that was an idea and he hoped they would give old Gandhi plain boiled rice next time he went on the wagon, as he used to get it for lunch at his prep school and it was a fair sickener, at which fine piece of reasoning Mrs. Bissell shook her head, but felt such a nice young man and who had raced jerboas with Matron's nephew, must be allowed to say what he liked.

The brief peace-time meal was over and as Everard had no port to offer they all adjourned to the drawing-room where a welcome fire was blazing to cheer the July evening.

"Do tell me," said Mrs. Birkett to Mrs. Bissell, "about Edna. We haven't heard any news of her for a long time."

Now Edna, for the benefit of those readers who did not have a brother, son or other relation at Southbridge School during the years of war, was Mr. Bissell's great-niece and distinctly a mental defective whom the Bissells who were childless, although they spoke of each other rather foolishly and touchingly as Mother and Daddy, had more or less adopted. No one had been able to take any real interest in Edna, but the Bissells had made themselves almost universally liked and respected and it had become a point of honour to inquire after the unprepossessing child.

"A sad story," said Mrs. Bissell, her kind face clouding, "but as Daddy and I often say, what is must be for the best. She seemed to be getting on and really sometimes almost bright, but when we got back to London she progressed backwards rather than forwards and after talking it over very seriously, Daddy and I came to the conclusion that she would be happier in an institute."

There was an uncomfortable silence for various reasons. Matron was burning to ask medical questions and determined to get Mrs. Bissell alone if possible. Kate, and possibly Everard, were thinking how dreadful it would be if Bobbie, or Angela, or Phil became mentally defective and had to leave home. Mrs. Birkett was rather hazy as to what exactly an Institute was. She knew that what used to be called the Workhouse in Barchester had been raised to the status of Institute after the '14 war and further bowdlerized to being a Hospital just before this war; but what kind of Institute little Edna was in she could not guess. Mr. Birkett, who was really very tired after his long day, thought vaguely of the Imperial Institute and the Institute of Mining and Metallurgical Engineers, knew he was being stupid, and resigned himself to that state.

"I say," said Mr. Shergold, "not the Ada Clotworthy Mental Institution? My father is one of the Governors. He had an old great-uncle who was quite dotty and left all his money to it. Father says it's a first-rate place, only he'd rather old Uncle Tom had left his money to him."

"The identical place," said Mr. Bissell, "and I really cannot tell you how wonderfully little Edna is cared for. When I say little, she's getting quite a big girl now, but mentally of course she will always remain the dear little girl we all remember."

Sympathetic murmurs rose from the party all of whom, except Mr. Shergold, had known little Edna when her uncle and aunt were living in Maria Cottage and had been variously terrified or revolted by her.

"And they are so well fed," said Mr. Bissell. "Their own cows and poultry and vegetables. A wonderfully healthy and bracing spot and many of the inmates are now well over eighty."

The thought of these struldbrugs living on his great-uncle Tom's money nearly made Mr. Shergold say what he thought, but he very wisely didn't, and Matron who took a deep interest in the milk question said the difficulty they were having now with the milk for the School was hardly feasible, and as this Government didn't seem to have any dried milk either at present, and why they called it Household Milk she did not know as what was milk if not Household, she really did not know what we were coming to.

"There is of course an extremely easy and sensible way of settling the whole question," said Mrs. Bissell in her precise, unemotional voice.

"Ah, trust Mother to see the practical side," said Mr. Bissell, looking at his wife with adoration in his lean, tired face; even leaner and more tired, thought Kate, than when he had first come down to Southbridge and was struggling to get the Hosiers' Boys' School going in unfamiliar surroundings.

Mr. Birkett asked what it was, rather expecting from the Bissells economic views which were or at any rate had been when they came to Southbridge of a severely academic Labour kind.

"If I were Minister of Food," said Mrs. Bissell, "I should at once stop all this very foolish nonsense about giving free milk to State-supported or State-aided schools. It is just the kind of silly thing a man would do. Men have no sense of values at all, Mr. Birkett." But she looked at her husband with an expression plainly showing that he had every sense of value in the world.

These subversive and unexpected words produced complete silence. If Mrs. Bissell had said that the Minister ought to refuse milk altogether to anyone who was not employed or controlled by the Government, or to impose a fine of a hundred pounds upon every capittleist who gave his children milk in their cocoa, her audience, though they might not have agreed, would have known where they were. But that Mrs. Bissell, well known to them all for her strong view on State ownership and her painstaking admiration of anything that came from Russia, should advocate taking the milk away from children at State Schools was very perplexing, not to say staggering.

"I say," said Mr. Shergold, voicing the general thought, so that everyone felt grateful to him, "that's a bit stiff, isn't it?"

"It is," said Mrs. Bissell, "no thank you, Mrs. Carter, I never smoke though Daddy will gladly light up his pipe if Mr. Carter is smoking his—it is merely common sense. You do not know the Lower or Working Classes, whichever you prefer to call them, as I do."

"Oh, I don't know about that," said Mr. Shergold, who would never have dared to use these words and was crimson with unnecessary embarrassment. "I mean kids want milk, don't they? At least we used to have oodles when we were kids. Milk puddings too. Lord! how we hated milk puddings. And milk too. But I've got quite fond of it now. Rather prefer it to beer sometimes, only one doesn't seem to be able to get it in England."

"Mr. Shergold has hit the nail on the head," said Mrs. Bissell, "and in more than one place. Normal children do not like milk. Most normal children have a definite revulsion from it and from milk puddings, though I do not entirely agree with Spurge-Mackworth in his analysis of milk-allergism as part of the Demeter-complex. In the upper and better-to-do classes, this revulsion is gradually conditioned by environment, and by the Zeus-Kronos complex which leads children to wish to out-do their parents in various ways. Now, in the socially inferior or less moneyed classes, the child rarely sees its parents drinking milk. Quantities of tea, yes; also beer. Therefore, the child looks upon tea, though not beer for some reason which is not yet fully understood—you were saying, Mr. Shergold?"

"I'm awfully sorry if I interrupted," said Mr. Shergold, "but I only said kids don't like the taste of beer. I remember drinking the remains of my father's beer when I was three and I nearly went Blue Ribbon for life. It's a funny thing, though, savages take to rum like anything. You'd think it would put them off, but

they lap it up like a cat with cream. Perhaps English children
don't get a chance to try it young. My mother was practically
teetotal, but she believed rum wasn't drink, bless her, and we had
lashings of it with hot milk whenever we started a winter cold.
That's really why I joined the navy for the war."

"Putting aside the question of rum," said Mrs. Bissell, inexo-
rably but not unkindly, "the child, as I was saying, looks upon tea
as a beverage to be coveted and milk as something sweet out of
a tin. If I told you the statistics of the amount of condensed milk
consumed by the majority of families before the war as against
cows' milk, you would be surprised. What happens now? The
child goes to school and from that moment is expected to drink
cows' milk. It does not wish to drink milk. If you had lived
among them as I have, Mr. Shergold, and seen the bottles of
milk that were delivered at the schools every day and the really
quite shocking waste that goes on and the amount that goes bad
or is thrown away, you would feel as I do about the whole
question. Now, I will tell you who do need milk. All the mothers
and aunts and grandmothers who do the housework and the
shopping and the queues and the cooking. If the Food Ministry
would stop pampering the children with milk and oranges and
bananas, which again no child likes by nature and I may add that
the nutritive value of bananas is a highly moot question, and
look after the housewives of England, they would show a little
sense. But that of course one cannot expect."

Mr. Shergold said not this lot anyway and for his part whenever he read about shiploads of bananas coming from Jamaica he
went hopping mad at the thought that it might have been rum.

"I see you are the Norm," said Mrs. Bissell, approvingly,
which frightened Mr. Shergold a good deal. "Like your nice
sister, Mrs. Carter," she added, graciously bringing her hostess
back into the conversation. "How is Mrs. Merton?"

Kate was delighted to tell Mrs. Bissell all about Lavinia's
measles and how Lydia was being so good and looking after her
and how they all hoped the little boy wouldn't catch it, and the

three elder schoolmasters fell into talk about the war as they saw it at Southbridge, while Mr. Shergold who had seen most of the war from H.M.S. *Flatiron* listened respectfully and Mrs. Birkett talked to Matron. The party broke up early, for everyone was tired.

"Our Mrs. Bissell is better than ever," said Mrs. Birkett to her husband as they walked back across the quadrangle with their umbrellas up. "If all the Labour party were like her, how different things would be."

"If the Labour party knew what Mrs. Bissell says about them," said Mr. Birkett, "and about the class to which she belongs, they would cut her head off. She is really a most remarkable woman. I wonder if there are many like her."

Mrs. Birkett said firmly that there were millions like her, only they hadn't all her gift of facing and stating facts, and it was perfectly true that the women of England needed milk much more than the children, and the oranges too, and the children could keep the cod liver oil. Then they telephoned to Captain Fairweather and heard that the baby weighed eight pounds and was a peach and perfectly hideous and Rose wanted to call her Glamora, but they needn't worry as he was going to have her called Mary, after his mother, and Rose was very well and sent her love.

"The Last Night in the Old Home," said Mr. Birkett as he went upstairs. But his wife said did he know where he had put that letter to the Duke of Omnium and this distracted his mind, so that he went to bed and forgot about the Old Home till the following morning, when it was too late.

"And a very nice party," said Everard Carter to his wife when the guests had gone and the Bissells had retired to bed. "I think Shergold will do. Matron likes him and that's half the battle."

"I like him very much too," said Kate. "It was so nice of him to take Bellinger to the station. I do hope Matron will keep an eye on him. Did you see that the top of his collar was frayed? He could trim it himself with his nail scissors this time, but it really needs turning before it goes to the laundry again, and Jessie is rather careless about that sort of thing. I do wish she would wear her spectacles."

"My love," said Everard, "for the dozen years or so that I have known Jessie she has never worn her spectacles when she ought to, or so Matron tells me, though whenever I meet her about the house she looks like the headlights of a motor. If you and Matron can't down her, nobody else will. Now don't worry about Shergold. Any man who has been in the navy can look after himself, and if he can't some woman will always do it for him."

Kate said that held true for men who weren't in the navy and would Everard be sure to give her his blue socks to mend before they went to the wash as there was a place that needed darning over and then it wouldn't go; a description which any sensible reader will understand.

"Do you remember the picnic to Parsley Island?" said Everard, his mind going back to a summer long before the war when he was staying with Kate's parents for the first time, "and how angry you were when you found that blue sock that Jessie had mended with black wool? I fell in love with you on the spot."

"Darling!" said Kate. "But that was Jessie all over. All right, I'll answer the telephone."

The telephone was Lydia to ask how Speech Day had gone off. Kate gave her a brief account of the ceremony, almost crying as she described the cheers and their singing, and then the conversation became slightly unintelligible as heard from one end only, but Everard never took much notice of Kate's long talks with Lydia and was not curious, so he began to write letters.

When Kate had finished talking she came to Everard and kissed the top of his head.

"Well, what is it?" said Everard, knowing that this wifely attention was not inspired by love alone.

"It's Lydia," said Kate. "Noel hasn't come back yet. Do you think he has had an accident?"

"No, goose, I don't," said Everard. "If he was dining with Peggy he is probably still there. It's only a quarter to ten. Our party stopped very early and no wonder after the day we've had. Was Lydia anxious?"

Kate admitted that her sister had not seemed anxious, but said she sounded pale.

"Now, do be sensible, my dear love," said Everard. "First you say Lydia sounds thin and then that she sounds pale. This is carrying affection too far. Lydia is one of the most sensible women I know and I can't have you beginning to worry about her. Today has been too much for you."

Kate said she was not worrying in the least, but on the following morning she rang Lydia up and was relieved to hear her sister mention Noel quite casually as working in his room and being obliged to go to town for a couple of nights that week. Lavinia was getting on but wouldn't be out of quarantine for some time and so far Harry seemed quite well. Kate asked Lydia how she was. Lydia said quite well, but she felt a bit meagre, which had been Rose Fairweather's catchword of a year ago and had made them both laugh.

Kate rang off feeling temporarily reassured, but in spite of the packing and getting away with the children her sisterly anxiety for Lydia would keep breaking in, and she mentioned to Everard as they were driving to the station that Lydia had said she felt meagre.

"Thin, and pale, and now meagre," said Everard almost impatiently.

Kate looked at him with the slightly exasperated affection that the most loving of wives may have for the best and most affectionate of husbands. For it is well known that men understand absolutely nothing.

CHAPTER II

Noel Merton had passed an agreeable evening with Mrs. Arbuthnot. Miss Arbuthnot had gone to supper at the Vicarage to talk about pictures with Colonel Crofts, so Noel and his hostess were alone and made a very comfortable and amusing job of it. And if any reader hopes that they were thinking of an elopement we may as well say at once that they were thinking of no such thing, for Noel was very fond of his Lydia and Mrs. Arbuthnot had carried through at least thirty-six delightful little flirtations without anyone's heart being even scratched, least of all her own. Noel had also made many excursions into Pays du Tendre in his time, but always with a first-class return ticket and very pleasant recollections of some pretty verbal fencing. He was a good deal older than Lydia and the charmers of his young barrister days were now thinking of bringing their daughters out and wondering whether their sons would do university or conscription, but his rapier had not rusted and with Mrs. Arbuthnot he gave himself the pleasure of philandering high and disposedly, knowing that his partner was taking it no more seriously than Mrs. Brandon had taken it in that hot summer when old Miss Brandon had died, and they both had to stop their talk from time to time to laugh at themselves.

"I thought," said Noel, "that Colin might be coming muffled in a cloak, his hat pulled well over his eyes and a naked sword in his hand to run me through the heart."

"I rather hoped he would," said Mrs. Arbuthnot with great frankness. "I remember once, when the regiment was stationed at Umbrella, Captain Fosbery and Major Hipkins would come to tea on the same day and tried to set each other out and in the end I had to ask them to go because I couldn't think of anything more to say. So I pretended I had a headache and they were so sympathetic that they knocked over one of those dreadful tables—a brass tray on eight carved legs that are never at the proper distance from each other because of folding up."

Noel said he knew those tables and hated them and that one of the many charming things about Editha was that there was nothing Indian in it, and what happened next.

"It was dreadful," said Mrs. Arbuthnot, making a delightful face of mock penitence, "but I laughed so much that they both lost their temper and went away and proposed to the girls the whole regiment had been expecting them to propose to. They were such plain girls," she added with a sigh.

"You are quite perfect," said Noel. "You always say exactly what one expects you to say. Would you think it impertinent if I said that I have known no one except Lavinia Brandon who so unfailingly uttered the right sentiment for every occasion?"

Mrs. Arbuthnot said she would consider it a compliment, as she adored Mrs. Brandon and thought Francis was so delightful and had been happier at Stories than she had been since Fred was killed. And this remark, Noel felt sure, was quite true. But curiously enough, though he was glad that she had enjoyed herself he felt that a woman of real delicacy would have shown more reticence. There was no need to drag Francis Brandon in.

Then Mrs. Arbuthnot spoke a little of her married life, which she rarely did in Barsetshire, and said how very nice Fred's grandmother had been to her.

"His father and mother died when he was fairly young," she said, "and old Mrs. Arbuthnot brought him up. She was extraordinarily good-looking, even in her old age and I believe she had been a terrific beauty and the whole regiment was in love with her. Fred was very good-looking too, which is such waste for a man. He ought to have been the girl and Effie the boy. She is just like the photographs of her father. Francis says his mother thinks Effie is very like someone she knew but she can't think who it is," which description of Mrs. Brandon rang so true that Noel could not help laughing again, though not at Francis Brandon's remark of course, merely at Mrs. Arbuthnot's amused rendering of it.

At about half-past nine Miss Arbuthnot came back escorted by the Vicar, and Noel said he must go and could he drive Colonel Crofts back to the Vicarage. Colonel Crofts said it was only a short distance but if Merton would care to come in and see Miss Arbuthnot's beautiful drawing of the stengah bird, he would offer him a glass of very good wine from the Vicarage cellar. Noel had only come across Colonel Crofts once or twice, but he had liked the soldier-vicar and he accepted the invitation.

"My love to Lydia," said Mrs. Arbuthnot. "I shall be in town most of next week, but after that I'd love to come and see her. I'm not a bit afraid of measles."

Noel said he had to be in town too so they might lunch together. And if his pleasure in her acceptance was tempered by her suggestion that Aubrey Clover and Jessica Dean should join them, he was too polite to show it.

Noel, who had occasionally been to the Vicarage when visiting the Carters, was much struck by the new Vicar's improvements and congratulated him on the agreeable and comfortable appearance of the house especially the study, where Bateman had drawn the Indian curtains against the horrid unreal twilight and a fire was burning. Colonel Crofts told Bateman to bring the port and proudly showed Noel the drawing of the Whisky-soda bird, which Noel much admired.

"Rum people those bird-lovers are," he said, with the comfortable background to his thoughts that the port was unusually good. "Rather inhuman."

Colonel Crofts, though not in the least taking offence, said he

did not think that epithet could apply to Miss Arbuthnot whom
he had found extremely kind and sympathetic, not only about
birds, but about practical matters such as having that door on the
top landing made to open inwards instead of outwards.

"I am perhaps a little jaundiced by Wickham, our agent," said
Noel. "He has a real passion for birds, but it takes rather peculiar
forms. He goes out at night sometimes with a very powerful
torch and photographs them, and to judge by the birds' expression in the photographs they will lay addled eggs for the rest of
their lives. And he is apt to throw a net over a hush so that they
can't get out and he can look at them at close quarters. He always
lets them go, but I expect their children are all born half-witted."

The Colonel said a kind of Colney Hatch, and he had met
Mr. Wickham once or twice and liked him. Noel said he was a
very good agent and apart from his devotion to birds and drink
one of the best fellows he knew. It would be very nice, he said, if
Colonel Crofts and the Arbuthnots would dine at Northbridge
when the measles were over and he would ask Mr. Wickham
too.

Then their talk meandered into the war and of course it
happened, as it so often does in novels which only copy real life
and even more often in real life which is but an untidy novel, that
Colonel Crofts's artillery had received very useful information
from Noel's Intelligence unit before the Fall of France, so that
they were able to indulge in the talk which Francis Brandon had
described as "old Robinson in the dugout," and with this talk the
time passed so swiftly that it was nearly twelve when Noel
reached Northbridge Manor, and Lydia was fast asleep.

August is one of the dullest months of the year, or has become
so since the war. It should be a holiday month, but lodgings had
become so expensive even if you could get them which you
couldn't, travelling so desperately uncomfortable, the probabil-
ity of being worse fed and housed than one would be at home so
acute, that most people remained where they were. The Carters
had gone to Everard's mother who like a proper grandmother

had a house near the sea, the Birketts had gone to their new home near Worsted, but hardly anyone else among our acquaintance had the energy to move and a good many could not afford it. Several hundred million people tried to go to Switzerland but could not get seats on the train or rooms in the hotel and gave it up, while those who did get there were so nervous all the time lest the seventy-five pounds which They allowed them to take abroad should not stand up to the Swiss exchange and the high prices of every extra from a cup of coffee to a funicular, that they could not really enjoy themselves. Some went to France and found that everything cost about ten thousand francs and could never remember how much that was in English money; some went to Belgium and lived in great comfort but were driven mad by the sight of all the delightful almost forgotten luxuries that They would not allow them the money to buy; a few went to Sweden or Portugal or Italy, but change their sky as they would, they could not change the war-ridden mind which took all its pleasures anxiously, never able to enjoy the moment, and most of them came back almost as tired as they went, to face the further attacks which They were preparing against their purses, their comfort and their liberty.

But in fairness to Them, let it be said that They had prepared a delightful pastime for the patient English public, namely the changing, alluded to by the Bissells, of Bread Units for food points. Horrid as the scenes outside the Barchester bread and cake shops had been when They deliberately withheld the dates of the various V-Days from the public to make it more difficult to get bread, they were nothing to the scenes which were being enacted in Barchester during the better part of a fortnight.

Three times did the Deanery make the attempt and three times was it baffled. On the first occasion Mrs. Crawley herself, who always got the family rations on Monday morning, stood in a queue outside the Food Office for three-quarters of an hour, only able to move from the public house to the undertaker's three doors up in that time. On the following day her housekeeper went at the advertised time of opening, found a long queue already established and had the pleasure of watching the girls at the Food Office arriving late with cigarettes hanging out of their mouths while the patient public stood in the rain. Once more did the Deanery, in the person of Octavia Needham its youngest daughter, try its luck, but even Octavia's stalwart and unimpressionable spirit was daunted after moving exactly eighteen inches in half an hour and the Bread Units were never changed. It was, however, a slight comfort to the Crawleys and all the other hard-working families of Barchester to know that, exactly as Mr. Bissell had said, the people who had patience enough and little enough to do and finally got their food points, had to spend them all on pilchards or semolina, for nothing else had the grocers got, thanks to Them.

However outside Barchester things were easier, for the bread still delivered itself three times a week at Pomfret Madrigal and Northbridge and Southbridge, and the grocer still called once a week and was considerate of his old customers. A great aimless wave of affection came over the female assistants, old, middle-aged and young, who all took to calling the customers "dear." Not, as Mrs. Villars said, that she particularly wished to be called madam, but dear, especially from the very insolent and customer-hating woman at the baker's, she could not stomach, and went so far as to say, "I am not dear, I'm Grannie." But the woman only thought she was an idiot and said dear more than ever, which Mrs. Villars said served her right for being conceited about having grandchildren. On the other hand the returned soldiers, whose healthy complexion and upright bearing marked them as being apart at any rate till the English climate and civil life had done their fatal work, were extraordinarily polite and efficient whether in shop, bus, or even civil service, and how grateful the housewives of Barsetshire were, only they can tell.

Miss Lavinia Merton made a very good recovery from her measles and Master Harry Merton did not catch them, which was considered by some people to be a mistake.

"For it stands to reason," said Lydia's old cook to Palmer the old parlourmaid who had now returned from her holiday, "that it's against nature if all the family don't have it. They say if you don't catch the measles when they're about, it drives them in. My old auntie when one of her children got the measles she shut them all up in the one room till they got it too, and the same with the whooping-cough. Now it's as likely as not Baby'll get the measles somewhere and if he'd got them off Miss Lavinia it would be more in nature. It's where you get the measles that makes all the difference." Palmer said no one knew where Miss Lavinia got hers. The cook said Ah well, we couldn't all know everything, but mark her word, if Nurse would let Baby take his sandals off in the garden we would see what we would see, and her old auntie always said to her dying day that to let a child go barefoot drew the measles; a scientific theory the more frightening for its obscurity.

At Noel's suggestion Lydia asked Colonel Crofts and the Arbuthnots to dinner quite soon, also Mr. Wickham. As Colin was clinging like a leech to Northbridge in spite of some very attractive invitations to Cromer and North Wales, a partner had also to be provided for him and Susan Dean was invited. Susan, who was taking ten days' holiday from the Red Cross, was to come out from Barchester by train after her work, spend the night, and be driven to Barchester next day by Noel who had to get the London train, by which means she would not have the long wait at Barchester, Central for the local to Winter Overcotes. Lydia had devoted herself perhaps unnecessarily to Miss Lavinia Merton, but the old Lydia Keith was still strong in her and she still threw herself with conscientious violence into whatever job presented itself; as she had thrown herself into war nursing with a vehemence whose result had been that Lavinia had never had the elder brother or sister who should have preceded her. Still, as Lydia said to Noel, someone had to be the eldest in a family or there wouldn't be any families at all.

"It's all very well madam looking after Miss Lavinia all the

time but the gentlemen don't always like it," said Nurse to Mrs.
Twicker, for the two ladies were on quite friendly terms when
not on their dignity. Which of them had the higher status it
would take the compilers of the Almanach de Gotha to decide.
Nurse had brought up several families and had Miss Jessica
Dean the popular actress to her credit and was queen of Northbridge nursery; but so few of her nurslings had children. Mrs.
Twicker, though she had lost status by marrying the gardener,
was as it were an honorary grandnurse, having been nanny to
Robert Keith, and much loved by all the Keith children. As for
Colin, Nanny Twicker deplored his bachelorhood but also
much enjoyed petting and scolding him and often said how nice
it would be when Master Colin brought a nice young lady back,
a remark at which Colin used to laugh, but which he now found
senseless and irritating, for no one in his or her senses could so
describe Peggy Arbuthnot. A bewitching woman if you like, a
fascinating charmer, even an accomplished and delightful flirt,
but not a nice young lady.

"When Miss Kate had the whooping-cough," said Nanny
Twicker, as if introducing an entirely new subject, "Mrs. Keith—
that was Miss Lydia's mother, Nurse, you wouldn't remember
her—was up for three nights with her. Every twenty minutes
the poor little thing was sick with that dreadful cough and we
took it in turns, Mrs. Keith and me. Now that *was* an illness.
Poor little Kate lost twelve pounds and looked so pale we all
thought she wasn't long for this world. But Mrs. Keith sent her
over to my cottage when she was better and the little lamb
picked up quite quickly. Such a darling child Miss Kate was—
she never gave any trouble at all."

Only those who have been forced against their will to study at
close quarters the insane jealousies and rivalries between faithful
retainers will appreciate to the full Nanny Twicker's masterly
tactics. To begin with, whooping-cough is far more spectacular
than measles, though measles have of late taken an unfair
advantage by becoming much more dangerous than they used to

be. Then Nanny Twicker had rubbed it well into Nurse that she had not known Lydia's mother and made it appear to be a social lapse. Then her charge had lost weight and looked ill, while Lavinia except for a couple of feverish days had been quite happy and eaten everything she was given! This was followed by the boastful statement which Nurse to her great annoyance knew to be true, that Kate had made a good convalescence in Nanny Twicker's own cottage, under her own eye, and topped by a deliberately provocative remark about Kate giving no trouble, obviously intended to imply that Lavinia did. Nurse was hopelessly outclassed and called to Harry to come along with Nurse and find his din-din.

Nurse on her return then retailed some of the passage at arms to Lydia, as part of the eternal game of giving one's fellow-servant, or in this case ex-servant, away, but got very little sympathy from Lydia who was conscious of being tired and irritable, states very foreign to her. But the foolish tale-bearing rankled and she wondered if she had been wrong in devoting herself to Lavinia. Had Lavinia been ill earlier in the year all would have been easy, for Noel was usually away for most of the week and Lydia reserved weekends for him. But in the Long Vacation, with Noel at home, the eternal question between good wife and good mother became urgent. She was already running Northbridge Manor as every house of any size was being run with a small and not very efficient staff; it was impossible for Nanny to look after an invalid, keep the nurseries clean and do all the tray-carrying, and there was the danger of infection for Harry. There was obviously nothing for it but to take over one of the children for the time being and hope that Noel would not feel neglected. Not that this worried her much, for she had a better opinion of him than to think he would feel neglected because his wife was nursing one of his children. But the insidious demoralization which six years of war followed by a peace which except for bombs and bloodshed had every malignity of war had brought to almost every British citizen, could not be escaped. Partly for the pleasure of playing a game at which he had been an adept in former years, partly because his house had become entirely childridden since Lavinia fell ill, partly driven by the unvoiced malaise to behave in a way foreign to his true nature, Noel had undoubtedly taken to Mrs. Arbuthnot as he might have taken to the whisky bottle and if it also annoyed Colin, well, Colin had been excessively annoying and boring about Mrs. Arbuthnot himself and it served him right.

It is possible that Lydia did not see much of what was happening, for she loved Noel and liked Mrs. Arbuthnot. To be a jealous wife would not have suited her and I think she was incapable of jealousy, but some sixth sense hitherto latent in her had told her that Noel was making himself fairly ridiculous and this hurt her pride deeply. Then her love told her pride in no uncertain terms that there was not room in the same house for both of them, but all the same she felt a dull ache of unhappiness and hopelessness. Had she been of a more forthcoming nature she might have found reassurance if not comfort from nearly everyone in the county, the country and indeed the whole world labouring under this same dull ache, but she said nothing. Kate was away, there was no one else to whom she could or would confide her anxieties, so she went on loving Noel and liking Mrs. Arbuthnot as much as ever, and there were dark marks below her eyes and a shadow below her cheek bones that might have reminded Noel of the year her father died, when she had come straight to his arms to be comforted. As a precaution Lydia had kept away from Harry even after Lavinia was well, but the dinner-party was to be the last night of her quarantine and the thought cheered her a good deal, though she was never free of the feeling of depression and guilt which can overcome the most worthy and candid natures.

Mr. Wickham had also made his plans, which were to fetch Miss Arbuthnot from Editha after lunch and take her to Nutfield where Roddy Wicklow, Lord Pomfret's agent and brother-in-law, who approved avimania as an essentially English occupation though his own interests were confined to game birds, was going to take them to a very private part of the estate where tradition had it that the last bustard in England had been buried, a wanderer from the colonies that were unsuccessfully reintroduced round the turn of the century. There was no basis at all for this tradition, some going so far as to say that the corpse was not that of a bustard, but a buzzard, shot by old Lord Pomfret's gamekeeper in the exercise of his duties. But as the lawful resting place of dead birds of prey is one of the farm or stable doors, where they are nailed with weasels and stoats as a deterrent to the animal world in general, nobody believed this story, nor indeed did anyone greatly care by now who or what was buried there except old Lord Stoke over at Rising Castle who enjoyed what he called "digging for bones" and would undoubtedly have insisted that the bustard or buzzard was a Viking had he come across its remains.

Accordingly Mr. Wickham drove up after lunch in his clanking little car and walked into Editha by the side way, for he was by now quite a friend of the house and on excellent terms with the sister-in-law. Mrs. Arbuthnot was pre-cooking the Sunday joint (if a bit of shank of a frozen lamb can be called a joint) just in case; a periphrase only too familiar to the British housewife, meaning in plain speech that it smells a bit queer doesn't it, but I'll just pop it in the oven and do it on the low gas and tomorrow I'll hot it through again and I do hope George won't make a fuss the way he did last week because it's the ration and that's that.

"Well, well," said Mr. Wickham. "It's like the place where the old horse died. Can I give a hand?"

Mrs. Arbuthnot, flushed and untidy but always pretty, said she was managing nicely and opened the oven door to baste the shank.

"Reminds me of the Tube in an air-raid," said Mr. Wickham. "Effie ready?"

And then Miss Arbuthnot came in all ready for the expedition in her old tweeds and strong shabby shoes and gloves and

Mr. Wickham said they had better be off as Wicklow had a meeting at three.

"Have a nice time," said Mrs. Arbuthnot, who had just been spat upon with hot fat while basting the lamb and was mopping her face with her apron. "Is your suitcase ready, Effie?"

Mr. Wickham said he didn't know they were staying at Northbridge Manor and in that case perhaps Effie would like to get up at three o'clock next morning and watch the dawn flight of handrails over the spinney.

"Oh, it's only Effie's evening things," said Mrs. Arbuthnot, who was beginning to do some rather greasy washing-up. "She can't dine with the Mertons in her bird things. Colonel Crofts is taking me. Good-bye till the evening."

"You'll like Roddy Wicklow," said Mr. Wickham as they drove towards Nutfield. "He's a quiet fellow. Never says much. Nor does his wife, but she's a nice little thing. Her mother is Mrs. Barton who writes those books about the Borgias and what not. A bit too highbrow for me," with which appraisal of Mrs. Barton's scholarly and exhaustingly documented historical novels about Italy in the fifteenth and sixteenth centuries, Miss Arbuthnot cordially agreed, as she did upon many subjects with Mr. Wickham.

"Funny Wicklow being Wicklow and my being Wickham," said that gentleman as they crossed the narrow high-backed fifteenth-century bridge which so far had been saved from being widened, though it was now only a question of time till They pulled it down and made it easier for motor coaches to roar up the beautiful High Street of Nutfield and turned the dignified brick of the houses into tea-shops and sham antique shops. "Another funny thing, I was in a sloop called *Walberswick* once. Things like that do happen to one. Queer things, things."

Miss Arbuthnot quite understood these last words and said she thought Wickham was a nicer name than Wicklow, adding, "don't you, Mr. Wickham? Really, I mean."

"I don't know," said Mr. Wickham. "My friends always call

me Wicks. It started in the *Walberswick*. I wish you'd say Wicks if you don't mind. Peggy calls me Wicks, so does Jessica."

Miss Arbuthnot said of course she would and he must call her Effie.

"I always do behind your back," said Mr. Wickham. "Have for a long time. Ever since you said you were F. E. Arbuthnot. There's Wicklow. Good, we needn't go in."

He drew up in front of one of the Georgian houses in the wide High Street which ran uphill from the river. In a front garden behind a low stone wall and elegant railings which had luckily escaped being made into cannon fodder, were Mr. and Mrs. Wicklow, three small children, several dogs and some very young puppies. The mother of the puppies wore a bland and fatuous expression of pride in her fat, wobble-legged off-spring while the elder dogs, including the puppies' father who had not the faintest idea that they were his own children, were frankly bored, and all the younger dogs who had never seen puppies before and did not remember how lately they had been puppies themselves, were looking with horror, disgust and in some cases terror on what they took to be a revolting exhibition of dog dwarfs.

Roddy Wicklow said Good, now they could be going. Introductions were briefly made. Miss Arbuthnot had an impression of a dark-haired, dark-eyed creature absorbed in her husband, her children and her home, a little frightened of strangers. Roddy got into the car and they drove over the hump-backed bridge, in at the West Lodge gates of the Towers and then, leaving the drive, branched off by a by-road through the home farm and so to where the shooting-land began.

Miss Arbuthnot, who had not seen that part of the county before, was overcome by its beauty. They had stopped in a long valley which curved gently away at each end. On the steep slopes behind were beeches rising to meet the sky. On the other side of the rich green valley the ground sloped less steeply but with pleasing irregularities where beech and wild cherry were judiciously interspersed with conifers. Drives for the guns were cut here and there, fern-carpeted, leading the eye to romantic interminable vistas at the end of one of which was an obelisk.

"I'd like to see this place in October," said Mr. Wickham, after a short silence.

"It's a jolly sight," said Roddy Wicklow. "A fine lot and jolly colours too."

Miss Arbuthnot said the beeches must be marvellous, with all that brown and gold.

"Not beeches, my girl," said Mr. Wickham, just as if Miss Arbuthnot were Black-eyed Susan. "Pheasant."

Roddy Wicklow then realized the mistake and the joke and laughed, though with the utmost good nature, and Miss Arbuthnot couldn't help laughing too though it was against herself.

"I'll tell you when you ought to see it, though," said Roddy suddenly becoming serious. "When the wild cherries are out. It's exactly like a Christmas card for a week. You know, white all over everything. It's a bit stupid, but I always make a point of coming here when they're out. Every spring you thing it can't happen again. But it does. It makes me feel things aren't so bad after all. Well, I must be getting on. I've got to see old Wheeler. You know your way, Wickham. Past the obelisk and down by the white paling. You can make a round by Hamaker's Spinney and get back to the car. It takes about two hours."

He strode away towards the far end of the valley where at a small farm of incredible Morlandesqueness a thread of blue smoke was rising from the thatched roof.

"He's a good chap," said Mr. Wickham approvingly, as he and Miss Arbuthnot walked across the valley towards the obelisk. "Likes horses better than cars. I expect he's got one waiting for him at the farm. A car's a useful thing, but give me a horse. By Jove, we could have fun here."

Miss Arbuthnot said the thing she most missed now, apart

from her brother, was the riding. In India she had ridden nearly every day.

"You'd look topping on a horse," said Mr. Wickham, looking at her tall, well-built figure as she walked easily up the fern-clad drive. "I wouldn't mind riding myself, though I mostly hold onto the mane now. I might be able to manage a mount for you. I know a lot of people round here who still ride or hunt a bit. Say the word and I'll get onto the job."

"Thank you very much, Wicks," said Miss Arbuthnot, "but I won't. I'm a bit old now and I haven't any riding things. And I think I'd miss Fred too much. We rode together a lot."

"Don't talk nonsense, Effie," said Mr. Wickham. "Old, indeed!"

"Well, I'm nearly forty," said Miss Arbuthnot, not boasting, not self-pitying, merely stating a fact.

"Comes to that I'm nearly fifty," said Mr. Wickham, whose voice seemed to Miss Arbuthnot to carry an implication that the ten years or so between them constituted some special bond. But the subject was dropped, for they had now reached the top of the drive and found themselves on a green plateau, behind them the beech woods, in front of them rolling land sloping away towards Harefield and the site of the new building for the Hosiers' Girls' Foundation School. It was all pure English and pure heartbreak, for no one, not the present Lord Pomfret nor Roddy Wicklow his faithful agent, knew whether Lord Mellings, aged about six, would be able to keep up any of the estates he would inherit, or provide for any of the old tenants to whom the Towers had for so long been a rock and a shelter, accompanied by a good deal of autocratic benevolence.

"Let's have a look at the obelisk," said Mr. Wickham. "The third earl won it at cards from the Duke of Omnium somewhere about 1760, and I believe it cost about two hundred pounds to get it moved and set up. Then he lost all his money gambling and it wasn't till the sixth earl that they really got going again with coal and marrying heiresses and built that hideous Pomfret

Towers. And now I suppose the next Lord Pomfret will have to be a Bevin Boy or join the trades union and they'll build prefabs all over the estate. Let's forget it. Can you read Latin?"

Miss Arbuthnot could not, so they gazed reverently upon an inscription carved on the base of the obelisk which said that the Goddess of Fortune had reft this Egyptian stone from Dux Omnium to bestow it upon Comes Pontefractus whose victories, not by the sword of Mars but by the peaceful dice, were here commemorated, and ended with the appropriate tag, 'Alea jacta est.'

"I can make out a bit here and there," said Mr. Wickham, "but I can't get much sense out of it—Latin's like that. They didn't seem to get the hang of putting the words in the right order. At least not when I was at school. Wicklow told me the Earl of Pomfret's private chaplain wrote it. I'd rather like to have something I'd written carved on a monument."

They looked backwards down the drive towards the beech-crowned cliffs on the far side and listened to the woodland silence, a silence made of a thousand tiny noises, and to the ever-present Barsetshire sound of melancholy sheep bells. Then they walked by the white palings talking about horses and birds and people, and Miss Arbuthnot told Mr. Wickham what fun she and her brother used to have in India before the war.

"He was younger than I am," said Miss Arbuthnot, "and frightfully good-looking. Everyone stared at him and Peggy wherever they went. Father wasn't a bit good-looking, but his mother, my grandmother who brought us up, was terrifically handsome. I believe she was very shocking when she was young and all the regiment was in love with her."

As she talked, more freely than Mr. Wickham had yet heard her, he had an impression that she had always been the man of the family and the good-looking Fred, in the words of a well-known ballad, nothing but a doggone pest who had probably borrowed what money his sister had and neglected his pretty wife, which perhaps accounted for the Arbuthnots' modest way of living. But he could hardly ask questions about such private matters, and by this time they had come to Hamaker's Spinney where they got out their field-glasses and looked at mippets, handrails, gallow-birds, spottletoes and other feathered friends to their hearts' content, for Lord Pomfret and Roddy Wicklow had managed to convey to the bird world that this part of the Pomfret Estate, though having no pretensions to be a bird sanctuary, would be regarded as bird property and respected accordingly. And this gave great pleasure to the birds of Barchester, for, as one of the Duke of Omnium's golden pheasants remarked at the yearly meeting of the Barsetshire branch of the Bird-lovers' Association, if you lived in a bird sanctuary people were always coming to look at you on Sunday afternoon, just when you had taken your boots off and were having a nice snooze on the couch in the lounge, whereas at Pomfret's place one could be practically sure of having one's privacy respected: and though the golden pheasant was a low fellow, living entirely on his looks, he spoke sense.

So much was there to see, to discuss, to photograph, for F. E. Arbuthnot was preparing one of her delightful articles for *Country Life* with illustrations, that the afternoon passed swiftly and it was well after five when they got back to the car. Mr. Wickham suggested that Miss Arbuthnot might come back to his cottage, look at some of his photographs of the great kitchen skewer, which inhabits the Boiler Range in Western Australia, have tea and then go on to meet her suitcase at the Manor. Miss Arbuthnot accepted with pleasure, was delighted to see Mr. Wickham's cottage, to admire its neatness and ship-shapeness, and glad to have the excellent bachelor's tea which he produced. Mr. Wickham on his side felt how peaceful it was to drink tea with a very intelligent woman who knew a bird when she saw one and to be able to say whatever came into one's mind with the certainty that she would understand, or if she didn't understand would sympathize. When they had finished their tea he put everything on the tray and carried it out.

"I'll just wash these up," he said. "I shan't be a minute."

"Quite right," said Miss Arbuthnot, getting up and following him. "Peggy and I decided never to leave the dirty things. They marry and have children if you leave them in the scullery. Shall I wash or dry?"

Mr. Wickham very sensibly accepted her offer and gave her two glass-cloths. Miss Arbughnot eyed his with the interest of an expert, approved his methods of rinsing, stacking and washing, his way of cleaning the sink after use. He liked her way of drying and admired the way in which she appeared to know by instinct where the china and teaspoons lived. They then returned to the sitting-room, where Mr. Wickham made up the fire and looking at his watch said what about a sun-downer.

"You haven't any whisky, I suppose," said Miss Arbuthnot.

For answer Mr. Wickham threw open the door of his corner cupboard.

"Good Lord!" said Miss Arbuthnot.

Mr. Wickham said he had a lot of good friends and set out two glasses.

"About two fingers," said Miss Arbutnot. "And hardly any soda. Thank you very much. It reminds me of Fred. We always had drinks in India. Not that he was a drinker. He just liked it."

Full of admiration for a woman who accepted whisky without protest and properly enjoyed it, Mr. Wickham remarked "Here's to F. E. Arbuthnot," and put his neat whisky down with promptitude and dispatch.

"I say, Effie," he said. "Why don't you come on the Royal Bird Watchers' Society's cruise to the Azores? There's some interesting work to be done there. We shall be almost the first in the field and the Bird Watchers are a quiet lot. I'm thinking of going myself. It's in September."

"I'd love to," said Miss Arbuthnot, "but I can't afford it."

"Nor can I," said Mr. Wickham cheerfully, "but I shall somehow."

"I can't, even somehow," said Miss Arbuthnot and there was a silence.

"I may as well tell you the facts," said Miss Arbuthnot, "and then we needn't talk about it again. Fred borrowed most of what money I had and that was that. I have one hundred and fifty a year. Fred ran through everything. I really don't know where it went. Chiefly in living beyond his means and giving presents and treats to pretty women. He only did one sensible thing in his life. Some old aunt or other left him ten thousand pounds and he settled it on Peggy before he could spend it. So she has the income on that minus the income-tax, and she had a bit from her people, so we get along all right. I don't mind, but I hate to see Peggy not having pretty clothes or new hats or lots of scent and face cream. F. E. Arbuthnot helps a bit and there's your publisher who may take my drawings. I wish Peggy would marry again. She ought to have luxury and fun."

"So ought you," said Mr. Wickham.

Miss Arbuthnot laughed and said she could do with another whisky.

"Look here, Effie," said Mr. Wickham, pouring a suitable amount of whisky for her and an equally suitable but quite different amount for himself, "it's all very well to talk of Peggy getting married, but what about you?"

Miss Arbuthnot said with perfect composure that she really didn't know and hadn't thought about it.

"Then it's time you did," said Mr. Wickham standing up in a rather threatening way. "I've got a bit of my own. I've got this house as long as I give satisfaction which I hope to go on doing. Why don't you think it over? Milk and eggs from the farm, our own vegetables, and we could do all the birding you like. I'm pretty even-tempered and I've a head like teak."

In pre-war India Miss Arbuthnot, although not beautiful nor superficially attractive, had had a fair experience of proposals though never one which had shaken her devotion to her brother. But this was something quite new, and for the moment she did not know what to say.

"Put it this way," said Mr. Wickham. "I love you. I'm sorry, but I do."

"Please don't," said Miss Arbuthnot. "It's no good."

"I know I'm not a patch on your brother," said Mr. Wickham, who had quite realized the depth of her affection for what seemed to have been an engaging and conscienceless ne'er-do-well, "but he is dead and I'm alive. Will you marry me, Effie?"

"I am sorry, I can't," said Miss Arbuthnot, very sadly, for she liked Mr. Wickham with all her heart and knew she would hurt him.

"Think again," said Mr. Wickham. "No reason why you shouldn't, you know. Peggy can come and live here if you like, but she's bound to get married again some time. Where would you be then?"

"I haven't the faintest idea," said Miss Arbuthnot. "Look here, Wicks, I can't and that's all. I am tremendously grateful and I think I'm going to cry, but I can't marry you."

"Look here," said Mr. Wickham. "The lesser gallowsbird *does* nest in Pockington's alder and nowhere else. Have you got that?"

"It's most generous of you to admit it," said Miss Arbuthnot, "but dear Wicks, I simply can't."

"You must," said Mr. Wickham. "Listen, Effie. The common fly-gobbler does say Too-pee-*terrip*-pip-a-rip-squee. I thought it didn't, but it does."

There was silence. Not for one moment did Miss Arbuthnot underestimate the sacrifice her admirer had made. For her sake he had renounced two of his cherished beliefs, and even if it was only lip-service it showed a depth of self-abnegation which touched her to the core. Not even for someone she loved very much would she palter with the truth about a bird's note. It was all more and more difficult.

"I daresay you're right," said Mr. Wickham. "I drink too much and I'm too old to stop. It's true I never get drunk, but it does run away with too much money. Anyone would turn me down and quite right too," which was an insidious and almost mean form of approach, putting Miss Arbuthnot in the position of a critic, a position she had never for a moment assumed. Her heavy face was contorted by her efforts to command her tears and to any unprejudiced observer she would have looked very ugly, but Mr. Wickham was not unprejudiced.

"I don't mind drink in the least," said Miss Arbuthnot. "But I don't love you, Wicks, and that's that. And now I'd better go to the Manor. Peggy will be coming with my suitcase and I've got to change. Thank you very much for the walk. I loved it and we'll do some more if you like."

"All right," he said. "God bless and all that, Effie. And now I would like to say that the common fly-gobbler does not say too-pee-terrip, it says too-pee-pirret. And what is more, the broad-tailed gallowsbird only nests in wych-elms, and if you thought you saw one in a variegated holly it was a lesser gallows-bird. There."

He drank another neat whisky, put the cork into the bottle, hit it down with the palm of his hand and put the bottle back in the cupboard.

"I'll walk over with you," he said. "I'll just lock up first."

He then put the chairs straight, shook up the cushions, shut his writing-table, put another shovel of coke on his kitchen boiler, gave a last look round and said he was ready. Miss Arbuthnot noticed that he had done everything except lock up and greatly admired a man who left his house neat and inviting for his return. So would she leave a house, if ever she had a house to leave. But it would not be Mr. Wickham's house. Avoiding such controversial topics as marriage and the exact words spoken by the common fly-gobbler, they walked to the Manor

"Well," said Mr. Wickham as they entered the garden by the white gate. "I've had it. But ever the best of friends and all that."

Miss Arbuthnot did not take the allusion, but she appreciated the spirit and shook hands with him. Mr. Wickham clung to her hand for a second and then they walked on to the terrace door, while Mr. Wickham reflected how hard and rough so many women's hands were now. Not like his mother's hands as he remembered them, though she was an excellent housekeeper and a very good cook when she felt like cooking. Still, mother didn't have to wash up and clean the brass and silver and quite likely wash the kitchen floor as Miss Arbuthnot probably did; though his love made him exaggerate, for except on Sundays and the days Mr. Dingle had had a drop too much the night before, Mrs. Dingle did what are known as "the roughs" as well as "the brights." Ruminating on this matter he opened the door and they went in.

At the Manor Mrs. Arbuthnot and Colonel Crofts with Miss Arbuthnot's suitcase had already arrived. The suitcase was up-stairs and Lydia took Miss Arbuthnot to her room, turned on the bath and told her not to hurry because Noel wasn't back yet. So Miss Arbuthnot was able to enjoy a very hot bath, put on the woolen dress she had packed (for only the youngest and most insensitive could wear cotton frocks that summer) and think quietly about Mr. Wickham. Not for a moment did she regret her decision. Everything, she knew, was in favour of her accept-ing him: or nearly everything. He was pleasant, competent, friendly, a lover of birds, a true countryman, an ex-naval man, of good Barsetshire stock, with a good and probably permanent job and a very comfortable little house. Anyone would say that Effie Arbuthnot, nearly forty, with one hundred and fifty pounds a year of her own, was a fool not to take him. Very well: she was a fool, and that was that. And as she brushed and knotted her hair in front of the glass (for one does not have a permanent wave with its ceaseless washings, settings, and re-newals on one hundred and fifty pounds a year), with the hard grey light of British-Summer-Time August casting it uncom-promising eye on her face, she thought it extremely improbable that any other man, however kind, however sympathetic, would ever think of her as a companion.

"You've had your chance, my girl, and you've lost it," said Miss

Arbuthnot aloud to herself as she unskilfully put some powder on her face and rubbed most of it off again. "So shut up."

Downstairs she found Colonel Crofts and Mrs. Arbuthnot talking with Lydia and a very comfortable party it made. Presently Colin arrived with Susan Dean, looking as Noel afterwards said to Lydia like the Stag at Bay.

"I am sorry," he said to Mrs. Arbuthnot, with a deep manly note in his voice which might have been taken by anyone who noticed it for a slight cold, "I was working."

Mrs. Arbuthnot said how splendid, which beautiful words so upset Colin that he nearly forgot to say how do you do to Miss Arbuthnot and Colonel Crofts.

"I expect," said Mrs. Arbuthnot, looking at Colin with a charm which almost cloaked her entire lack of interest, "that you have to work quite hard in the Long Vacation or you'd forget it all," which original point of view overheard by Noel nearly upset his gravity. To Colin, when he had sternly repressed the natural irritation felt by his saner self, the remark seemed wholly beautiful, the expression of an innocent and credulous mind, ripe for cultivation by a finer intellect, say for example that of a barrister-at-law of the Inner Temple.

"It was not so much tat," he said, "as My Own Work."

Mrs. Arbuthnot said of *course*, with an emphasis which quite clearly showed that she had forgotten what it was. But Colin, who had for some months been in no condition to see anything clearly, obligingly explained to her the very tricky nature of running powers, instancing the lines from Marylebone and Paddington as far as Princes Risborough, over which two railway companies have joint control. Mrs. Arbuthnot listened with the same deceptive air of appreciation that had ensnared her late husband's regiment, who all expounded to her their views on polo, women, cricket, the Government, horses, the way Major Potter played that last hand at bridge, obscure Indian dialects, fellers that came out for a season and wrote books, the Mess Secretary's failings and a hundred and one other interesting topics; which expositions left her as unmoved as Ianthe, passing like wind over the grass; but very pretty, flower-strewn, scent-laden grass.

"I know," she said, just as Colin had got well into a detailed description of Princes Risborough Junction. "I went to Oxford that way once. I can't think why, except that I missed the proper train at Paddington and the porter said there was another, and I remember Princes Risborough perfectly well, because it was Ascot week and the engine driver waited till the station-master gave him the winner on the wireless, so we were a little late. And there is a charming station at Bledlow with the station-master's house right on the platform with lace curtains. I simply adore railways."

Palmer then announced dinner, which thanks to the Home Farm was very good, including a boiled bit of the Merton's own pig with broad beans over which Colonel Crofts, whom no one had suspected of being greedy, became quite lyrical.

"I am going to keep a pig at the Vicarage," he said to Mrs. Arbuthnot who was next to him. "My man is a farmer's son and he has managed to keep in touch with pigs all the time he was in the army. I believe his great ambition is to cross a White Porkminster with a Cropbacked Cruncher. He has a theory that he could get more good streaky bacon that way than anyone has yet produced."

"Pigs are so nice," said Mrs. Arbuthnot, "but I don't know much about them. You ought to talk to Effie. She was brought up in the country and adores them, but we haven't got room at Editha. At least we really have, but Chives wouldn't like it."

Colonel Crofts asked who Chives was.

"Our gardener one afternoon a week," said Mrs. Arbuthnot. "He doesn't hold with anything but vegetables and a few roses for the ladies. We did try to keep hens, but he wouldn't let us."

Colonel Crofts said he thought his man knew Chives, down at the Red Lion, and he must certainly talk to Miss Arbuthnot about pigs after dinner. And then Mrs. Arbuthnot left him and sparkled upon Noel, who enjoyed himself very much. Their talk was mostly about friends in town and about Aubrey Clover's new play in which Jessica Dean was as usual going to play the female lead.

"She is coming to your lunch on Tuesday, isn't she?" said Mrs. Arbuthnot. "I do so adore her."

"I will adore anyone that you adore," said Noel, "but I am a little frightened of Jessica. I have a horrid feeling that she has rather a low opinion of me. She may be perfectly right, but I don't like the feeling."

Mrs. Arbuthnot said nonsense, and Jessica was very fond of him and Lydia, and then she and Noel began to talk nonsense. There was no harm at all in the nonsense, but it was all London talk about London people and the others had not much clue to it, and Miss Arbuthnot on Noel's other side had to talk to Mr. Wickham next to whom she had by Fate's usual unintelligent arrangements been placed. To talk on general subjects to a man whom you have just refused and for whom you have a sincere liking is not the easiest job in the world, but they both brought good will to it and gradually from birds they worked round to pigs, which pleasing creatures Mr. Wickham had known pretty intimately in his boyhood. Colonel Crofts, who was opposite them, overheard something of what they were saying and with an apology for speaking across the table asked Mr. Wickham if he knew anything about White Porkminsters.

"I knew them very well, sir," said Mr. Wickham, "when I was a lad. My father is a farmer and I was brought up on the farm. There is a kind of squareness about White Porkminsters that you don't get in any other pig. When I say square I mean cube, only of course much longer."

Like two cubes put together with a pig's face and a curly tail, Colonel Crofts suggested.

"That's what I mean, sir," said Mr. Wickham. "And so low in the undercarriage you can hardly see their trotters. What are you doing with your trotters, Mrs. Merton?"

Lydia, who was feeling a little annoyed with her dear Colin for taking no pains to talk to that nice Susan Dean, said she proposed to have the trotters parboiled and then finished in the oven with bread crumbs and a little fat: unless, she said, making one more effort to drag Colin into the conversation, he preferred them plain boiled with parsley sauce. But Colin said he did not mind which way they were cooked; perhaps the most tactless and stony-hearted answer a guest can make. So Lydia gave him up and joined in the pig talk, but not with quite her usual gusto, for she felt oppressed without knowing why. It was not that Colin was being very trying at present, for she had a large and affectionate toleration for her brother; it was not that Mrs. Arbuthnot and Noel were having apparently such fun over private jokes about people she didn't know, for she had long been accustomed to his London interests being a world apart from her life. Perhaps, she thought, as the tides of pig and London washed over the table, she ought to have tried to go to London more, but she did so hate London, and here there was so much to do. The house, the nursery, the farm, the animals, the garden; always shorthanded in the house, always the chance of a cold or a measle in the nursery, Mr. Wickham doing three men's work on the estate and often glad of her help, old Twicker getting past his work as a gardener with no young men under him to train. In every part of Northbridge life Lydia was needed to fill the gaps made by the war and the far worse peace. In Barchester demobilized men who might have been on the land were blowing new-fangled soap bubbles at street corners, photographing shoppers as they walked down the High Street and thrusting cards into their hands, peddling elastic or saucepan cleaners. Colonel Crofts could have told her that this is the aftermath of every war and that no amount of labour exchanges, no lavish expenditure of the taxpayers' money will create labour when it does not wish to be created. He had seen the poison at work after 1918. Now it was at work in a worse form and among far greater numbers. The whole world was sick and tired, and the people who were doing the jobs had to make a greater effort every day to accomplish each day's routine. Or so Lydia felt, overconscious of Colin's dead weight at the party, of the gulf that lay between her and London life, though with her accustomed honesty she admitted that this last was her own fault, for she so disliked London that she had made every excuse not to go there, even to please Noel.

Susan Dean had watched Colin with some concern realizing that his sulks, for that was what his behaviour amounted to, were worrying his sister Lydia and becoming increasingly obvious. As a member of a large, good-humoured, intelligent family and in her work at the Red Cross she had learned to talk pleasantly whether she felt like it or not, she decided that something must be done about Colin.

"Do you know Lincolnshire at all?" she asked.

Colin said only High Tide on the Coast of. As Susan's education had not included the works of Miss Ingelow she thought he alluded to sea-bathing and perhaps having had his clothes washed away by a wave, but the fascinating speculation was foreign to her purpose and would have got her nowhere, as she continued firmly, "I was there last Easter at a place called Muckby-cum-Sparrowby where there's a little branch railway with a twelve-inch gauge. I wondered if you knew it. The grandfather of the people I was staying with built it."

Colin, his whole demeanour softened and much improved, said he knew the little mineral railway from Ravenglass to Eskdale where the driver sat, as far as he remembered, all crouched up in the tender to drive the tiny engine, but the Muckby one was new to him.

"It's only three miles long," said Susan, "and you sit in a little open truck that holds two people face to face. It goes from Muckby to the sea. It's really almost as quick to walk, but it's great fun. We used to go by it to bathe."

"I must go into this," said Colin seriously. "I suppose it belongs to the Great Eastern Railway?"

Susan said it did and it didn't. It was really the private property of her friends, but the Great Eastern had a ninety-nine years' lease of it and as they were putting their own motor buses on the same route everyone was afraid that it would be closed down altogether before long.

"I would like to know more about that," said Colin, now again the intelligent and rising barrister who was going to make a considerable name for himself in cases affecting the railway world. "I know the Company's solicitor. I'll get him to lunch one day and pump him. Who built it?"

Susan said she had told him. Her friends' grandfather.

"I mean the engineer," said Colin. "It must have been Hornby or Basset-Lowke," at which names of power, honoured all over the model railway system world by men from seven years old to seventy, he would have raised his hat had he been wearing one at dinner.

Susan said her brothers used to have a Vasset-Lowke train with all its rails, signals, and other appurtenances and they were allowed to fasten the rails to the wooden floor of an attic to make a really permanent way.

Colin's face clouded as he confided to Susan that his parents, though in other respects God-fearing and law-abiding people, had never let him nail his rails to the nursery cork carpet, and that the most searing moments of his boyhood were the days, once a week, when the nursery floor was washed and all his lines and rolling-stock had to be taken up and put away.

"Nanny used to tell me to clear away my toys and things," said Colin, his face darkening. "She even said my rubbish some-times."

"How *ghastly*," said Susan. "I say, the twins have still got their model railway and they always get it out when they come on leave from their ships. Would you like to come and help to run it next time they are at home? It's all electric."

At these words Colin's heart, but lately a dry and crumpled affair, began to expand like a new bath sponge. Some people, even quite sensible grown-up people, would have spoken of a Toy railway and asked him if he would like to play with it. Fools! A model railway was a very sacred thing and to run it a privilege not to be granted lightly to one's younger brother, or children if any. His heart warmed to the Dean twins and he asked Susan more about them and their railway. For a woman he found Susan surprisingly well informed, able to describe an engine by its class and its wheels, sound on the matter of steel-built coaches, versed in the gauges of the Dominions and abroad.

"I see," said Colin, "they are beginning to standardize the Australian railways at last. Is it four or five different gauges they have? The one real advantage of the change of gauge between the different states was of course that if the Japs had landed they would have had to change so often to get anywhere that it would have held them up considerably, unless they had been able to land millions of lorries and jeeps."

And then he described to Susan the little railway in Yorkshire where the compartments have seats on one side only and a kind of prie-dieu with a brass handrail on the other, and the engine is at the back and the driver drives from the guard's van by a system of wires and pulleys, with a kind of red birdcage on the roof labelled Fire, containing chickens, and Susan listened with interest and was pleased to see Colin so absorbed in something outside himself, but at the same time thought how silly men were when they thought they were in love and had a shrewd suspicion that Mrs. Arbuthnot felt much the same. Also she was fond in her own undemonstrative way of Lydia Merton and thought Lydia looked tired and what a bore it must be for her to have Colin being sorry for himself all through the Long Vacation. Spurred by this reflection, she asked Colin if he was going abroad. Heaps of people were, she said.

"I don't think so," said Colin, casting what can only be described as a sheep's eye at the other end of the table where Mrs. Arbuthnot was laughing with Noel. "I've rather a lot to do."

"Well, you ought to go abroad," said Susan. "Everyone needs a change even if they don't think they do. I'm going to Switzerland at Christmas. That's why I'm only taking a week now. They're awfully decent at Barchester and giving me a fortnight at Christmas. Why don't you book for Christmas if you're really too busy to go now?"

There was something about her use of the word really that offended Colin's opinion of himself, and he said rather stiffly that he had his book to finish.

"Oh, your book on *Lemon*," said Susan. "Well, anyway you can't get it published at Christmas even it it's finished, because of no paper and everything. Even Mrs. Morland's next book is hung up she told me, because of a bottleneck though I've forgotten which kind of bottleneck it is this time."

Colin, pleased that Susan remembered about *Lemon*, though she might have been more tactfully hopeful about the prospects of publication, said it wasn't a bad idea and it would be fun to go on all the Swiss mountain railways and if possible ride in the driver's cab and talk to him.

"I daresay Daddy could help you," said Susan. "He knows a lot of the Swiss railway engineers. But talking's a bit awkward. You'd have to know railway-French and railway-German and then you'd find drivers that talked one of those extraordinary private languages they keep in Switzerland. Anyway, let me know if Daddy can help"

So much did the idea of ten days spent entirely on mountain railways appeal to Colin that he forgot to be annoyed at Susan's slightly masterful attitude and said he would be very glad if he could talk to Mr. Dean about it.

Mr. Wickham had very handsomely brought a bottle of port over two days previously, which port had been sitting on a shelf getting over the excitement of the journey till late that afternoon when Noel decanted it. It was not real vintage, Mr. Wickham had explained, but one needn't be ashamed to drink it, so in its honour Lydia had said she would make it a real dinner-party and take the women away for their coffee, leaving the gentlemen to do whatever it is they do when alone.

"It's very good," said Noel to Mr. Wickham, "but Colonel Crofts—or do you prefer to be called the Vicar, sir?" he added, to which Colonel Crofts replied that if Merton would just say Crofts it would promote friendly feeling.

"Crofts then, since you insist, sir," he threw to his guest in parenthesis, though addressing the company in general, "Crofts has a superb port. It had been in the Vicarage cellars since goodness know when. I must warn you, Crofts, not to let Wickham have any. His palate is ruined by spirits."

"Wickham has offered me pre-war sherry," said Colonel Crofts, "so the least I can do is offer him my port."

"We'll make a night of it, sir," said Mr. Wickham, "or better still, two nights of it. You dine with me and then, as you have been kind enough to suggest it, I'll dine with you."

Colin, suddenly inspired by an evil demon to a piece of showing-off, said claret was his drink. Very few people appreciated a good claret now, he added. To which Mr. Wickham, who read his Boswell through at least once a year, said he agreed with Dr. Johnson. Is was not a very kind remark and Colin, taking the point, flushed angrily; but Mr. Wickham had got so tired of Colin's moods since the star of Mrs. Arbuthnot rose over Barsetshire that we cannot blame him. Colonel Crofts who saw that something was a little wrong, said the old sexton at Southbridge was very ill.

"Poor old Propett," he said. "He lived for his work in the churchyard and the Vicarage gardens, and I may add he has been quite incapable of both for the last two years as I gathered from Admiral Phelps and have seen with my own eyes. But he can't bear anyone else to ring the bell and he has insisted on tottering up to the church when he wasn't fit for it. I do what I can for him, but he most reasonably dislikes me because I am a newcomer," but he did not say anything about the laurels and the trees that darkened the Vicarage, for those were matters personal to him, and old Propett's peace of mind was more important.

Noel sympathized, saying that he and Lydia were in much the same position, as old Twicker the gardener was really past heavy work but whenever help was offered he took offence and Lydia was doing far too much. And after that the talk shifted to the war, and old Robinson in the dug-out was discussed and everyone felt better for the backward glimpse into a world where England's name had stood high, though she only thought of grumbling her way through what had to be done. But at least one could look forward then. Now, except for the brave-new-worlders who were perfectly happy with prefabs, plastics, cinemas, wireless and several million too many people wherever one went, one had to look back to recapture some kind of content, for looking forward might daunt the stoutest courage.

"Enfants perdus, that's what we are," said Mr. Wickham, who occasionally surprised his friends by his knowledge of army French, picked up round the French Mediterranean coast in the last war, by which we mean 1914-1918 as no one has yet invented a satisfactory name for either of the wars, "and jolly well perdus too. No one is going to rescue us. Funny to think we fought for freedom, or thought we did. A damned lot of freedom we got. We've bought it all right. Well, I suppose we must just carry on."

"Verlorner Posten in dem Freiheitskriege," said Noel, who had never quite lost the young romantic love for Heine.

"I didn't know anyone read German now," said Colonel Crofts. "I had a semester at Göttingen as a young man and I've found my German useful."

"His heart broke in the end, if you remember," said Noel.

"God helping us, ours won't," said Colonel Crofts, and such was the honest simplicity and unselfconsciousness of his nature that no one felt uncomfortable; which is the best tribute that we can pay to him. And then the talk went to other matters.

Meanwhile the ladies had been very comfortable round the

August fire, as ladies always are when relieved of the delightful society of men. Mrs. Arbuthnot, who had noticed with kind concern how tired Lydia looked, asked about the children and told Lydia some amusing stories about Aubrey Clover and made her laugh which was very good for her, for our Lydia, fond though we are of her and have always been, had not, if the truth has to be faced, very much sense of humour.

"Aubrey is coming down to stay with the Deans round the end of the month," said Mrs. Arbuthnot. "He needs a real rest when he is doing a new play and he finds the Deans perfect. Mrs. Dean goes gently to sleep, Mr. Dean is always away on business, and the family in general look upon him just as a friend of Jessica's and walk and talk right in front of him. He says it is the one house in England where he can really relax."

"I wish Colin could relax," said Lydia, whose fatigue had the effect, so common in women, of making her work physically and worry mentally up to the limits of her powers. "He really ought to get away for a bit. You couldn't do anything about it, could you, Peggy? He's awfully fond of you."

"I'll try with the greatest pleasure," said Mrs. Arbuthnot, "but I can't promise much result."

"Oh, I did hope you could do something," said Lydia disappointed. "I think he thinks he is in love with you. Of course I'd love it if he were, but I don't think he can really be or he wouldn't be so very cross all the time. He is my favourite brother, though I'm awfully fond of Robert too, and it does worry me to see him being horrid."

"If men are in love with one," said Mrs. Arbuthnot, looking compassionately at Lydia, a fellow sufferer from the selfish and exhausting regiment of men, "they are usually so silly that one can't do anything with them at all."

"I thought," said Lydia, "one could wind them round one's little finger."

"My dear child," said Mrs. Arbuthnot, who was probably about Lydia's age, from the depth of her vast experience, "you can't do anything with them at all. Not unless you are quite unprincipled. A man in love with one is usually a perfect pest."

Lydia said with great candour that she didn't know much about it because no one but Noel had ever been in love with her. And, she added, after what Peggy had said she hoped no one ever would be, because it would be too ghastly.

"I think I can promise you, my dear," said Mrs. Arbuthnot, "that no one except Noel ever will be. You are far too nice," with which enigmatic words she kissed her own fingers and carefully deposited the kiss on Lydia's hand.

"Peggy," said her sister-in-law, "Susan and I have a splendid plan. When Aubrey Clover comes to Winter Overcotes, couldn't you and he get up one of his sketches for the Red Cross Hospital Libraries' fête?"

"Oh, do," said Susan. "You've no idea how people would love it and we could charge them twice as much for the tickets with Aubrey's name. Do say yes, Peggy."

It was so obvious that Mrs. Arbuthnot asked nothing better that it was decided on the spot to force Aubrey Clover to act, whether he wanted to or not. One of his little triangle plays, said Mrs. Arbuthnot, at once assuming command. *Three for a Letter* perhaps, or *Hic, Hac, Hoc*, or even *Out Goes She*. Miss Arbuthnot objected that it would mean a third player and did her sister think there was anyone who could act Rollo Pertwit, or Oliver Lights, or Phil Parradene. Not at the moment, said Mrs. Arbuthnot, but she was sure she would find someone and it would be all right on the night, which professional touch made her hearers feel she was already behind the footlights. The whole affair being now arranged, with the trifling exception of a second male lead, the three guests talked at once, their voices rising shriller and shriller according to the custom of the educated middle class, while Lydia thought how amusing it was and how lovely it would be when they were all gone and she could go to bed.

When the men came in they had a nervous feeling of being so

many Orpheuses among the Thracian women, but Susan Dean who appeared to be head priestess for the occasion rode on the whirlwind and talking her fellow priestesses down explained their plan.

"We've only got to get another man and it will be perfectly easy," said Susan. "If we do *Out Goes She* Aubrey will do his own part of Henley Marlowe, Peggy will do Mrs. Calliper and we'll get someone for Phil Parradene. Can't you act, Noel? After all, you've got nothing to do and frightfully long holidays."

Noel, unmoved by this appalling and subversive view of the Long Vacation and a lawyer's leisure, said he had been, so his mother had told him, an extraordinarily beautiful and brilliant Helena in his prep. school performance of *Midsummer Night's Dream*, but since then had got a bit out of practice.

"No, Wicks, not you," said Mrs. Arbuthnot firmly, as Mr. Wickham opened his mouth. "We all know you were the Widow Twankey's charwoman in the *Gridiron* Christmas pantomime, but this is a bit different. Not in your line, Wicks."

Colonel Crofts surprised everyone by saying that he used to take the chief baritone parts when the regiment got up Gilbert and Sullivan, but even this wasn't much help.

"And you aren't any good, Colin," said Mrs. Arbuthnot, now entirely the female actor-manager uninfluenced by any personal considerations. "But we'll easily find someone. It's a heavenly plan of yours, Susan. Aubrey must do it whether he likes it or not. Clothes will be a bother but I'm sure I can find something. Mrs. Brandon always has heaps of things put away and I'm sure she would help. Noel, you must sit in front and clap very hard and Colonel Crofts too. Lydia darling, *might* I ring up Mrs. Brandon? It is all too heavenly."

Lydia, sympathizing with her friend's excitement though it was all a strange world to her, asked Noel to take her to the pantry telephone where she wouldn't be disturbed, and they left the room together while Susan, Miss Arbuthnot and Mr. Wickham argued about the play. Colonel Crofts, who felt real concern for his hostess's exhausted appearance, sat by her and told her about his married sons in India and his plans for having them and their children to stay at the Vicarage when they next got leave, which would not be for some time unfortunately. They both, it appeared, had country homes of their own in England and Lydia gradually received the impression that Colonel Crofts for all his simple manner of life and his entire lack of any outward show of wealth must be very well off, even by present-day standards.

But who is to describe the feeling of Colin Keith who appeared to be looking placidly at last week's *Country Life* in which one of F. E. Arbuthnot's delightful articles on birds appeared, with a reproduction of one of her water-colour drawings?

Mrs. Arbuthnot, for Peggy was too good a name for her, had told him he was no good, and before a roomful of people. He knew very well that he could not act. He had never acted except at his prep. school when he was one of supers in *The Shoemaker's Holiday*; he had never wished to act; he would go so far as to admit that he felt himself quite incapable of acting and would be struck dumb and much embarrassed by his arms and legs and body if he so much as walked on with one line. But all this was not for Peggy Arbuthnot to say. He admitted the woman's charm, superficial it is true; she was certainly pretty in that fluffy kind of way, no more; doubtless she could act, but that did not interest him. In fact he had done with the woman. For him serious work on *Lemon*, now nearly finished. He would take *Lemon* up to London and work in his chambers where he would be undisturbed and then accept a few country invitations. At Christmas he could go to Switzerland, armed with introductions to Swiss engineers which Susan could get for him through her father. Vistas of enthralling work on railway law opened before him; an agreeable bachelor life with dinner-parties and weekends, taking his various nephews and nieces to the pantomime, pursued by delightful hostesses, briefs marked higher and higher. Away with women.

When Mrs. Arbuthnot came back she was nearly speechless with excitement and could only say "My *dears!*" To the company, so Noel got her some soda water.

"As Peggy has apparently gone mad," he said, "I will tell you what has happened. Mrs. Brandon is able and willing to dress Peggy from head to foot as Mrs. Calliper and what is more Francis has played Phil Parradene with the Barchester Amateur Dramatic and would love to take the part, providing Clover approves."

"Of course Aubrey will approve," said Mrs. Arbuthnot, quite drunk with soda water and excitement. "I am sure Francis can do it perfectly. Parradene is absolutely his type and we can do a little bit of dancing to the gramophone, you know, Wicks, when Parradene reminds Mrs. Calliper how they were lovers for one night in Valparaiso and danced the tango, and she has had so many men she has forgotten him, but when they begin to try the tango she remembers him by the way he dances—that's the only way she knows her lovers apart because she has had so many. I can *see* it. Oh, heavenly!"

Her hearers were deeply interested by this dramatic outburst, a new aspect of Mrs. Arbuthnot which Barsetshire had not yet seen. For a moment Colin felt the attraction of the moth to the star but the mention of Francis Brandon recalled him to his better self. If Peggy wished to dance at the Town Hall in what sounded a quite revolting piece of Aubrey Clover's clever stuff, let her; with Francis Brandon. And so relieved was he by his new-found freedom that his sister Lydia, whose head was aching with fatigue, felt quite comforted to see her dear Colin himself again though feeling too unwell to wonder why. Mrs. Arbuthnot then apologized and said they must really be going or they would talk all night and if Colonel Crofts would not mind they would say good-bye.

"You ought to take Lydia's temperature," she said to Noel as he saw them into the car. "She doesn't look well a bit."

"Oh, I think she is all right," said Noel. "Lavinia's measles were rather a strain. I'll make her have breakfast in bed to-morrow if she is tired."

The Southbridge party drove away and Noel went back to the drawing-room.

"Lydia's gone to bed," said Susan, "and she said not to bother to say good-night because she's taken an aspirin and wants to go to sleep. It's been a lovely evening. Do you mind if I go to bed too, Noel, because I'm so sleepy? It's all the excitement I expect. Good-night Colin. Good-night Mr. Wickham."

Mr. Wickham also said good-night, leaving Noel and Colin to talk legal shop. He walked through the garden and back to his cottage, went to his sitting-room, got out a bottle of navy rum and sitting in his comfortable old chair solemnly drank Mrs. Arbuthnot's health.

"And a damned good little actress she is," he said, for he liked to commune aloud with himself when no company was present. "And a fine girl Effie is."

He then drank Miss Arbuthnot's health and read the *Country Estate and Agents' Journal* which had a very informative article about White Porkminsters.

"I might as well drink my own health too," said Mr. Wickham, putting the paper aside. "I've been damned lucky. Suppose Effie had accepted me. She's a fine girl, a splendid girl, but she might have said yes. Wicks, you're a lucky man and don't go and do it again. The luck doesn't always hold." He drank he own health, put away the rum, and went up to bed.

CHAPTER 12

Next morning when Susan Dean came down to breakfast she found Noel and Colin in consultation and obviously glad of her coming.

"Lydia doesn't look at all well," said Noel. "I tried to take her temperature but I can't shake the wretched thing down, nor can Colin."

He held up a clinical thermometer, saying that he had shaken it nearly to death with no result.

"It's quite easy," said Susan, giving the stubborn creature a flick of the wrist to which it immediately responded. "You need only know how to do it. I'll go up and see her. Has she had any breakfast?"

Noel said he was just putting some on a tray.

"Not coffee and fish-cakes if she's running a temperature," said Susan. "Tea and toast. And some butter and honey in case she feels like them. You can bring them up in five minutes."

Having issued these orders she went upstairs brandishing the thermometer, which was now thoroughly cowed and huddling in the basement. Lydia's voice, croaky and weak, told her to come in.

"You look horrid," said Susan appreciatively. "Keep this in your mouth for a minute. Yes. Nicely over normal. I expect you've got measles. Here's your tea."

She took the tray from Noel, shut the door, and made her flushed, languid patient take a little light nourishment.

"I can't eat any more," said Lydia, who had nibbled a piece of toast very ungratefully. "Oh dear, Noel his to go to London and he was to take you to Barchester. You'd better hurry. And please tell Nurse I can't see the children till we know what I've got. And Colin's socks wanted mending. I can do them in bed. And I ought to write to Kate and——"

"I'm not going to Barchester with Noel," said Susan. "I've got a holiday and I'm going to stay here. I've done all my First Aid and been a V.A.D. and I've had measles. And you're not to do anything or think of anything."

On hearing this, tears began to roll down Lydia's face.

"You'll need another handkerchief if you do that," said Susan, and at once found the handkerchief-drawer and put two clean ones by Lydia's bed. "Cheer up. It's rather fun really."

Lydia wiped her eyes and felt better. She wanted to explain to Susan that she wasn't crying because of having measles and having to stay in bed, but because it was so heavenly to be able to stay in bed and be quiet with herself for a little. But to explain all this was too tiring. Susan then washed Lydia's face and hands, brushed her dark shining hair, rearranged the bed-clothes and took the tray away. In the hall she found Noel waiting.

"I'm awfully sorry," said Noel, "but you'll have to hurry or I'll lose my train. Is Lydia all right, or do you think I'd better not go to London? Or I could come back tomorrow instead of Friday."

"Of course you can go to London," said Susan. "And don't come back till Friday. I expect Lydia will be all right then. I'm going to stay here and look after her. You might ring Dr. Ford up, Colin, and tell him I think she's measling."

"Susan! The children!" said Noel. "Won't they get it?"

Restraining herself with an effort from saying, "don't be an idiot," Susan said Lavinia had just had measles and Nurse would look after Harry and he would lose his train, and gently pushed him out of the house. Colin was already telephoning, so Susan went up to the nursery where breakfast was over and Nurse was washing-up the breakfast things.

"Hullo, Nursie," said Susan. "Lydia's got the measles. At least I think it is, so I've sent for Dr. Ford. I'm going to stay here."

Nurse expressed sorrow and said, quite untruthfully, that she had said all along that Mrs. Merton would get them.

"I don't see why," said Susan stoutly. "When Jessica and Robin and I had measles, mother didn't get them. Do you remember how Jessica screamed when the doctor came?"

Nurse said it was play-acting, and she had always said Jessica would be an actress some day. Of course Mrs. Dean didn't get the measles, she said, because she had had them. Mrs. Merton hadn't ever had them, but nobody knew till Mrs. Carter mentioned it. She was by this time obviously longing to tell Susan about measles which had left mothers of about Lydia's age blind, deaf, deformed and mentally deficient, but Susan had no time to waste.

"Look here, Nursie," she said. "I'll do Lydia and you can do the children. Lavinia's all right; she's had hers. But what about Harry?"

On hearing his name Harry looked up from his business, which was beating the leg of the nursery table with a drumstick, and said "Hoy." Nurse said proudly he would be talking before they knew where they were, saying his name so plain, and then looked worried.

"I was thinking," said Susan guilefully, "that we ought to get Harry away. If only Mrs. Carter were at Southbridge you could give me a hand with Lydia."

Nurse's eyes gleamed at the thought of looking after her employer.

"Of course there is Mrs. Twicker," said Susan, carelessly. "But I daresay it would be rather a trouble for her. Well, if Harry is here of course I'll have to do Lydia alone. Oh, she sent you her love, Nursie, and said she was sorry she wouldn't be able to see you because of baby."

During this artfully calculated speech Susan had overtly observed Nurse's face, which had faithfully reflected jealousy of Mrs. Twicker and jealousy of Susan in about equal proportions. To let the old ex-Nannie have one of her charges was unthinkable; on the other hand to let Miss Susan do it all, for Palmer would be no use and someone must look after poor Mr. Merton and poor Mr. Keith, and to be excluded from the joys of a sick-room, was more than she could bear.

"I was just thinking," said Nurse, with the air of one who had suddenly evolved a brilliant and original scheme, "that if Harry went to Nanny Twicker for a few days it would be quite a nice change for him and seeing he didn't get Lavinia's measles it would be a pity if he got Mrs. Merton's. Then I can help you, Susan. I don't know what your mother will say."

But this was such an obvious piece of hypocrisy that Susan ignored it altogether, knowing well, as did Nurse, that Mrs. Dean accepted with perfect placidity all that her large adventurous brood did, reserving her very small worrying capacity for her husband.

"Right," said Susan. "I'll tell Mrs. Twicker." And before Nurse could change her mind, she had left the nursery and gone to the kitchen where she broke the delightful news to Cook and Palmer and the daily woman, all of whom had foreseen and foretold it, but there were some people that if you told them a thing twenty times you might as well tell the cat.

"I'm sure I'll do my best, miss," said Palmer, already resenting Susan's authority, "but of course it's my afternoon off today," to which Susan, who through long dealing with Red Cross voluntary helpers was quite used to people's days off and the fantasies they performed on the same, replied that everything would go on just as usual and she and Nurse would manage very well, which roused both Cook and Palmer to such jealousy of Nurse that they decided to stay in all that week in case Nurse came to the kitchen or the pantry during the absence of one or the other.

After lunch Dr. Ford came and said it was a very mild attack and the rest would do Mrs. Merton good; collected from Susan some Winter Overcotes gossip to retail at High Rising and went away, his last words to Susan being, "It'll do Mrs. Merton good to have measles. Keep her quiet for a bit. Better measles now than a breakdown at Christmas." Harry was taken to Mrs. Twicker who received him with Nannie-grandmotherly joy, and there, to Nurse's chagrin, he settled down at once with Nanny Twicker's cat who allowed very small children to pull her tail; and after this peace descended upon Northbridge Manor.

To Lydia, who was more tired and unhappy than ill, bed with very mild measles was like heaven. Her strong shoulders had ever since the war began taken every burden. Since the war ended her burdens had not been lessened and she had been driving herself mercilessly all through the last year, spending recklessly the capital of her youth and strength. Noel had always let his Lydia take her own way, being confident that it would be a good one. Under more normal circumstances he might have interfered with the authority that Lydia's deep love for him recognized, but with the war over and his practice increasing daily he had been less and less at Northbridge and perhaps did not realize that Lydia was doing, like most women, far more than she should simply because there was no one else to do it. He had perhaps found Northbridge with its local interests a little duller than it used to be as his London life grew more and more absorbing, and certainly he had found Mrs. Arbuthnot's company more amusing than anything else the neighbourhood could provide. And possibly, manlike, he thought that Mrs. Arbuthnot found his society more amusing than that of other neighbours, not understanding that everything and everybody amused Mrs. Arbuthnot, who had in her the most delicate possible touch of the adventuress, a quality which in a pretty woman who is also a lady can have great fascination. That Lydia might feel a little out of it did not occur to him.

The time passed peacefully. Susan and Nurse were a strong combination against Cook and Palmer. Lavinia appeared quite happy without Harry. Colin worked very hard at *Lemon* and told Susan about it at breakfast, lunch and supper, who listened with every appearance of interest. Noel rang up twice a day and hearing that Lydia was doing very well and quite happy, accepted an invitation to a weekend party at the house of a high officer of the Crown, which excited Lydia very much, and she and Susan wondered if Noel was to made Attorney-General on the spot, which led to a very ignorant discussion as to who the present Attorney-General was; but, as Susan said, there wasn't anyone that one knew or one's people knew in this Government, so how could one know?

The Arbuthnots, who had had measles and also most tropical diseases without turning a hair, had been shopping in Barchester and came by train to Northbridge Halt to see Lydia in her convalescence, and Mrs. Arbuthnot was so pretty and so gay and so excited about the play, that Lydia couldn't help liking her more than ever.

"We had such an amusing lunch with Aubrey Clover," said Mrs. Arbuthnot, who had been in town. "He is nearly as keen on the play as I am. He is coming down to the Deans next week and you will be quite well by the time the play is acted. Jessica was quite livid with envy and Aubrey is going to write in a little part for her. She says she always wanted to play a soubrette, so she is to be Mrs. Calliper's personal maid and Aubrey is writing a song for her. I hope Noel enjoyed the party."

Lydia said he hadn't said anything about it, but when people telephoned they never said anything they wanted to say.

"I like Noel awfully," said Mrs. Arbuthnot. "But I like you better. There is something so comfortable about talking to women."

"But I thought people like you, I mean people who have had lots of experience," said Lydia, fumbling for words to express her thoughts, "I don't mean in a horrid way, but just like in general, liked men better than women. I don't mean to be rude."

"Bless your heart, I do like you," said Mrs. Arbuthnot. "You are such a lamb that one really doesn't know where to begin.

Men are quite amusing, but they will fall in love with one, and then it is *quite* dreadful and such a bore. And they will tell you about themselves which is quite crashingly dull. Fred wasn't dull. But then he told all the other women about himself and apparently they liked it. Perhaps if he had been a little duller— oh, well, one never knew. The kind of man I really like is someone that laughs at my kind of joke and never loses his temper. Of course one would like him to dance well and have some money, and he can fall in love with one, but he mustn't be serious. Aubrey is never serious except about the stage, and as the whole of his life is the stage," said Mrs. Arbuthnot reflectively, "I suppose he is always serious. Dear me, what a muddle. And how are the children?"

Her sister Kate, said Lydia, on hearing of the measles had at once come up from Devonshire and taken Lavinia and Harry back with her and Nurse was to follow in a few days. It was a little lonely, said Lydia, but all the same very peaceful, and she wondered perhaps if Noel got a little tired of everything being so domestic. And Mrs. Arbuthnot, looking at Lydia with a theatrical eye, thought how good her bones were and what an excellent thing it would be if the hollows in her face filled out, even at the expense of her nobly ravaged air. Lydia asked where Effie was.

"Oh, she went to see Wicks about the bird book she is illustrating," said Mrs. Arbuthnot.

Lydia, reflecting on what her visitor had lately told her, said Mr. Wickham didn't talk about himself. He usually, she said, talked about the farm, or drink, which Mrs. Arbuthnot said was much the same thing. Lydia, an apt pupil, said she supposed talking about birds was also the same thing, and Mrs. Arbuthnot laughed and asked after Colin.

"He is working," said Lydia. "Susan is typing some of his book for him. They'll be here for tea in a minute. I can't tell you how kind Susan has been to me, I wonder——"

She stopped, conscious that a speculation on the possibility of

Susan and Colin falling in love would be misplaced, but encouraged by Mrs. Arbuthnot's very kindly air of amusement she added, "I think Colin has quite fallen out of love with you, Peggy. He is so much nicer now," at which Mrs. Arbuthnot laughed again in a perfectly delightful way and said nothing could be nicer, which gave Lydia a very exciting conspiratorial feeling of a League of Women against Men.

"How incredibly young you are, my dear," said Mrs. Arbuthnot, but with no touch of condescension. Almost wistfully, Lydia thought.

Palmer then brought in tea and Colin and Susan came in with Miss Arbuthnot whom they had met in the hall as she returned from the agent's cottage.

"I do wish Susan weren't going," said Lydia. "It hasn't been much of a holiday for her, but it has been heavenly for me."

"I enjoyed it frightfully," said Susan. "I like looking after people and it was great fun to order Nursie about. I shall never be frightened of her again. Jessica is still terrified of her. Still, if she is going to Devonshire, perhaps it's all for the best."

"I'm awfully sorry you're going too," said Colin. "It has been perfectly splendid to have you to work for me," at which words Lydia and Mrs. Arbuthnot nearly had the giggles.

Then Miss Arbuthnot, after being pressed to do so, told them about the book she was illustrating and with a child's pleasure in a toy mentioned the quite generous payment she was getting. Colin said he wished he were as lucky, for his little book was still in search of a publisher, to which Miss Arbuthnot modestly and seriously said that after all her book would only be to amuse people, and his book would be very learned and not get out of date.

"Of course Colin's books will get out of date," said Susan. "Books about law and history and things always do. But pictures of birds are much more real, because birds don't alter, so Effie's pictures will be just as good in a hundred years."

"They'll probably be cut out of the book and made into

lampshades or table-mats by then," said Miss Arbuthnot cheerfully.

"No they won't," said Mrs. Arbuthnot, "because everything
will be those horrible plastics then. When I was in London,
Lydia, I got out of the Tube at South Kensington to go to a little
dressmaker, and there I saw a great dreadful queue of people
outside the museum, about half a mile long and seven or eight
deep, and they were all shuffling along at about half a mile an
hour to see a lot of hideous things that they weren't allowed to
buy even if they liked them because they were all for export,
though what the foreigners will think of them I cannot imagine.
The children looked so dreadfully tired, poor little things, and
everyone was eating, which is so depressing in the street."

Colin, becoming rather legal, said how could she tell from
outside that the things were hideous.

"I didn't," said Mrs. Arbuthnot, "I had lunch at that hotel
opposite the museum with General Cumberboard and he is in
business now and had a trade card, so we got in quite easily, and
got out as quickly as we could. I don't think the crowd really saw
anything. They just liked being in a crowd and getting along
very slowly in lumps. Pinky Cumberboard said it was a peristal-
tic action, but I don't know what he meant," at which Susan,
who was pretty well up in medical terms though she had
switched over to literature, burst into a rather unrefined laugh in
which she was joined by Colin, owing to his acquaintance with
Greek. The other ladies looked and felt bewildered and Miss
Arbuthnot hoped Peggy had not unconsciously said anything
very dreadful, as she not infrequently did.

Lydia, suddenly anxious on her friends' behalf, asked how
they were getting back to Southbridge, because the connection
with Barchester was so bad, and could Colin drive them back.
At which Colin, his mind on *Lemon*, tried to look pleased.

"Oh, didn't I tell you?" said Miss Arbuthnot. "The Vicar is
having tea with Mr. and Mrs. Villars, so he said he would drive
us back."

Lydia asked which vicar, and then suddenly realized that it was Colonel Crofts who one was apt to forget was a clergyman, largely, she supposed, because his beard hid his collar. And sure enough, in came Colonel Crofts, who had had a very agreeable tea-party with the Vicar of Northbridge and his wife.

"I met Villars's second-in-command, Father Fewling," said Colonel Crofts. "An ex-naval man, I gathered, so we got on very well."

"Oh, Tubby Fewling," said Colin. "He is frightfully high church, but a very good sort. I went to St. Sycorax once. It was like being abroad, only just all wrong and nothing but women there and I couldn't make out what it was all about, so I didn't go again. Fewling is a great friend of Wickham's, because they were both in the navy. I believe they both drink navy rum till all is blue without turning a hair."

Mrs. Arbuthnot laughed, as she usually did, but Colonel Crofts looked rather grave and changed the subject, and presently he said he must be getting back to Southbridge if it was not inconvenient to the ladies. So good-byes were said and the Arbuthnots were driven away.

Colonel Crofts stopped the car at Editha Cottage for Mrs. Arbuthnot to get out, but Miss Arbuthnot accompanied him back to the Vicarage to inspect the water-colour drawing of the School which he had done, according to his promise, for the Birketts. In the hall Bateman met them and saluted.

"Beg pardon, sir," he said to the Vicar, "but old Propett's very bad, sir. The doctor says he won't last through the night. I thought you'd like to know, sir."

"You will forgive me," said Colonel Crofts to Miss Arbuthnot, "but I must go and see the old sexton. You will let me have the pleasure of showing the picture another day?"

Miss Arbuthnot said she would walk down to Propett's cottage with him and see if she could do anything for Mrs. Propett, so they went down the lane, past the end of Wiple Terrace and down the High Street into a kind of village slum of very picturesque cottages which had been condemned before the war. But their inhabitants were much attached to them, being in some cases, as Everard Carter said, so grimed into their houses with dirt that they had become inseparable, like a snail and its shell. In one of the most tumbledown of these cottages Propetts had lived, probably since the cottages were built at the end of the sixteenth century, and the old sexton was the last of his name.

The front door was open, so Colonel Crofts knocked on it and went in. Miss Arbuthnot, shy of intruding, remained just outside. The little room was black and greasy with age and soot from the open fireplace. A very small window was masked by dirty, torn lace curtains and several pots of geraniums, which appeared to be doing very well in the close atmosphere. Some heavy old-fashioned furniture filled most of the room. A half-open door in the corner revealed a box staircase which led to the upper floor, and below the window on a very uncomfortable-looking bed lay the sexton, covered with a large horse-blanket and a tattered patchwork quilt, and looking malevolently at his Vicar.

"Good evening, Propett," said the Vicar. "I am sorry to find you so poorly."

Propett was understood to say that there were some as wouldn't be sorry if he was dead. That there Bateman, he said, would give a silver sixpence to hear he was dead, he would.

"May I sit down?" said the Vicar, laying his hand on a Windsor chair with a broken back, but for all answer the old sexton called, "Come down here, Polly. Come down, you old Poll," to which his wife's voice from the room above said it wasn't time for his tea and he could wait.

"Come on down, you old fool," said Mr. Propett, "it's the Vicar."

And down came Mrs. Propett, who looked even older and dirtier than her husband but moved with terrifying agility.

"Oh dear, oh dear, who'd have thought of you coming, sir," said Mrs. Propett. "Propett's been that bad I did think of sending for you, but he wouldn't hear of it, sir. So I saw your man at the end of the lane, sir, and I said to him, 'Propett's very bad.' Not that chair, sir, it's only got the three legs. Take this one, sir."

"You go outside, you old Poll," said Mr. Propett. "I've got to talk to his reverence and it's not seemly you being here."

So Mrs. Propett, remarking that Propett could kill hisself his own way if he liked, went outside the cottage and the Vicar asked Propett what he could do for him.

"There's one thing, sir," said Mr. Propett, looking as if Death already had his hand on his coat collar, "one thing I'd like before I die."

Colonel Crofts said he would be glad to help him.

"It's that new man up at the Vicarage, sir," said Mr. Propett. "Bateman he calls himself. I can't abide the sight of him."

The Vicar said he was sure Bateman had perfectly friendly feelings towards the Propetts.

"Maybe," said old Propett, "but I've not got no friendly feelings to he. He wants to cut down my shrubs. He wants to ring my bell. I've rung that bell man and boy for sixty years and I won't have no one ringing my bell. Thirty year old I were when I first rang that bell and I won't have no one ring it. Don't you let that Bateman touch my bell, sir, not so long as I'm sexton here."

The Vicar gave his word to that effect and old Propett retired into a kind of coma, murmuring half-aloud. "He thought he'd ring my bell but I bested him, I did, drat and drabbit him."

The Vicar, feeling that he could not do much more, called to Mrs. Propett who came back followed by Miss Arbuthnot, and said he was afraid her husband was very weak and he would come again at any time she sent for him.

"That's very kind of your reverence," said Mrs. Propett, in whose wrinkled old face every wrinkle was marked with dirt as if drawn with ink. "It's hard work looking after Propett, sir. Sixpennorth of gin, that's what I want, sir, to keep my strength up. I asked *her* for sixpennorth of gin, but she said he hadn't got none," said Mrs. Propett, looking malevolently at Miss Arbuthnot.

As Mrs. Propett appeared to be living mentally in a Golden Age when gin was still the cheap drink of the happy poor, and to be quite unaware that gin was now practically unprocurable and in any case sixpennorth would go nowhere, the Vicar said he would see what he could do and moved to go. At the same moment old Propett, who had only been reassembling his wits and his strength, opened his eyes and said quite distinctly, "Don't give her no gin, sir. She's an old sinner. Calls herself Mrs. Propett, she does, but I never married her. More nor sixty years we've been living together, but the parson didn't have nothing to do with it. Old Mr. Benson he never meddled with me, nor me with him. Don't you give her gin, sir. You bring another nice bottle of port like you did before and old Propett'll drink your health and your good lady's. And don't you let that Bateman bring it, sir."

The Vicar, ignoring these revelations about old Mrs. Propett, very courageously took the old man's filthy hand and said a short prayer, while Mrs. Propett muttered a kind of response of sixpennorth of gin.

"Thank you kindly, sir," said old Propett. "It won't do me no harm I dessay. There's one other thing, sir. I'd like the passing-bell rung for me. Ninety-two strokes, that's me. But don't you let that Bateman ring it, sir. I'll come out of the grave and knock him down if he does. Wants to cut down my laurels. Meddling young fool."

The Vicar gave his word that Bateman should not ring the old sexton's soul to heaven, and with a final mumble of "Propett's cooked his goose, the meddling young fool," the old sexton relapsed into his state of coma.

"I don't think we can do any more," said the Vicar and made to go, much impeded by old Mrs. Propett who demanded gin with all the authority of a lawfully wedded wife, so that it was the greatest luck that the district nurse came up in her little car.

"That's all right, Mrs. Propett," said the nurse. "You leave the Vicar alone. He's going to get your gin. Never mind her, Mr. Crofts, it's only her way. The doctor says it's only a question of hours."

With terrifying brightness and competence she disappeared into the dark living-room and the Vicar and Miss Arbuthnot went away.

"Poor old fellow," said the Vicar. "I'll send Bateman down with some port. How lucky it is that we found that wine in the cellar."

Miss Arbuthnot, who had been educated in a tradition of respect for good wines, felt that a bottle of Government-controlled Pure English Winporto from the grocer would have done just as well, but did not say this aloud, much as she would have liked to protect the Vicar against his better self.

"Dear, dear, that won't do though," said the Vicar. "If he sees Bateman it may make him much worse. I'll take it down myself, later."

They were now walking up the High Street and as they passed Jutland Cottage Admiral Phelps came out, carrying a bottle.

"Good evening, Phelps," said the Vicar. "I've just been to see old Propett. "There isn't much to be done for him, but I've promised him some port."

"Old sinner," said Admiral Phelps, though not unkindly. "He screwed this out of me and probably he has got something out of Miss Hampton. It's a pity Mrs. Carter is away. She would have taken him chicken broth and seen that he drank it too. There's nothing like a kind unselfish woman for getting her own way. I shall miss old Propett, though he has been more than difficult and as obstinate as a mule. By the way, Crofts, we shall be looking for a new sexton. Have you any views?"

The Vicar said he had hardly got to know people well enough to make a choice and would be very glad of the Admiral's advice.

"I have given a lot of thought to it in the last year," said the Admiral, "and I don't see anyone very suitable. The fact is, most of the men about here don't go to church. There was one idea I had—but I fear it might inconvenience you."

The Vicar said he would be glad of any suggestion from the Admiral and that, if he might put it that way, he was there to be inconvenienced and looked upon it as a duty and a pleasure. An officer, he said, always tried to think of his men first.

"That's very nice of you," said the Admiral. "It's your man Bateman. I've had a talk with him from time to time at the British Legion and in the village. He tells me he knows something about bell-ringing, an I know he's a regular churchgoer. It's simply a question of whether he can do a sexton's work without neglecting the Vicarage. It's not a heavy job, or old Propett couldn't have kept it as he did."

The Vicar said he quite agreed that Bateman would be an excellent man and he would consider the suggestion and speak to Bateman about it. Of the private inconvenience to himself he said nothing, for that was all in the day's work.

"Good," said the Admiral, much relieved. "I'll take my port down to Propett now. It's only Algerian, but I daresay Propett won't notice. I can't get the real stuff now. I'll ask Nurse to let us know if anything happens to the old man. She is spending the night there."

Miss Arbuthnot said she was a very brave woman, at which the gentlemen laughed and agreed with her.

The Admiral then raised his hat courteously to Miss Arbuthnot and hurried on.

"Perhaps," said the Vicar to Miss Arbuthnot, "it is rather late now to show you the picture. Your sister may be expecting you," but Miss Arbuthnot said Peggy never worried and it was the kind of supper that would keep hot in the oven. So they walked back to the Vicarage.

At the garden Bateman was talking to a man unknown to the Vicar.

"It's our jobbing gardener," said Miss Arbuthnot. "At least he is lots of people's jobbing gardener. He is frightfully good at vegetables."

"Beg pardon, sir," said Bateman, standing to attention. "This is Corporal Chives, sir, ex-Barsetshire Regiment. I've seen something of him at the British Legion and the Red Lion, sir. He'd like to have a word with you, sir, if convenient."

"It won't be one word; it will be more like a thousand," said Miss Arbuthnot. "I'd like to see how you deal with him. There's no hurry," with which words she sat down on a large stone cannon-ball to await events.

"Salute the Colonel, you fool," said Bateman, digging Chives in the ribs.

Chives, upon whose slow, earth-loving Barsetshire nature the Barsetshire Regiment had made very little impressions, saluted, though with a lack of smartness that made Bateman draw in his breath with a hissing sound.

"You were a corporal, my man?" said the Vicar. "Where did you serve?"

Chives let his powerful frame relax and leaning like a symbolic figure upon his spade, embarked upon a long, rambling exordium, of which the purport roughly was that old Chives he'd a-gone into the army because they told him to and he'd a-liked to layout a few of them perishing Germans, but the perishing doctors at the depot said old Chives had something wrong with his stomach and wouldn't let him go to Germany and they'd sent old Chives to foreign parts up Essex way, dreadful flat country that was, perishing hard to dig and enough to make a man burst his perishing guts begging Miss Arbuthnot's pardon, and now he was doing jobbing work, but he'd had words with some of his ladies as didn't understand vegetables and were all for perishing new-fangled flowers, that he didn't hold with and what was the use of a man getting a nice load of manure for the ground and then to be asked to put flowers in he'd like to know when he could use it for spuds and nice sound spuds too old Chives he put in, not some of these perishing new-fangled spuds that fair broke a man's heart.

To Miss Arbuthnot who was used to Chives and his flow of talk this was all in order, but the Vicar in his military capacity had had enough and firmly interrupted Chives to ask what he wanted to say.

"Beg pardon, sir, but he's a bit soft," said Bateman, "though he's a first-rate gardener, sir. It's just this, sir. He wants to know if you will be wanting a gardener. He wants to take a regular job, sir, not jobbing."

"What old Chives said,——" the ex-corporal began, but Bateman remarking in the audible aside, "You shut your trap," took the matter into his own hands and added, "I said I'd let you know, sir. That's all, sir."

"Look here," said Miss Arbuthnot to Chives, "what about Editha? You can't give up the garden just when you've got the vegetables going so well."

"Now, lady, don't you be hasty," said Chives, changing his attitude for one of equal picturesqueness. "Old Chives he never said nothing about Editha. Old Chives isn't going to let Editha down. If I thought young Brown," said Chives, alluding to the Red Lion's nephew who did a lot of jobbing work, "was a-going to get his hands on old Chive's vegetables, I'd hit him over the head with my spade, I would, and flatten him out and bury him. Old Chives is coming to Editha every Saturday afternoon, lady."

"Well, that's all right," said Miss Arbuthnot.

"Thanks, my man," said the Vicar. "I'll have a word with Bateman and let you know. Good-night."

Chives gave a salute which had a strong family resemblance to pulling a forelock, winked at Miss Arbuthnot and went away.

"Thanks, Bateman," said the Vicar. "I'll have a talk with you later. I think it might suit me. By the way, old Propett looks very ill. He wishes to have the passing-bell tolled for him when he dies. I'll have a word with you about that too. And get up a bottle of port. And now, Miss Arbuthnot," he said, assisting her to rise from the cannon-ball, "if your patience is not worn out, may I ask your opinion of the little drawing."

Accordingly they went to the Vicar's study, where he showed her a charming water-colour prospect of the meadows with the School beyond, which might have been painted by a painstaking pupil of Varley. Miss Arbuthnot admired it whole-heartedly and the Vicar consulted her about the frame.

"There is something I wanted to ask you," said Miss Arbuthnot. "When Colin Keith was talking about Father Fewling and said he drank rum with Mr. Wickham, I couldn't help seeing that you were displeased. I'm sure Colin would hate to say anything to annoy you. You know, we are all so fond of you that we are apt to forget you are a clergyman."

She then became conscious of how very silly her remark sounded, though she had meant it in all earnestness. However, much to her relief, the Vicar said he quite understood and though he valued his priesthood very highly he did not wish it ever to be a barrier between himself and his friends or, if he might borrow Miss Arbuthnot's kind words, those he was fond of.

"That's all right then," said Miss Arbuthnot, strangely moved. "I only thought he might have shocked you."

"I may as well make it clear that it wasn't the rum," said the Vicar, marching straight up to the batteries. "I'm all for good drink, moderately used. It was Keith's account of Fewling's ritual. I would not pass judgment on any fellow priest and Fewling is as good a man as I know, but as for his practices, I simply cannot away with them. You will forgive me for speaking so plainly."

"I am so glad you did," said Miss Arbuthnot. "I think Father Fewling's church is quite *dreadful*. Peggy likes it rather, but I like yours. It's exactly right."

Had the Vicar been a clergyman of longer standing he would have been a little suspicious of the violent and usually ill-informed religious zeal which animates ladies of the English middle classes to adoration or condemnation of what they mostly knew very little about. But he had, luckily for him, had little experience of the voluntary and unwanted intromission of women into church affairs and took Miss Arbuthnot's words at their face value. In which he was perfectly right, for Miss Arbuthnot was only expressing a personal point of view and saw no reason why her sister-in-law should not prefer Father Fewling at Northbridge or Mr. Miller at Pomfret Madrigal if she wanted to.

"Thank you very much," said the Vicar.

And then Miss Arbuthnot said good-bye and went back to Editha, where her sister-in-law had kept supper back, and the Vicar ate his good but solitary dinner and had a long talk with Bateman. He considered taking the port to the old sexton, but as Admiral Phelps had already taken a bottle he decided to leave it till the following day.

Early next morning Southbridge heard a solemn note, often repeated, from the church tower. To the younger part of the village it meant nothing, and if they thought about it at all they thought what a long time that bell was ringing. The older inhabitants recognized a sound not often heard now, the passing-bell. Most of them, to their great annoyance, had not begun to count till too late and so were in doubt as to whether it were old Propett at ninety-two or Mr. Brown of the Red Lion's uncle at eighty-seven. But Miss Arbuthnot, who had thought a good deal about the events of the previous evening, counted every stroke and felt very much relieved that the malevolent old man was no more. In any case she was going to early communion that morning, so she slipped out while her sister-in-law was still asleep, and got to the church a full fifteen minutes too early, owing to her mind being elsewhere.

In the churchyard she met the Vicar and his churchwarden, both looking guilty yet proud, and at once guessed what had happened.

"It was for old Propett," she said. "And you were ringing the bell."

Both gentlemen looked more ashamed and even prouder.

"Old Propett's last wish———"

"I had promised him that Bateman———" said Admiral Phelps and the Vicar simultaneously.

"So I suppose you tolled the bell yourselves," said Miss Arbuthnot severely.

"You see, Miss Arbuthnot," said the Admiral, "the district nurse came in early this morning to say the poor old fellow had died in the night, and the last thing he said when I took the port down last night was that he wanted the passing-bell rung, so I came up to the Vicarage———"

"And when Phelps asked about ringing, I told him old Propett particularly didn't want Bateman to do it," said the Vicar.

"So we thought the best thing was to do it ourselves," said the Admiral. "And I must say, Crofts, it was a delightful experience. I've always wanted to ring a bell ever since I left the navy, but I never knew if it was a job a churchwarden was allowed to do."

"So I took the responsibility on myself," said the Vicar. "Bateman stood by. I think he was afraid we would hang ourselves or be pulled up through the rope-hole into the belfry. Phelps, we must do something about bells for the church. One bell isn't enough."

The Admiral received this suggestion with enthusiasm but said he was afraid it would cost a good deal. This, the Vicar said, they could discuss later, but if it would be of any help he would be prepared to contribute very substantially. Admiral Phelps, who had the affairs of Southbridge church very near his heart, nearly danced a hornpipe on a tombstone in his ecstasy.

"What about Mrs. Propett?" said Miss Arbuthnot, suddenly thinking of the dirty old woman who had never been married to the sexton.

"She drank the whole bottle of port and a bottle of gin that

Miss Hampton had brought, while Nurse was laying her husband out," said the Admiral, "and the doctor had to ring up Barchester General for an ambulance, but he doesn't think she'll live."

"Do you know if they were really married?" said Miss Arbuthnot.

"I've often wondered," said the churchwarden. "A man called Benson was parson here for about thirty years, which would cover all possible years for their marriage and there is no entry in the register. But Benson was notoriously careless, one of the old port-drinking, fox-hunting parsons that still survived. He might easily have omitted it."

The Vicar said he was a port-drinker himself and though he didn't hunt he had done a lot of pig-sticking in India, and then went away to prepare for the service and Admiral Phelps and Miss Arbuthnot went into the church. The Admiral, in spite of his private feeling that he would like to be conducting the service from his quarter-deck, followed the words with rapt attention, but we fear that Miss Arbuthnot's mind was in a sad jumble. Old Propett, old Mrs. Propett now probably dead of a surfeit of spirituous liquors. Colonel Crofts, his kindness, his water-colours, his reassuring air of authority in a time when authority had formed the base habit of saying, "Would you like to do this?" instead of "Do this"; Admiral Phelps taking the bottle of Algerian port he could ill afford to the old sexton; Colonel Crofts putting aside the real port which he could probably afford but could hardly like to sacrifice, all for the benefit of an ungrateful, malevolent old man; the two gentlemen ringing the bell from respect to the dying wishes of the same ungrateful man; Chives's Shakespearian monologue and the Vicar's firm cutting short of the same; Bateman's ambitions; Colonel Crofts and his charming water-colour, also his very sound views on Father Fewling's mode of worship; quite suddenly a lonely feeling because Peggy was so entirely absorbed in her theatricals, though one was delighted to see her looking so gay and happy;

then memories of Fred who had been such a perfect brother that one must forget that he was a bad husband, though being a generous woman she forgot that he had also taken and wasted her little patrimony; then again Colonel Crofts and the austere beauty of the early service, to which she really must pay proper attention; and so her thoughts went squirrelling round and round and returning to one point.

Old Propett's death, followed twenty-four hours later by the death of Mrs. Propett from alcoholic poisoning, was naturally a perfect godsend to Southbridge with the School shut for the holidays and so many people away. Miss Hampton and Miss Bent gave special party in honour of the event, but without Birketts, Carters and junior masters it was not very exciting. The appointment of a new sexton was discussed with some interest, as was the approaching Red Cross Fête in Barchester for which Miss Hampton had taken tickets.

"Clever young man, Clover," said Miss Hampton. "He and I have much in common, only we're on different sides of the fence. I know his mother quite well."

This new light on Miss Hampton deeply interested her hearers, though most of them weren't quite sure what she was talking about, or alternatively thought they knew what she meant but felt they oughtn't to.

"A very nice woman," said Miss Hampton. "She was the widow of the bank manager in my father's parish and Aubrey used to sing in the choir when he was a boy. Yes, that's how he started," a remark whose possible implications made such her guests as had considered them ashamed of themselves for doing so. "Mrs. Lover—can't think why Aubrey calls himself Clover though it suits him very well—has never seen Aubrey act. She doesn't approve of the theatre. But Aubrey always goes down there at Christmas. So do Bent and I. To my old aunt. Have to keep up family ties, you know."

"Hampton's aunt has never read any of her books," said Miss

Bent, almost proudly, as one who was connected with a valuable museum piece.

"Quite right too," said Miss Hampton. "Sensible women my aunt and Aubrey's mother. Know what they don't like and don't do it. Trouble with people is broadmindedness. They want to prove all things but haven't the sense to hold fast that which is good. You'll agree with me, Vicar."

The Vicar, who liked Miss Hampton as a good fellow and considered that her literary activities were no business of his, said he rather agreed.

"So do I," said Admiral Phelps. "When people say they are broadminded they usually mean sloppy. In the navy you know your duty and do it."

"The Bishop," said Mrs. Phelps, who had come on after a meeting of the Southbridge Goat Club to pick up her husband, "just shows. There's not a single silly idea he isn't broadminded about. Did you read about his visit to Germany? If I had my way I'd tie him to a stake and let the billies loose on him to stamp on his feet and butt him in the apron."

Her hearers, who had not been at all edified by the report of the Bishop's sermon in Strohwasser about the wickedness of England in general and the Army of Occupation in particular with special reference to the Germans as more sinned against than sinning, which sermon had of course been relayed by wireless to every part of the world in which it would do most harm, felt that Mrs. Phelps had the root of the matter in her and various other ingenious suggestions for Bishop-baiting were put forward, Miss Arbuthnot's plan that he should be perpetually shadowed by Chives, whose determination of words of the mouth was inexhaustible, being very favourably received. Mrs. Phelps then took her husband away and the rest of the party left.

The Vicar said he would see Miss Arbuthnot home, which was very nice of him, and Miss Arbuthnot wished the journey were a little longer than from one end of Wiple Terrace to the other. But even in that short distance, such is the press of life in

little country towns, they met with a diversion, which was Mr.
Feeder trimming his hedge in his little front-garden who pounced
out on Miss Arbuthnot to ask if she had heard of any little house to
let in Southbridge, or even any rooms, as his mother wanted to
come and live near him.

"Not with me, she couldn't stand that," said Mr. Feeder, with
justifiable filial pride, "but somewhere near. If only I could get
Traill out of Maria, she would be just the right thing, but he
won't think of it. He says the house is only held together by his
gramophone records and if he had to move them it would fall
down."

Miss Arbuthnot was full of sympathy and while regretting
that she did not know of anything, promised to make inquiries.

"Thanks awfully," said Mr. Feeder. "I'm staying here for most
of the holidays because it's so nice to be in my own house and not
hear Traill's gramophone."

Miss Arbuthnot and the Vicar then walked on to Editha.

"May I come in for a moment?" said the Vicar. "I have some
news which will, I think, interest you, on which I would like
your opinion."

Miss Arbuthnot said she would be delighted and how sorry
she was Peggy had gone over to Stories for a couple of nights to
rehearse with Francis Brandon. It happened not to be quite so
cold that day, so they went into the little garden and sat on a seat
against the back of the house where it was fairly warm.

"And what is the news?" said Miss Arbuthnot.

"It is about Bateman," said the Vicar. "He is going to be
sexton, and as you were so kind as to assist me when I saw old
Propett for the last time, I thought I would like you to be one of
the first to know."

Miss Arbuthnot said she was so glad, but what about the
Vicar. Wouldn't he be rather neglected?

"I have thought about that," said the Vicar. "Not selfishly, I
hope, but from a practical point of view. Your man Chives is
coming as my regular gardener and odd-job man. Bateman isn't

really much good at gardening and was only doing it because he is a good servant. That will give Bateman plenty of time to attend to his duties as well as look after me. And as a matter of fact I believe he is walking out with Eileen who is, so he tells me a first-rate cook, so I may have a man and wife in the house."

"Do you mean Eileen at the Red Lion?" said Miss Arbuthnot. "She's our Mrs. Dingle's niece, though I never know how they manage it," and indeed the difference between the Red Lion's barmaid, a dazzling blonde with hair crimped like a skate and blood-red finger-nails, and Mrs. Dingle who did dirty work wearing her husband's cap and a shapeless cotton frock, was very great.

The Vicar said he believed that in spite of Eileen's appearance she was very kindhearted and he had heard from several reliable sources how good she had been with evacuated children during the war, delousing them with quite maternal vigour again and again, and what a splendid help she had been to Matron at the School Christmas-party for evacuees.

"If Matron approves I am sure it is all right," said Miss Arbuthnot. "I am very glad you are to be so comfortable."

"A good officer," said the Vicar, "looks after his own men first, but he is a very foolish man if he doesn't look after himself as well, for if he lets his own affairs go his men will suffer in the long run."

There was a pause. Miss Arbuthnot looking absently down the garden noticed a stirring among the runner-beans, realized that Chives was there and hoped that he would not see them, or he would infallibly come and give them the benefit of his conversation.

"I think we had better talk quietly," she said to the Vicar. "Chives is down there."

"That will suit me very well," said the Vicar, "for I have some rather quiet, dull things to say. I had some letters from my sons in India today and want you to give me your advice, if you will be so kind."

Miss Arbuthnot wondered what use her advice could be, said she would be delighted to do anything in her power, and felt her heart banging against her ribs.

"My boys were very fond of their mother," said the Vicar. "I need not tell you how fond I was of her, but it is twelve years since she died and even the most beloved memory is dimmed by time. We have to live in the present day if we are to do our duty. My boys have never urged me in so many words to marry again, nor had I thought of it."

Miss Arbuthnot politely said of course not, and immediately repented such an inane remark.

"But for various reasons I have asked them to tell me frankly whether the thought of a stepmother was distasteful to them. Their answer would not have affected my own opinion, but I thought it only fair to them," said the Vicar.

Miss Arbuthnot knew what was coming. In some, perhaps in most women, the Vicar's words would have roused a kind of spiky pride but Miss Arbuthnot, most of whose life had been passed in considering and looking after other people, did not find them unreasonable.

"Yes?" she said.

"Will you do me the honour to marry me?" said the Vicar.

"Yes," she said.

And as this word seemed to be entirely adequate to the occasion, nothing more was said for a few seconds.

"If you have anything else to say, you had better say it," said Miss Arbuthnot suddenly, "for Chives may see us at any moment."

And indeed, as she spoke, Chives's powerful form came slowly up the garden, scenting an audience.

"Do you want me, Chives?" said Miss Arbuthnot.

"Old Chives always wants the ladies," said Chives gallantly, "but this time it's the gentleman he wants. It's manure I've got in my mind, sir, begging the lady's pardon. I can lay my hands on the sweetest load of manure heart could wish. I was telling

Bateman about it, sir, at dinner-time, and when old Chives tells a man about anything, that thing is a good thing, and you can take your Bible oath on it," he added, apparently feeling that this religious aspect of the manure would appeal to the Vicar.

"Thanks, my man," said the Vicar. "I'm busy now. You can report at the Vicarage tomorrow morning. That will do now."

The command gradually worked its way into Chives's slow mind. He looked at the Vicar and Miss Arbuthnot, smiled his slow Barsetshire smile and saying that old Chives wasn't a perishing spoil-sport, retreated in very good order to the bottom of the garden.

"How could you?" said Miss Arbuthnot, but in admiration of his courage, not in blame. "I didn't know anyone could stop him."

"You can't. I can," said the Vicar. "His voice was a little disturbing. Will you make me feel quite sure that I am honoured by your affection? It is true that you said you would marry me, isn't it?"

"Yes," said Miss Arbuthnot. A look of agony then passed over her face and she added, "I am so sorry, I mean no."

Instead of flying into a rage, or to Timbuctoo, the Vicar who had never turned his back in a military or a moral way upon Don or Devil yet asked her which she did mean, to which Miss Arbuthnot replied that what she meant was yes, but there was Peggy. The Vicar, keeping a cool head, rightly interpreted her muddled explanation."

"You mean you don't feel you ought to leave your sister-in-law," he said.

"Fred did ask me to take care of her if he was killed," said Miss Arbuthnot, her eyes filling with tears.

"And you said you would," said the Vicar. "Take my hand-kerchief, my dear. It is quite clean. Very well. But if Peggy didn't need your care, you would feel free?"

Miss Arbuthnot, whose face was almost covered with the

Vicar's large handkerchief of fine Indian linen, nodded violently.

"I shall be quite content with that," said the Vicar, who felt very little doubt that Mrs. Arbuthnot would marry again before long, either in Barsetshire or London. "And as we have settled that point, I would like to tell you that my sons both wrote to say that they would like to think of me with a companion. Money is an unpleasant subject, but I may as well tell you at once that they are both quite independent of me, as they inherited money from an uncle and have married wives with money. And I am quite comfortably off myself and can make a settlement upon you which will leave you independent when I die."

"But you *mustn't* die," said Miss Arbuthnot. "I couldn't *bear* it. Oh, and I don't know your name."

The Vicar said his name was Francis Edward Crofts, but his friends and relations always called him Edward.

"Edward," said Miss Arbuthnot, savouring the name. "I like Edward. It sounds like someone with a beard and very safe and comfortable. Oh, Edward!"

"What is it?" said the Vicar.

"We both have the same initials," said Miss Arbuthnot. "F.E. It will be very confusing."

The Vicar pointed out that if she did not marry him the confusion would not arise, to which Miss Arbuthnot replied that he knew perfectly well what she meant and she could not possibly marry till she knew Peggy would be well cared for, which was all rather silly and like a hen, but the Vicar appeared to find her hennish folly entirely to his taste and said he would leave the decision about an engagement entirely in her hands.

"There is only one serious question that I must ask you," he said. But before Miss Arbuthnot had time to be alarmed by the word serious, he added, "Will you mind being kissed by a man with a beard?"

Miss Arbuthnot said she didn't know. Fred, she said, was the only man who had ever kissed her since her father died, and he had an ordinary army moustache. The Vicar said he used to have one too when he was a gunner, but he felt a beard would look more venerable when he decided to become a priest and was also far less trouble. He then kissed her, very kindly, and Miss Arbuthnot having survived the ordeal seemed none the worse.

"Oh, Edward——" she began.

"I like to hear you say my name," said the Vicar, as if he were quite young and foolish. "What were you going to say?"

"Chives!" said Miss Arbuthnot.

The Vicar looked down the garden and saw Chives still among the bean-stalks. Whether he had been looking or not, it was impossible to say and the Vicar felt it would be better not to inquire. So he reassured Miss Arbuthnot and they had a delightful talk about some rearrangements of the Vicarage, on the distinct understanding that Miss Arbuthnot was not in the least engaged and might still be looking after her sister-in-law in 1966, till it was time for the Vicar to go back to the Vicarage.

Miss Arbuthnot went on with her usual avocation, shopping, doing some housework and cooking, working on her next article for *Country Life* and beginning the series of bird paintings for Mr. Wickham's cousin the publisher. In spite of knowing that she could never marry as long as her sister-in-law needed her, she felt very happy and secure, and when Mrs. Arbuthnot came back from her little visit to Stories, flushed with rehearsals, she at once guessed what had happened to Miss Arbuthnot and having a good deal of worldly wisdom of a benevolent sort she gave no hint of what she guessed and allowed Miss Arbuthnot to hide her head in the sand to her heart's content. If she sometimes felt a little desolate it was not for long, for she was unselfishly enough fond of her sister-in-law to wish her to be happily married, and as for herself, something always turned up and there were lots of friends and lots of fun and the performance of *Out Goes She* was in any case occupying most of her mind. That Colin Keith had stopped falling in love with her she barely noticed, and if she gave it a thought, that thought would probably have been that Colin was quite a lamb but such a nuisance and thank goodness he had cooled off, for young men in love were so troublesome when they took it seriously.

Meanwhile at Northbridge Lydia had made a good recovery from her measles. Kate insisted on keeping the children and Nurse and though Lydia missed her nursery it was also very nice to know that they were happy and to have a little leisure to be lazy. Mr. Wickham, who was very fond of his employer's wife, made a point of turning up in the garden or on the farm unexpectedly, just when Lydia had done enough work, and forbidding her to do any more and she was really quite glad to be ruled for her good. Colin worked very hard and was his old self again, visiting the Deans for tennis at weekends and often going to Barchester where Susan Dean was hard at work again and taking her out to lunch.

But Lydia, perhaps because of measles, felt that the world was grey and chill. As far as the weather went nothing could have been more true, nor did public affairs at home or abroad, though Lydia did not trouble greatly about them except as they affected her family and the house and farm, offer any kind of cheering-up. For the first time in her life Lydia felt uncertain and did not like the feeling at all. It was not that she felt ill, or really unhappy, her life had not suddenly crumbled away beneath her feet as people's lives do in novels, but the vitality which had carried her through all the years of war, through her hard work on the land and in hospital, through the arduous, exhausting and bitterly disappointing months of peace, suddenly flagged and she was a little frightened. And for the first time in her life she did not tell Noel about it. This was perhaps a mistake on her part, but her instinct told her that at the present time Noel might be a little impatient. Ever since Peggy Arbuthnot had come into their lives things had been altered. Lydia's generous nature did not for a moment blame Mrs. Arbuthnot whom she liked very much and who had always been very nice to her, but it seemed to her that the charming creature had brought a slightly disturbing influence with her. Colin had been more than trying in his selfish devotion to her, which she certainly had not encouraged, merely accepting as she probably always did the attention of a personable young man. Mr. Wickham obviously admired her, though his admiration took the form of a kind of back-slapping, glass-clinking camaraderie. The Brandons had practically adopted her. The Deans, who safely shut up in the atmosphere of a large affectionate family did not as a rule trouble very much about outsiders, had accepted her at once. And, it was useless to try to shut one's eyes to it, Noel had found her extremely attractive. Not for one moment did Lydia think that he had found her anything more, for her nature was on the whole unromantic and almost uninfluenced by fiction, a rare state of mind, and she would have repudiated with honest indignation the faintest idea of his being even in temporary love with Peggy Arbuthnot, while she could not help seeing how amused and slightly flattered he was by her pretty ways and her trick of looking up at people under her dark lashes.

There were hours in which Lydia reproached herself for not having tried to share Noel's London life more since he had gone back to the bar, and then her robust common sense told her that her home and her family belonged to Northbridge and that London was no place to drag children to unless it were necessary. So she blamed herself for everything, after the fashion of some women, and quite left out of her balance-sheet the fact that Noel, like Colin but not with Colin's unrestrained selfishness, had found Peggy Arbuthnot an extremely amusing interlude in the drab post-war world and had taken to her as one might take to going to the cinema, or any other form of amusement which required no mental effort and gave one a false feeling of escape. It was all a storm in a teacup and Lydia knew it, but the prison of the six-years' war and one year of so-called peace in a country which had given itself into the hands of irresponsible doctrinaires, was breaking down the resistance of the strongest and most sensible. One safe anchor remained to

Lydia in this turmoil. She had once said to Philip Winter on the brilliant early summer day after Dunkirk, before she had opened the telegram which contained life or death for her, that whatever it was she would love Noel just the same; and to this star she was true.

The Red Cross Cabaret and Fête at the Town Hall of Barchester, with the glittering attraction of a play by Aubrey Clover, music and lyrics by Aubrey Clover and featuring Aubrey Clover (we apologize for these barbarisms), while reminding a few educated people very forcibly of Mr. Toad's programme for the entertainment at Toad Hall, was proving an immense attraction. All tickets for the play were sold a week before the day. Lady Fielding was lending her very good piano for the accompaniments. Several frightful rows had risen on the question of who should entertain Aubrey Clover's accompanist who, it was discovered, always made a point of going back to his mother in Ealing from wherever he was playing, if money could hire a car. The General Fête Committee and the Cabaret Sub-committee sat like the fathers of the city, practically all night and day, being very businesslike and referring matters back like anything, while Aubrey Clover and Mrs. Brandon, whom no one had suspected of such energy, ran everything exactly as they pleased. How Mrs. Brandon, who had never taken any part in Barchester affairs, had come to the front nobody could quite explain, least of all that lady herself. But as her son Francis was acting second male lead and Peggy Arbuthnot of whom she was very fond was the female star, she felt a proprietary interest in the play and had long talks with Aubrey Clover wearing what Francis called her mysterious mischief face. No one quite knew what they talked about, but the general impression was that they compared their embroidery and that Aubrey Clover was going to put her in a play. The former guess was probably correct. As for the latter, anyone who has written a play or a novel will be familiar with the invitation, usually made with a kind of half-witted archness, to meet so-and-so because he or she is just like one of your characters and I know you'll jump at the chance of putting him or her in your next play or book. To which the answer is of course the reply which Mrs. Morland once thought of making but very kindly did not make to old Lord Stoke, that any book or play containing such a person would fall dead of its own weight.

Among all this Susan Dean went and came with matter-of-fact efficiency, for though she was not on the Committee, the business sense which she inherited from her father had been remarked in her work for the Barsetshire Red Cross Hospital Libraries and she found herself becoming a kind of Court of Appeal whenever the Fête Committee got into a muddle. Colin Keith, who had finished *Lemon* and sent it to be typed, constituted himself a kind of honorary A.D.C. and was able to give valuable assistance with his trained mind, now untroubled by the tender passion. There were moments, it is true, when he felt convinced that his manuscript would be lost or deliberately destroyed by the office in Barley Street who were typing it, but he usually managed to get the better of these crises, familiar to all writers, with the help of Susan who simply told him not to be silly.

Francis Brandon and Mrs. Arbuthnot were not, in spite of that lady's over-excited words about it's being all right on the night, of those who believe in a divine providence where the stage is concerned, and in any case to act with Aubrey Clover was a perilous honour for which vigil must be kept. So they rehearsed their own parts together, especially the tango scene so vividly described by Mrs. Arbuthnot, with unflagging energy at Stories at Winter Overcotes under Aubrey Clover's mournful, fish-like eye, on the little stage at the Town Hall and in fact, as Francis said, danced the fandango all over the place. And as for their song,

> Argentina tango
> Makes a girl and man go
>   Where you and I have been,

every one of their friends and relations was heartily sick of it, with the exception of Mrs. Brandon who embroidered placidly through several evenings of it at Stories and Jessica Dean who scolded and bullied them both at the week-end until they might have passed, so she said, for professionals at the Wigan Empire. All of which they took in very good part and appeared to be enjoying themselves very much.

Noel, his work in London being now at an end, was apt to turn up at the rehearsals and sometimes drove Mrs. Arbuthnot back to Southbridge. There was no harm in it at all, but if one lives in the county one must be prepared for the county to notice one's behaviour. To do Mrs. Arbuthnot justice we must say that she merely looked upon Noel as an amusing person with a car, and so occupied was she with theatricals that she never stopped to reflect upon the amount of petrol he had used on her behalf and there was no one who would point it out to her. Miss Arbuthnot sometimes looked anxious, and though most of her anxiety was in case Peggy landed herself in a scrape again, a little of it was for herself; for Noel Merton was certainly not going to marry Peggy. But no one would have known her trouble by her manner or her face.

Jessica Dean, the brilliant young actress, was at her parents' house the weekend before the Fête and ordered Aubrey Clover to take her to Northbridge to see Mrs. Merton. She looked on Lydia with a critical eye, was not altogether pleased, and asked after her children. Lydia said they were in Devonshire with Kate and Nurse, who had been having the most soul-splitting rows with Kate's nurse about all sorts of things like tomatoes and a piece of soap and who sent that vest to the wash we always did it at home, but Kate didn't seem to mind a bit. She then apologized to Aubrey Clover for being so dull, but Aubrey Clover who was looking like any not quite young man one didn't know who had been brought to tea, said his mother used to have a lot of trouble with nurses, and gently absorbed these incidents of domestic life which in course of time probably appeared, transmuted by his theatre mind into terms of the stage, in one of his comedies. And meanwhile Jessica looked at Lydia without appearing to look and drew some conclusions from what she saw.

They had just begun tea when Noel came in with Mrs. Arbuthnot, explaining that he had met her coming out of the Town Hall and was taking her back to Southbridge when she had had some tea. Mrs. Arbuthnot kissed Lydia in a very friendly way and sat down, blowing kisses to Jessica and Aubrey Clover, who was handing cake and looking as undistinguished as the second footman in the days when such beings existed, so that the party almost forgot he was there.

Lydia asked how the play was going.

"Quite dreadfully," said Mrs. Arbuthnot, who seemed however to be in her usual spirits. "Francis muffed his entrance and I fluffed my lines and Aubrey put in a new little bit that upset it all. We shall never get through. Only a week off. Aubrey will kill us."

"Not you, Peggy darling," said Aubrey Clover. "I'll kill Jessica perhaps. She is worth it."

Lydia, though careful of her guests' welfare, took very little part in the talk and Mrs. Arbuthnot looked quickly at her more than once and on one occasion caught Jessica doing exactly the same thing.

"Under the blasted oak at midnight," said Jessica to Mrs. Arbuthnot and then turning to Aubrey Clover said she knew he wanted to see the garden.

Aubrey Clover said he had quite forgotten but of course he wanted to see it most frightfully if it wouldn't be a bore. So they all went into the garden which was at its very worst, between the late summer and the autumn, and Jessica hung behind with Mrs. Arbuthnot while Aubrey Clover went through a very good performance of a dull guest being shown a garden.

"Well?" said Jessica.

"It's all such a bore," said Mrs. Arbuthnot. "He doesn't care for me in the least of course. The fact is he hasn't enough to do. Why lawyers have such long holidays I can't think. And I am so fond of Lydia."

"She is a lamb," said Jessica. "How she came to marry such a stupid man one does not know. I suppose she fell in love. What are you going to do about it? She is the silent suffering sort and that sort are very difficult. They sit like Patience on a monument only they don't smile at grief because they won't admit it. They lose their looks. Drat the man."

"I know," said Mrs. Arbuthnot, her pretty face full of anxiety. "Didn't I know what it was like when Fred was running after Mrs. Colonel Matcham, or whoever it was at the time. Of course the whole regiment knew about Fred and so did Effie, bless her, but so far I don't think people have noticed this great tom-fool," for so did Mrs. Arbuthnot lightly allude to the very successful barrister who was marked for promotion.

"I expect they have," said Jessica coolly. "They always do. Well, Peggy, what are you going to do about it? It's partly your fault, you know. You never will look where you're going."

Mrs. Arbuthnot said she really didn't know. Anything she said to Noel might and probably would further hurt Lydia, and it was all so silly that she could scream and she was a fool not to have done something about it sooner, and tears of annoyance rose to her attractive eyes.

"Well, I'd better do it," said Jessica. "As mother says, 'Darling Jessica is so young, but in some ways she seems like my mother,' which usually means that she wants me to do something for her that she doesn't want to do herself. All right, Peggy, I'll buy it. Out Goes He. Isn't it a delightful garden, Aubrey?"

Aubrey Clover, who had quietly become a dull country gentleman interested in dairy herds, said the garden was charming and they had looked at some Jerseys in a field Jolly little things, he added, his fish-like eyes fixed on Jessica with no expression at all.

"If Noel is taking you to Southbridge, Peggy, I'll come too," said Jessica. "Aubrey you can stay with Lydia if she'll let you.

And mind you say what a find chap Noel is, blast him," she added under her breath.

Aubrey Clover, who by one of his rapid changes of character was becoming the useful friend of a Pinero play under the eyes of Jessica who knew him well though to the rest of the party he appeared as undistinguished as ever, said he always liked a character part. Mrs. Arbuthnot, also taking her cue quietly, said to Lydia that she must be going as Noel was being kind enough to drive her, and Lydia must promise to come and see her act, which Lydia promised faithfully to do.

If Noel had anticipated some refreshing verbal badinage with Mrs. Arbuthnot, he was the more deceived, for the ladies sat in the back seat and talked shop till they got to Southbridge.

"We'd adore to come in, darling," said Jessica to Mrs. Arbuthnot, "but Noel must take me back at once. You know what rages Aubrey gets into if he is neglected."

To which Mrs. Arbuthnot, delighted by the little conspiracy and Jessica's abandoned lies about Aubrey Clover, said good-bye and disappeared into the cottage where she found her sister-in-law and the Vicar in the drawing-room. Colonel Crofts, Miss Arbuthnot said, was showing her his plans for altering the top floor of the Vicarage as soon as he cold get a permit, to make it more convenient for visiting grandchildren. So Mrs. Arbuthnot looked with amiable want of comprehension at a ground-plan of the top floor and wondered when Effie would tell her.

Jessica, now the rather dim, dowdy, devoted maiden aunt, beguiled the journey by telling Noel how unwell dear Lydia looked.

"I so well remember," she said, with a boringness that quite deceived Noel, "coming with mother to see her in the summer of Dunkirk, when you were still missing. I was quite a child then, but I remember so well the strained look in her face. She was just as sweet and gentle as ever, but one saw Pain looking out of her eyes, just as one does now," which interesting rehash of Jessica's lucky recollection of a visit to Northbridge during which she had naturally noticed nothing at all, being too young, except that there was a little pond with goldfish in it, annoyed Noel a good deal. So he said rather crossly that the measles had pulled her down.

"Of course," said Jessica. "Still it's wonderful for her to have you at home. You must find the Long Vacation awfully boring. If I had nothing to do for—how long is it? much longer than anyone else's holidays anyway—I'd go mad. I expect that's why lawyers, not you of course, darling, are always so dull. Darling Colin has been quite impossibly dull this summer mooning about after Peggy, who was bored stiff with him, poor lamb. Why do men always think that Peggy has nothing to do but listen to them making sheep's eyes at her? The trouble is that there is no one near Southbridge who is in the least amusing for her. She is frightfully fond of Lydia, only, as she was saying to me, it's such a bore if you go to see a woman you like and her husband is about all the time. Do you know the Lord Chancellor? He is such a lamb and a frightful pet of mine. I shall tell him he really must make your holidays shorter and then you won't get into so much mischief."

Noel was by now white with anger. Little Jessica Dean, whom he had vaguely known ever since she was in the nursery, was presuming to criticize him, and not only himself, but the whole sacred edifice of Themis. And what was far worse, he knew what she meant. He knew that he had found Mrs. Arbuthnot amusing and attractive. He knew that he had run after her, if one could use so horrid an expression about oneself, in a lukewarm way, and it began to dawn upon him that his conduct had been observed. There was nothing for it but to pretend to Jessica that he did not know what she meant, knowing all the time that she had planted every one of her barbs deliberately and was coolly watching their effect. And accustomed though he was to masking his feelings and controlling his emotions in his public career to do this in the narrow confines of a car with Jessica's theatre-trained eye upon him taxed even his acting powers.

However they got back safely to Northbridge, where they found Aubrey Clover telling Lydia about his flat in London and his old nurse who looked after him, while Lydia contributed an account of her struggles for supremacy in her own nursery.

"But of course you come out on top," said Aubrey Clover. "You are the sort that always does in the end. I wish I had your courage. My Nurse will call me Master Aubrey, *so* mortifying in front of company and I have to pretend I like it and say what a marvelous period piece she is."

"It's fairly easy to be brave with servants and nurses," said Lydia. "It's people one is fond of that it's difficult with."

"May I use that?" said Aubrey Clover, allowing the playwright to get the upper hand of the Useful Friend for a moment.

"Put it in a play, do you mean?" said Lydia. "But I thought all your people said clever things."

"Smart clever things, not unusual clever things," said Aubrey Clover. "When I use it, will you let me send you a box for the first night? And if I am acting in the play I'll wink at you when your line is said."

Lydia, not much accustomed to verbal homage and still one of the happy many who are dazzled by Stage-land, was almost confused. She thanked Aubrey Clover as a child might thank an uncle for the offer of seats at the pantomine, and by the time Noel came back they were talking together like old friends and Aubrey Clover had begged to be allowed to come over and see Nanny Twicker, a promise which, though the date of its fulfillment is outside the limits of this chronicle, we are glad to be able to say he kept, giving great pleasure to Nanny by asking her to call him Mr. Aubrey, and subsequently sending her a signed photograph of himself at three years old as page at a cousin's wedding.

Jessica and Noel came in just like a lady and gentleman who have been for a little drive and Jessica then carried Aubrey Clover away. Noel, left alone with his Lydia, felt for the first time in his life a certain embarrassment in her company and while mentally cursing Jessica Dean was compelled as a barrister to admit that she was right in equity, even if over-riding common law. The rest of the day passed uneventfully and happily. Lydia looked the better for her glimpse of a different world and the subtle flattery that Aubrey Clover had administered. Noel, honestly trying to see her as outsiders might see her, felt a distinct pang at his heart as he realized the shadows under her eyes and under her cheekbones, caused doubtless by measles but also, perhaps, by his own want of thought. But being a man of common sense as well as very fond of his Lydia, he did not go down on his knees and confess that he had been rather silly and make a great reconciliation scene. He began, however, to plan in his own mind a reparation which was almost theatrical, so far-reaching had his brief association with Jessica Dean and Aubrey Clover been, but in his desire to give Lydia a delightful surprise he did not reflect that what she really needed was an immediate sign, a word, an arm round her shoulders which would assure her that everything was all right. Instead of which he said it was a nuisance, but he would have to go to London for a night. Lydia's heart fell so fast, so deep, that she felt almost sick. Then she reproached herself for even imagining that Mrs. Arbuthnot was also going to town and only said she hoped Noel would not miss the Red Cross Fête as they must see Peggy act, which was quite a courageous way of grasping a nettle. Noel said with a little too much emphasis that of course he would be back, so that Lydia almost regretted her words. But nothing that might give pleasure to Noel was regrettable, she said to herself, and did her very best to be happy for the rest of the evening, so that Noel felt even more uncomfortable than before.

CHAPTER 13

Mrs. Brandon, with the view of promoting general happiness and forwarding the rehearsals of *Out Goes She*, had invited the Arbuthnots to stay at Stories for the Red Cross Fête. The Fête was on a Saturday, so Mrs. Arbuthnot and her sister-in-law came into Barchester by train on Friday morning and were driven out to Pomfret Madrigal by Francis who was taking a long weekend off. What exactly his business was we do not know and probably wouldn't be much the wiser if we did, but it was, so his mother said, something to do with merchanting, which sounded rather well. In any case it was an old Barchester firm which had always moved on with the times and Francis was now a director and in a fair way to be very well off, quite apart from his father's money which would eventually be divided between his sister Delia Grant and himself.

It had long been a matter of speculation in Barchester and Pomfret Madrigal what bride, if any, he would choose. In his younger days he had amused himself with everybody. The war happened, and he was in Africa and Italy, and people either forgot about him or said, Ah, he would probably marry a foreigner. But luckily he did not, and he had settled down again to work and such play as the peace afforded quite happily, for as yet he had found no one more charming and amusing than his mother. Not that he as one of the mother-ridden sons marked down by possessive mothers as permanent gentlemen-in-waiting, for Mrs. Brandon in her generous way would have liked to see her son and indeed everyone including the Pope married with large healthy families. So far her grand-maternal wishes had only been satisfied by Delia who had two delightful children, and as we know she was a little afraid that if no more babies turned up Nurse might feel it her duty to go to a younger family or even, as she had darkly hinted from time to time, take a place at the nursery school which was now safe in its new home in Sussex.

For a year or so that part of the county had observed Francis Brandon and Susan Dean with some attention. It all seemed very suitable. Both families were well off. Neither was quite county; not as the Thornes, the Leslies, the Greshams were. Francis really ought to be settling down, people said, and though girls were marrying late now it was considered that Susan Dean ought to be settling down too. Still even round about thirty and twenty-seven respectively neither of them seemed to be doing anything about it and the county's attention had relaxed. It is probable that Mrs. Brandon would have welcomed any wife of Francis's with enthusiasm and she liked Susan very much, but of late she had taken a particular affection for Mrs. Arbuthnot whose nature seemed to fit admirably with her own. She loved good looks in other women with all her warm heart and large nature, and in Mrs. Arbuthnot she found a capacity for harmless flirting quite equal to her own and an equal passion for clothes, so she and her new friend enjoyed long and delightful talks about nothing in particular with a good deal of laughter.

As for Susan Dean she was modern enough, though it is a sad kind of modernity, not to consider matrimony as her necessary fate. All the Deans had brains, inherited from their engineer father. Her elder sister Helen Fanshawe who knew more about cars than most men was happily married, but had driven for the Wrens through part of the war and still liked cars nearly as much as her husband and children. Her sister Betty who had married an American, was her husband's right-hand man in the reorganization of the peanut export trade. Jessica, the baby, was Aubrey Clover's leading lady, worked like a slave, and had never shown any symptoms of falling in love. And Susan, between Betty and Jessica, had done first-rate work under the Red Cross Educational Scheme for Prisoners of War and was now Depot Librarian of the Barsetshire Branch of the St. John and Red Cross Hospital Libraries and a considerable power in that world, for she was highly competent and never petty or jealous. Whether she really wished to leave this position for the delights of married life we cannot say. Possibly she did not know herself, for to feel slightly giddy at the touch of someone's hand on one's shoulder is not now necessarily a prelude to matrimony and in any case Susan had a very clear mind; not always the happiest sort of mind for a woman, one may say, but it depends very much on the woman.

However none of the above speculations troubled the mind of Francis Brandon as he drove Mrs. and Miss Arbuthnot through the chill September day to Pomfret Madrigal, arriving in time for lunch. Mrs. Brandon enfolded her guests with her own peculiar soft kind atmosphere, there was a log fire in the sitting-room and a good lunch in the dining-room and both guests relaxed gratefully to their surroundings.

"I love Editha," said Mrs. Arbuthnot, "but it is so heavenly not to know what one is going to eat. Effie is much more sensible than I am. She makes up her mind what we are going to have and sticks to it. I think of one thing and then I think of something else that might be nicer and I get quite addled. Of course in India I never had to think, because the servants did it all."

"You are just like mamma," said Francis. "She makes all sorts of delightful plans and then Cook does exactly as she likes."

"You are quite unfair, Francis," said Mrs. Brandon indignantly. "I said yesterday to Cook that plum pie would be very nice and we are having plum pie."

"Don't take any notice of my mamma," said Francis. "What

really happened was that Cook came in and said, 'I was thinking, madam, we ought to use up some of those plums we bottled as there's two bottles looks as if they had a little bit of mould on them.'"

"She didn't," said Mrs. Brandon. "I said fruit would be nice if she had enough fat for pastry, and she said she had just been saying the same thing to Rose. And here it is," said Mrs. Brandon, with a judicial air of having proved something.

But so concerned was she at Mrs. Arbuthnot's confession of liking her food to be a surprise that after lunch she sent her up to rest with a hot bottle, a treat exactly to her guest's mind. Francis said he must write a few letters, so Mrs. Brandon and Miss Arbuthnot settled very comfortably by the fire in the sitting-room, for the big drawing-room though it had been refurnished and recarpeted after the nursery school had gone was not much used except on warm days. Their talk was on general topics, on the play, on the dress which Mrs. Brandon had got Nurse to alter for Mrs. Arbuthnot and so by a natural transition to Mrs. Arbuthnot herself. And gradually under the spell of Mrs. Brandon's very kind and uninquisitive interest, if this expression is clear, Miss Arbuthnot spoke about herself, which she rarely did, and told Mrs. Brandon about her only brother, younger than herself, how she had kept house for him in India and how fond she had been of him.

"Did you mind very much when he married Peggy?" said Mrs. Brandon, though from her the question did not seem so much curiosity as a genuine and warm-hearted interest.

"I couldn't," said Miss Arbuthnot. "You know what Peggy is now. She was just the same then and Fred simply had to fall in love with her. And she was frightfully in love with him. It ought to have been perfect."

"Wasn't it, then?" asked Mrs. Brandon, looking up through her owl-like spectacles from her embroidery.

"No," said Miss Arbuthnot. "I'd like you to know, because you are fond of Peggy. Fred was the nicest brother that anyone could have, but he simply couldn't keep away from pretty women. He made Peggy very unhappy. Perhaps it is a good thing he was killed. I really don't know."

As she spoke, her heavy face once more assumed the fierce, sullen look that had puzzled Mrs. Brandon earlier in the summer, and again Mrs. Brandon wondered why it was familiar to her, but in her desire to comfort Miss Arbuthnot she put this thought aside.

"I am very sorry, Effie," she said. "I believe a nice brother is a very special thing. I never had any. Francis's old aunt, Miss Brandon, had a very special brother she adored. He was killed in India pig-sticking years and years ago, and she kept all his letters. She gave me this ring that he had given her," and she stretched out her pretty hand upon which shone the diamond that Captain Frederick Brandon had given to his younger sister long, long ago, on the last leave he ever had. "She lived in a dreadful house full of horrors. I must show you some photographs of them."

Full of her kind wish to distract Miss Arbuthnot from her mood of black remembering, she laid down her work and got from a shelf a handsome and hideous photograph album.

"Old Aunt Sissie had the Abbey photographed inside and out for her brother," she said opening the book, "and she gave me this copy. Isn't it a *dreadful* house, all turrets and pointed windows. She threatened to leave it to Francis once, and to Hilary Grant who married Delia—he was a sort of cousin of hers too—but thank goodness she left it for some kind of home and anyway the Government took it over and have got it still. She had two terrifying wooden gorillas with hats on that always stood in the corridor outside her bedroom. I must find them," and she turned the pages till she came to the photograph. "They were holding a kind of tray and I think they were meant to put flowers on, or to leave your cards on if you called, but quite dreadful and the children used to be terrified of them."

"But I know those gorillas," said Miss Arbuthnot.

"Do you?" said Mrs. Brandon. "Aunt Sissie left them to her maid who lives at Southsea. Could you have seen them there? I mean, military people live in extraordinary places sometimes."

"Fred had them," said Miss Arbuthnot. "Photographs of them, just like these. Our grandmother gave them to him. How very funny."

"What an extraordinary thing!" said Mrs. Brandon. "Perhaps your grandmother knew Miss Brandon," which indeed seemed a reasonable supposition. "I must show you a photograph of her."

She turned to the end of the book where were several photographs of the redoubtable Aunt Sissie; not as the heavy, helpless, pain-racked old woman that Mrs. Brandon had known, but as a young middle-aged woman in the dress of the late nineties with a curled fringe.

"She was about forty then," said Mrs. Brandon, looking at the heavy unhandsome face, "but I didn't know her till she was much older, and all the end of her life she was in bed, poor thing. Our Vicar's wife was her companion the year she died."

Miss Arbuthnot made some reply, but Mrs. Brandon did not hear it, for quite suddenly she knew what the likeness was that had eluded her. Miss Arbuthnot when her face looked annoyed or sullen was exactly like the photograph of Aunt Sissie in about 1897: which was obviously ridiculous.

"Have you any stamps, mamma?" said Francis coming in.

His mother looked at him kindly, but her looks and her thoughts were very far away and for a moment Francis wondered if his mamma had lost her wits.

"A most extraordinary thing, Francis," said Mrs. Brandon. "Effie knows the gorillas quite well!"

"God bless my soul!" said Francis, sitting down.

"My grandmother had that photograph," said Miss Arbuthnot.

Francis suggested that Miss Brandon had sent a copy to Miss Arbuthnot's grandmother. People, he said, did send photographs to people, and if Aunt Sissie had that ghastly Brandon Abbey photographed, what more natural than to send the photographs to her friends.

"I know she had them done for her brother Fred," said Mrs. Brandon. "He was a Captain in the Indian Army and she adored him. He was a good deal older than she was. How very funny."

"And my brother was Fred, and I adored him," said Miss Arbuthnot, to no one in particular.

"Good gracious!" said Mrs. Brandon suddenly.

"My dear mamma, you mustn't say things like that," said Francis. "What is there to be gracious about?"

"I don't know if I ought to say it, but it's all too extraordinary," said Mrs. Brandon, her dark eyes appearing to grow to twice their size with excitement.

"Well, if it's anything you oughtn't to say, let's hear it," said Francis. "Do you agree, Effie?"

Miss Arbuthnot said by all means.

"I hope I am not making myself liable to be prosecuted or anything," said Mrs. Brandon, looking straight into space in a most alarming way, "but I suddenly thought of something."

"It's quite all right," said Francis to Miss Arbuthnot, "she just goes like that sometimes."

"Now do be serious, Francis," said Mrs. Brandon, "because this is important. When Aunt Sissie gave me this ring, she said her brother Fred would have liked me to have it because he liked pretty women to have jewellery. I was pretty then," she added with a graceful melancholy.

"Yes, darling, and you are now," said Francis. "But do get on a bit if you really have anything to say."

"And she said he gave a diamond bracelet to a Mrs. Colonel Arbuthnot in Poona in seventy-six and had to exchange into another regiment," said Mrs. Brandon.

"Our grandmother had a very beautiful diamond bracelet," said Miss Arbuthnot, interested and rather puzzled. "She left it to Fred and he gave it to Peggy. I think she is going to wear it for the play. Could it have been Captain Brandon's? How funny."

"It's more than funny," said Francis, with a warning note in his voice for which neither of his hearers could account. "Shall I put the photographs away, mamma?"

His mother said yes, and how curious it was that Effie had such a look of that photograph of Aunt Sissie when she was about forty, and it had been worrying her for quite a long time.

"But it was all more and more peculiar," she said. "Francis, you remember the village fête the summer Aunt Sissie died and how Noel Merton came in afterwards and told us about her will and how she had left ten thousand pounds to Miss Miller because she was her companion, I mean Miss Miller was *her* companion."

Francis said he remembered quite well, and what about it.

"Well, if you remember that, you *must* remember that he said she had left ten thousand pounds to a Captain Arbuthnot in the Indian Army."

"Fred did have ten thousand pounds left to him just before the war," said Miss Arbuthnot. "That was the money he settled on Peggy. If he hadn't, she wouldn't have had a penny, so it was a lucky thing. But I thought it was some kind of old aunt. I didn't know it was Miss Brandon. Why should she have left him money?"

Mrs. Brandon had by now thought of a very probable and very possible reason why old Miss Brandon should have left money to a young officer in the Indian Army whom she had never seen. Every piece in the puzzle was clear, but she was not sure if the solution would be acceptable to her guest.

"Perhaps because her brother had liked his grandmother," said Francis, also seeing the final shape of the puzzle, but anxious not to hurt Miss Arbuthnot.

There was a rather embarrassed silence, during which Mrs. Brandon and Francis began to be a little nervous of the spirit they had raised, while Miss Arbuthnot sat thinking.

"Wait a moment," she said, though neither of them had shown any wish to hurry her. "Miss Brandon's brother had to exchange into another regiment because of some scandal about Mrs. Colonel Arbuthnot—that's what they used to call my grandmother."

"Mrs. Miller, who was Miss Morris then and Miss Brandon's companion, said her last words were 'Mrs. Colonel Arbuthnot,'" said Mrs. Brandon interrupting, "and she said Miss Brandon laughed in a pleasant kind of way, though she was too weak to say any more."

"And then," continued Miss Arbuthnot, her likeness to old Miss Brandon again very apparent as she knit her brow with the effort to follow her thought, "Mrs. Colonel Arbuthnot had a son and a grandson, my brother Fred. And Miss Brandon left ten thousand pounds to Fred. And you say that I am like Miss Brandon."

Mrs. Brandon hurriedly protested that she had not exactly meant what she said and photographs could be most misleading, but her voice trailed away to nothing before Francis's look and Miss Arbuthnot's complete absorption in her own train of thought.

"Then probably father was Captain Brandon's son," she said, apparently rather pluming herself upon the deduction.

Francis was really terrified. If what she had said was true, and it all seemed very reasonable, he and his mother between them had proved that Miss Arbuthnot's father was illegitimate, which though it may sound romantic must be very awkward at times. Mrs. Brandon, suddenly inspired by common sense, said if Mr. Colonel Arbuthnot, Mrs. Colonel Arbuthnot's husband she meant, said his son was his son, he was his son, legally.

"I don't care in the least what my grandfather said," said Miss Arbuthnot. "If my father was really Captain Brandon's son, it makes all the difference."

Such a note of triumph was in her voice that Mrs. Brandon and Francis thought she might have gone mad, which would have seriously deranged the theatricals, but her next words reassured them.

"You see," said Miss Arbuthnot, "if Fred was Captain Brandon's grandson, it makes everything all right."

Francis said he was now prepared to believe absolutely anything, but if Miss Arbuthnot would explain why it made everything all right he would be very grateful and he felt like a teetotum.

"Don't you see," said Miss Arbuthnot. "Fred could not keep away from pretty women and it made Peggy dreadfully unhappy and I couldn't bear to think that Fred could be so unkind. But if his real grandfather was Captain Brandon, which I think he must have been, because I know that it was Grannie who insisted on his being called Frederick, he obviously couldn't help it. If only we had known about Captain Brandon we wouldn't have minded so much. Now I know it wasn't really Fred's fault, I am so very glad," of which state of mind she suddenly and most unexpectedly gave the very feminine proof of beginning to cry.

"Don't, Effie," said Francis, much alarmed. "Think of Mr. Churchill, or the clubfooted sparrowhawk, or anything you like. If Peggy sees you have been crying, she will ask why."

This plea made Miss Arbuthnot dry her eyes in a rather defiant way and she agreed with Francis that this suspicion must at all costs be kept from her sister-in-law which, providing they kept their heads and didn't let it out by mistake, would be quite easy; though, as Francis pointed out, to keep one's head while quite easily physically except for people like Charles the First or Louis the Sixteenth, was very difficult mentally, because if one's tongue could get one into trouble, it always did.

"But why shouldn't Peggy know?" said Mrs. Brandon, who had not taken much part in the discussion. "She might think it was rather fun. And don't tell me not to say things like that, Francis, for I know Peggy *much* better than you do."

"Perhaps you are right," said Miss Arbuthnot. "She was always good at facing facts."

"And talking of facts," said Francis, "I have just thought of one. If all this extraordinary story is true, you are a cousin of ours, Effie."

"Of yours and Delia's, not of mine," said Mrs. Brandon in a dignified way. "Aunt Sissie was your father's aunt and no relation to me at all."

"Never mind, darling," said Francis. "You were the one that was kind to Aunt Sissie and used to go and see her, so you can be a cousin too. I must say I think it all a very good plan."

After a little more consideration of the subject it was decided that Mrs. Arbuthnot should be told when a favourable occasion presented itself, and that although the whole story was now old history and could not hurt anyone, there was no need to make it public.

"After all, Poona in eighteen-seventy-six is a long way off," said Mrs. Brandon. "Aunt Sissie is dead, and her brother, and your grandmother and your father."

"And Fred," said Miss Arbuthnot. "How he would have laughed. He used to tease our grandmother about her good looks and all the officers that must have been in love with her, but none of us knew about Captain Brandon. Grannie cared for Fred much more than she cared for me. I suppose he reminded her of the diamond bracelet."

Then tea came in and Mrs. Arbuthnot followed hard upon, looking particularly pretty after her rest. Presently she took out of her bag a shabby red morocco case.

"Do you think it would look too showy if I wore this for the play?" she said to Mrs. Brandon, opening the case and showing her a bracelet glittering on the faded red velvet.

It was indeed a most handsome piece of jewellery, a little on the heavy side perhaps but of beautiful design and what Mrs. Brandon, who knew something about jewellery, declared to be very good diamonds.

"Do put it on," said Mrs. Arbuthnot to Mrs. Brandon. "It will look lovely on you. Put it on for her, Francis."

Nothing loth, Francis took the bracelet and clasped it with courteous reverence upon his mother's arm. Mrs. Brandon looked with great satisfaction at the glittering bauble, turned her elegant wrist this way and that the better to admire the stones, and said Mrs. Arbuthnot must certainly wear it for the play as it would make a very good effect upon her black frock.

"Your black frock, dear Mrs. Brandon," said Mrs. Arbuthnot, for Mrs. Brandon had produced from her still well-stored wardrobe a filmy affair of black chiffon and black lace which Nurse hardly had to alter at all. And of course after this the talk ran upon clothes and Miss Arbuthnot was a little out of it, for though she loved to see her sister-in-law prettily dressed she was not deeply interested in her own clothes, liking to be neat and not liking to be noticeable. Also she was preoccupied with a thought which had come to her, a thought about which she wanted some advice; but she was patient by nature and her thought could quite well wait till the play was over and they were back at Editha.

Presently Mrs. Brandon unclasped the bracelet and put on her spectacles the better to examine it from every aspect. On the gold behind the largest diamond a heart was engraved with a monogram inside it.

"L. F.," said Mrs. Brandon.

"Fred and I used to wonder what it stood for," said Mrs. Arbuthnot. "His grandmother's name was Lily, but her maiden name was Elliman. We thought perhaps a bottom bit of the E had got worn away, but it is quite clearly an F."

"One can't help admiring his impertinence," said Francis, quite forgetting the pact of conspiracy. "And one admires her impertinence in wearing it even more."

He then realized that his tongue, just as he had said before tea, had made trouble for him. Mrs. Arbuthnot said she didn't quite understand. Who was impertinent? Francis said no one.

"Don't be silly," said Mrs. Arbuthnot. "What is it all about?"

Francis and Miss Arbuthnot would have involved themselves

in several unconvincing subterfuges not to say lies but Mrs. Brandon, whose real common sense was out of all proportion to her deceptive air of being a charming fool, said Peggy had better know and briefly told her the story of Mrs. Colonel Arbuthnot's romance, to which Mrs. Arbuthnot listened with intense interest.

"How lovely!" she said with a deep breath of satisfaction when Mrs. Brandon had finished her exposition; at which Francis couldn't help laughing and we regret to say that the whole party laughed, some at Mrs. Arbuthnot, some at the story, and Mrs. Arbuthnot at herself.

"Yes, mamma darling, I am going to say it before you can," said Francis. "All this is quite shocking and we ought to go into mourning and wear weepers, whatever they are. Bless your heart, Peggy. I wish Aubrey Clover were here."

"And Fred was called after Captain Brandon, I suppose," said Miss Arbuthnot. "How like Grannie to have it done. She had my father under her thumb and my mother too. How she must have loved Captain Brandon."

"I don't know," said Mrs. Arbuthnot, suddenly thoughtful. "One can't always go on loving people who are always falling in love with someone else. But then of course she had the baby, and Captain Brandon was killed. I wish we knew what your father was really like, Effie."

Miss Arbuthnot, who knew only too well what her sister-in-law had felt about a husband who ran after other women and how she had quietly regretted having no child, said it was very difficult to guess what he was like as she had been quite small when he died, but Grannie always spoke of him with a sort of kind want of interest and she thought he must have been quite ordinary and respectable. Mrs. Arbuthnot sighed.

"I know, darling," said Miss Arbuthnot, who but rarely showed emotion; and she got up and kissed her sister-in-law, half-wishing that her adored brother had been killed sooner so that his widow might have retained her illusions about him.

"It's no good," said Francis. "Even Clover couldn't do justice to it. And now let us run through the tango, Peggy, just to clear the air."

So the bracelet was put back in its case, the gramophone turned on. Francis and Mrs. Arbuthnot danced and sang. Mrs. Brandon took up her embroidery and Miss Arbuthnot thought of her own private difficulty and decided to let it wait.

By some gross oversight of Providence the day of the Fête was fine and almost warm, which raised Lydia's spirits a little. It was high time too, for Noel had been in London and although she knew that Mrs. Arbuthnot was at Stories she could not help imagining journeys to town and meetings at lunch. Also she had expected Noel on the previous evening and he had telephoned from London to say he would come down on Saturday morning and sounded preoccupied. So it was with great relief that she heard the car drive up to the house before lunch and then Noel came into the room with an expression that she could not quite interpret.

"Well, my precious love," said he, kissing her. "Here I am, all ready to go to the Fête. And I have brought you a little present."

He laid on the table a large rather heavy parcel.

"For me?" said Lydia. "What is it?"

"Open it," said Noel.

He sat down and watched Lydia while she undid the string and made a neat loop of it and took off the outer layer of brown paper and folded it; for war habits of economy in paper and string were not lightly shed, and good paper and string still very scarce. The present, whatever it was, was still wrapped in some whitish paper which Lydia loosened and brought to view a roll of purple silk, satin on one side, dull on the other, of just the rich colour that Lydia could wear.

"Silk!" said Lydia, silk-starved as all the women of England were by the years of war and the worse peace when everything good made in England was sold to foreigners.

"Yes, silk," said Noel. "Best Lyons silk too. Pre-war."

"But how?" said Lydia, touching the silk as tenderly as if it were her first-born child. So would not Miss Lydia Keith have fingered or valued a length of silk, but Mrs. Noel Merton had learnt a great deal since her marriage, though the old Lydia was still violently alive in her.

"I know a man who was in Germany," said Noel. "He said that there is any amount there still. All French loot of course. Do you like it?"

But all Lydia could answer was, "Oh, Noel!"

"I rather wanted you to have some silk," said Noel, looking at her a little mockingly though very affectionately, "because some is coming my way and I like to share everything with you."

"Do you mean you can get some more like this?" said Lydia. "I could have heavenly pyjamas made for you, if you don't think it would look too rich. What colour?"

Noel said black, at which Lydia's face fell and she begged him to take her purple for his pyjamas and she would have a black evening dress.

"As a matter of fact," said Noel, "the King is making me a present of it. At least I shall have to buy it myself, but I shall have His Majesty's permission to wear it. And if I have a silken gown, my wife shall have one too. That sounds like poetry."

"Do you mean you are going to take silk?" asked Lydia, deeply excited by the magic words which must float in the mind of every barrister's wife.

Noel said he expected to write K.C. after his name and wished Lydia could write it after hers, and could not understand why she began to laugh until she explained that the magic letters K.C. stood for that stuff one put into the washing-up water now that soap was rationed, though what the letters meant she had never known. Nor, we may add, did any of the thousand other users.

"And that's that, my precious love," said Noel, who with the obtuseness of even the best and nicest husband thought that a present would make all his past foolishness melt into oblivion. Only this time he happened to be right, for Lydia's true joy at hearing the good news and her pleasure in the web of silk, combined with her own generous and loving nature, made her faith vanish into sight and her hope be emptied in delight. And we must say for Noel that though he had been quite silly during the last weeks he had the sense and the grace not to make any apology, for an apology would only have reopened old wounds. What Lydia left unspoken he would leave unspoken too, and seldom had he done a wiser thing.

All through lunch they talked of the excitement of Noel's rise and how well K.C. would look after his name, though Noel said wistfully that there was a cachet about Q.C. that could never be equalled, cheering up however when Lydia said that very likely Harry might be a Q.C. when he grew up.

"Of course," said Noel, "I shall now look down on Colin like anything. Is he still not in love with Peggy?" which was a good way of introducing her name.

Lydia said he was still being very nice so she supposed he was quite out of love, and she did think perhaps it might be Susan Dean, which would be very nice.

Noel said he had a strong feeling that Lydia had been right when she described Colin as a perpetual uncle, but they would see; and now they really ought to be starting for the Red Cross Fête.

"And I do truly adore you, my precious love," he said, putting an arm round her shoulders.

"So do I," said Lydia and rubbed her face against his coat. "It is frightfully exciting to be going to see Peggy acting with Aubrey Clover."

Noel said that was at least two present participles too many and kissed her.

The Red Cross Fête was going very well. All tickets were sold, all the right people were there, the weather had remained fine though not hot enough to make the hall uncomfortable. Mrs. Brandon and Miss Arbuthnot had good places in the middle of the fourth row and were prepared to spend a very pleasant afternoon, for both had complete confidence in the success of Aubrey Clover's play and were not suffering from the vicarious stage-fright which mothers and other near relations know. The seat next to Mrs. Brandon had been empty and now Colonel Crofts, who had arrived just before the end of the first part and did not wish to disturb people by squashing his way in, came and took his place. Whether Mrs. Arbuthnot had told Mrs. Brandon in good-night confidences that she wondered when Effie would tell her about Colonel Crofts we cannot truthfully say, but we think it extremely probable, the more so that Mrs. Brandon, most untruthfully alleging a wish to talk to the very dull woman on his other side, presently got him to change places and sit between herself and Miss Arbuthnot.

"I am sorry to be so late," said Colonel Crofts to Miss Arbuthnot. "It was all Bateman's doing."

Miss Arbuthnot inquired how. Colonel Crofts said he had been away for a night and Bateman, together with Chives, had conspired to cut away the shrubbery and had made a very good job of it.

"I cannot tell you," he said, "how much improved the drawing-room is already and by the greatest good luck they found all the verandah posts were rotting, so I don't think there will be much difficulty about having the whole thing removed," upon which piece of good luck Miss Arbuthnot congratulated him warmly.

"I left them tackling those two depressing trees," said Colonel Crofts. "I would have liked to give a hand myself but I knew you would be here and I felt, selfishly, that I must come. I didn't know my seat was next to yours. When are you coming back, my dear?"

Miss Arbuthnot said she and her sister-in-law were spending the week-end at Stories and would be back on Monday and then there was a good deal of excitement while Lady Fielding's piano, which had been biding its time in a corner of the Town Hall, was pushed forward to take the part of orchestra for Aubrey Clover's play.

"Edward," said Miss Arbuthnot, feeling that this was a safe moment to speak of her private difficulty, "I have very much wanted to see you——"

"Bless you, dearest," said Colonel Crofts, "but not half so much as I have wanted to see you. Forgive the interruption. I could not resist it."

"——because," said Miss Arbuthnot, "there is something I want to tell you about."

Colonel Crofts expressed general willingness to hear anything she wished to say and prepared to listen with loving attention. But even while he was speaking Miss Arbuthnot, with the astounding amount of thinking that one's mind can cram into a few seconds when it has nothing else to do, came to the conclusion that what she had to say was not worth saying. If, as certainly appeared probable, a Captain Brandon of whom she had never heard had rashly made himself her illegitimate grandfather at Poona in eighteen-seventy-six, what did it matter, to whom did it matter? The answer was that it did not matter at all. It was a curious piece of scandal and everything fitted in, but it affected no one now, and even if it were shouted from the house-tops no one would be interested. With an inward blush she had to admit to herself, in those seconds of swift thought which confuse all one's ordinary notions about time and space, that she had been dramatizing herself and had only just in time realized it. There was really nothing to disclose to Colonel Crofts, nothing to hide from him. In its time and place the story might be told to him, an old, foolish, far-off thing, but not one which could in any way affect their relationship. And as this very common sense point of view filtered into her mind, she began to laugh at herself inside; an excellent way of treating oneself.

All this had passed so swiftly in her mind that Colonel Crofts had hardly begun to notice a pause before she said that it really was not important and what did he think about leaving one section of the verandah at the east end to keep the wind off, which Colonel Crofts thought a good idea. And he was just beginning to expound his views on a rose-garden where the shrubbery had been, when Aubrey Clover's accompanist, an expressionless man of no particular age, took his seat and contemptuously threw off a kind of Brock's benefit of arpeggios, trills, chromatic scales, crashing chords and a final glissando which merged with a bang into the overture. A feeling of delightful anticipation ran through the hall, the curtains parted and Aubrey Clover as Henley Marlowe was discovered in his service flat, looking exactly like the part he was acting.

Out Goes She is too well known to require a detailed description and Aubrey Clover said afterwards that he had never enjoyed a busman's holiday more. He and Mrs. Arbuthnot shimmered like sheet lightning, dazzled like forked lightning, did their verbal fencing as well as the most accomplished cross-talk comedian of the halls. Mrs. Arbuthnot in black chiffon and lace, the bracelet of sin as Francis called it flashing on her wrist, was more ravishingly pretty than ever. Francis, with a slight but engaging touch of the amateur, was a worthy Phil Paradene, and when he and Mrs. Arbuthnot swayed and dipped in "Argentina Tango," all their friends were agreeably shocked and found themselves suddenly letting out spurts of laughter against their better and more refined selves. But the great success of the afternoon was that brilliant young actress Jessica Dean, who nearly made Aubrey Clover forget his lines, though winning his profound respect, by suddenly producing an entirely new reading of her part. The smart personal maid, the well-trained automaton with pretty legs who knew too much about human nature, about her employer's in particular, and had one or two good lines, in fact the conventional soubrette, suddenly came to life in her hands as the complete village idiot with a face vacant of all expression, obviously thinking if she thought at all of nothing but the movies and the boys, and putting into her few lines a wealth of meaning that left Barchester several bars behind with its laughs and even made Aubrey Clover fluff one of his entrances. But she had saved her final effect for the end and when Aubrey Clover, amid the roars of the audience, led his little company to the footlights to sing "Argentina Tango," Miss Jessica Dean in cap and apron with a perfectly imbecile face, sang right through the song on one note, never losing pitch; a tour de force which commanded the unwilling respect of all musicians in the audience. The curtain fell for the last time, the everyday world resumed possession of several hundred people who had been blissfully transported to Escape, and the audience began to disperse.

Mrs. Brandon and Miss Arbuthnot, taking Colonel Crofts with them, of course went behind the stage where Jessica was listening unmoved to Aubrey Clover's denunciations.

"Devil!" said Aubrey Clover as Mrs. Brandon and her party came in. "Never again! Making me miss a cue in my own play! Fiend!"

Jessica, quite unperturbed, said the maid was really like that only Aubrey hadn't known it. It took a really great actress, she said, to disentangle what the dramatist thought he had written from what he really meant to write. Aubrey, she said carelessly, but with a wink at Mrs. Arbuthnot, had better in future let her read all his plays before rehearsal and then she could tell him what his characters were really like.

"Hell-cat!" said Aubrey Clover.

The accompanist came up, said he didn't know Miss Dean had absolute pitch and he must say good-bye now as Mums was expecting him back for supper. "And I was right about that F sharp," he added to Aubrey Clover and so departed.

"I have only heard that done once in my life," said Colonel Crofts admiringly to Jessica Dean. "It was when the Follies were at the Apollo Theatre in King Edward the Seventh's time. They brought one of the property men on in his working-suit and a bowler hat and he sang right through the chorus on one note. I think it was 'I'll never have another Mother, If I live ten thousand years,'" to which Jessica made a suitable reply, but Mrs. Brandon was the only person present who remembered the Follies and she at once got Colonel Crofts to herself to talk about them.

Then another great irruption of friends took place, among them the Mertons and Colin Keith.

"The First Noel," said Jessica, making a proper soubrette's curtsy and moue. "Do you remember me, or are you proud?"

"I'm not a bit proud," said Noel, managing to back Jessica into a corner, "and I do remember. I remember everything. You were a perfect devil, Jessica, but I deserved it. A stitch in time saved me. Lydia, will you break the news to Jessica? It might be too much for her in her present state of congenital idiocy."

"You were frightfully funny," said Lydia, kissing Jessica warmly. "And it is all heavenly, because Noel is to be a K.C. and he gave me a roll of most beautiful French silk from Germany."

"So you will walk in silken gown. And siller have to spare," said Jessica, looking with kind mockery at her friend's happiness. "And I am a doggerel bard. All right, Noel. Next time I won't let you off so easily."

Lydia asked Noel what Jessica meant and he said actresses were often like that after a performance and they went on to congratulate Mrs. Arbuthnot, who was so carried away by her triumph that she kissed everybody, including Noel and Colonel Crofts.

"Come on, Jessica," said Susan Dean, suddenly appearing. "I've left father's big car at the back of the Town Hall and you and Aubrey can take him and mother home. I've got to clear up a bit and I've got the little car. I'll see you later on."

So with a final round of indiscriminate kissing the two professionals went away and the rest of the company began to disperse. The competent Depot Librarian of the Barsetshire Branch of the St. John and Red Cross Hospital Libraries then went to the committee room which the Town Hall had lent for the occasion, thanked all the voluntary helpers and said she would see to the rest of the business. So she tidied everything and collected the programme money to take it to the bank on Monday, and then in walked Colin Keith.

Being almost of their period, they said, "Hullo," which is rapidly becoming the Basic English for all greetings, morning, noon or night; friend to friend; lover to lover, parent to child and child to parent.

"I always feel ashamed when I've said hullo," said Colin, sitting on the edge of a table.

Susan said she did too. She did not naturally say it, she added, but in the Red Cross it didn't do to be unlike other people. Then, knowing that a good secretary thinks of others and not of herself, she inquired how *Lemon* was getting on.

"Johns and Fairfield," said Colin, mentioning a firm of good repute who had published Mrs. Rivers's novels and old Lord Pomfret's *A Landowner Under Five Reigns*, and whose senior member was Mr. Wickham's cousin, "have accepted it. I don't think it will have large sales, but one hopes the right people will read it. It all helps."

Susan, who was checking the sixpences and shillings and half-crowns, made no answer.

"Peggy was quite good," said Colin.

"She was very good," said Susan rather sharply and added under her breath, but only just under it, "and much too good for you."

Colin heard what she said, which put him in a horrid position. Either he hadn't officially heard, which meant that he must not only tell or imply a lie but also go to the trouble of keeping it up; or he had heard, in which latter case he didn't know what he ought to do. So he fidgeted with everything on the table and swung his legs, while Susan went on with her tidying.

"There," said Susan, putting the last of the papers into a very professional accordion-pleated case. "Are you coming, Colin? I'm just going to shut up."

So Colin dismounted from the table and helped Susan to take the money and the account books to the Mayor's Parlour where an official was kindly waiting to put them in the safe til Monday morning. Susan thanked the official for his help in exactly the right way and after inquiring warmly after his wife and his little boy shook hands and took Colin away.

"How well you do it," said Colin.

Susan said do what.

"Saying the right things to the right people in the right way," said Colin, to which Susan, the competent impersonal librarian, answered that if one was doing a job one might as well do it thoroughly. She unlocked the little car and got into it.

"Good-bye," she said to Colin, as she started her engine. "Come to tennis one Sunday. Not tomorrow because Aubrey will be there and he is going to read us his new play. He goes to London with Jessica on Monday to start rehearsing."

This was not to Colin's taste. Aubrey Clover might be a genius, a portent, a wonder-man, but he, Colin Keith, had written a commentary on Lemon's great work on running powers, which would probably become a standard text-book.

"And don't sulk," said Susan sharply, causing the little car to make as horrible a noise as possible.

"I'm not sulking," said Colin, in a loud sulky voice.

Susan turned the tap that stops the noise and lowering the window asked what he was saying.

"I said I wasn't sulking," said Colin, in a louder sulkier voice. "Do be human, Susan."

"I've been human quite long enough," said Susan Dean, the competent careerist. "I've listened to you going on about railways and I've watched you mooning about after Peggy Arbuthnot. When you've grown up a bit I'd like to see you again."

At this well-founded reproach Colin went pale.

"I'm sorry," said Susan, "but it's quite true and it's high time someone told you. Good-bye."

"But Susan," said Colin, grasping the edge of the window as if to stop the car. "I thought you liked railways."

"I do," said Susan, moved by his distress, though not touched to the quick. "But you've got to get Peggy out of your head if you want me to be interested in your railways."

"I have got her out of my head," said Colin, "and out of my mind and my heart and liver and lights and gall and all. I really have, Susan. I stopped caring for her quite a fortnight ago."

"Well, keep it up for another fortnight," said Susan firmly but not unkindly, "and we'll see. I shall be frightfully busy for the next few weeks as our accountant is having her holiday. Ring me up at the beginning of next month and we might have lunch."

Colin, chastened and subdued, said he would like to give her lunch and put his hand in at the window.

"Lydia may be right," said Susan giving his hand an impersonal pat, just as if he were a nice, boring dog. "She thinks you are a permanent uncle."

With these discouraging words she drove off. But Colin for some reason did not find them discouraging and walked to Barchester Central where he caught the local to Northbridge Halt and so walked back to the Manor, planning a dedication for his book on *Lemon*. So abstracted did his literary thoughts make him that his sister Lydia wondered for a moment if he had measles, but as she did not see any spots she dismissed his affairs from her mind and devoted her thoughts and her love to Noel. And all Noel could do was to accept them with deep gratitude, for he knew that he must never try to explain his short-lived folly; and this was quite as much punishment as he deserved.

In spite of its being early autumn, the general atmosphere of Stories was that of Christmas. The short-lived fineness of the day was over. Bitter blasts of wind and sleety rain and a leaden sky were enlivening the landscape to such an extent that Francis insisted upon drawing the curtains and pretending it was dark, which made the sitting-room quite Dickensishly cosy. Francis begged Mrs. Arbuthnot to put on for dinner the black dress which she had worn in the play and the diamond bracelet, and furthermore asked his mother to wear his old sweet-pea frock if she knew what he meant, which she apparently did. As for Miss Arbuthnot, it is with great liking and profound respect that we are obliged to state that whatever she wore would have looked dull, which did not for one moment prevent the essential good-ness of her character from shining through her attire. After refreshing cups of tea the ladies retired to have a short rest, while Francis visited what was left of the cellar and occupied himself in other ways till eight o'clock when the party reassembled.

To oblige her son Mrs. Brandon had got Nurse to take down and press a frock which she had worn in the first winter of the war. It was a chiffony cloud of every sweet-pea colour and cunningly arranged so that if Mrs. Brandon wanted to occupy a whole sofa she could do so with great ease, but could fold herself up into quite a small space for anyone she liked, the anyone in this case being Mrs. Arbuthnot. And just as the two ladies were about to discuss the play all over again, Francis came in wearing his real, proper evening dress with white tie and white waistcoat and a white camellia in his button-hole. Both ladies showed flattering surprise and pleasure.

"I am delighted that you approve," said Francis, admiring in his turn the sweet-pea cloud and the black lace cloud that reposed so lightly on the sofa. "And I have taken the liberty of bringing a small floral offering for each of you. Mamma, here is an orchid, because I think you ought to have one and there is no chivalry left except in your tall and fascinating son. Peggy: stephanotis, if not considered too cloying, is I think exactly the thing. May I put them on?"

He brought a hassock to the ladies' feet, tweaked the knees of his evening trousers up a little, knelt, and in a very workmanlike way pinned each lady's flower exactly where it should go. He then stood up, gave the knees of his trousers an encouraging pat and put the hassock back in its place.

"Francis, you are an idiot," said Mrs. Arbuthnot, smelling her stephanotis with every air of enjoyment. "Your mother looks heavenly with orchids. She always ought to have them."

"I did have some orchids once," said Mrs. Brandon, "years ago, from a dreadfully dull cousin of your father's, Francis."

"I don't know why it is," said Francis, addressing Mrs. Arbuthnot, "that mother always speaks of father like that. It makes me feel so responsible for him, especially when I hear about the very dull cousin. Mamma, I cannot help my father having had a dull cousin and if he was my father it is entirely your fault and I will take no responsibility whatsoever. Who was he, anyway? The cousin, I mean."

"Oh, a dreadfully dull man, only a second cousin, I think," said Mrs. Brandon, "because your father didn't have any first cousins. He took us to dinner at Claridge's and then to a play, and he gave me some orchids all rather tightly done up with a large black-headed pin to fasten them on with, and it was a dreadfully dull play about people in Lancashire. I remember it because we were in a box, so of course we couldn't see anything and the orchids fell into the stalls, so I said I felt rather faint and could we go home. It was not long before you were born, Francis," she added, looking accusingly at her son.

"Good heavens, mamma, how coarse you are," said Francis. "That also was no fault of mine. And here is Effie to whom I shall have the honour of giving an orchid, but a quite different one from yours, mamma."

Mrs. Brandon, much enjoying the entertainment provided by her son, felt that he could not have chosen better. Miss Arbuthnot was wearing a woollen dinner-dress of a suitable dark green and the highly respectable greenish orchid which Francis was pinning on her shoulder somehow looked quite in place; and if Mrs. Brandon had been pressed to say what her thoughts were at the moment, she would probably have said that the orchid, by mere association with Miss Arbuthnot, looked as if it had been very cleverly made by cripples and almost took one in.

Rose now announced dinner.

"I know what there is tonight," said Francis to Miss Arbuth-not when they had taken their places, "because it smelt so divine while I was having my bath that I went to the kitchen to ask Cook."

"It is extraordinary," said Mrs. Brandon plaintively, "how smells from the kitchen do come into the bathroom. I suppose it is because the bathroom is above it only a little further along and the smells come up slanting. I remember before you were born, Francis——"

"No, mamma," said her son, outraged, "not again. If you will go on being Gampish I shall simply refuse to have been born at all. I am going to tell you the menu, Effie, and the others may listen too. First there is this divine soup which is all thick and oniony with a large rather scrunchy piece of bread fried in fat and lots of cheese. When we have finished this—no, Rose, not yet: I must go round the side of my plate again first—we are going to have a roast chicken with everything that a chicken should have except that the bread sauce will be dark grey, to please the Food Minister. And then an ice-pudding out of the frigidaire with hot chocolate sauce. And then, if we are still alive, a small, very hot, crisp savoury. And with the meal will be served some of the white wine that mamma would never have bought in 1939 had it not been for her gastronomical son's foresight, and later the last dying remains of a bottle of Cointreau. Coffee of course."

If Mrs. Brandon thought her son was rattling away more than usual, she made no sign. The theatricals had been very exciting and Francis had acted charmingly and there was a very good dinner and some good wine and two nice guests, one of whom was very pretty and an enchanting actress. So there was really every reason for Francis to be a little over-excited, and she thought of him as a little boy, his pink cheeks flushed at children's parties and his fair hair curling like the tendrils of a vine. And though his cheeks were no longer pink though neatly shaved, and his hair was kept in such strict subjection that only after a bath did it misbehave itself, she saw the small Francis in his green linen party-suit quite distinctly, which access of maternal sentiment caused her to say to the company at large that Francis was nearly always sick at parties.

"My dear mamma," said Francis, "if you go on like that Peggy will never marry me."

"Is she going to?" asked Mrs. Brandon, no whit discomposed and taking an intelligent interest in the question.

Mrs. Arbuthnot said she really couldn't, because Francis hadn't asked her, and then Rose was in the room taking away chicken-bones and serving ice-pudding and so hovered about the table that talk had to be on more ordinary subjects, and they all fell to and discussed the play again till they could escape from Rose and go to the sitting-room and coffee and liqueur.

Peace and repletion then descended gently upon the party and with equal gentleness the talk veered to the ever-enthralling subject of Captain Brandon and Mrs. Colonel Arbuthnot.

"But of course," said Mrs. Brandon, with the air of one who had plumbed the depths of the Indian Ocean and brought up a pearl, "that explains *everything*."

"I am sure it does, mamma," said Francis. "But which everything in particular do you mean?"

"You need only look at Peggy and me," said Mrs. Brandon with great dignity.

"Yes, darling," said Francis, "and a nicer sight I couldn't see. But it doesn't get us any forrader."

"You know perfectly well, Francis," said his mother, looking at him through her spectacles like an owl schoolmistress, "that Peggy is rather like me, or I am rather like her if you prefer it. Everyone has noticed it."

"Quite right, mamma, and it does you both great credit," said Francis. "Very often it doesn't do anyone credit, like Miss Pettinger being so like the Giant Panda. But even so, I fail to see your point."

"If Peggy and I are like each other, which is very nice for me," said Mrs. Brandon, casting an affectionate and admiring look on Mrs. Arbuthnot, "this explains it all."

Her audience said nothing at first for her train of thought, though perfectly clear to herself as one's train of thought always are, was dark as Erebus to everyone else till light broke upon Miss Arbuthnot.

"But, dear Mrs. Brandon," she said, "you and Peggy are not related in the least. Even if all this old story is true, Peggy doesn't come into it at all. If anyone is like you it ought to be I, and goodness knows I'm not. Peggy isn't any relation of the Arbuthnots. She only happened to marry one."

"And may I add," said Francis, "as holding a watching brief for the Brandon family in this cause célèbre, that my mother is not a Brandon at all. She was Miss Lavinia Oliver and married my father, not with my connivance I may say, for I wasn't born then. I am very sorry, mamma, but you and Peggy are as unrelated as ever. Effie and I," he added proudly, "are illegitimate cousins possibly, but proud as I am of the relationship it leaves you and Peggy out altogether."

Mrs. Brandon, who had been frowning in her efforts to disentangle what Francis was saying, gave it up, placidly resumed her embroidery and said it was all very disappointing because she had meant to give Peggy her other pearl necklace, but if she wasn't a relation it spoilt it all.

"Listen, mamma," said Francis, perhaps for the first time in his life a little nervous with his mother. "If it is only the pearl necklace that is worrying you, let me provide the solution for all your troubles. If Peggy marries me she will be your daughter-in-law, and it will then be your obvious duty to give her all the family jewels and retire to the Dower House."

"But is Peggy going to marry you?" said Mrs. Brandon, pleased, surprised, interested.

"I don't know, mamma," said Francis, "but Our Mr. Brandon,

as we say in the office, will at once proceed to take steps to assure confirmation of same."

He then got up, put the little hassock at Mrs. Arbuthnot's feet, gave his trousers a slight hitch at the knees, knelt down before her and said, "Could you bear to marry me, Peggy? If you want to please my mamma, say yes."

We do not attempt to conceal the fact that Mrs. Arbuthnot had expected something of this kind all evening, indeed for some days past, but when it happened she was more moved than she would have thought possible. Bright tears came to her lustrous eyes, her pretty face flushed, and impulsively she leaned forward, put her hand on Francis's shoulder and her arms round his neck and began to cry.

Mrs. Brandon and Miss Arbuthnot, who were not greatly surprised, watched the tableau with affectionate sympathy and each lady confessed afterwards to that kind of pricking behind her eyes. It was of course inevitable that Nurse, who dearly liked to go to the sitting-room upon some pretext during the evening just to show Rose, which gap in the sense the reader will quite well understand if she gives her attention to it for a second, should come in with one of Francis's shirts. There was no need for anyone to tell her what was happening, though she after-wards said in the kitchen, most untruthfully, that you could have knocked her down with a feather and knowing how upset Madam must be, though she was sure in this case Madam would gain a daughter and not lose a son; to which Cook replied daughter-in-law she supposed Nurse meant, and Rose said if *she* went into the sitting-room without Madam ringing she would keep her tongue quiet whatever she saw. However, these bick-erings were but part of the protocol consecrated by usage of the relations between the sewing-room, the pantry, and the kitchen, and the three ladies united in a hearty meal of cocoa, bread and a large piece of American cheese out of a tin, and within half an hour had wedded and bedded Francis and Mrs. Arbuthnot and provided them with a large family who were to spend their whole time at Stories.

Francis, who had seen Nurse out of the corner of his eye, said indignantly into Mrs. Arbuthnot's hair that this was a deliberate and put-up job to ensnare bachelors, and if Peggy wouldn't marry him he would be the laughing-stock of Pomfret Madrigal.

Mrs. Arbuthnot sat up again, wiped her eyes with Francis's handkerchief which he obligingly produced, and going over to Mrs. Brandon said, "Would you mind, dear Mrs. Brandon?"

It was evident that Mrs. Brandon wouldn't mind in the least, and prolonged, soft, scented embraces took place, while Mrs. Brandon, so her son very discourteously said, looked just like a half-wit hen who had laid a double-yolked egg.

"And that," he said, "reminds me of my manners. Mamma, Effie has been left out of this too long. I can't tell you how enchanted I am, Effie, that you are going to be my sister-in-law. That is really why I proposed to Peggy," and he gave her an affectionate brotherly hug and kiss which Miss Arbuthnot very much enjoyed, though she felt that older men, men with handsome beards, understood the job better.

"Oh, but Francis!" said Mrs. Arbuthnot, tearing herself from her future mother-in-law, "Effie! I *can't* leave her all alone."

"You must all come and live here," said Mrs. Brandon, seeing her chance. "I have been thinking about it and planned it all. You and Francis can have the Green Room and Green Dressing-room and Effie can have the Pink Room."

"It all seems very unorthodox," said Francis. "I thought a husband was expected to find a house for his wife so that she and his mother shouldn't quarrel, though anyone who could quarrel with mamma would quarrel with a feather-bed."

His mother said he should not say such things and everyone talked at once till Miss Arbuthnot, who had something she wanted to say herself, managed to make her voice heard.

"It's absolutely all right about me, Peggy," she said to her sister-in-law. "I didn't tell you that Colonel Crofts and I are going to be married. I hated not telling you, but I couldn't think of leaving you. Fred did ask me to take care of you."

And at these words Miss Arbuthnot, worked upon by the emotional scenes past and in progress, had to turn her head away.

Mrs. Arbuthnot of course pretended to be overcome with surprise, and everyone kissed and congratulated Miss Arbuthnot with such affection that she could hardly speak.

"There is only one thing," said Mrs. Arbuthnot suddenly. "Editha. It's a three-year lease."

"That's all right," said Miss Arbuthnot. "We can sub-let it. I know that Mr. Feeder is wanting a cottage for his mother."

"Then that's all right," said Mrs. Arbuthnot. "Oh, but one other thing, Effie, you must please let me give you that money that Fred settled on me. I am sure I could sign a paper or something. You really ought to have had it. It was Brandon money and I'm not a Brandon, nor an Arbuthnot except by marriage."

Miss Arbuthnot, deeply touched by her sister-in-law's generous and foolish words, said that as a matter of fact Colonel Crofts was very well off and she could not think of taking Peggy's money even if it were legally possible. This news pleased everyone, for though Francis would willingly have taken Mrs. Arbuthnot without a penny, it was gratifying to know that his bride's sister-in-law of whom she was so fond was going to be well looked after. For, to be quite truthful, poor relations are no inheritance.

"And now, mamma," said Francis, "and Peggy and Effie too, I think champagne. We still have a few bottles."

He went away to the cellar while the ladies had a delightful talk, undisturbed by men, about houses and drains and clothes and weddings, and again clothes, and were almost annoyed when Francis came back with a bottle of champagne and four glasses.

"I just looked into the kitchen, mamma," he said, "and gave them a bottle of that Colonial sherry that no one much liked. I had to leave them at once as Nurse was obviously about to ask how many children I proposed to have and how soon," at which Mrs. Arbuthnot laughed and appeared no whit discomposed, which led Francis to say that he thought the elder Mr. Weller was wrong in his advice about widows.

"Something you have all forgotten," said Mrs. Brandon severely, when everyone's happiness had been drunk. "The Vicar."

"My good mamma, it is half-past ten at night," said Francis. "Mr. Miller can't come round and marry us with a curtain-ring at this hour and in any case Mrs. Miller wouldn't let him, as he has to go to bed early on Saturdays after wrestling with his sermon."

"I don't mean Mr. Miller," said his mother, "and you really ought to know that, Francis. I mean Colonel Crofts."

"Good God, though that isn't the way to speak of the clergy, how right you are, mamma," said Francis. "Effie, if I ring up Southbridge will you give Crofts our love and tell him how happy we are about your engagement? Not half as happy though, as I must candidly admit, as we are about our own."

He accordingly went to the hall to telephone, got through to the Southbridge exchange, told the girl on night duty that if she listened in she would hear something worth while, and so got onto the Vicarage.

While this conversation was going on Mrs. Arbuthnot had become very thoughtful.

"It really makes one almost believe in things," she said, looking into space.

"What does?" said Mrs. Brandon.

"Do you remember, Effie," said Mrs. Arbuthnot, "when we were getting into Editha and the old Vicar's aunt came to see us and said neither of us would live there long."

"So she did," said Miss Arbuthnot. "And we thought she meant we were going to die."

"And then she said it would not be death, but another life," said Mrs. Arbuthnot. "How funny."

And then Francis came in with the news that Colonel Crofts was waiting to speak with Effie. Miss Arbuthnot was away for about twenty minutes, at the end of which time she came back full of cordial messages from Colonel Crofts and as excitement and champagne were making everyone yawn, Mrs. Brandon said they had better go to bed.

When, after a great deal more kissing and a few more agreeable tears, the guests had been safely seen to their bedrooms, Francis went round the house as usual to see that everything was locked, for even in Pomfret Madrigal far too many undesirable characters had been spewed up by the peace, and one didn't want anyone at Stories to be shot or knocked on the head for the sake of the small amount of silver now in use. When he had satisfied himself that all was in order he went upstairs and tapped at his mother's door.

Mrs. Brandon was reclining upon a great many soft pillows and looking very young and attractive in the shaded light with a cloud of dusty pink chiffon about her head and shoulders.

"Good-night, darling," said Francis. "You are perfect. And I may say that there isn't another mother-in-law in the whole world that Peggy and I could possibly consider living with."

"It's not forever," said Mrs. Brandon, who in spite of her apparent vagueness had a sound bottom of common sense. "You'll find a house presently. Or I might let you have Stories and take Nurse and Rose to a smaller house when things are easier. But we will see about all that in time."

"Bless you, darling," said Francis. "There's plenty of time to think about your being a dowager. And meanwhile Peggy and I and all the children will love to live here."

Mrs. Brandon looked with great affection upon her son, already planning in her mind a life which they would not share under one roof. There was however no hurry, and there were occasionally families in which a joint household was a harmonious manner of life, but this was not a thing she was going to count upon as enduring.

"I have had one thought, Francis," she said, taking off her spectacles and laying down her book.

"Out with it," said Francis. "They do say suppressed ideas do the most outlandish things to one."

"You know that ten thousand pounds that Peggy's late husband settled on her," said Mrs. Brandon.

Francis said he did, feeling at the same time a certain compassion for the late Captain Arbuthnot who had been so firmly relegated to the past by his mother's words.

"Well, Aunt Sissie left it to him," said Mrs. Brandon, "so it is Brandon money. And now it has come back into the family, which is really very suitable. I wonder if Aunt Sissie Knows," said Mrs. Brandon, drawing a veil between herself and any definite theories about the unseen.

"My dear mamma, you must not say such things," said Francis, and after kissing his mother with great affection he went to his room. While undressing his eye was caught by the green chiffon handkerchief lying in the box where he kept his best studs. For a moment he toyed with the dashing idea of taking it to Mrs. Arbuthnot's room and giving it to her as a betrothal present. But the thought of Nurse, who was quite certain to be about if she was not wanted, made him reconsider this romantic plan. After a few seconds' thought he put the handkerchief into an envelope and addressed it to Mrs. Francis Brandon. The name, he considered, looked very well; striking, yet in good taste. So he put the envelope in the drawer and went to bed.

COLOPHON

This book is being reissued as part of Moyer
Bell's Angela Thirkell Series. Readers may join
the Thirkell Circle for free to receive notices
of new titles in the series as well as a newsletter,
bookmarks, posters, and more. Simply send in
the enclosed card or write to the address below.

The text of this book was set in Caslon, a typeface
designed by William Caslon I (1692-1766). This
face designed in 1725 has gone through many
incarnations. It was the mainstay of British
printers for over one hundred years and
remains very popular today. The version used
here is Adobe Caslon. The display faces are
Adobe Caslon Outline, Calligraphic 421,
and Adobe Caslon.

Composed by Alabama Book Composition,
Deatsville, Alabama.

Private Enterprise was printed by Edwards
Brothers, Ann Arbor, Michigan on acid free paper.

Moyer Bell
Kymbolde Way
Wakefield, RI 02879